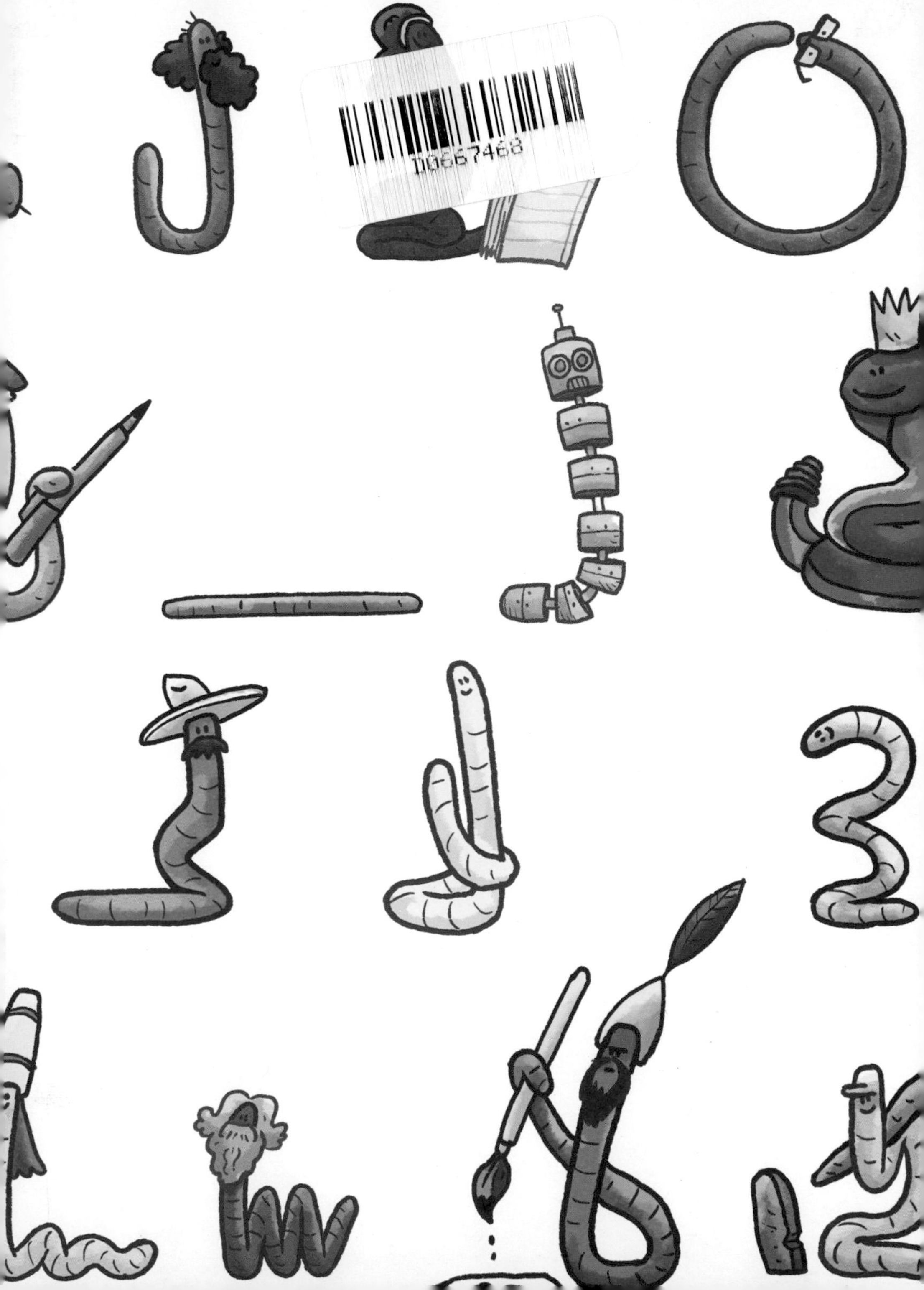

Blue, Barry & Pancakes

&

BIG TIME TROUBLE

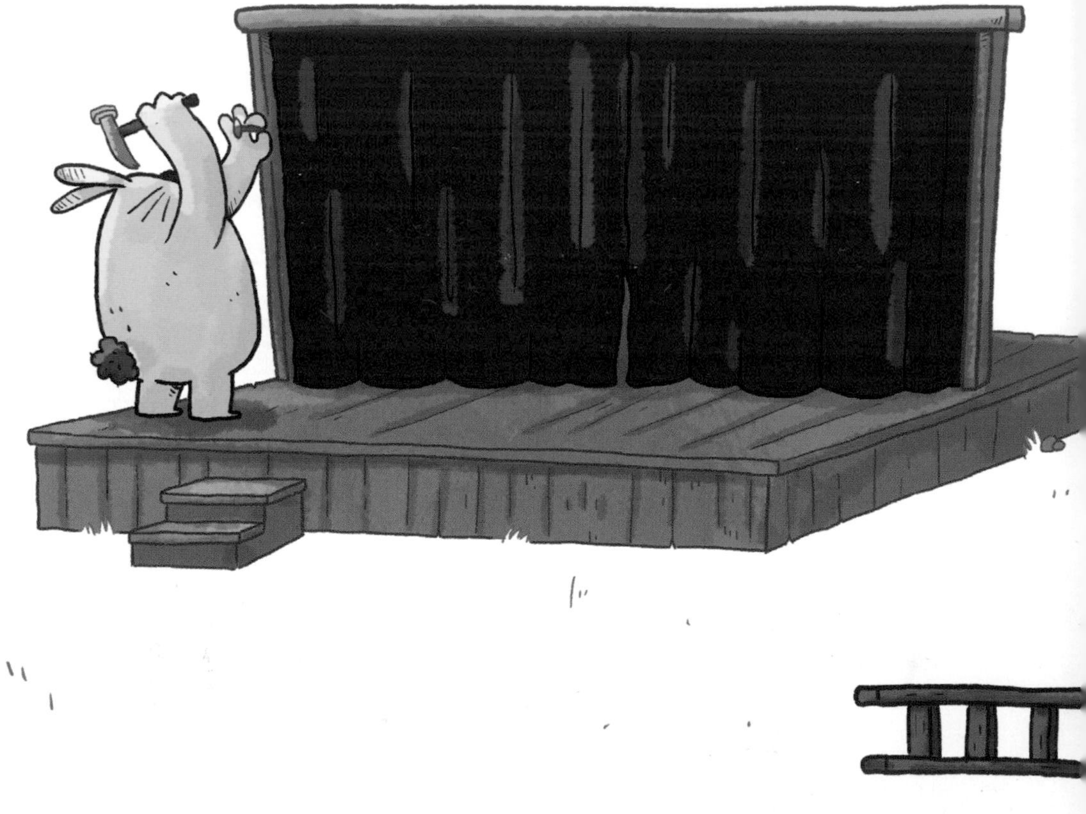

Blue, Barry & Pancakes
BIG TIME TROUBLE

by
Dan & Jason

POETRY
READING
by
BLUE

:01

First Second
New York

This book is dedicated to Alex,
Calista, and Sunny.

Without their limitless talent and undying patience,
these books would never exist! —D.A. & J.P.

First Second

Published by First Second
First Second is an imprint of Roaring Brook Press,
a division of Holtzbrinck Publishing Holdings Limited Partnership
120 Broadway, New York, NY 10271
firstsecondbooks.com
mackids.com

© 2023 by Dan Rajai Abdo and Jason Linwood Patterson

Library of Congress Cataloging-in-Publication Data is available.

Our books may be purchased in bulk for promotional, educational, or business use. Please
contact your local bookseller or the Macmillan Corporate and Premium Sales Department
at (800) 221-7945 ext. 5442 or by email at MacmillanSpecialMarkets@macmillan.com.

First edition, 2023
Edited by Calista Brill and Alex Lu
Cover and interior book design by Sunny Lee
Production editing by Avia Perez

This book was drawn mostly on a Wacom Cintiq and iPad Pro. Dan & Jason write,
draw, color, and letter together in Photoshop and Procreate. The font is a
unique Blue, Barry & Pancakes typeface created specifically for these books.

Printed in China by RR Donnelley Asia Printing Solutions Ltd.,
Dongguan City, Guangdong Province

ISBN 978-1-250-81697-9 (hardcover)
10 9 8 7 6 5 4 3 2 1

Don't miss your next favorite book from First Second! For the latest
updates go to firstsecondnewsletter.com and sign up for our enewsletter.

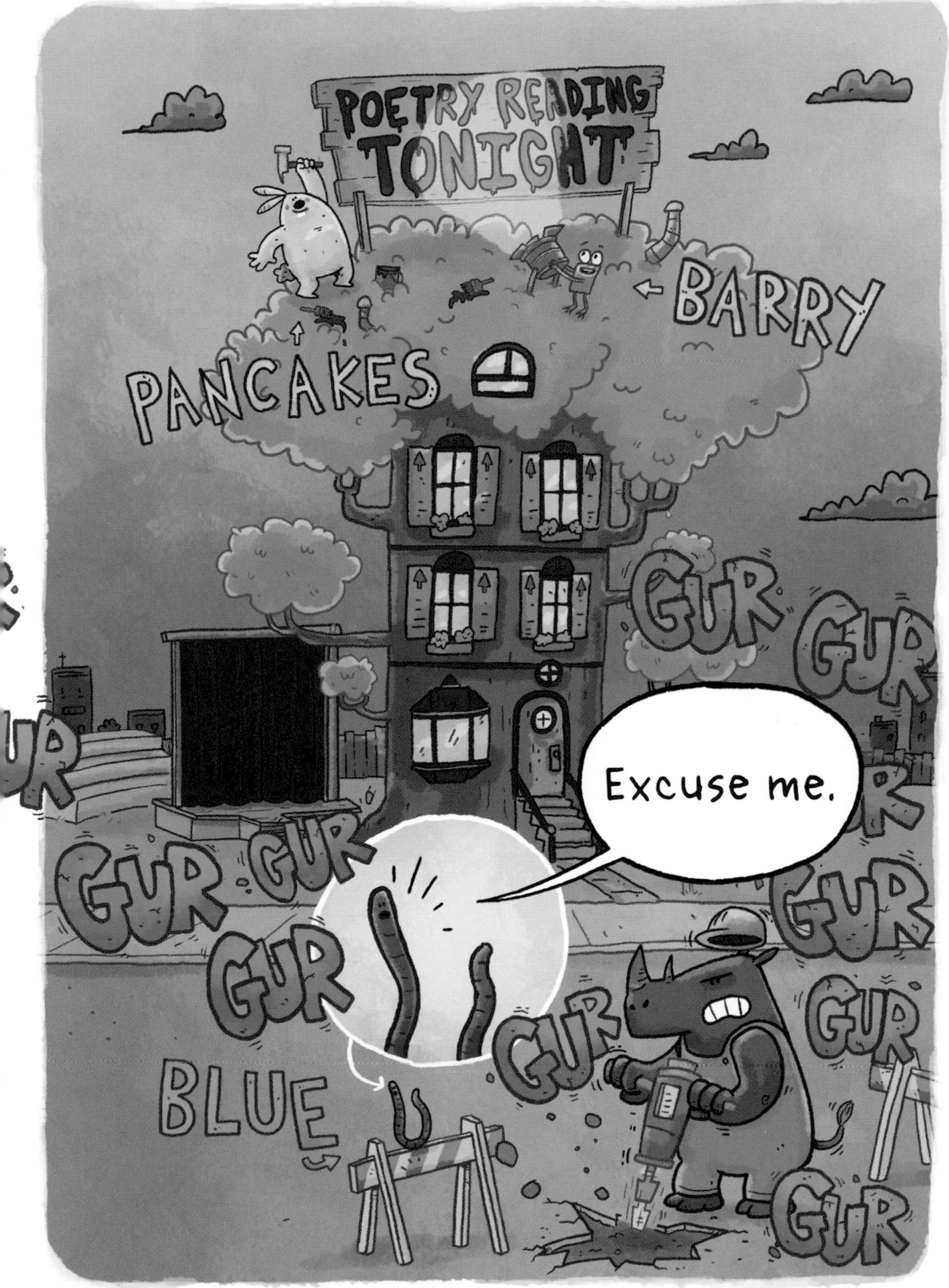
POETRY READING
TONIGHT
PANCAKES
BARRY
GUR
GUR
GUR
GUR
GUR
GUR
GUR
GUR
GUR
Excuse me.
BLUE

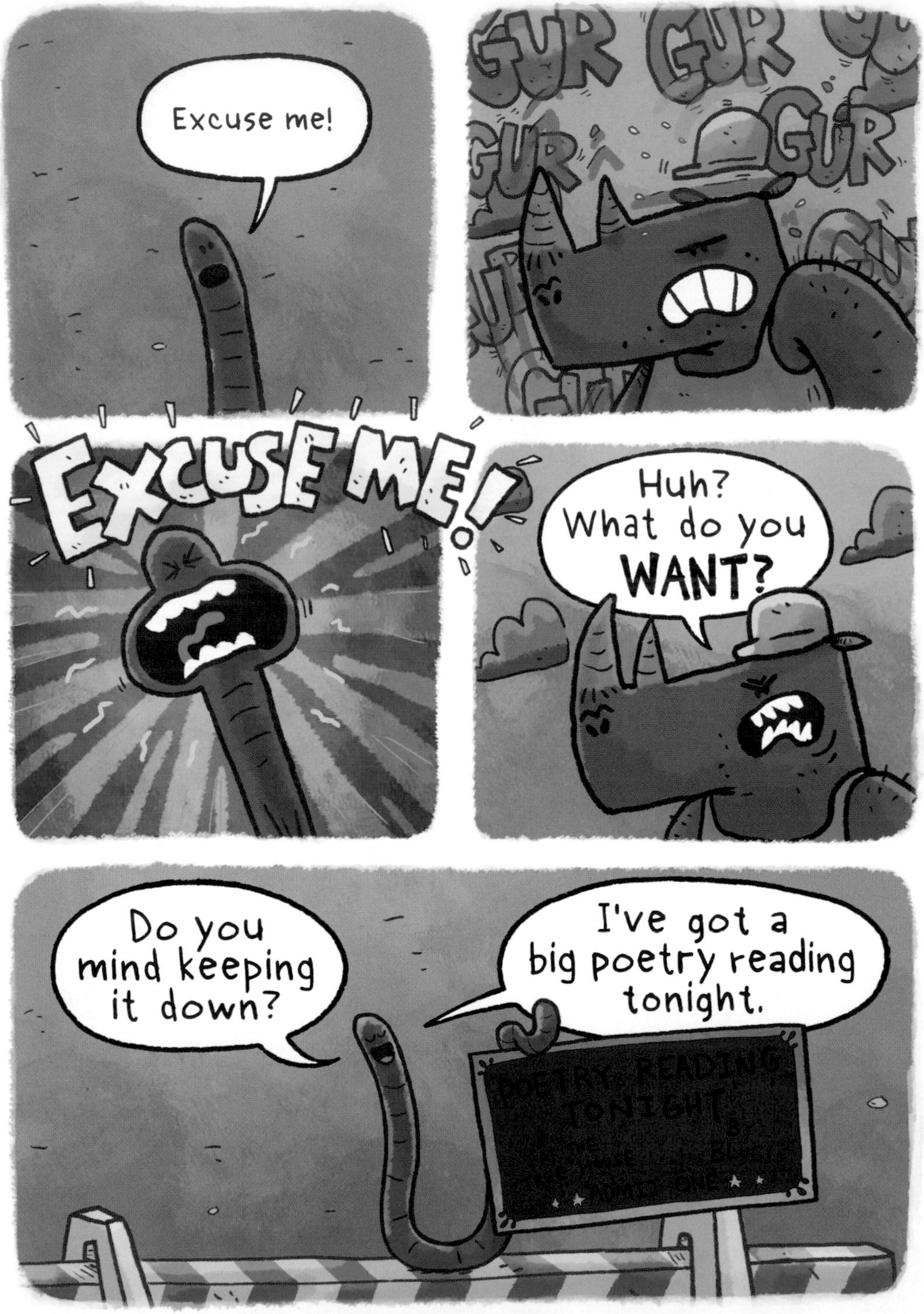
Excuse me!
GUR GUR
GUR GUR
EXCUSE ME!
Huh? What do you WANT?
Do you mind keeping it down?
I've got a big poetry reading tonight.
POETRY READING TONIGHT

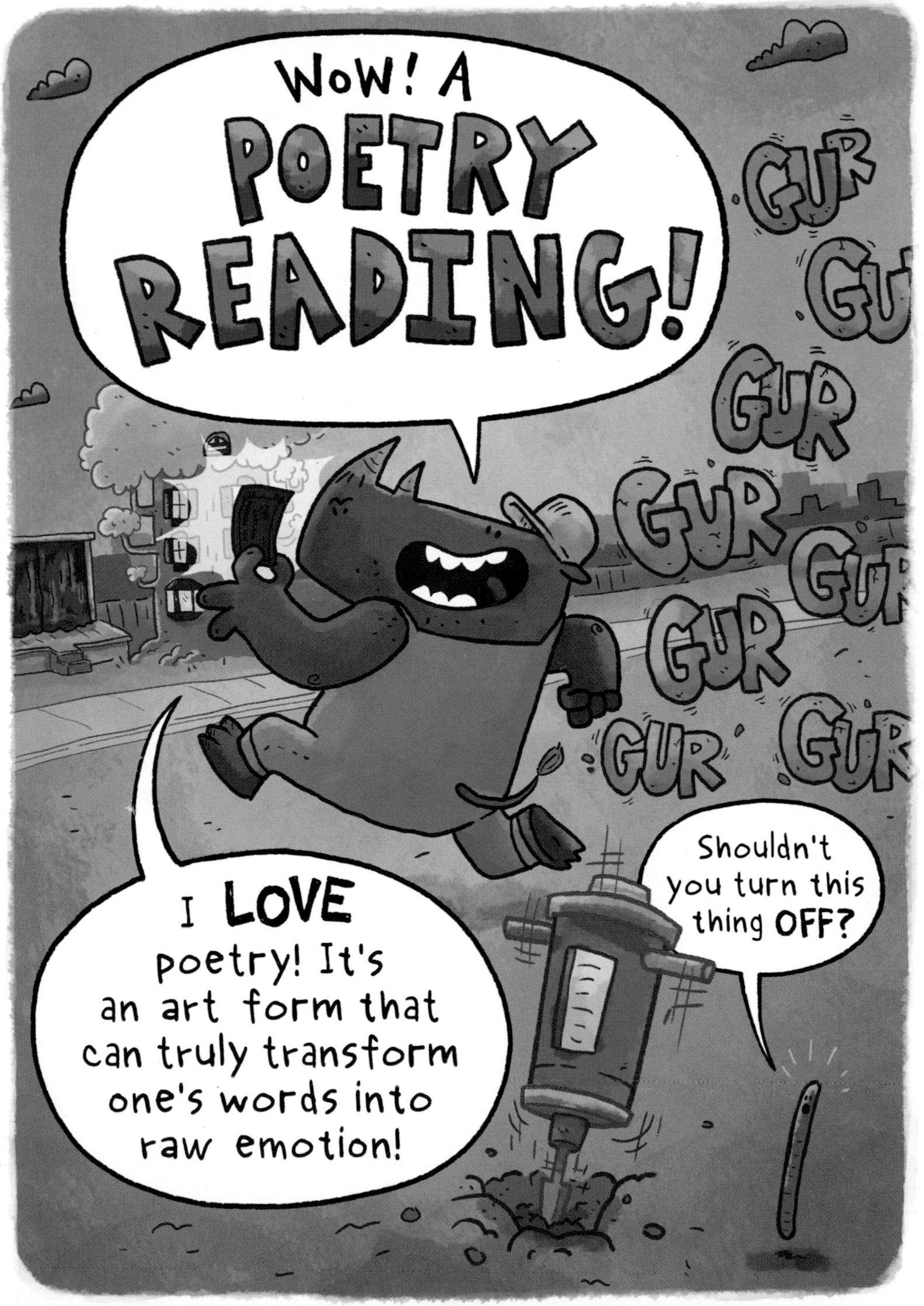
WOW! A POETRY READING!
GUR GUR GUR GUR GUR GUR GUR GUR
I LOVE poetry! It's an art form that can truly transform one's words into raw emotion!
Shouldn't you turn this thing OFF?

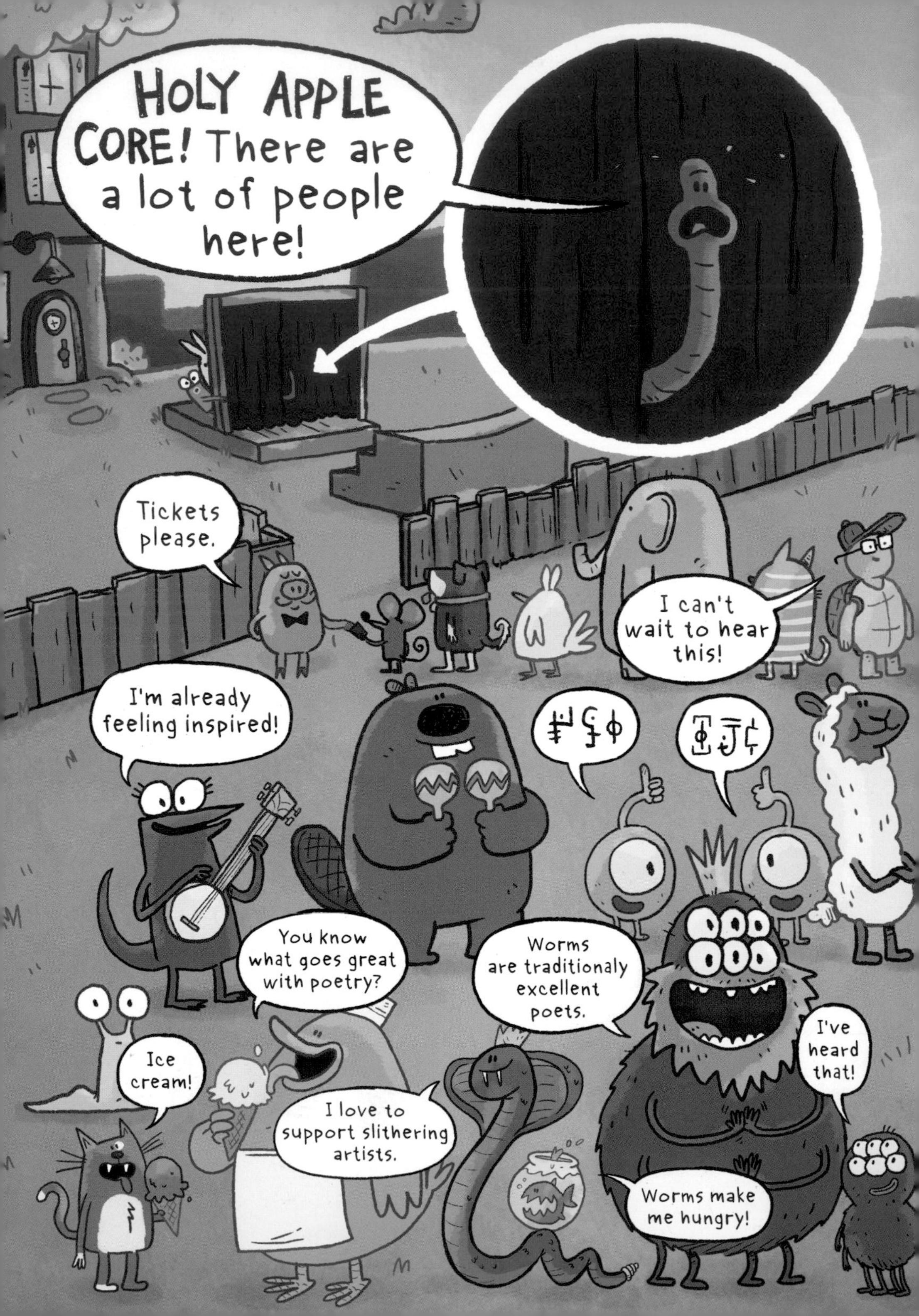
HOLY APPLE CORE! There are a lot of people here!
Tickets please.
I can't wait to hear this!
I'm already feeling inspired!
You know what goes great with poetry?
Worms are traditionaly excellent poets.
I've heard that!
Ice cream!
I love to support slithering artists.
Worms make me hungry!

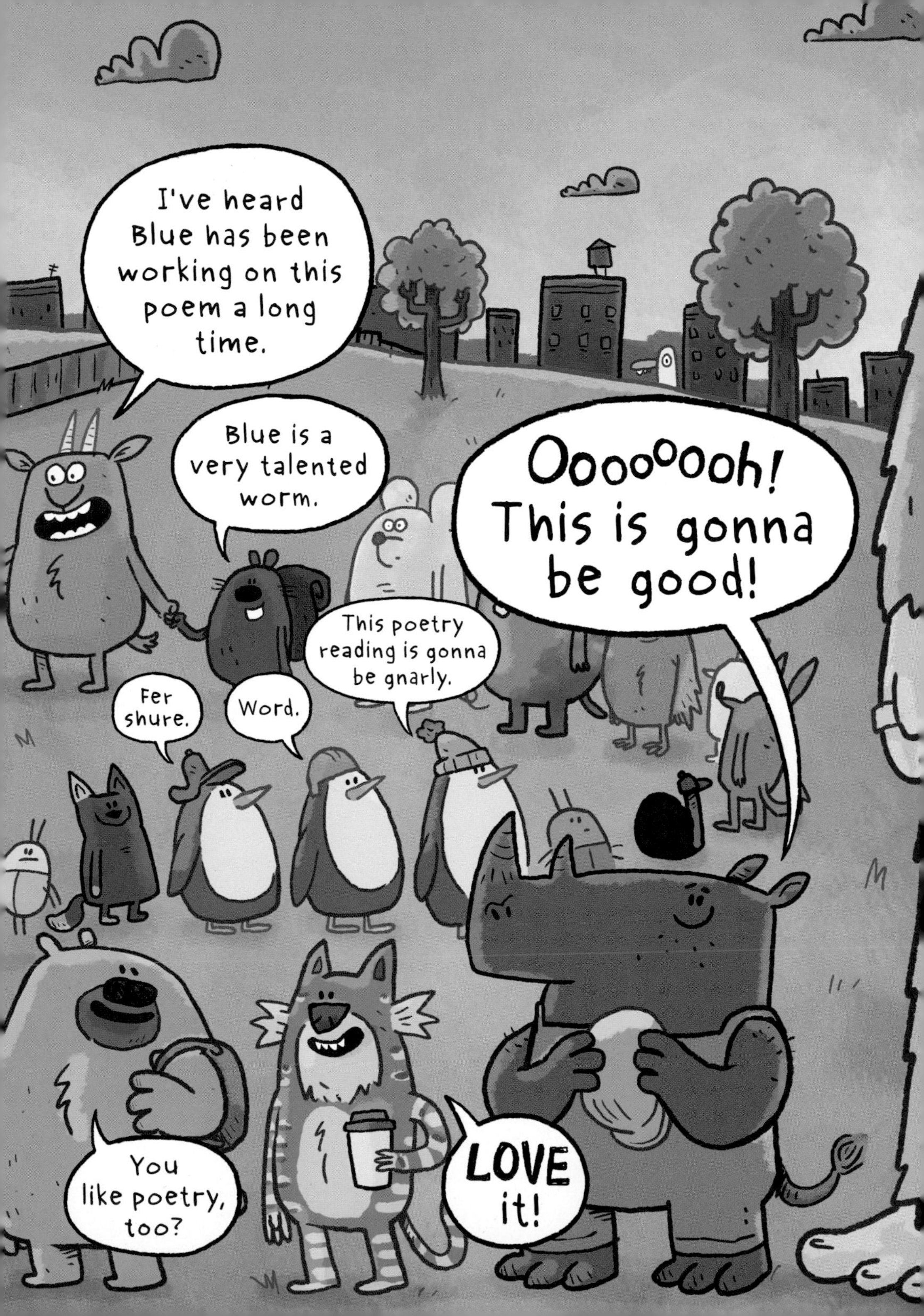
I've heard Blue has been working on this poem a long time.
Blue is a very talented worm.
Ooooooooh! This is gonna be good!
This poetry reading is gonna be gnarly.
Fer shure.
Word.
You like poetry, too?
LOVE it!

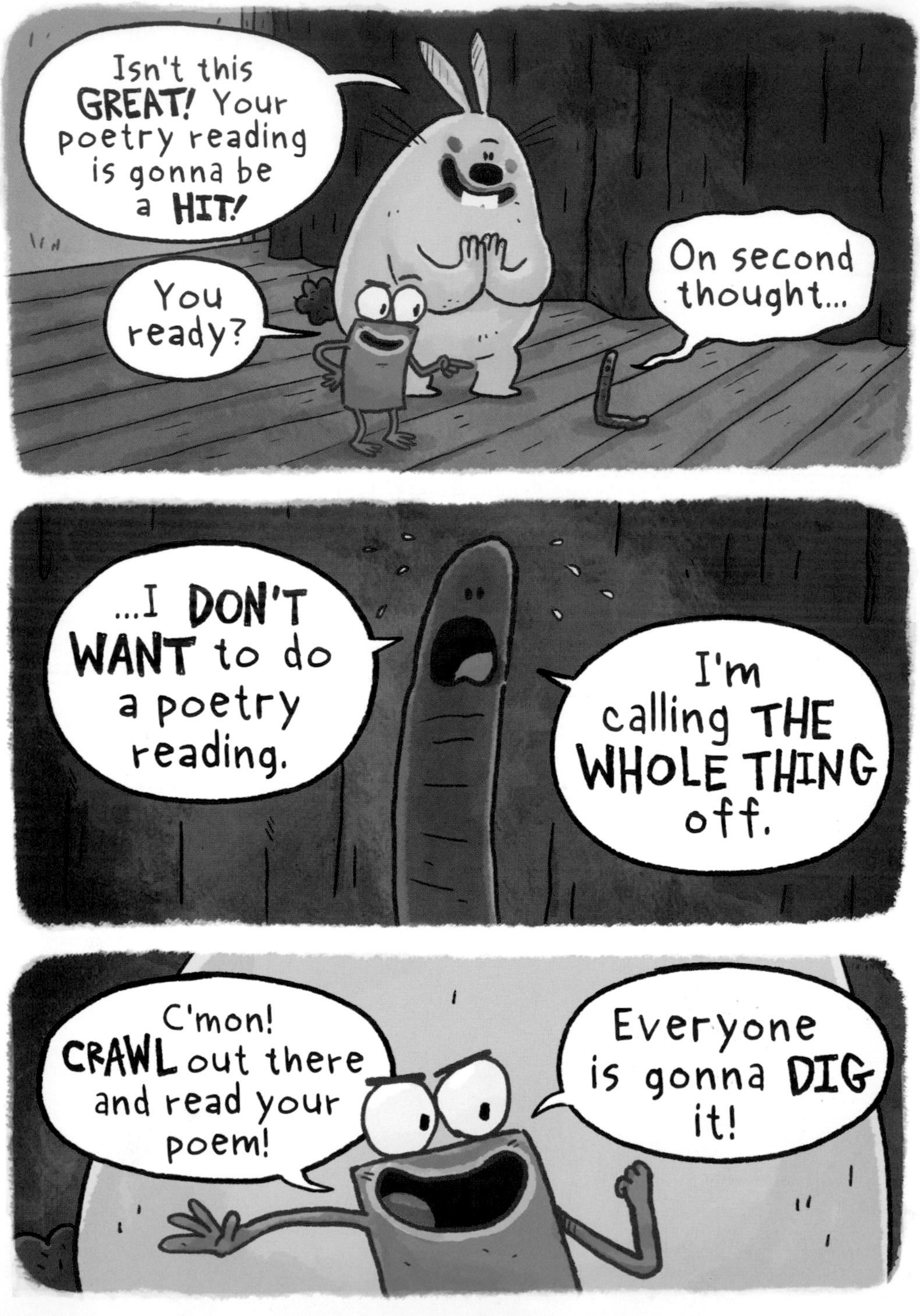
Isn't this GREAT! Your poetry reading is gonna be a HIT!
You ready?
On second thought...
...I DON'T WANT to do a poetry reading.
I'm calling THE WHOLE THING off.
C'mon! CRAWL out there and read your poem!
Everyone is gonna DIG it!

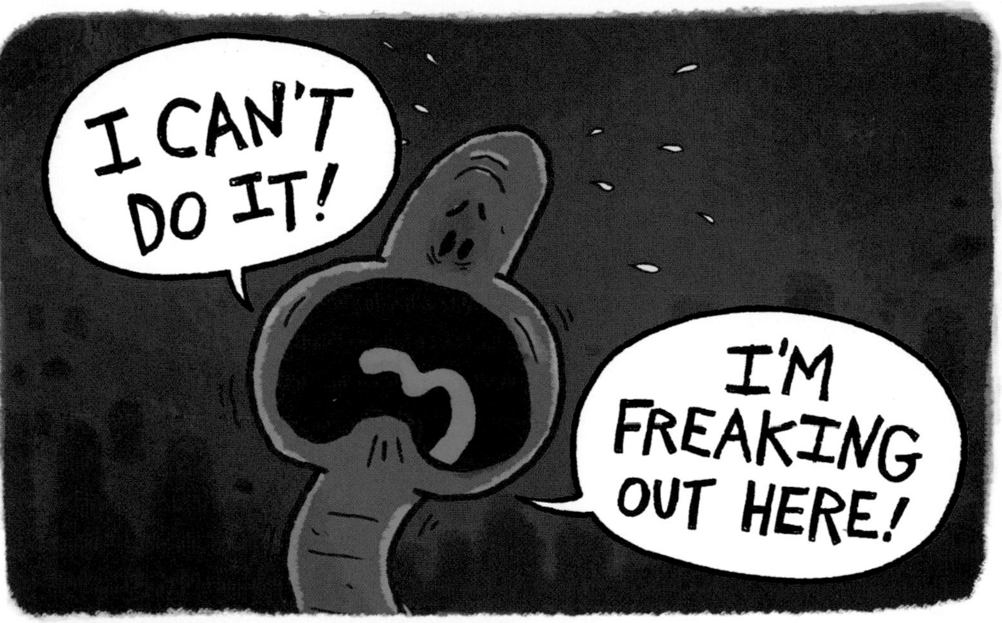
I CAN'T DO IT!
I'M FREAKING OUT HERE!

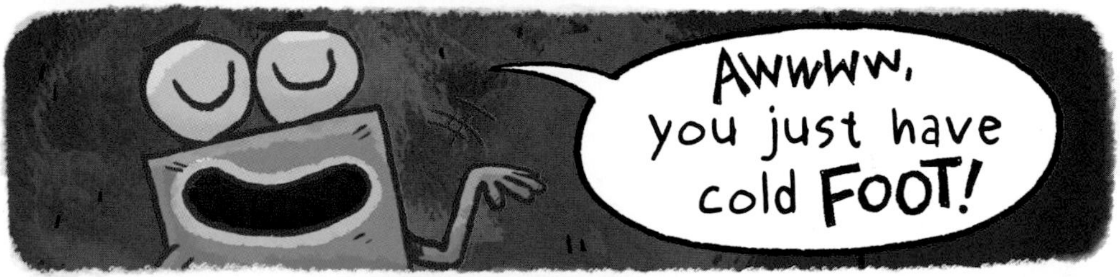
AWWWW, you just have cold FOOT!

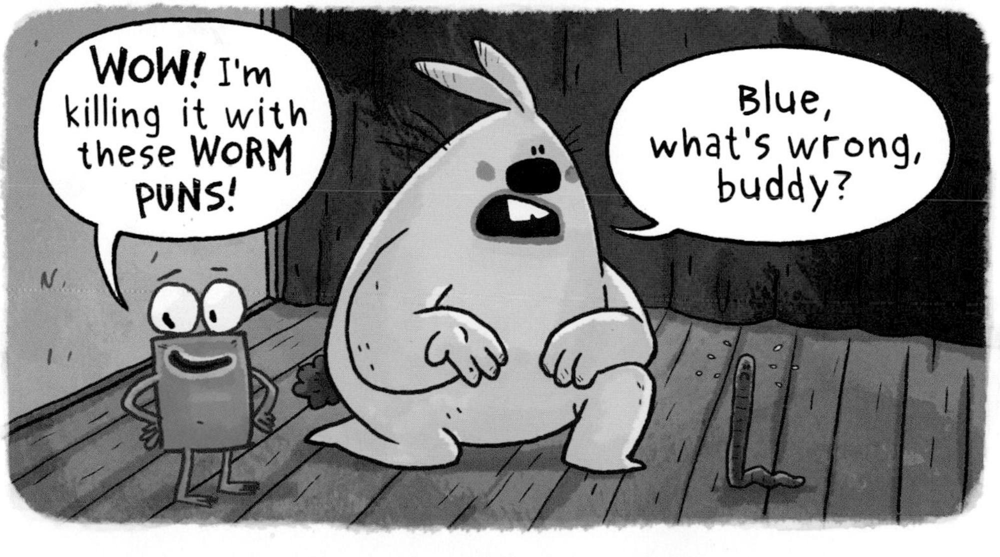
WOW! I'm killing it with these WORM PUNS!
Blue, what's wrong, buddy?

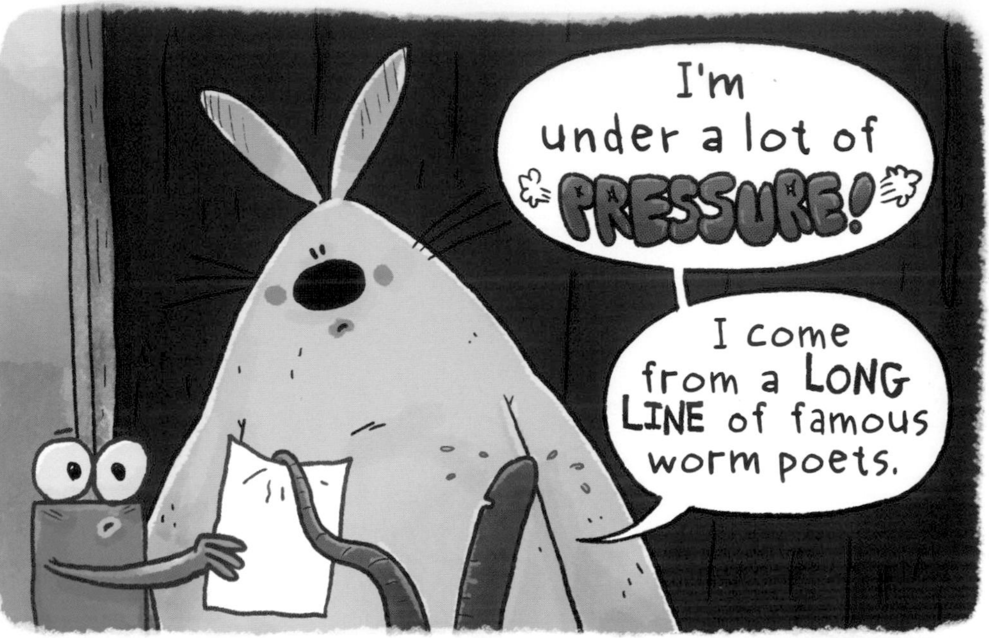
I'm under a lot of PRESSURE!
I come from a LONG LINE of famous worm poets.

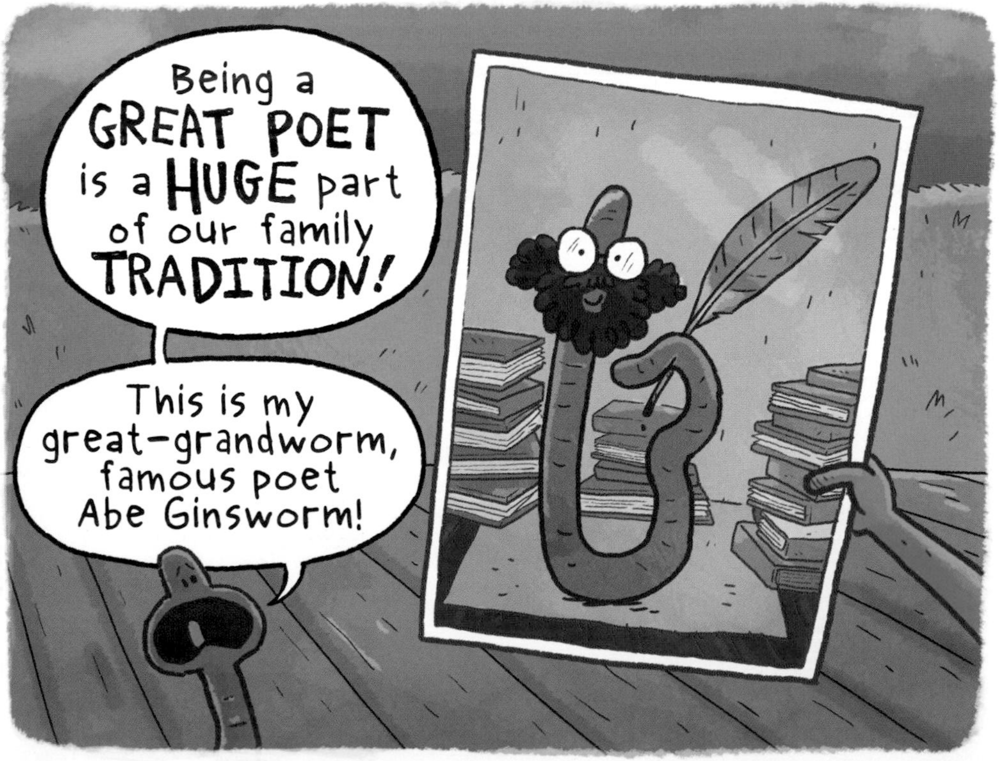
Being a GREAT POET is a HUGE part of our family TRADITION!
This is my great-grandworm, famous poet Abe Ginsworm!

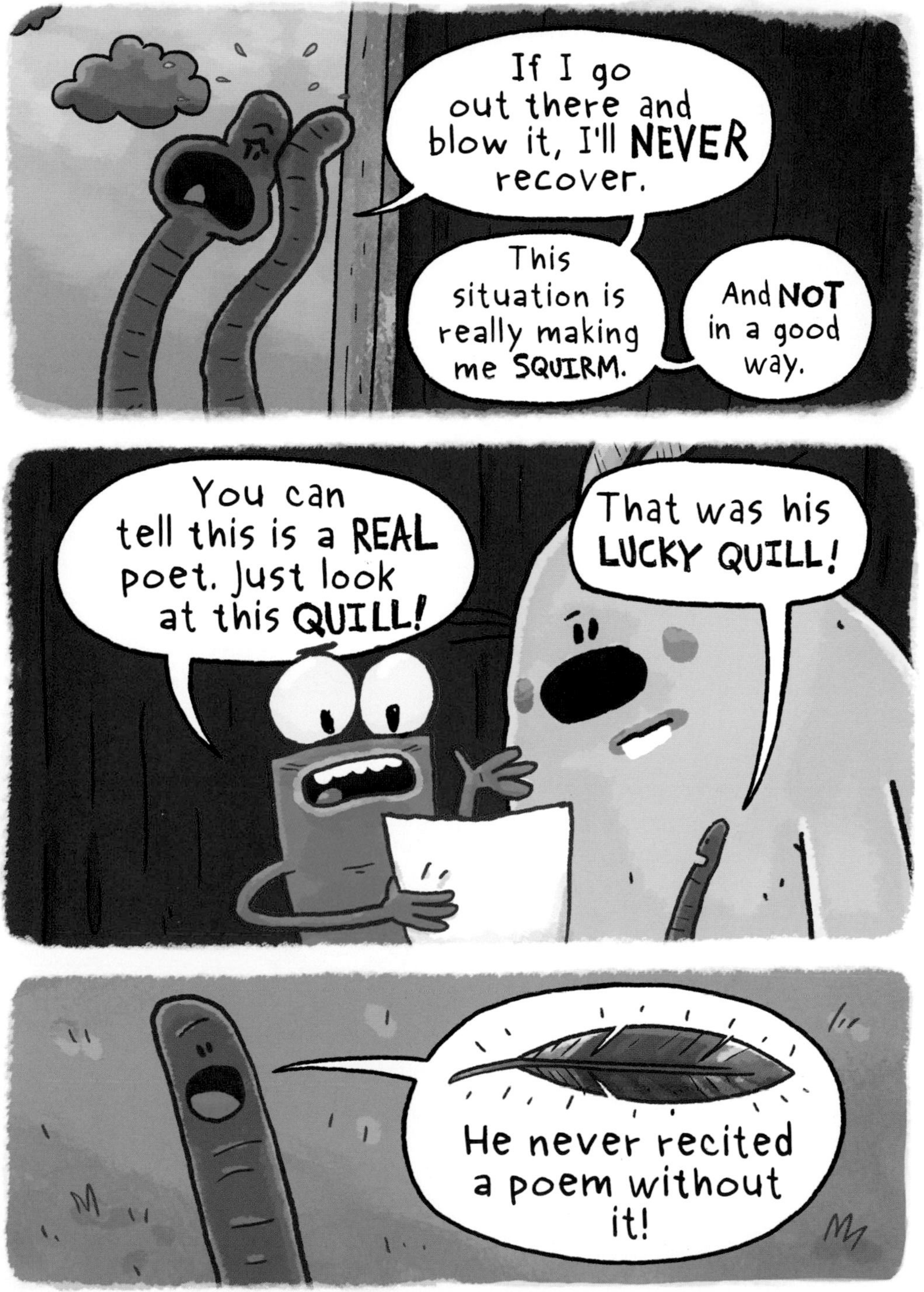
If I go out there and blow it, I'll NEVER recover.
This situation is really making me SQUIRM.
And NOT in a good way.
You can tell this is a REAL poet. Just look at this QUILL!
That was his LUCKY QUILL!
He never recited a poem without it!

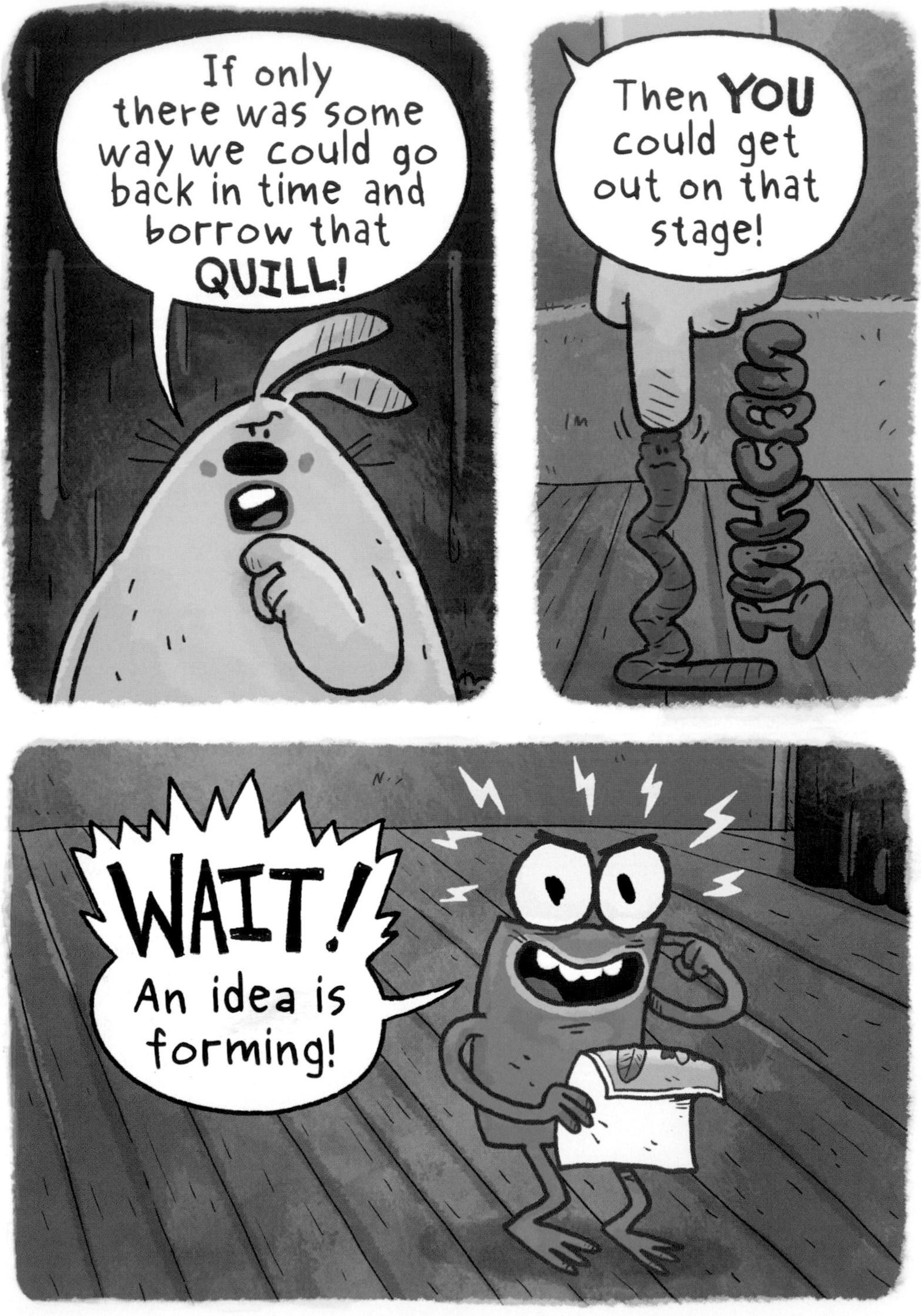
If only there was some way we could go back in time and borrow that QUILL!
Then YOU could get out on that stage!
INKCREDIBLE
WAIT!
An idea is forming!

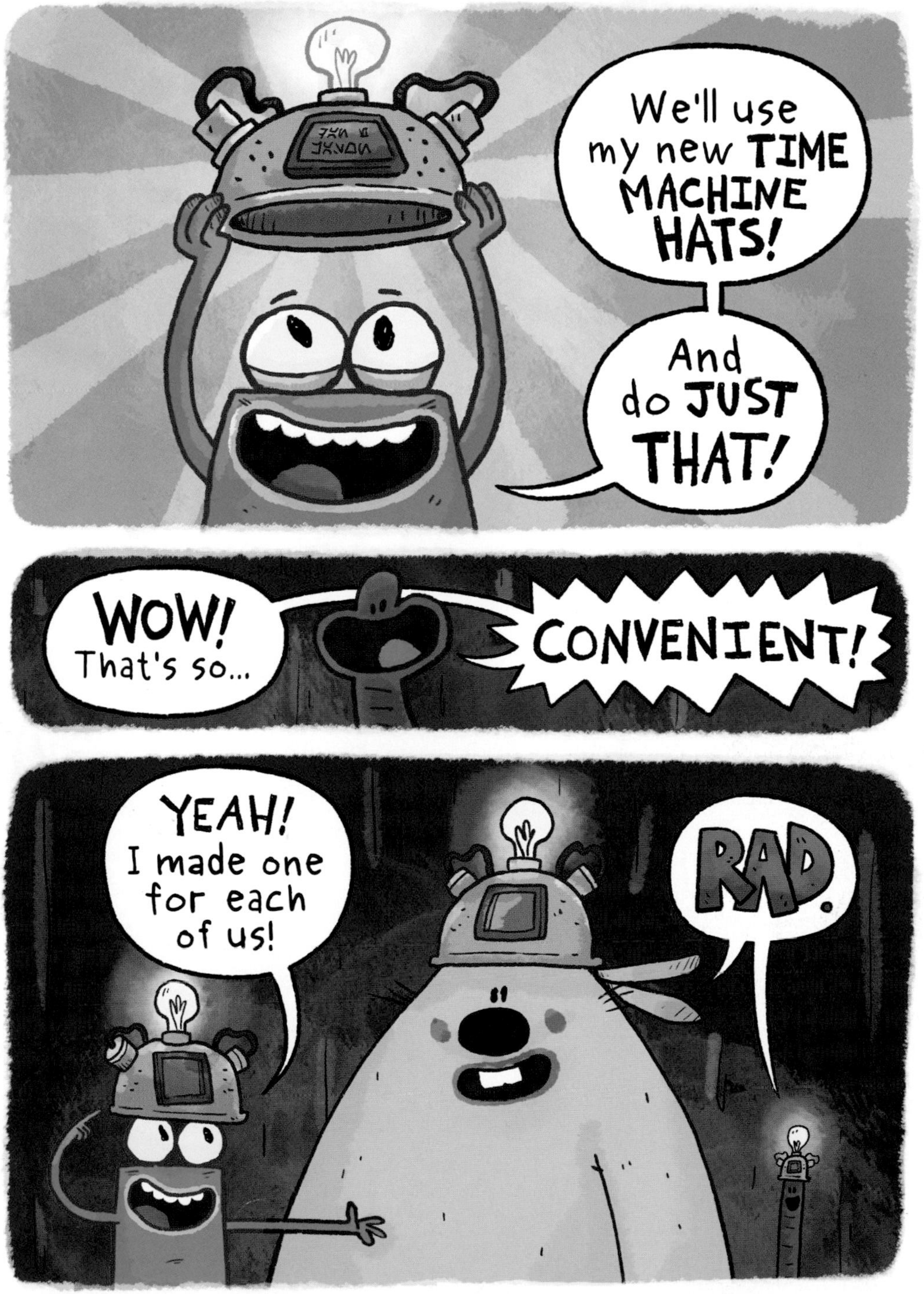
We'll use my new TIME MACHINE HATS!
And do JUST THAT!
WOW! That's so...
CONVENIENT!
YEAH! I made one for each of us!
RAD.

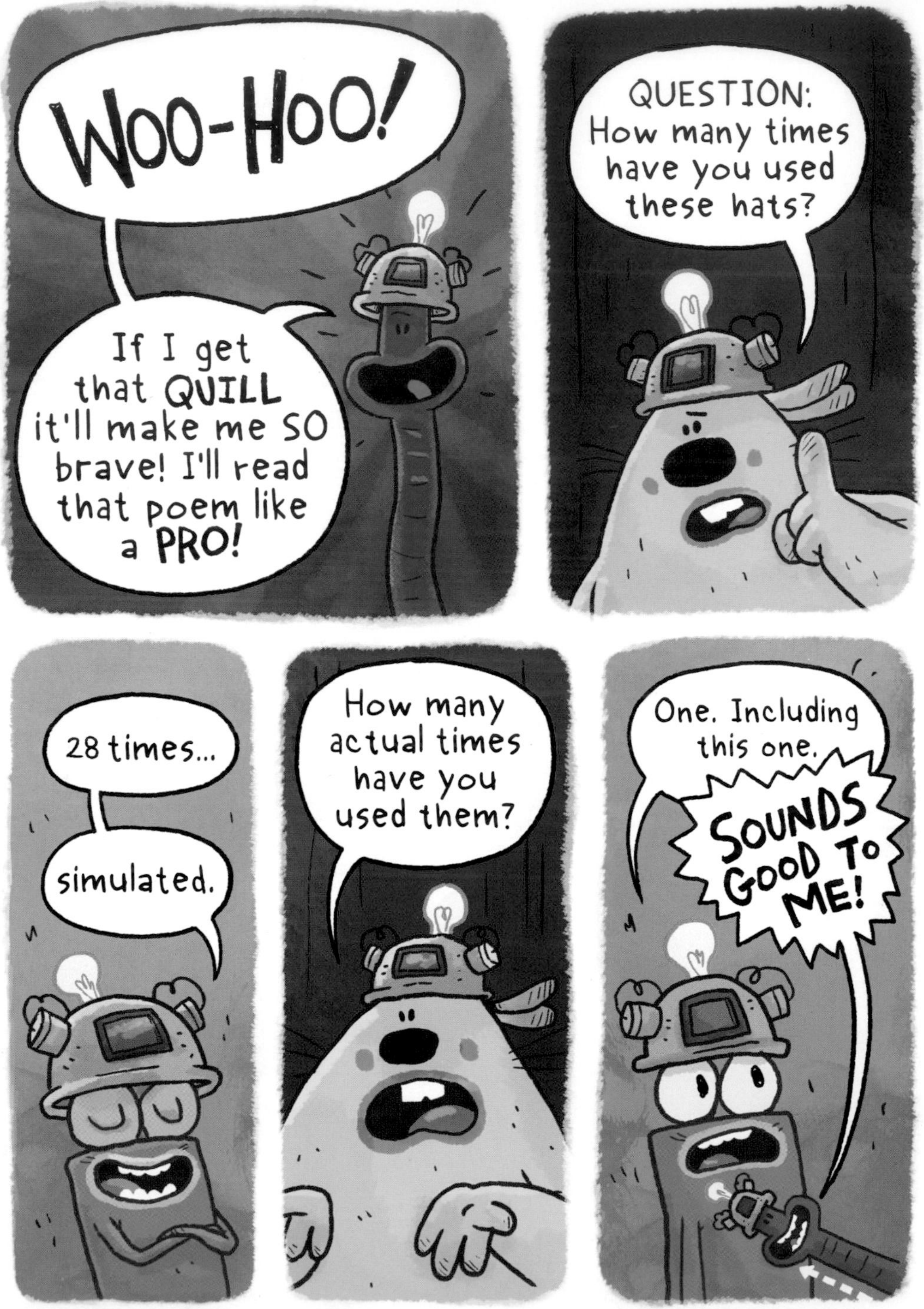
WOO-HOO!
If I get that QUILL it'll make me SO brave! I'll read that poem like a PRO!
QUESTION: How many times have you used these hats?
28 times...
simulated.
How many actual times have you used them?
One. Including this one.
SOUNDS GOOD TO ME!

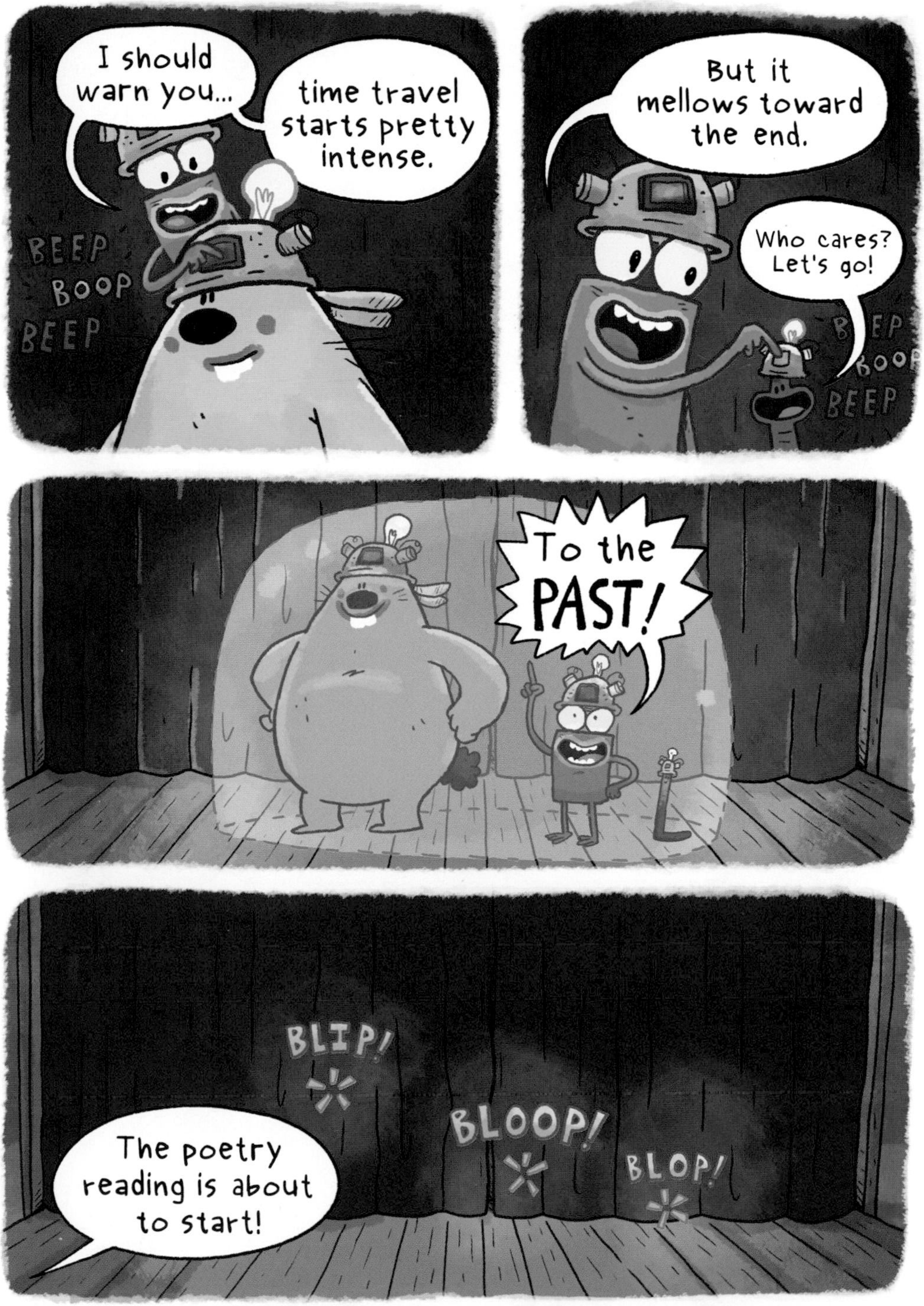
I should warn you...
time travel starts pretty intense.
BEEP BOOP BEEP
But it mellows toward the end.
Who cares? Let's go!
BEEP BOOP BEEP
To the PAST!
BLIP!
BLOOP!
BLOP!
The poetry reading is about to start!

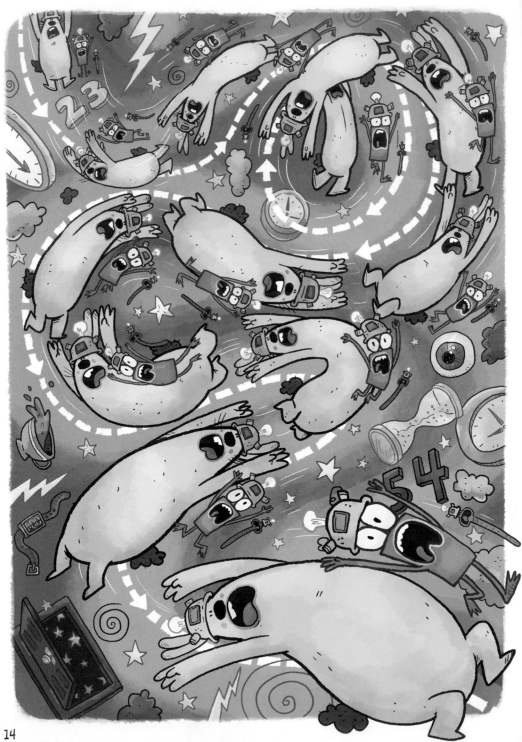

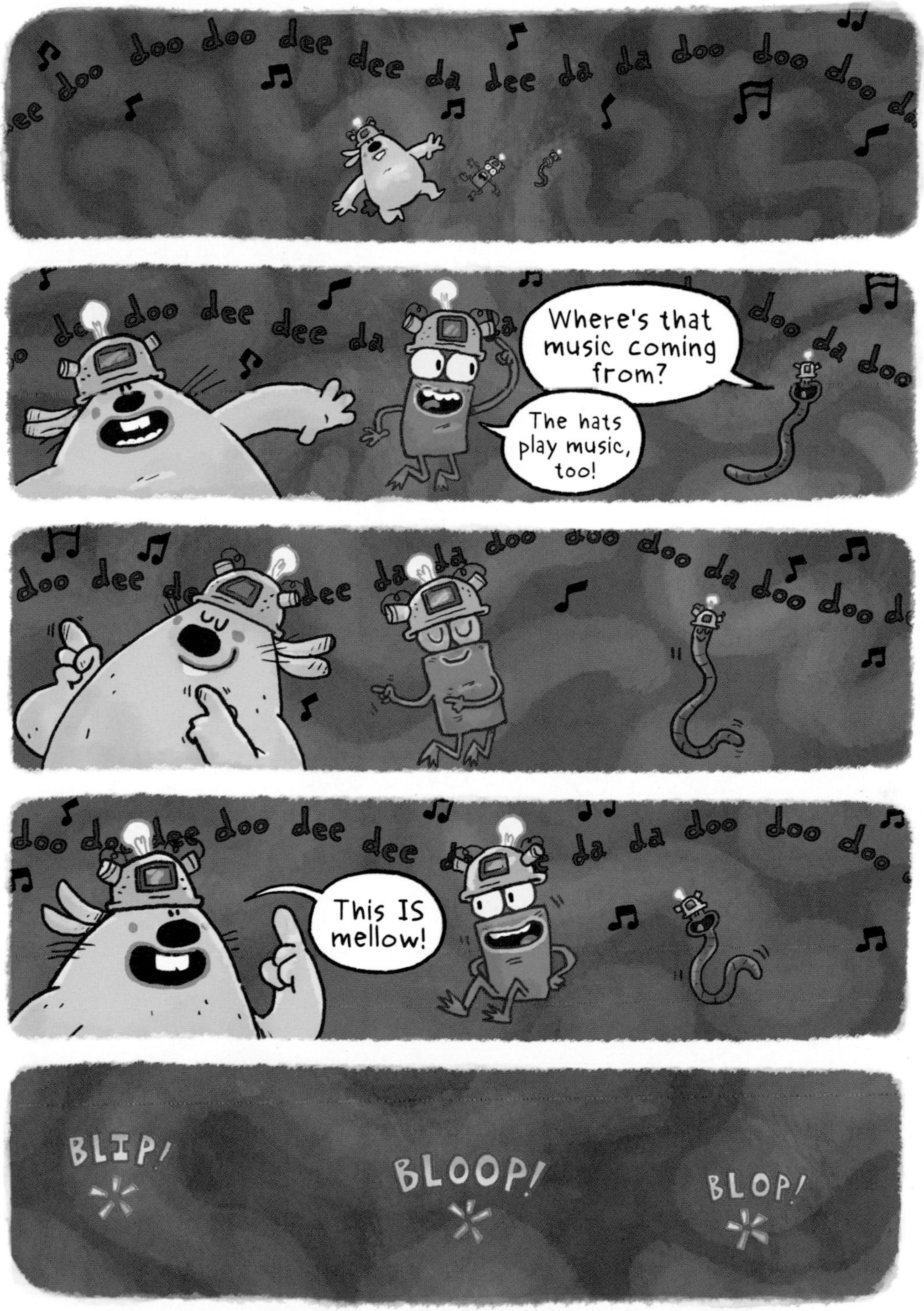
Where's that music coming from?
The hats play music, too!
This IS mellow!
BLIP!
BLOOP!
BLOP!

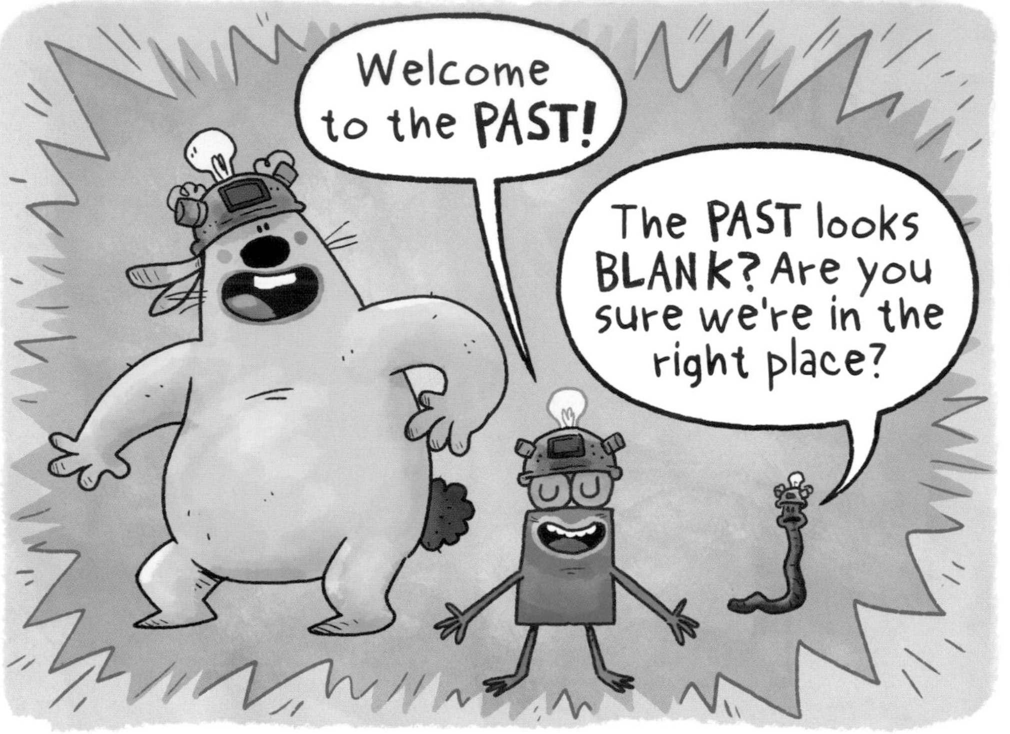
Welcome to the PAST!
The PAST looks BLANK? Are you sure we're in the right place?

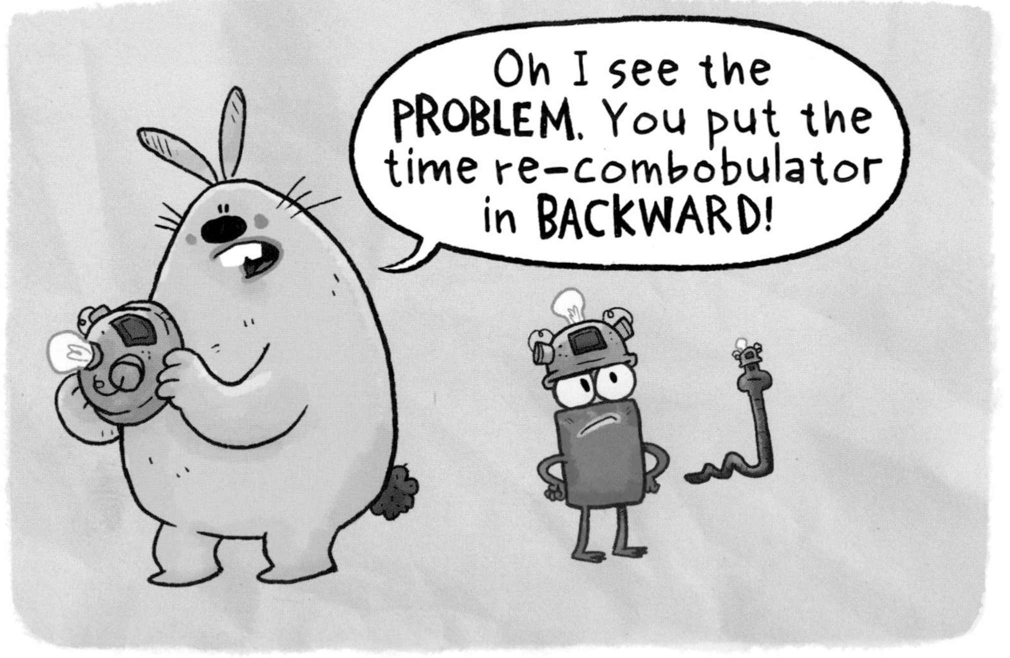
Oh I see the PROBLEM. You put the time re-combobulator in BACKWARD!

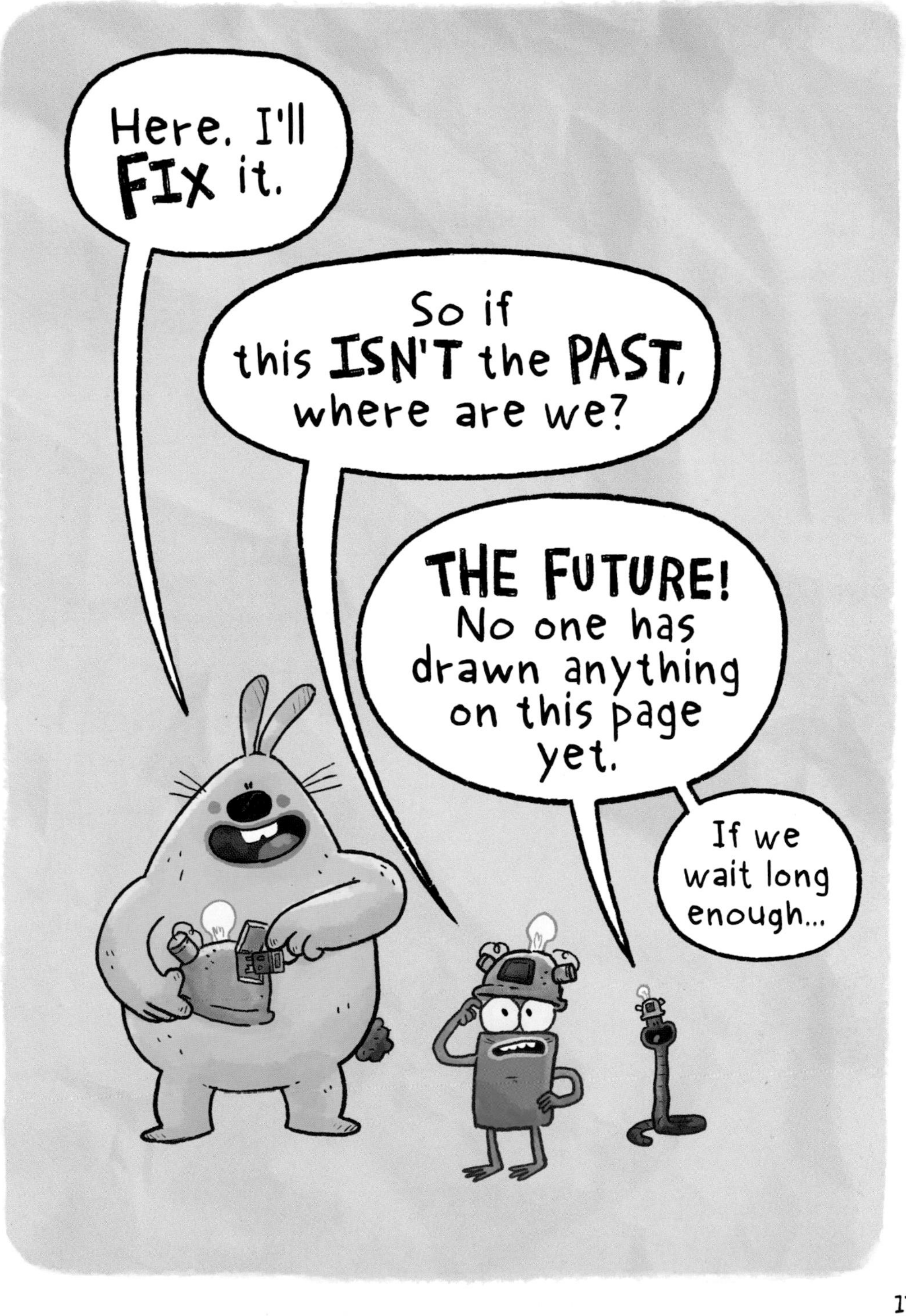
Here. I'll FIX it.
So if this ISN'T the PAST, where are we?
THE FUTURE! No one has drawn anything on this page yet.
If we wait long enough...

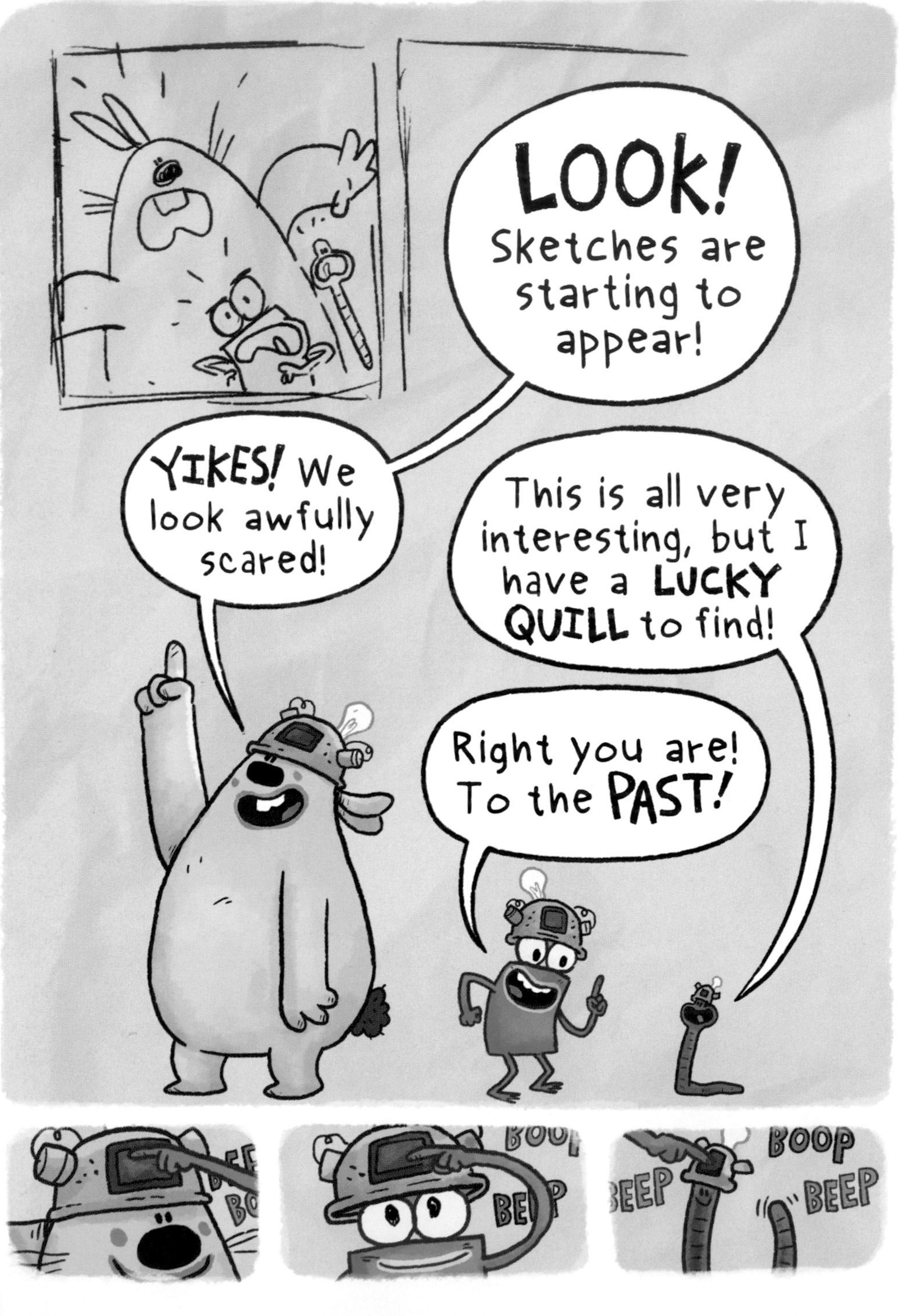
LOOK! Sketches are starting to appear!
YIKES! We look awfully scared!
This is all very interesting, but I have a LUCKY QUILL to find!
Right you are! To the PAST!
BOOP
BEEP
BEEP

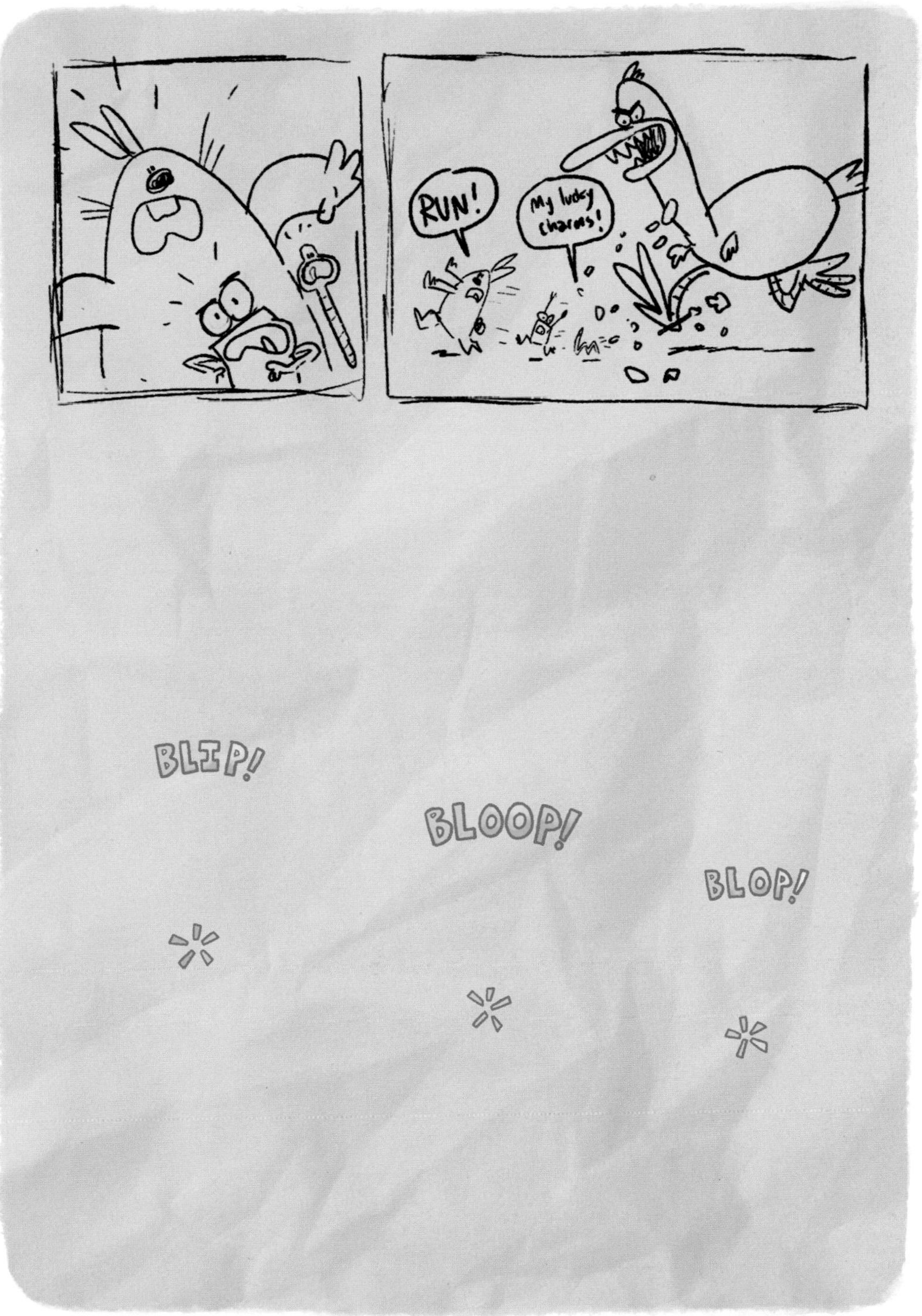
RUN!
My lucky charms!
BLIP!
BLOOP!
BLOP!

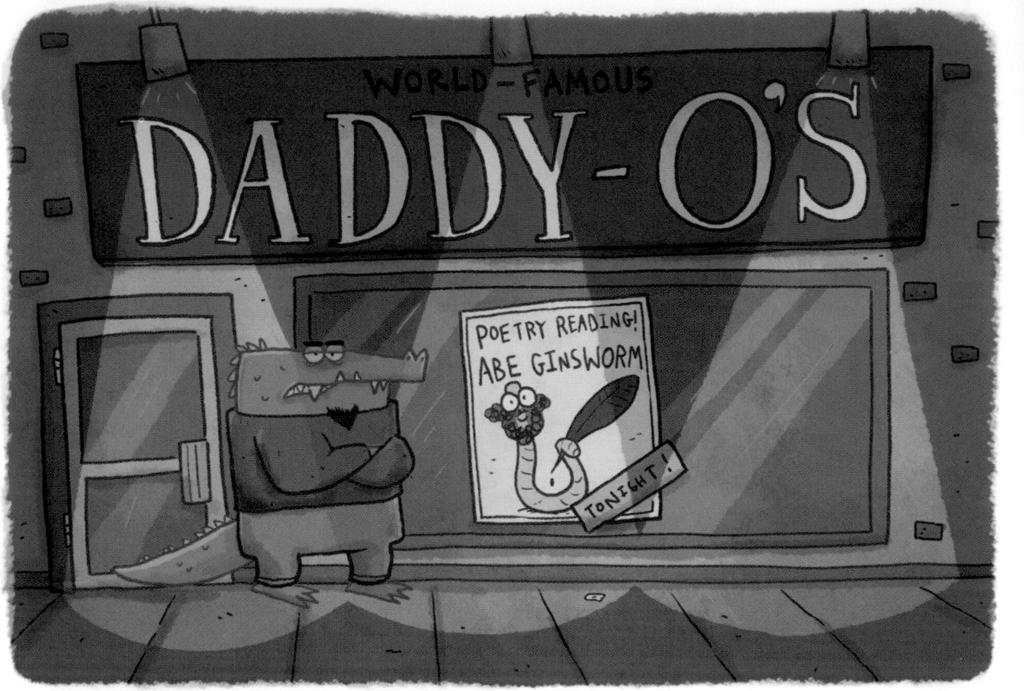
WORLD-FAMOUS
DADDY-O'S
POETRY READING!
ABE GINSWORM
TONIGHT!

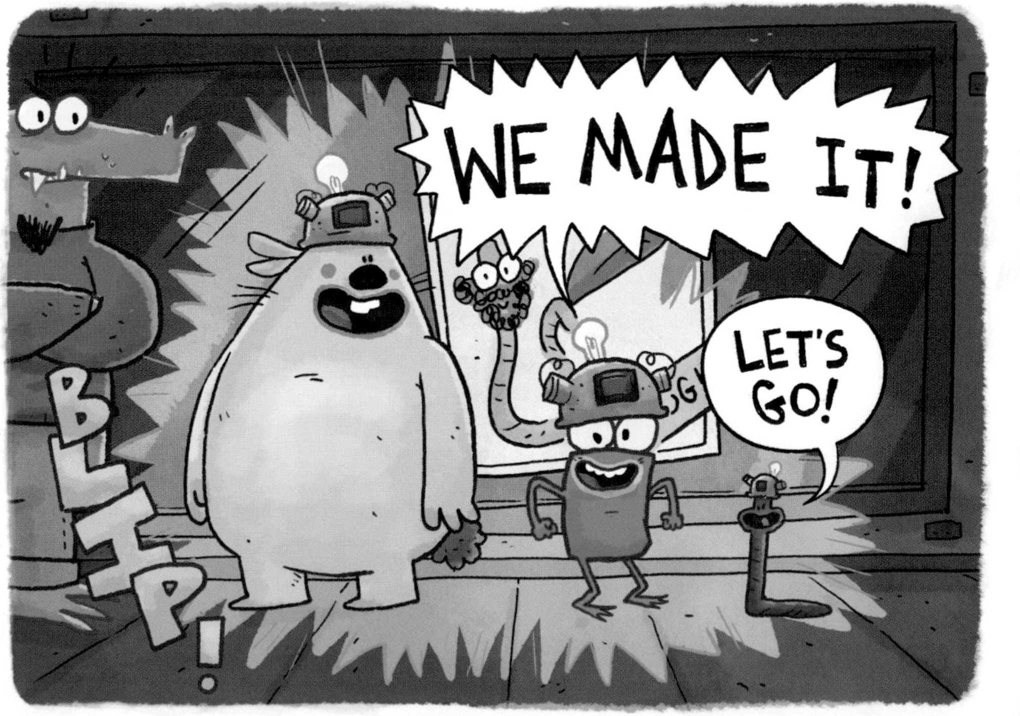
WE MADE IT!
LET'S GO!
BLIP!

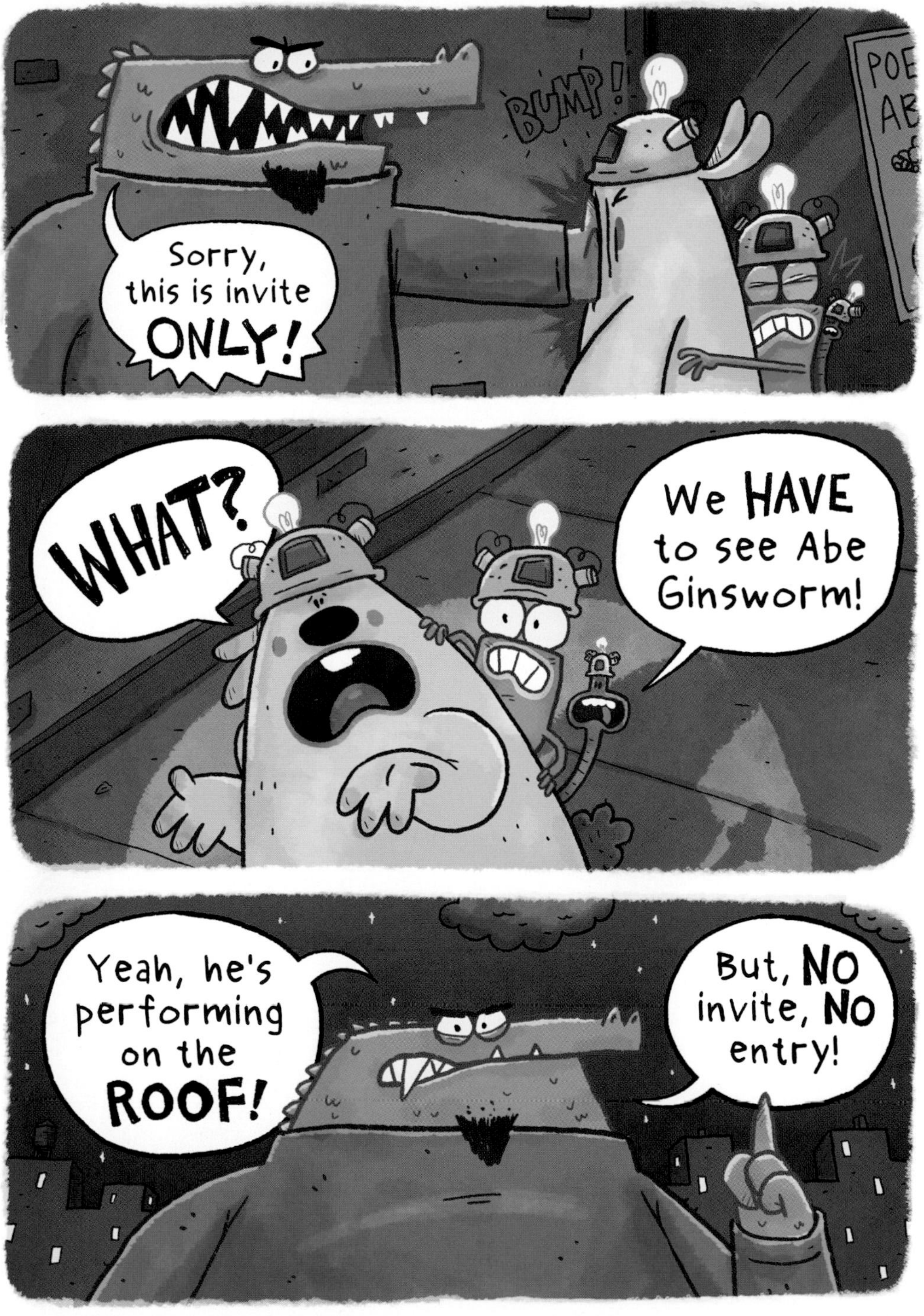
BUMP!
Sorry, this is invite ONLY!
WHAT?
We HAVE to see Abe Ginsworm!
Yeah, he's performing on the ROOF!
But, NO invite, NO entry!

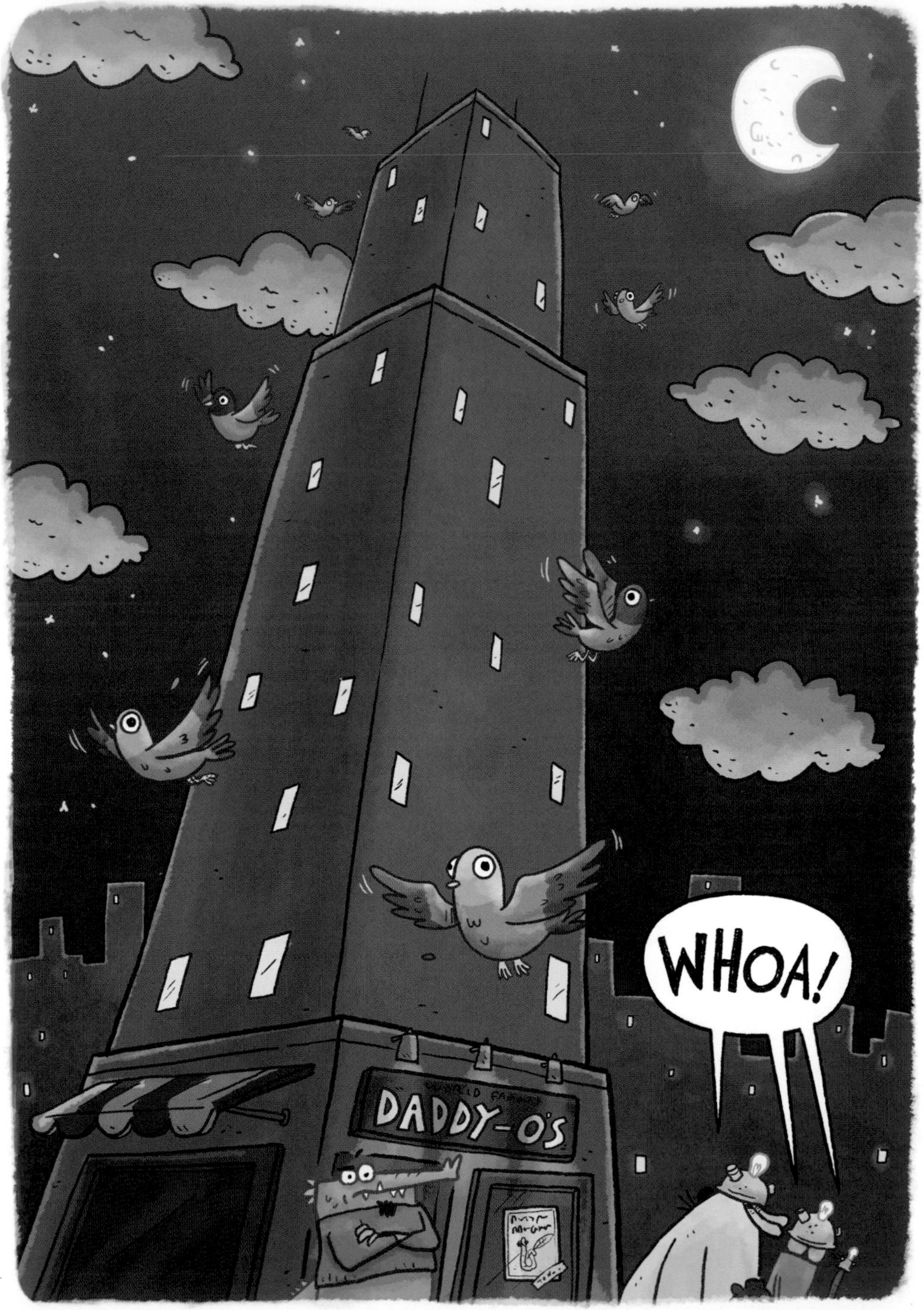
DADDY-O'S
WHOA!

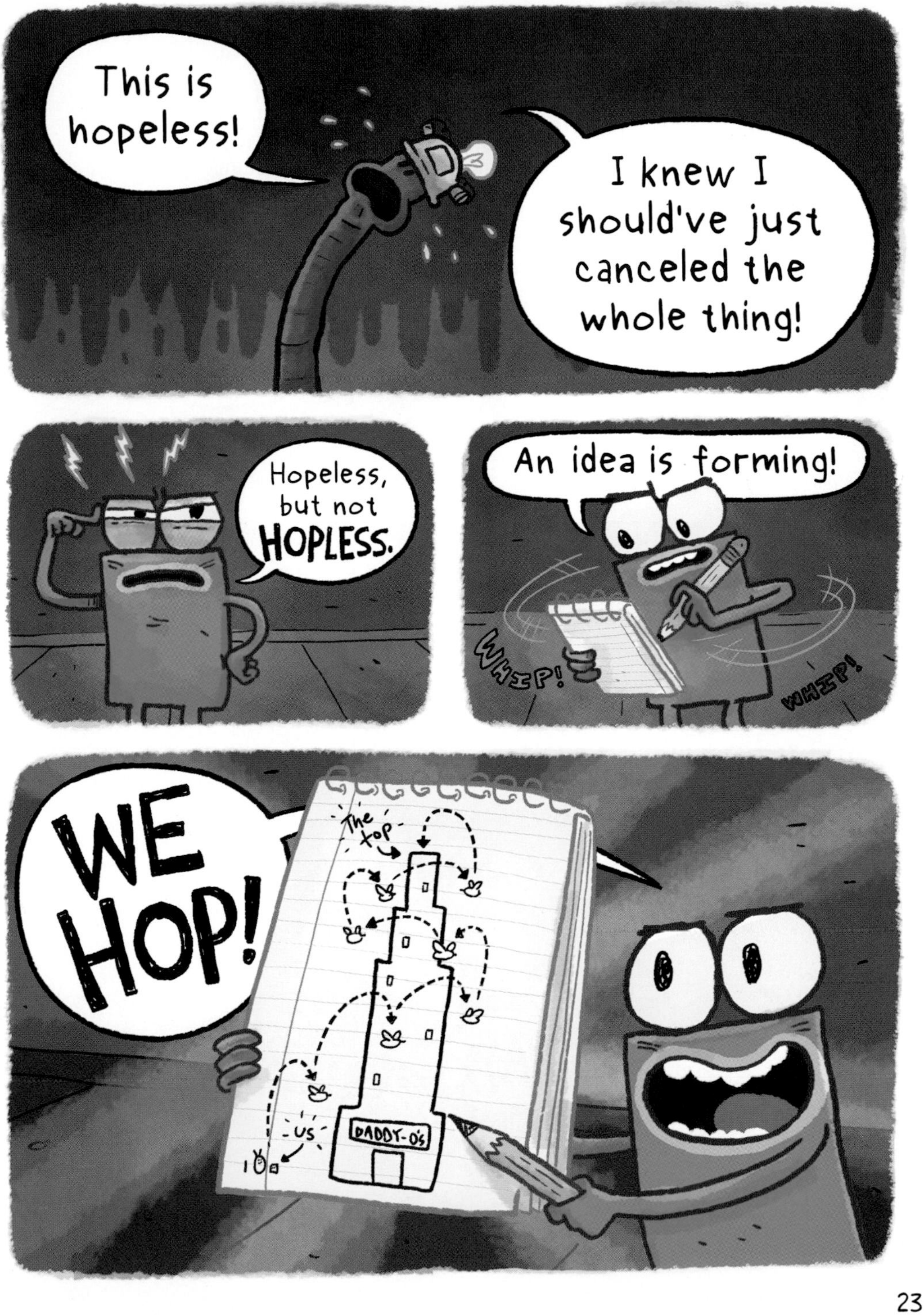
This is hopeless!
I knew I should've just canceled the whole thing!
Hopeless, but not HOPLESS.
An idea is forming!
WHIP!
WHIP!
WE HOP!
The top
US
DADDY-O's

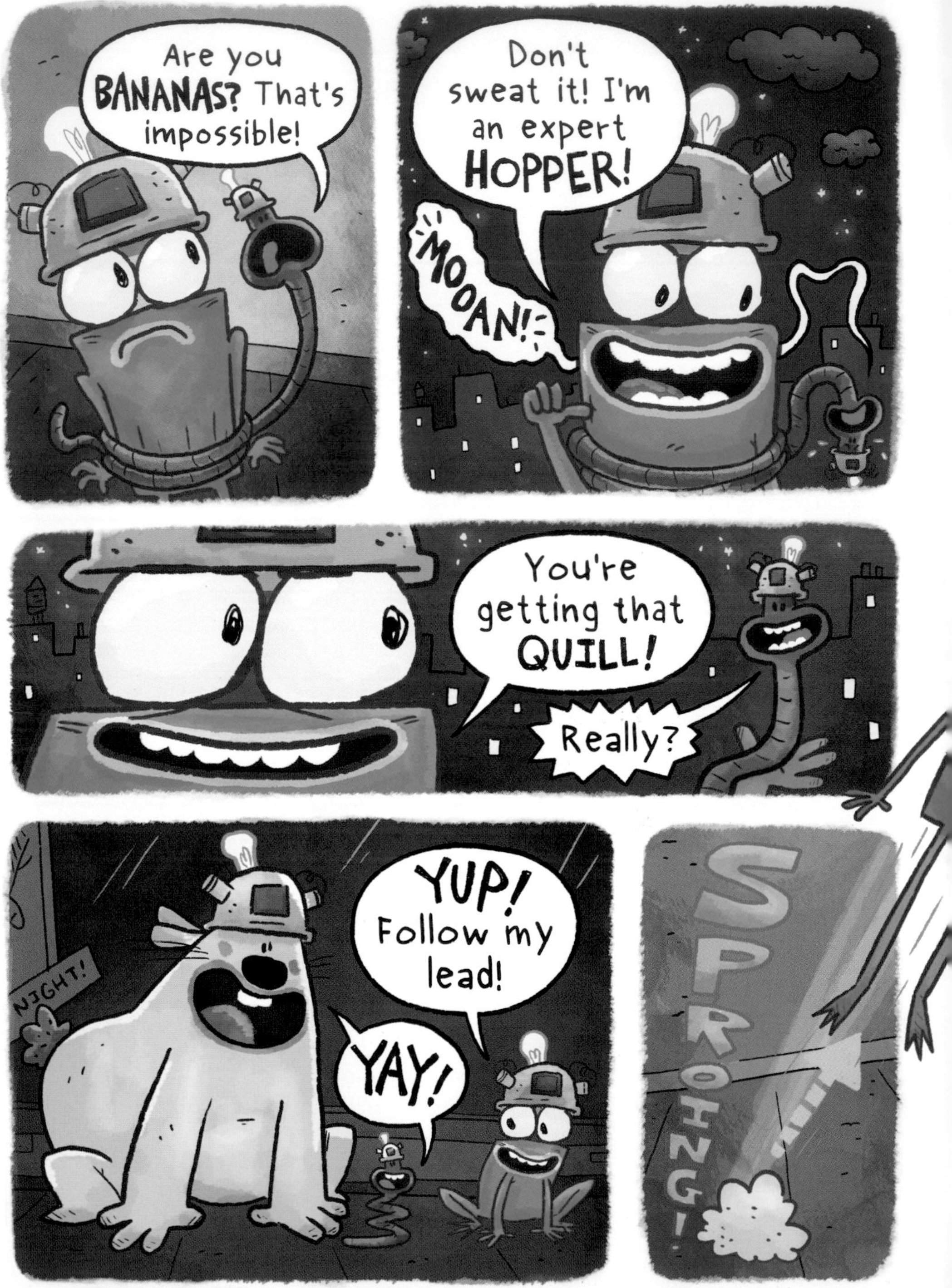

Are you BANANAS? That's impossible!
Don't sweat it! I'm an expert HOPPER!
MOOAN!
You're getting that QUILL!
Really?
NIGHT!
YUP! Follow my lead!
YAY!
SPROING!

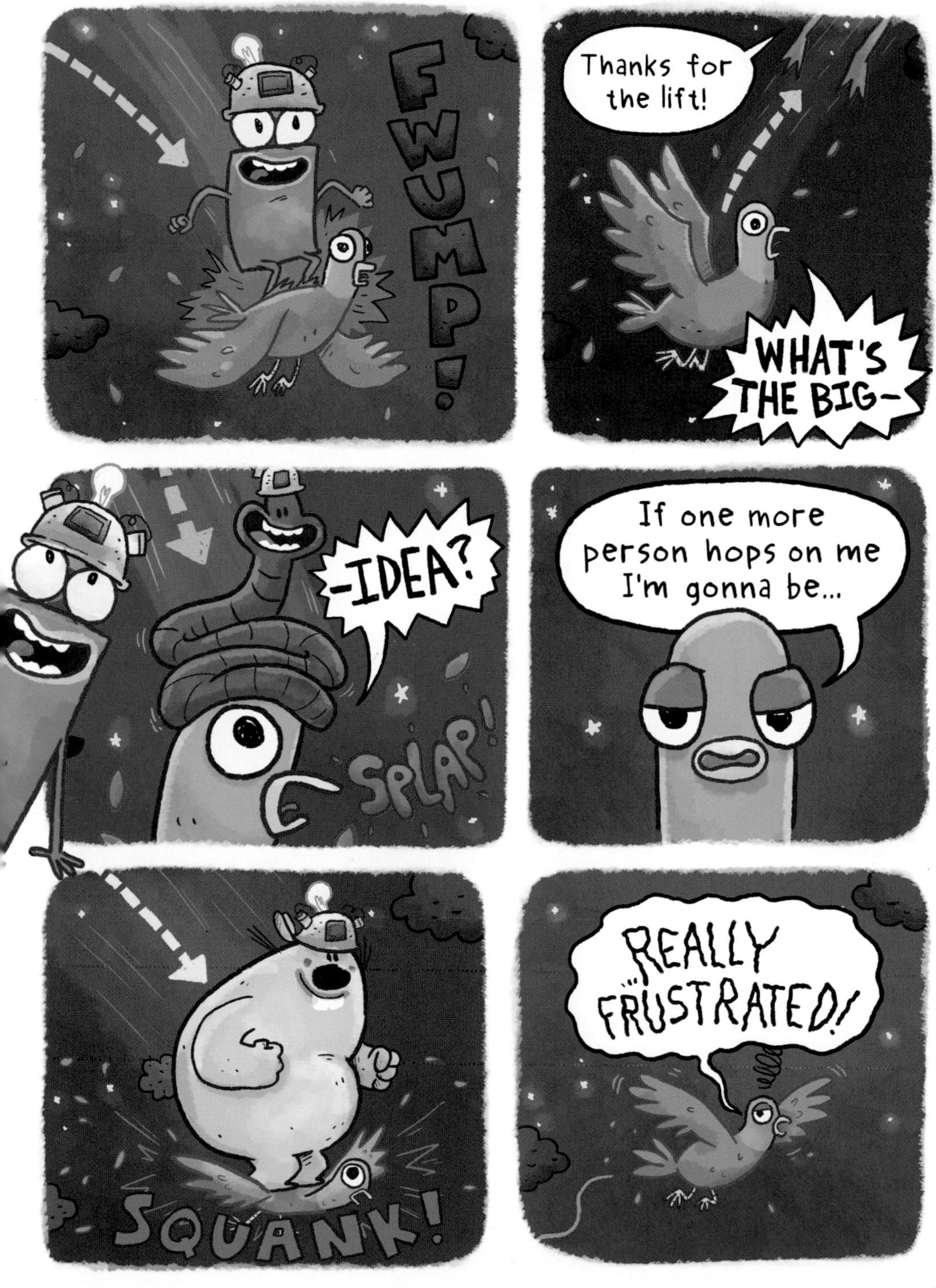
FWUMP!
Thanks for the lift!
WHAT'S THE BIG-
-IDEA?
SPLAP!
If one more person hops on me I'm gonna be...
SQUANK!
...REALLY FRUSTRATED!

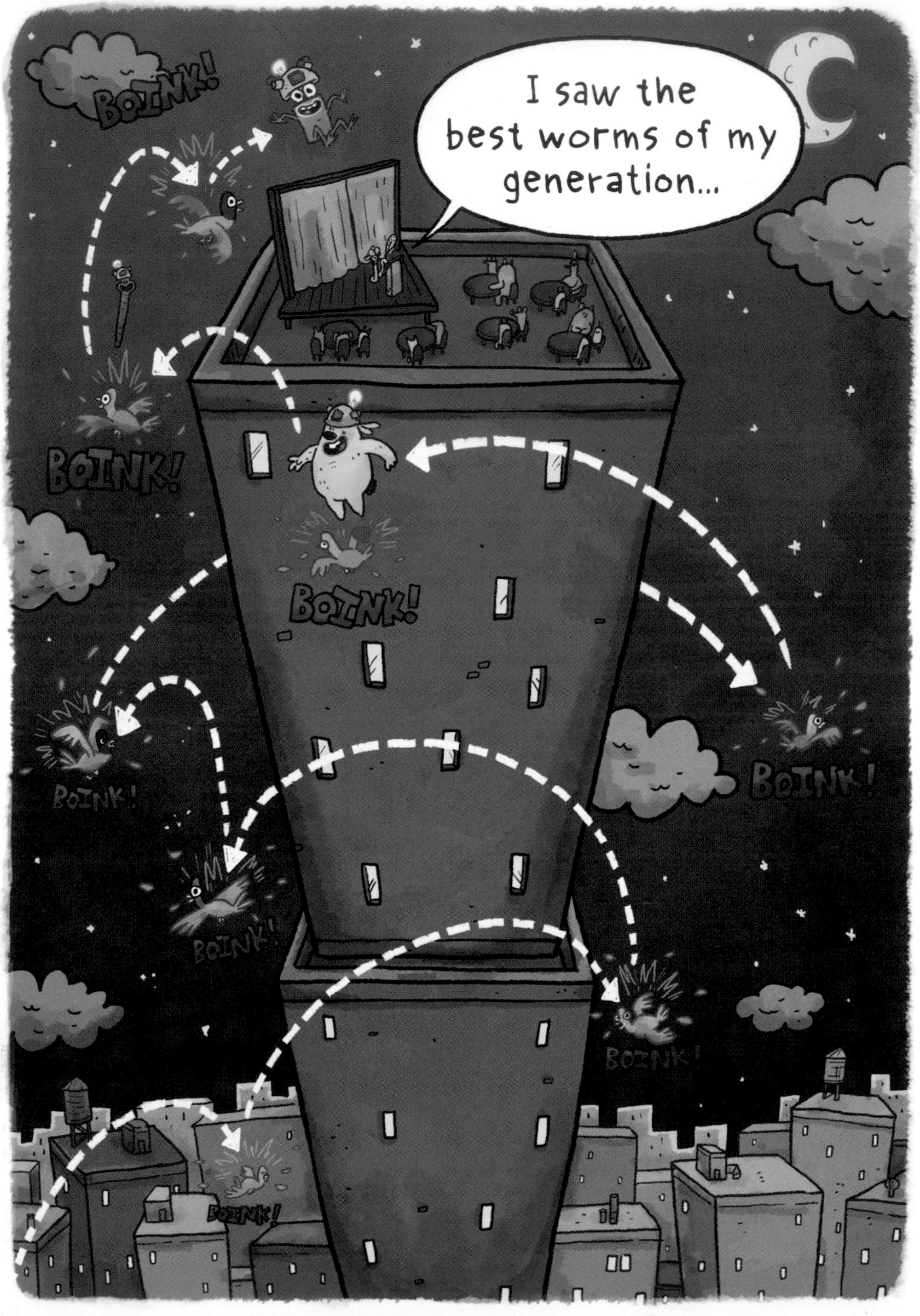
I saw the best worms of my generation...
BOINK!
BOINK!
BOINK!
BOINK!
BOINK!
BOINK!
BOINK!
BOINK!

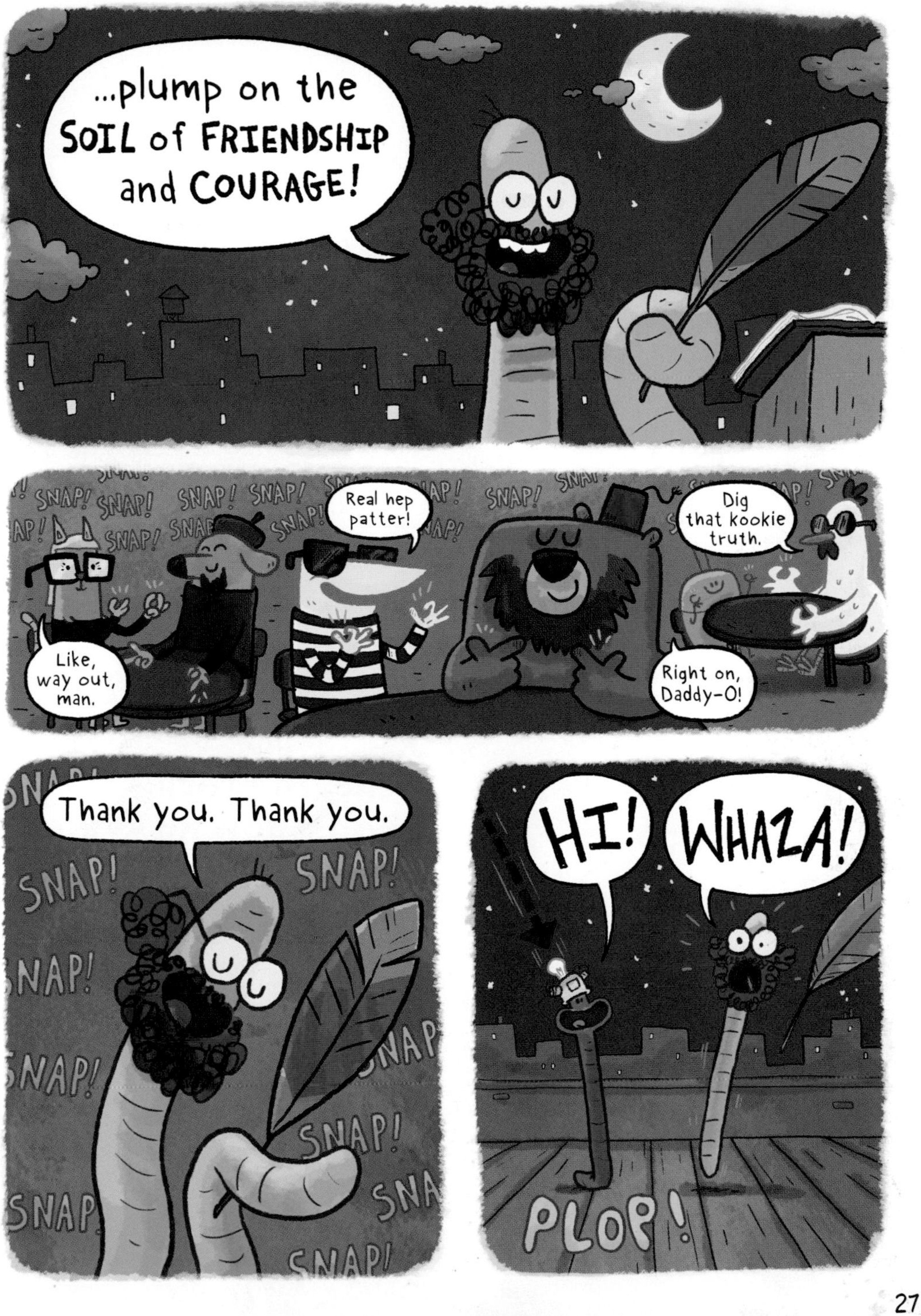
...plump on the SOIL of FRIENDSHIP and COURAGE!
SNAP! SNAP! SNAP! SNAP! SNAP!
Like, way out, man.
Real hep patter!
Right on, Daddy-O!
Dig that kookie truth.
Thank you. Thank you.
SNAP! SNAP! SNAP! SNAP! SNAP!
HI!
WHAZA!
PLOP!

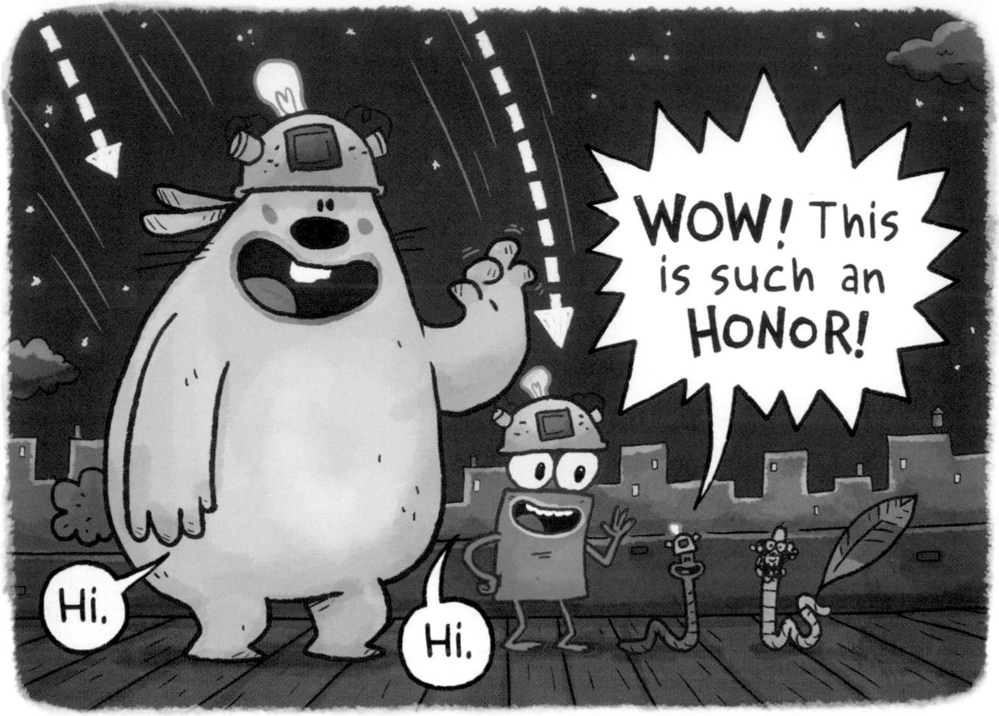
WOW! This is such an HONOR!
Hi.
Hi.

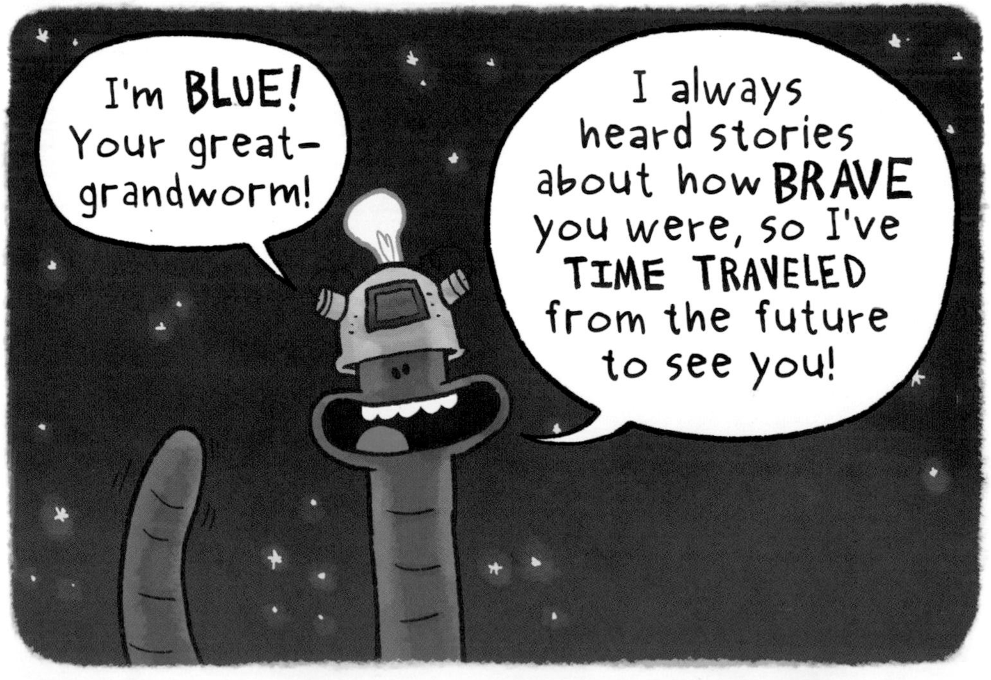
I'm BLUE! Your great-grandworm!
I always heard stories about how BRAVE you were, so I've TIME TRAVELED from the future to see you!

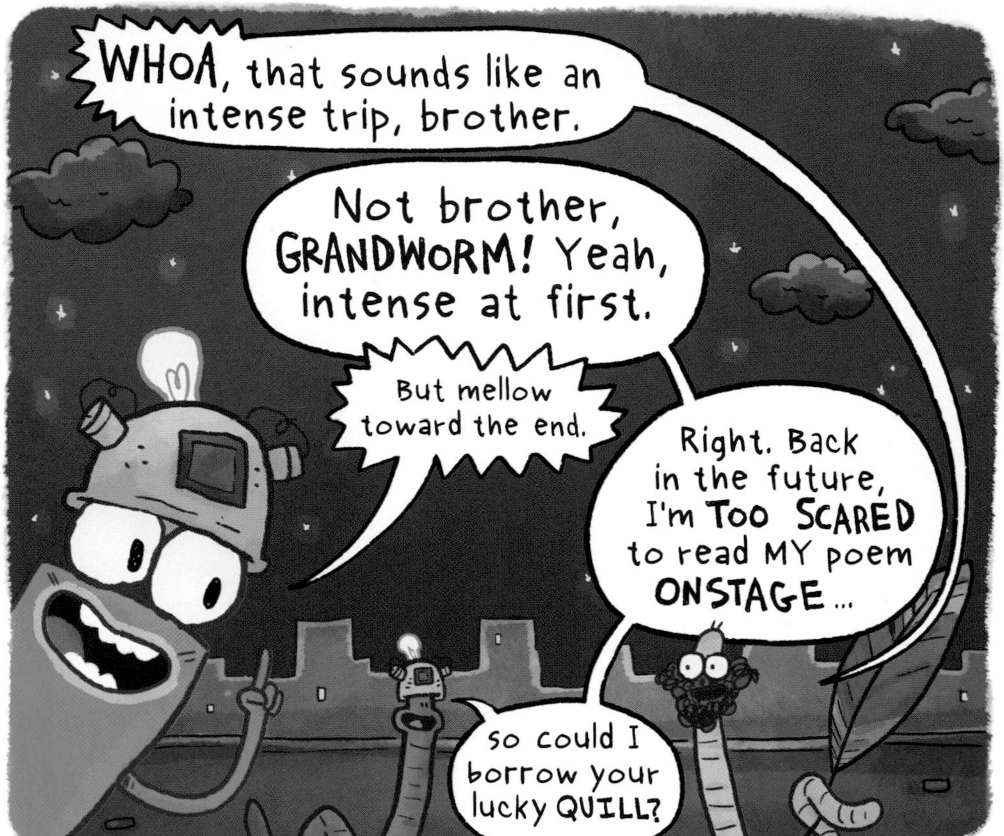
WHOA, that sounds like an intense trip, brother.
Not brother, GRANDWORM! Yeah, intense at first.
But mellow toward the end.
Right. Back in the future, I'm TOO SCARED to read MY poem ONSTAGE...
so could I borrow your lucky QUILL?

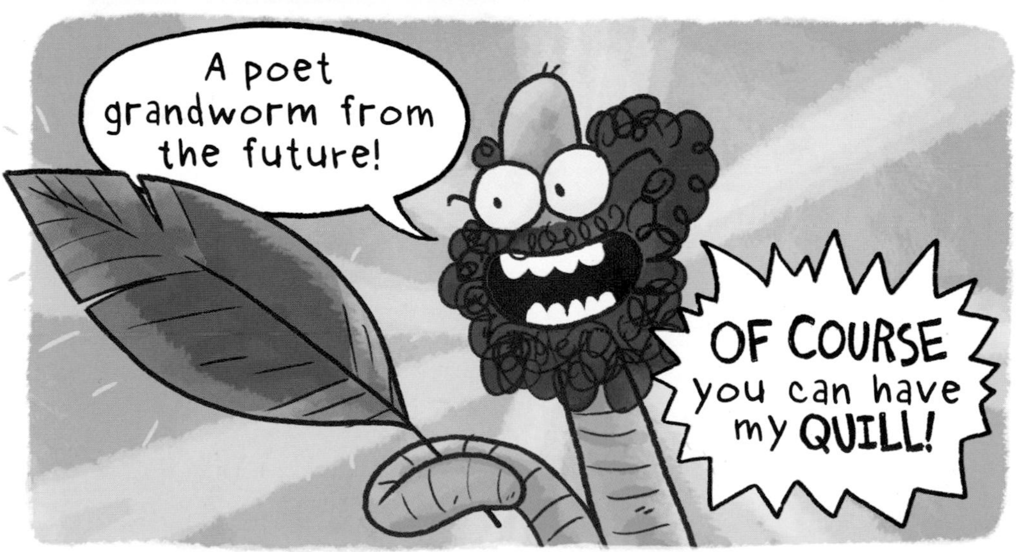
A poet grandworm from the future!
OF COURSE you can have my QUILL!

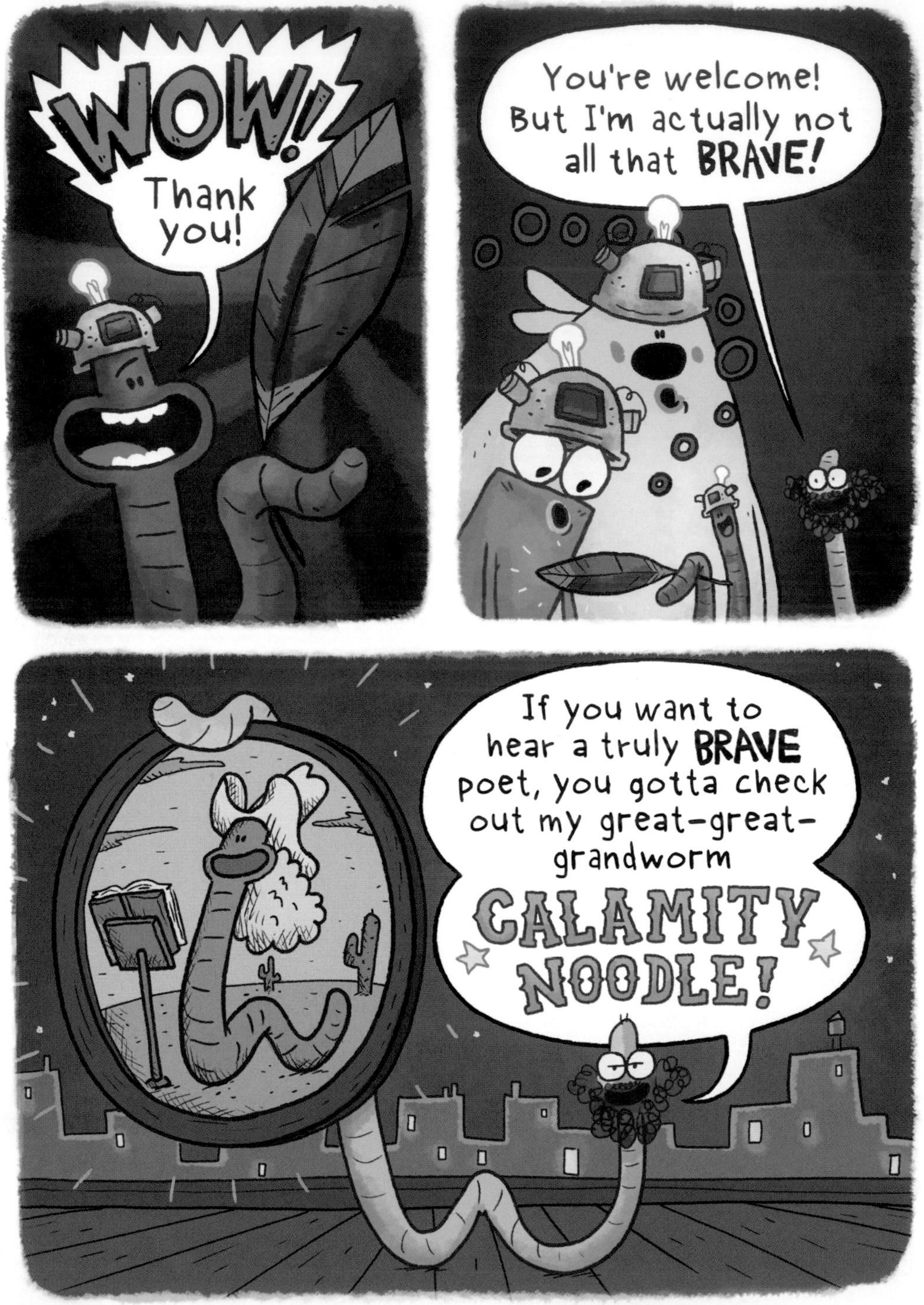
WOW!! Thank you!
You're welcome! But I'm actually not all that BRAVE!
If you want to hear a truly BRAVE poet, you gotta check out my great-great-grandworm
CALAMITY NOODLE!

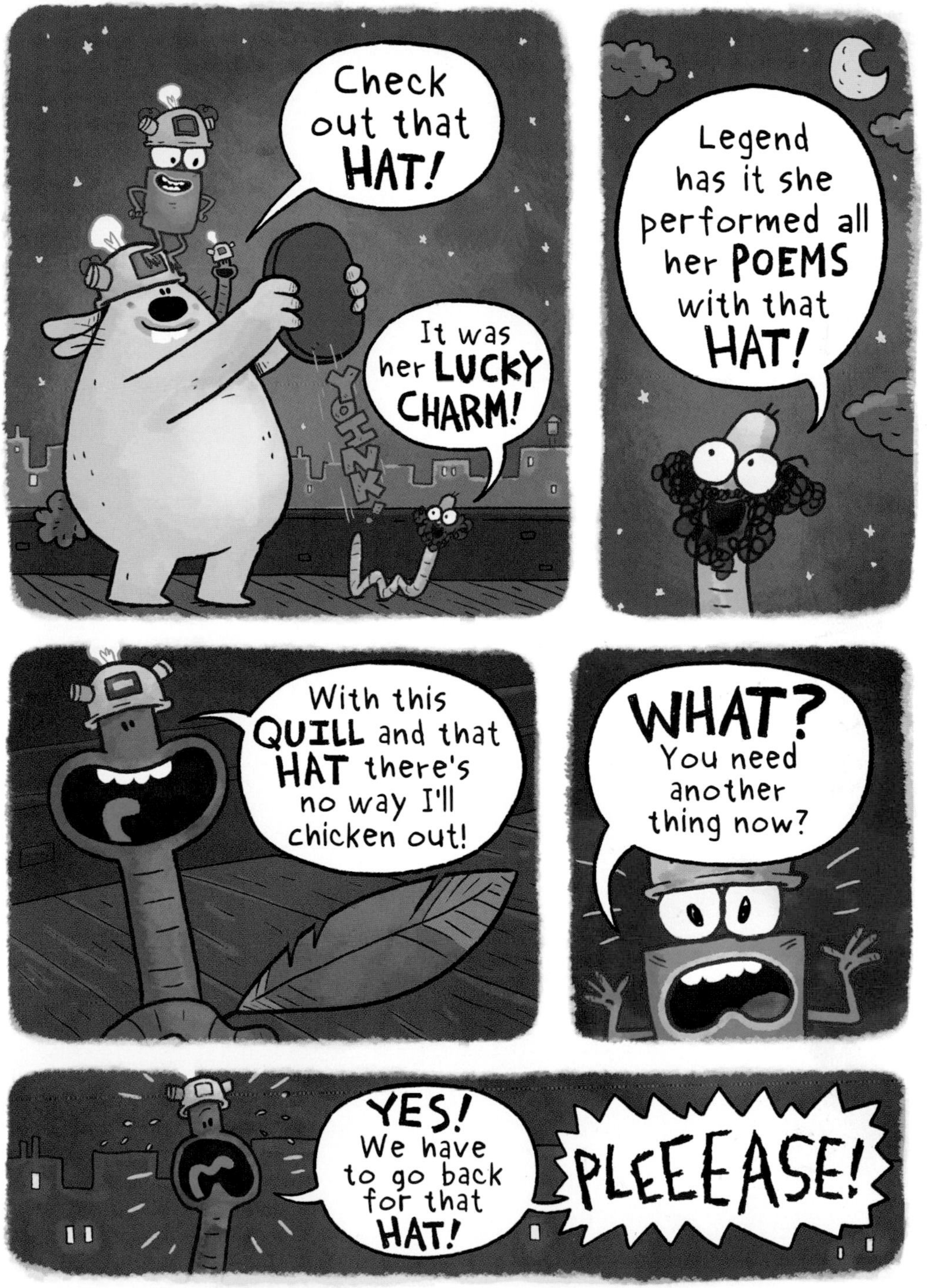
Check out that HAT!
It was her LUCKY CHARM!
YOINK!
Legend has it she performed all her POEMS with that HAT!
With this QUILL and that HAT there's no way I'll chicken out!
WHAT? You need another thing now?
YES! We have to go back for that HAT!
PLEEEASE!

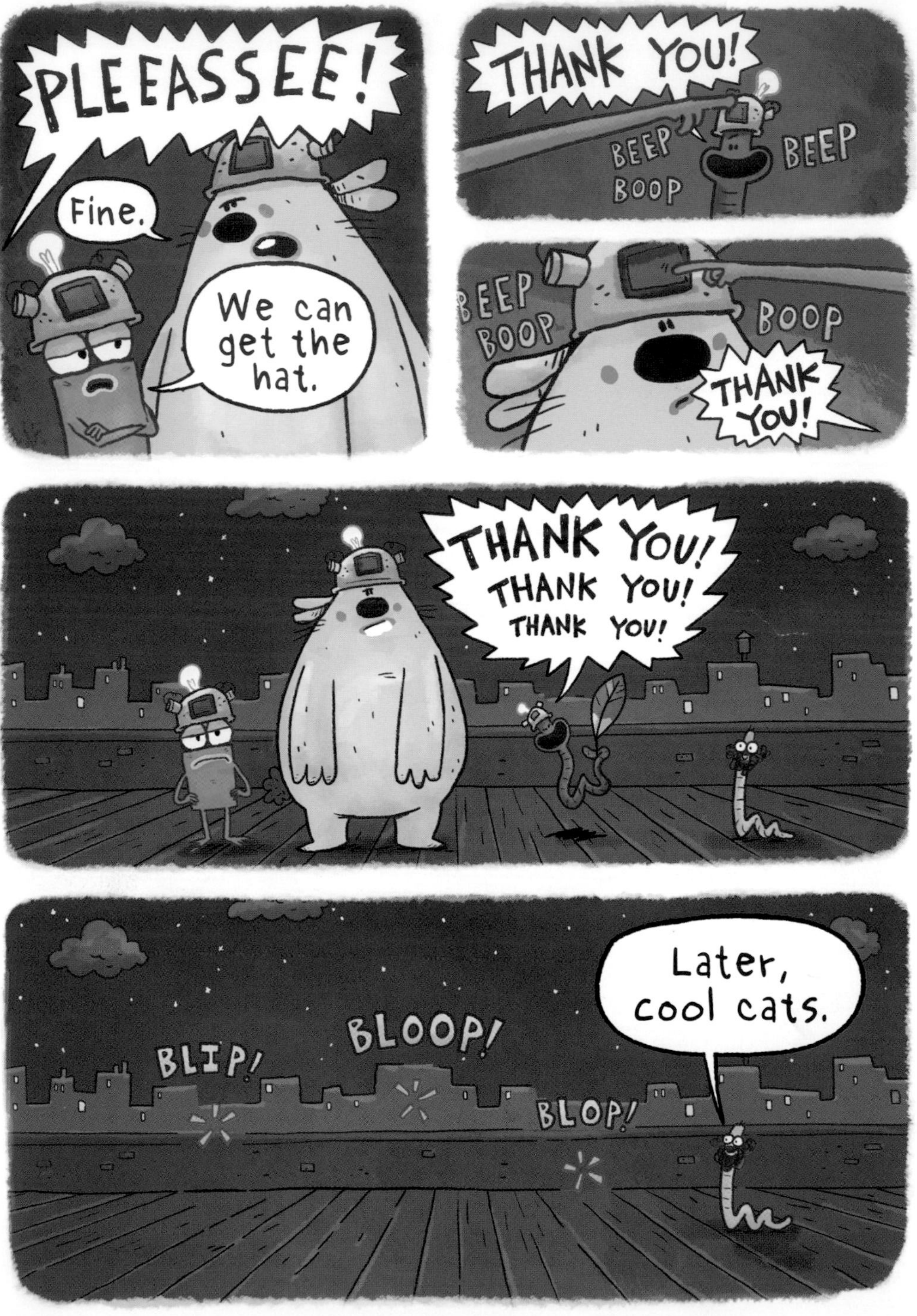

PLEEASSEE!
Fine.
We can get the hat.
THANK YOU!
BEEP BOOP
BEEP
BEEP BOOP
BOOP
THANK YOU!
THANK YOU! THANK YOU! THANK YOU!
BLIP!
BLOOP!
BLOP!
Later, cool cats.

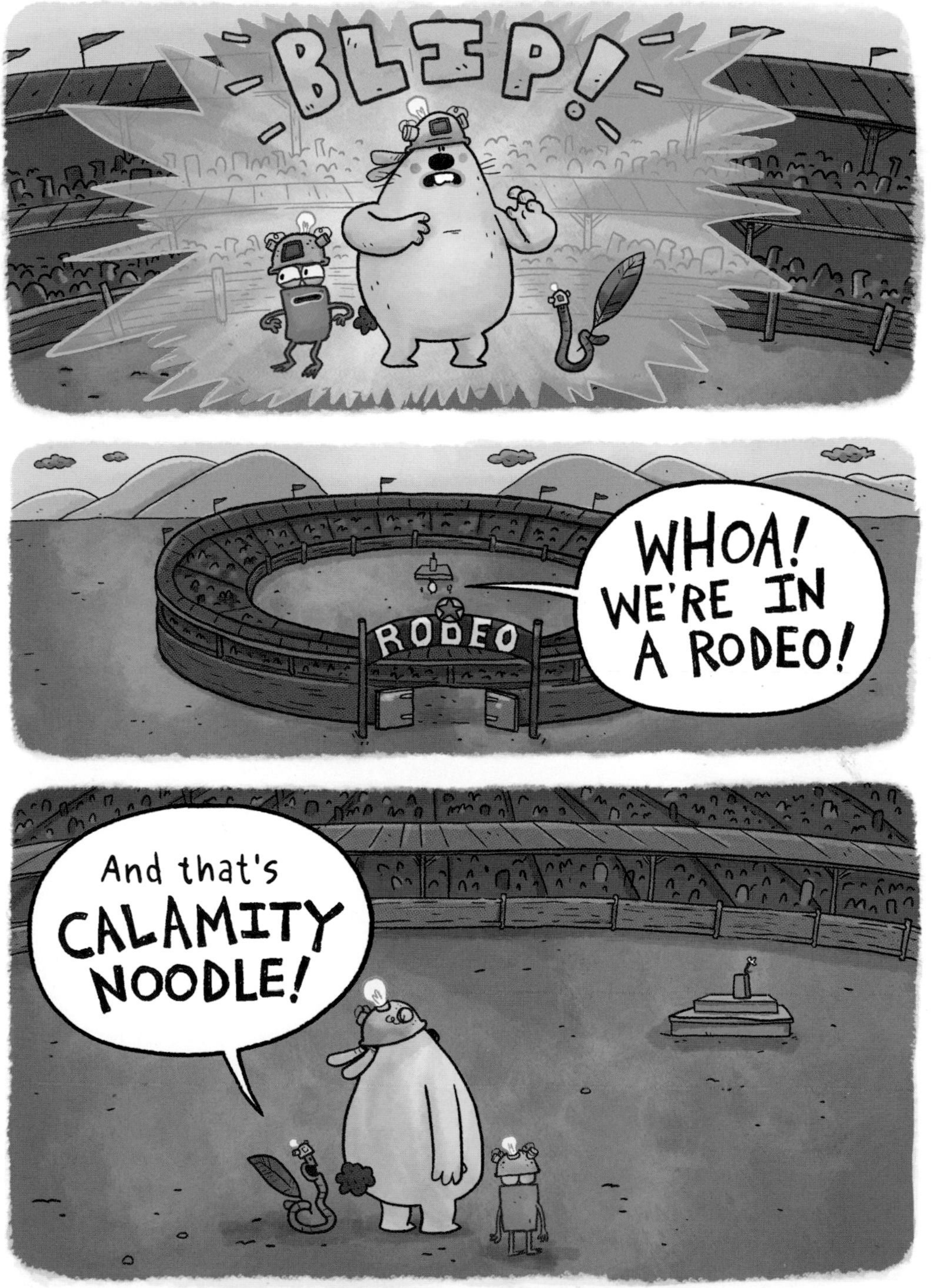
BLIP!
WHOA! WE'RE IN A RODEO!
RODEO
And that's CALAMITY NOODLE!

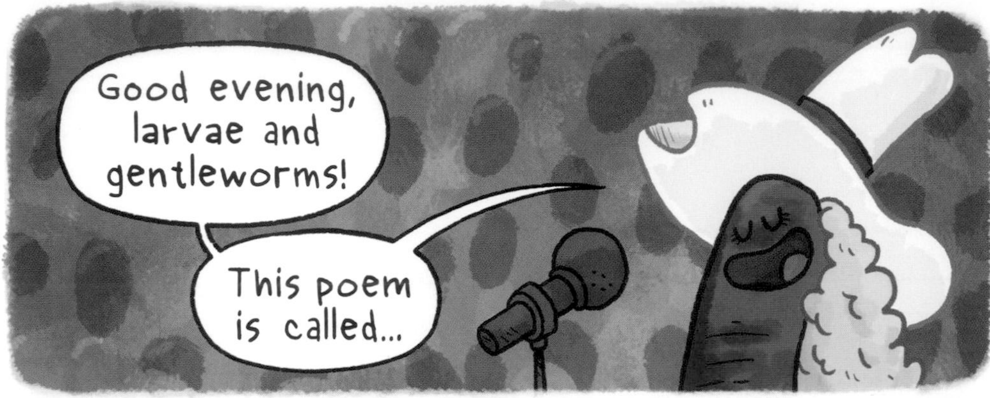
Good evening, larvae and gentleworms!
This poem is called...

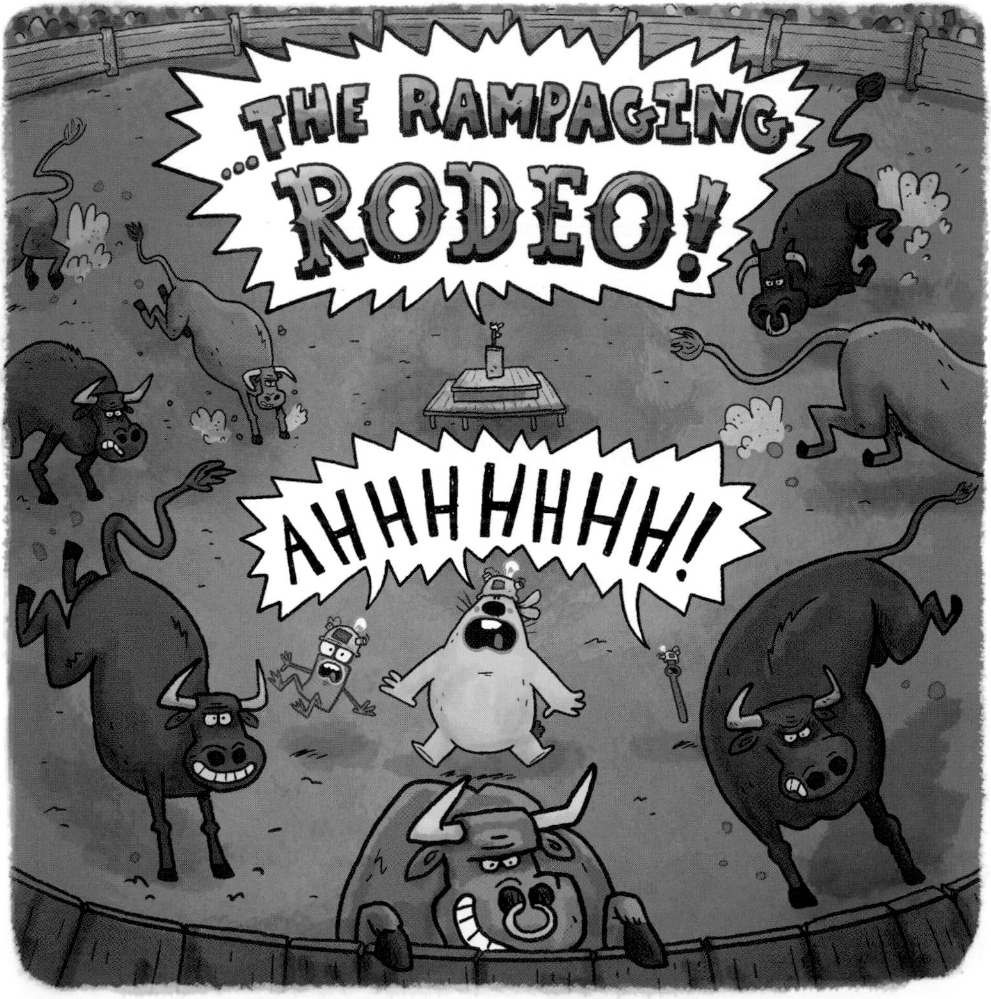
...THE RAMPAGING RODEO!
AHHHHHHH!

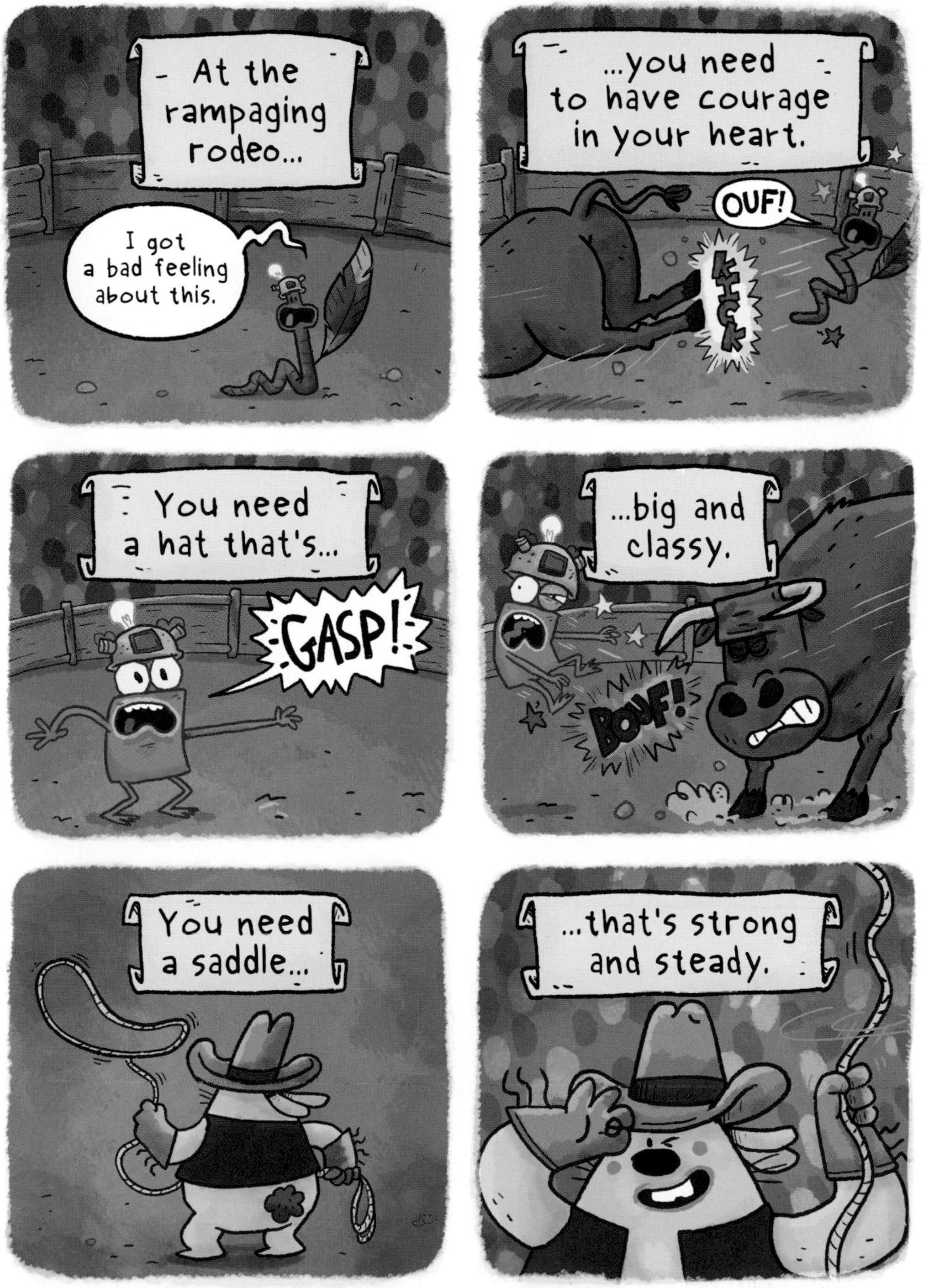

At the rampaging rodeo...
I got a bad feeling about this.
...you need to have courage in your heart.
KICK
OUF!
You need a hat that's...
GASP!
...big and classy.
BOUF!
You need a saddle...
...that's strong and steady.

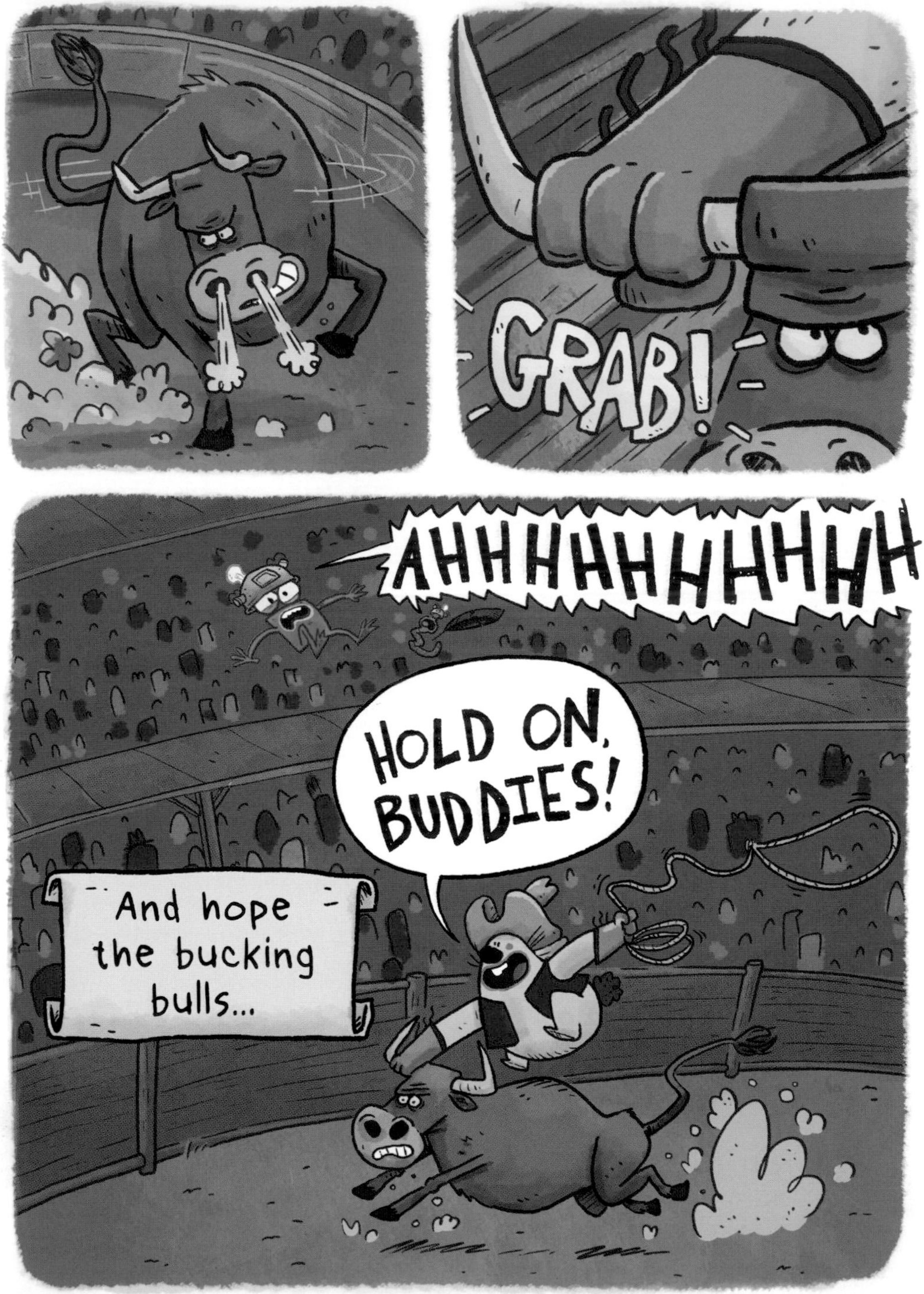
GRAB!
AHHHHHHHHHH
HOLD ON, BUDDIES!
And hope the bucking bulls...

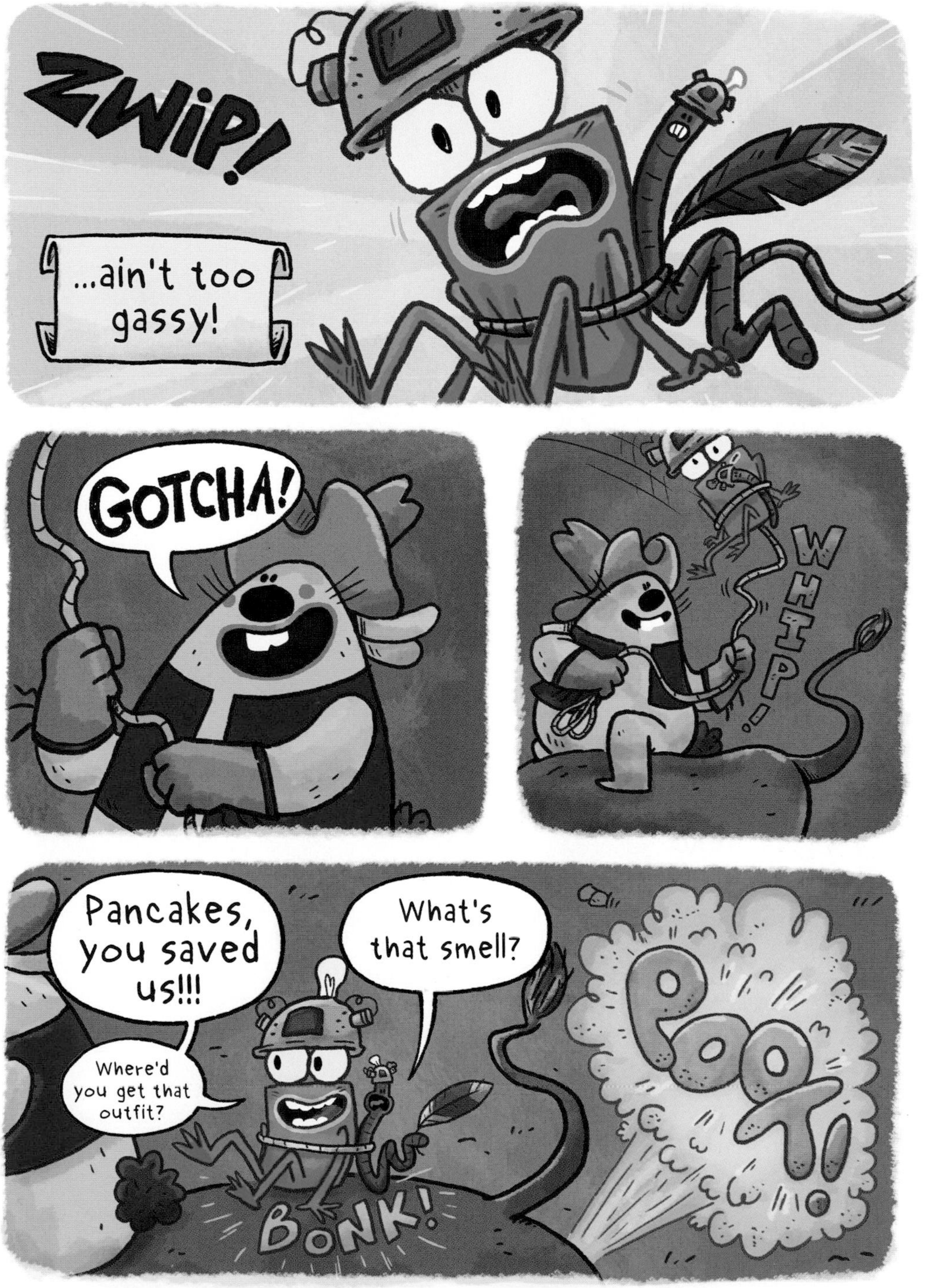
ZWIP!
...ain't too gassy!
GOTCHA!
WHIP!
Pancakes, you saved us!!!
Where'd you get that outfit?
What's that smell?
POOT!
BONK!

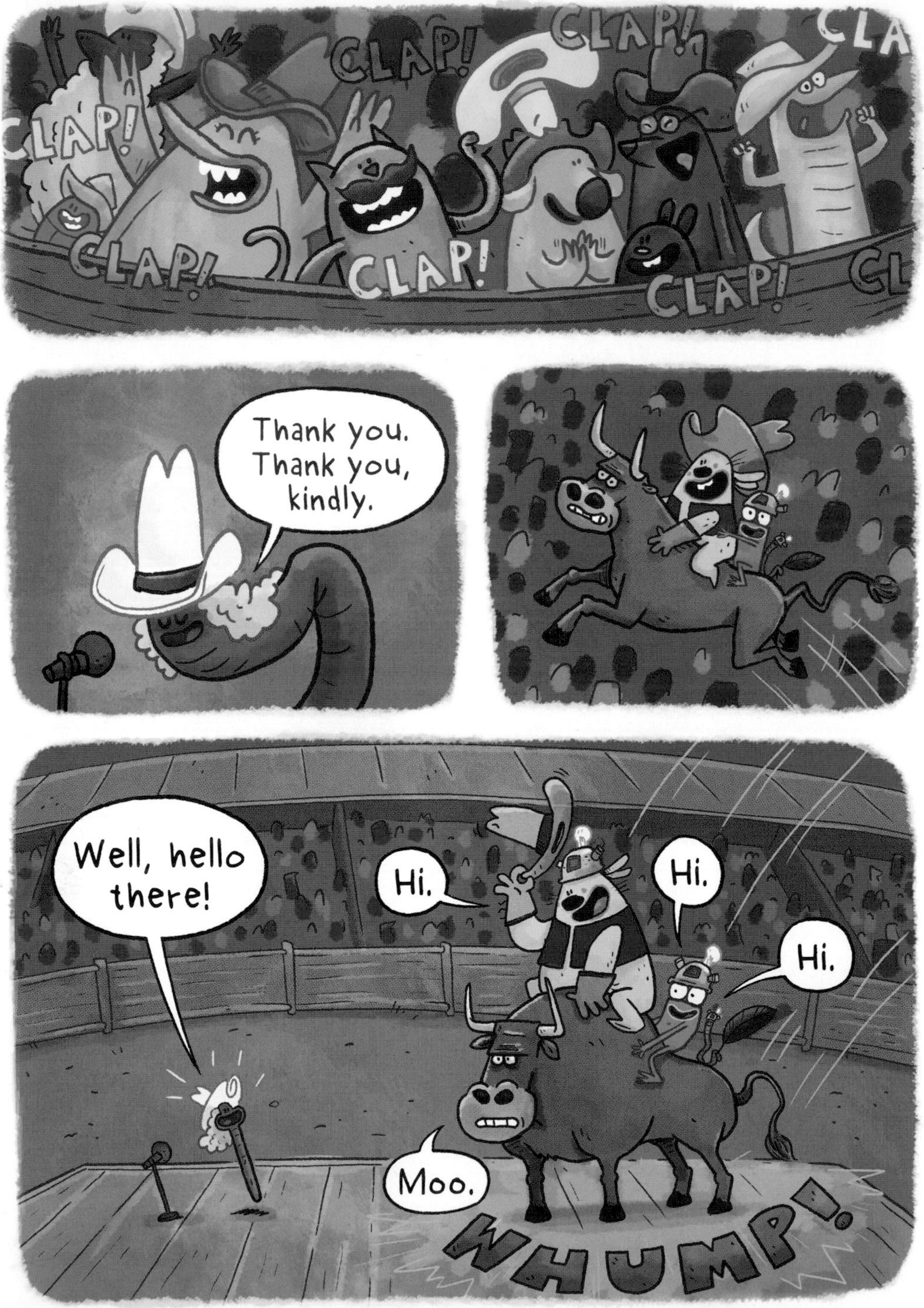
CLAP!
CLAP!
CLAP!
CLA
CLAP!
CLAP!
CLAP!
CL
Thank you. Thank you, kindly.
Well, hello there!
Hi.
Hi.
Hi.
Moo.
WHUMP!

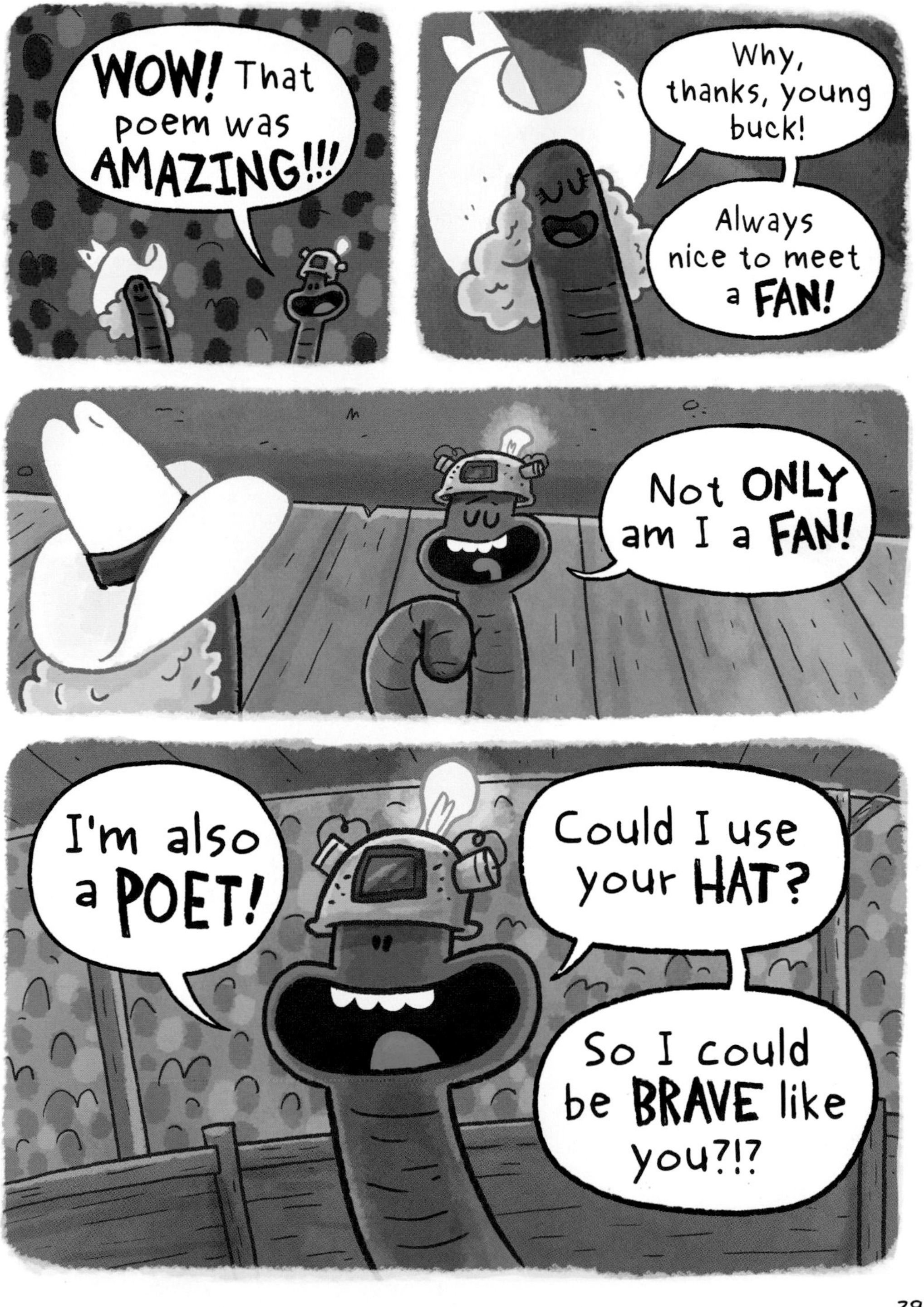
WOW! That poem was AMAZING!!!
Why, thanks, young buck!
Always nice to meet a FAN!
Not ONLY am I a FAN!
I'm also a POET!
Could I use your HAT?
So I could be BRAVE like you?!?

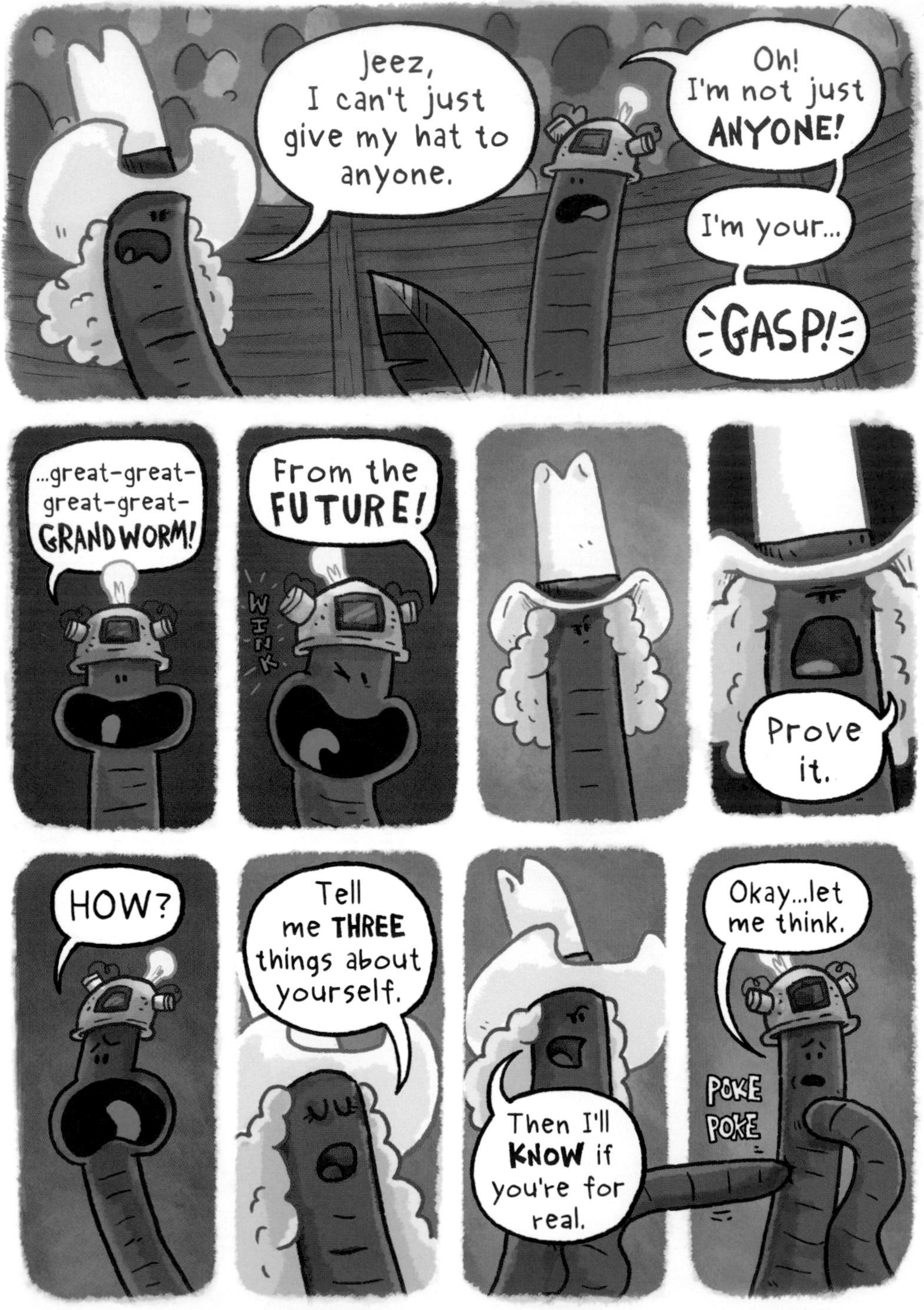
Jeez, I can't just give my hat to anyone.
Oh! I'm not just ANYONE!
I'm your...
GASP!
...great-great-great-great-GRANDWORM!
From the FUTURE!
WINK
Prove it.
HOW?
Tell me THREE things about yourself.
Then I'll KNOW if you're for real.
Okay...let me think.
POKE
POKE

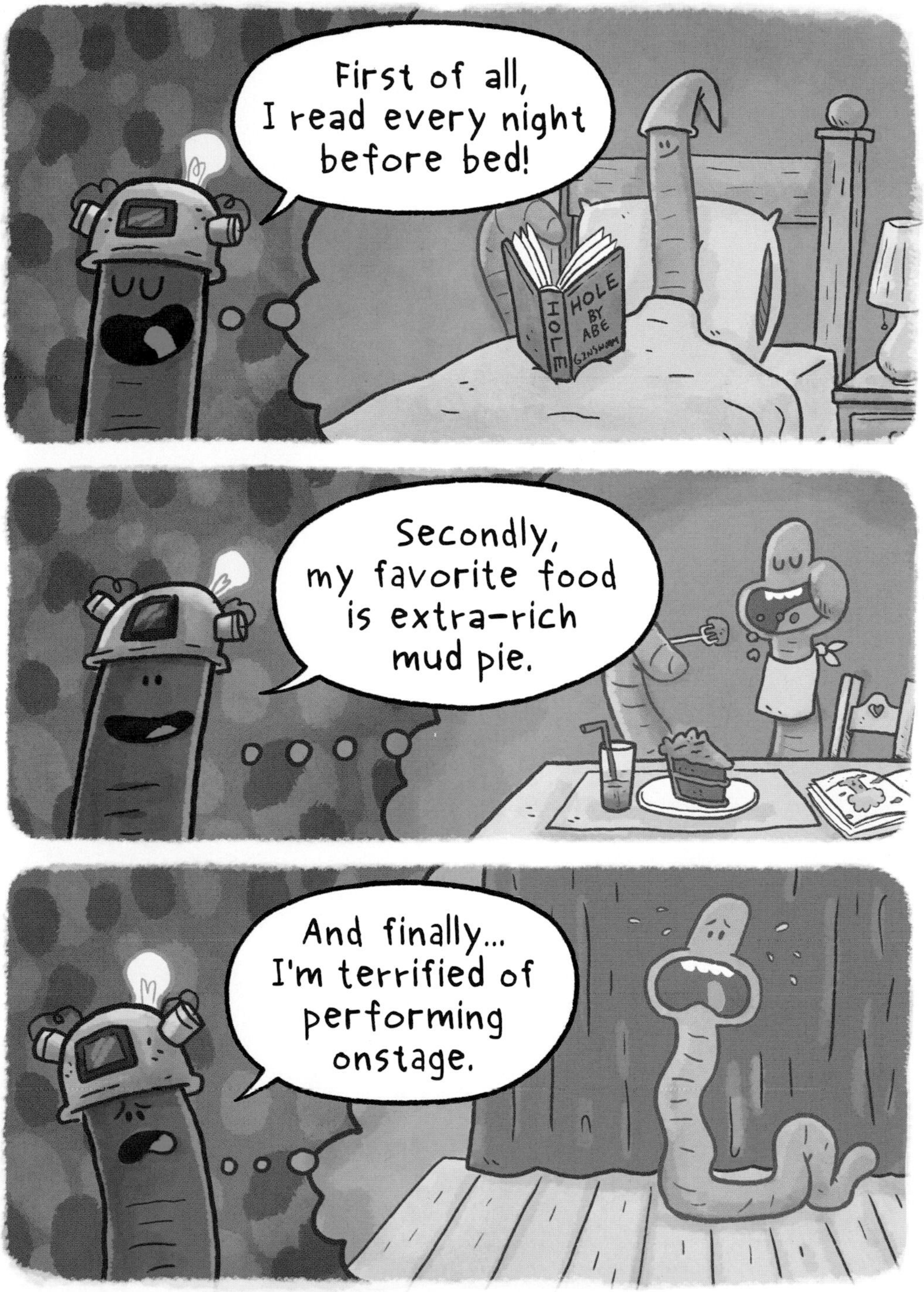
First of all, I read every night before bed!
HOLE BY ABE GINSWORM
HOLE
Secondly, my favorite food is extra-rich mud pie.
And finally... I'm terrified of performing onstage.

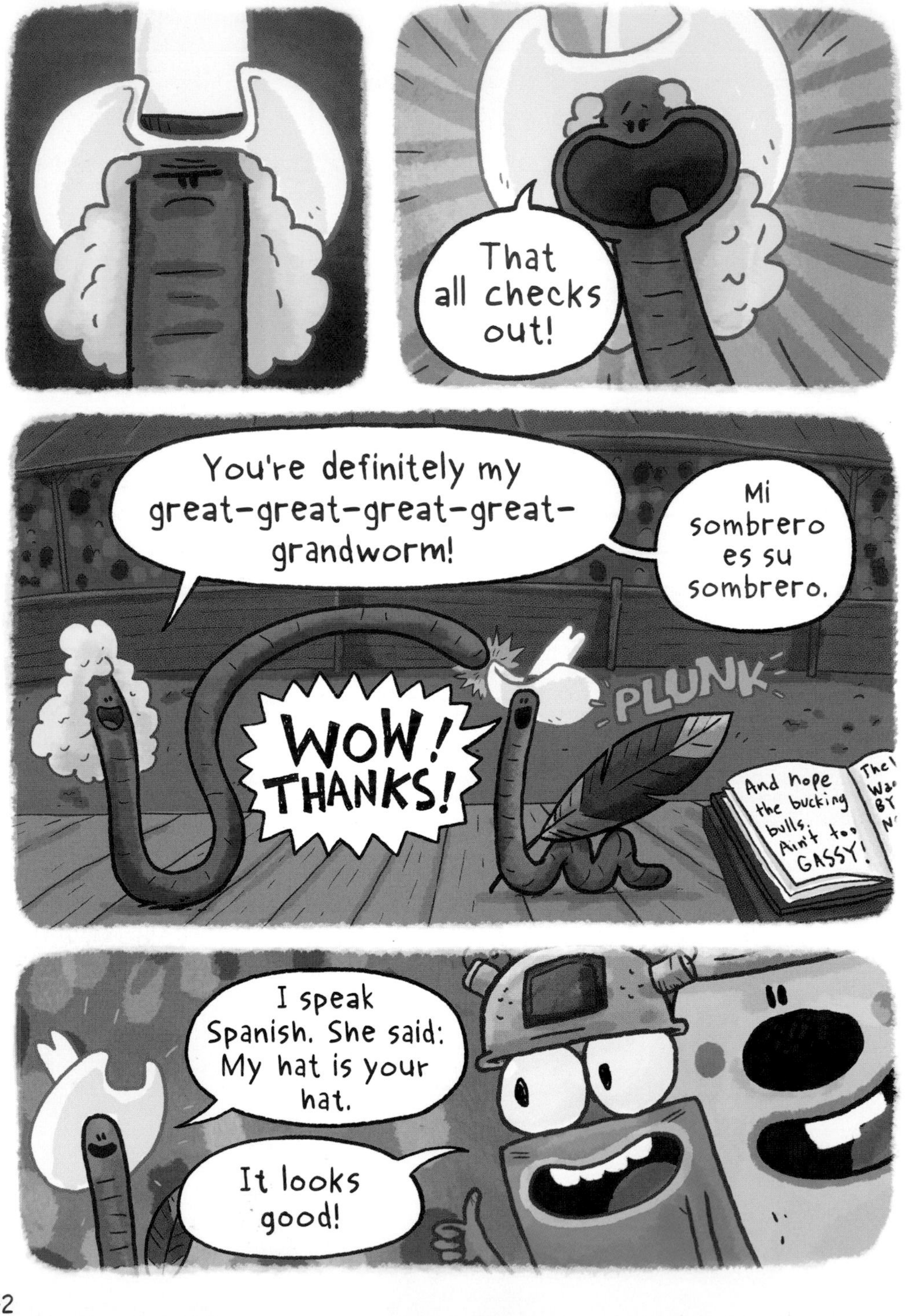
That all checks out!
You're definitely my great-great-great-great-grandworm!
Mi sombrero es su sombrero.
WOW! THANKS!
PLUNK
And hope the bucking bulls Ain't too GASSY!
I speak Spanish. She said: My hat is your hat.
It looks good!

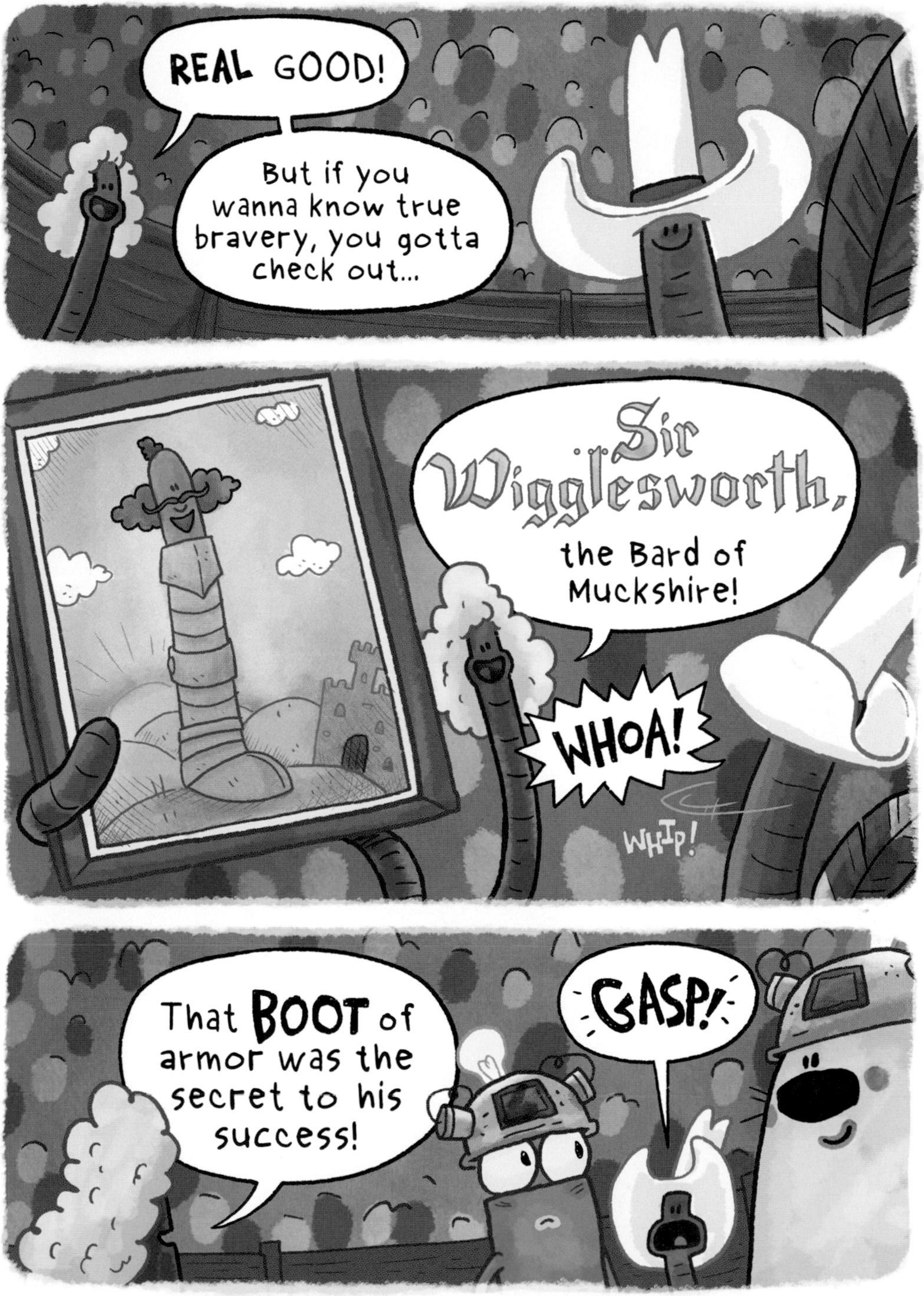
REAL GOOD!
But if you wanna know true bravery, you gotta check out...
Sir Wigglesworth, the Bard of Muckshire!
WHOA!
WHIP!
That BOOT of armor was the secret to his success!
GASP!

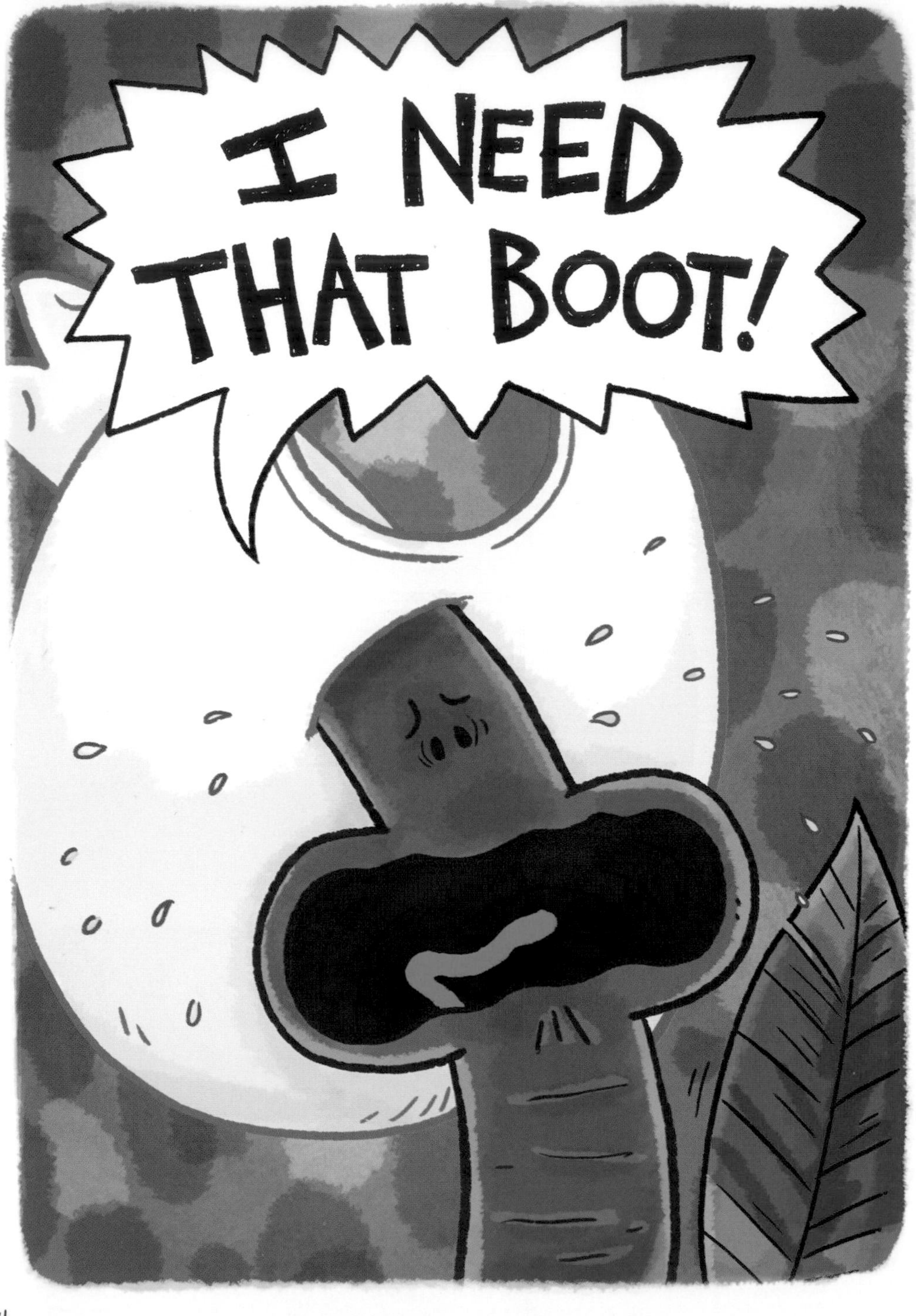
I NEED THAT BOOT!

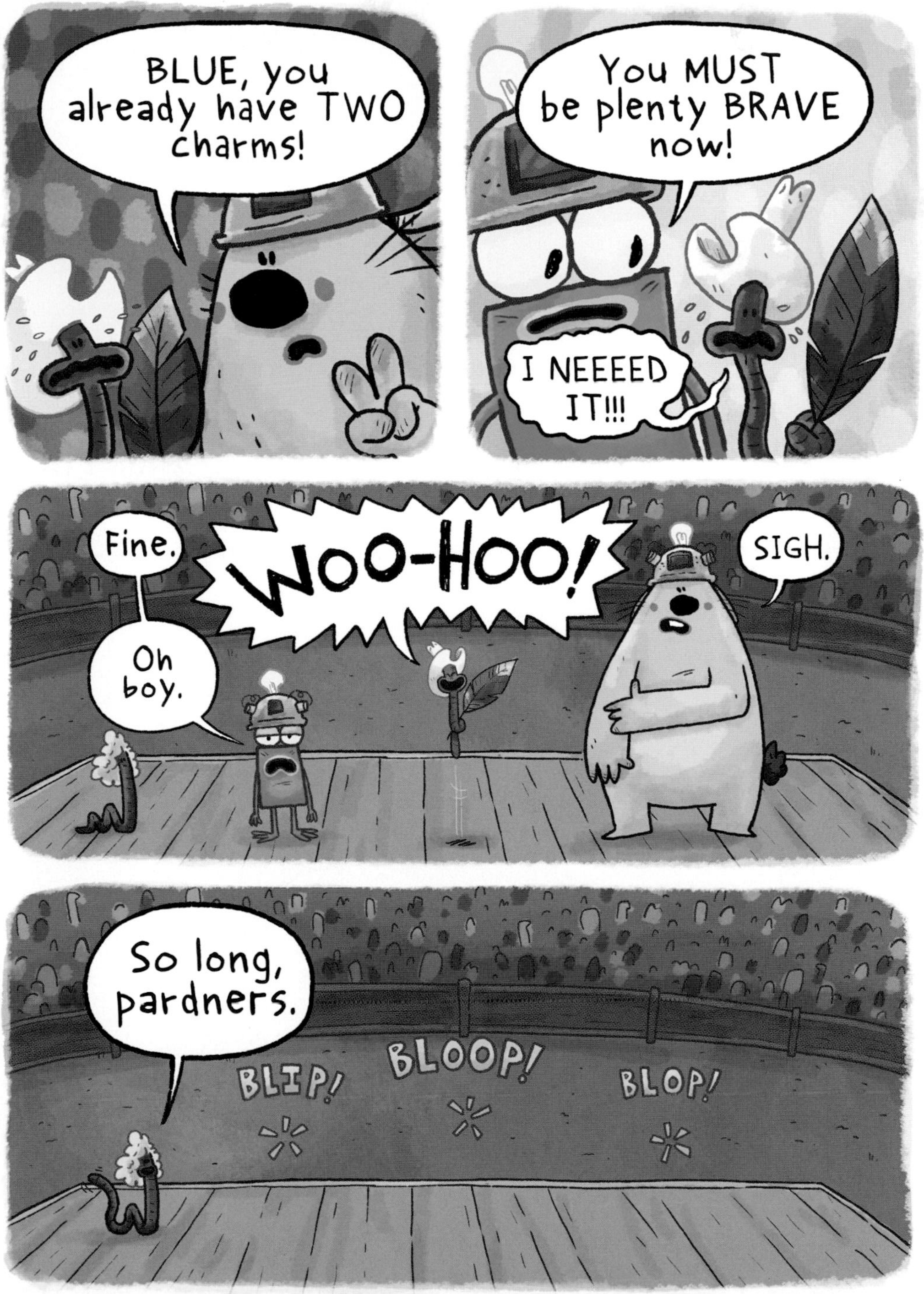
BLUE, you already have TWO charms!
You MUST be plenty BRAVE now!
I NEEEED IT!!!
Fine.
Oh boy.
WOO-HOO!
SIGH.
So long, pardners.
BLIP!
BLOOP!
BLOP!

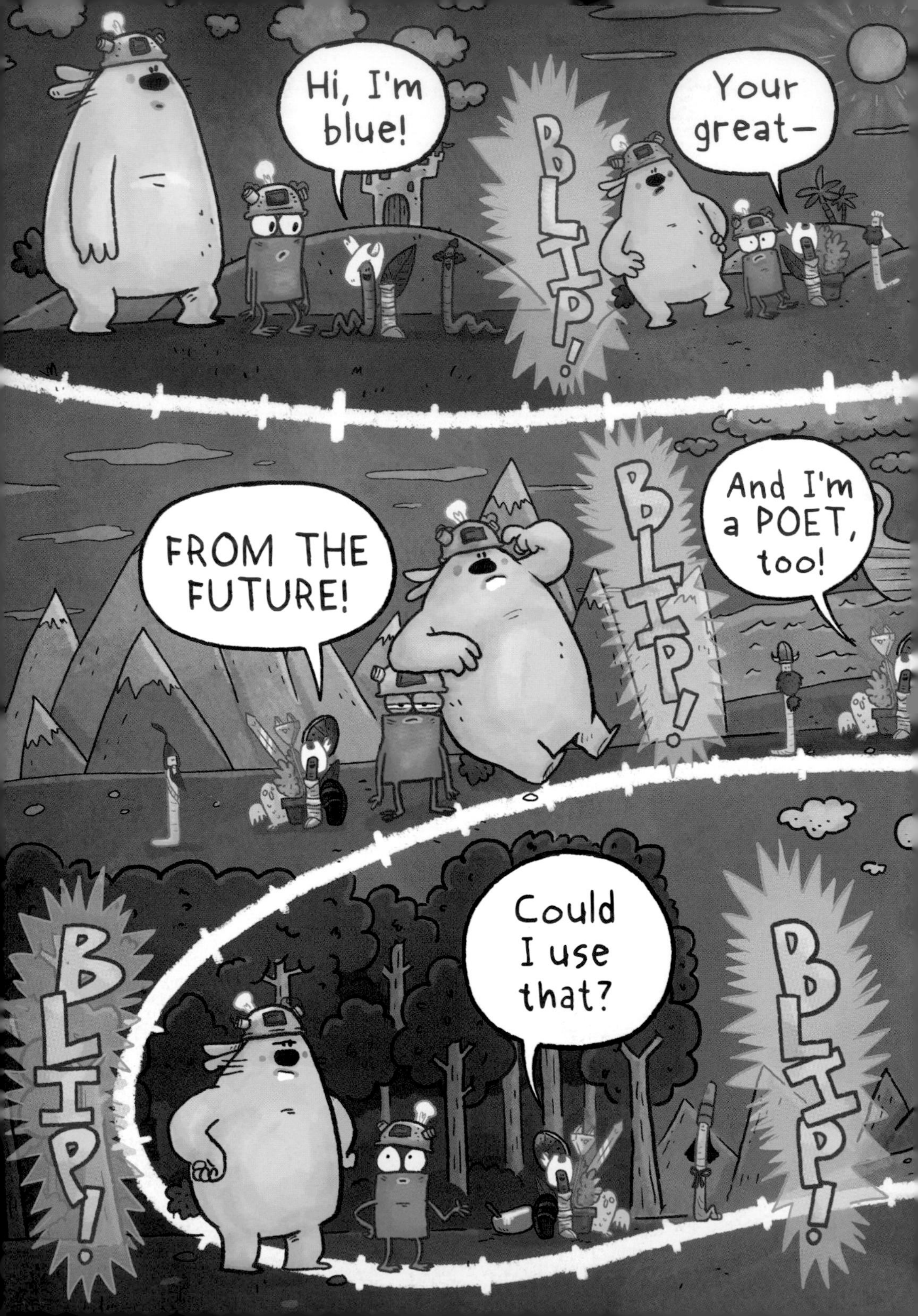

Hi, I'm blue!
BLIP!
Your great—
FROM THE FUTURE!
BLIP!
And I'm a POET, too!
BLIP!
Could I use that?
BLIP!

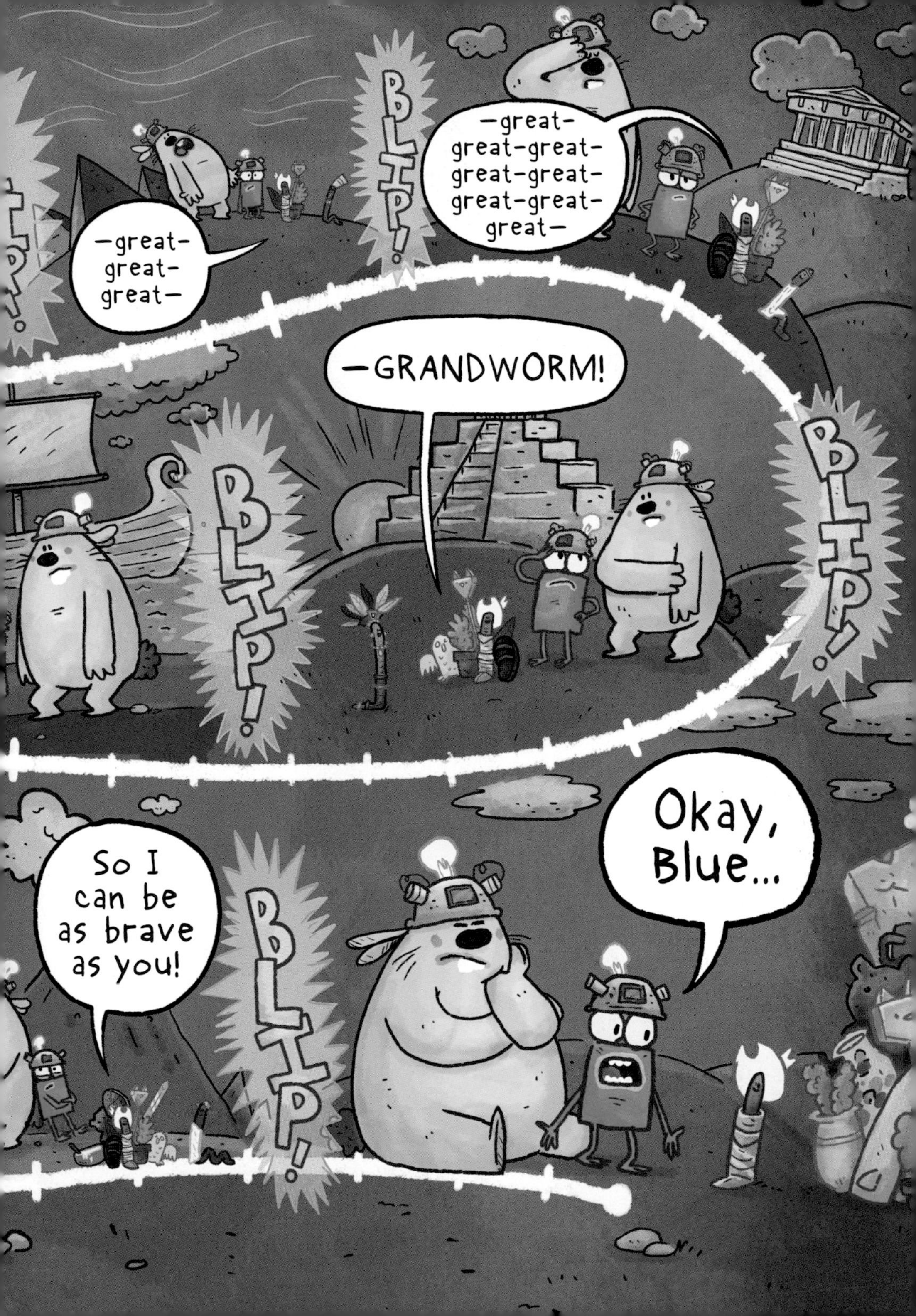
BLIP!
-great-
great-
great—
BLIP!
—great-
great-great-
great-great-
great-great-
great—
—GRANDWORM!
BLIP!
BLIP!
So I
can be
as brave
as you!
BLIP!
Okay,
Blue...

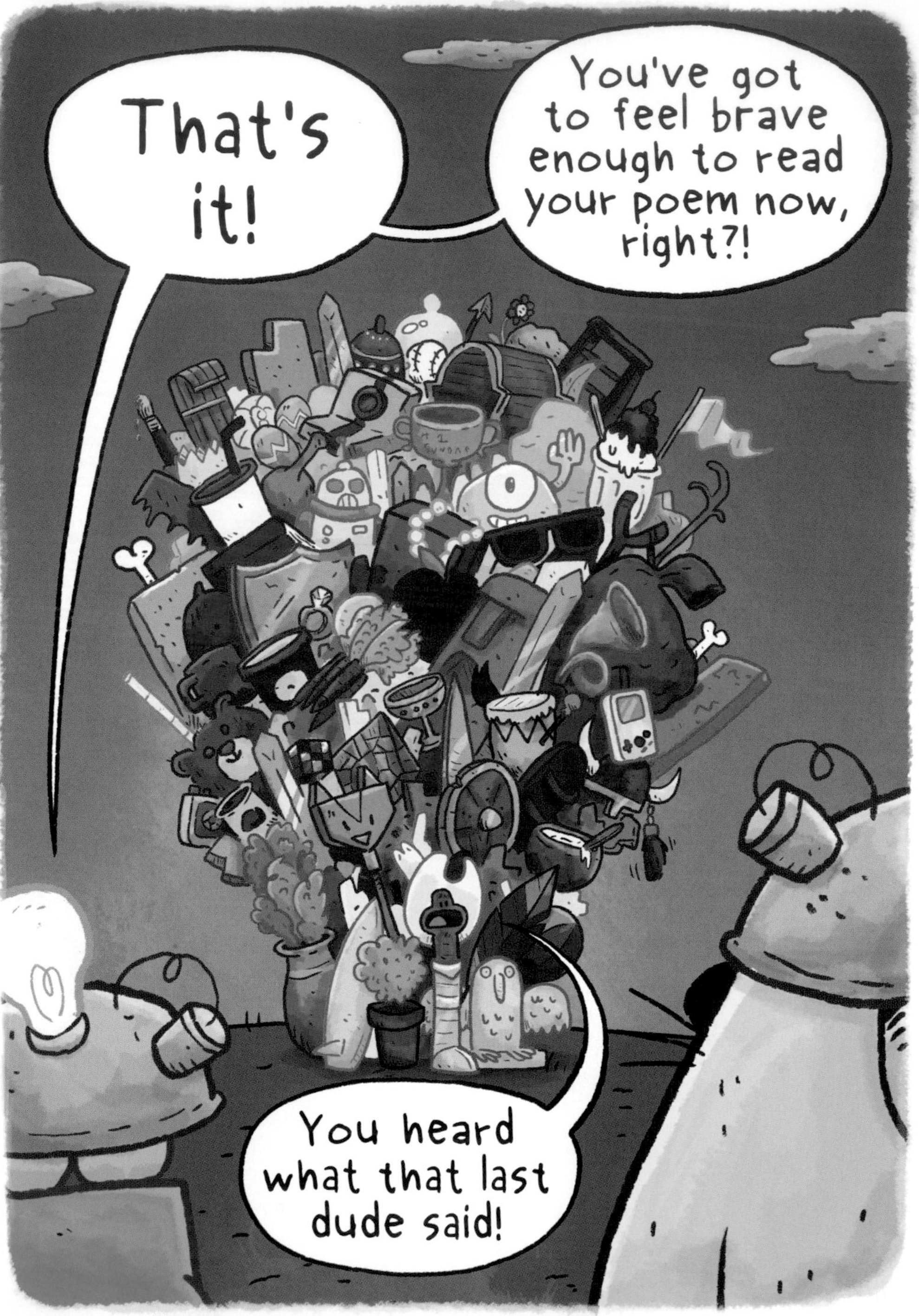
That's it!
You've got to feel brave enough to read your poem now, right?!
You heard what that last dude said!

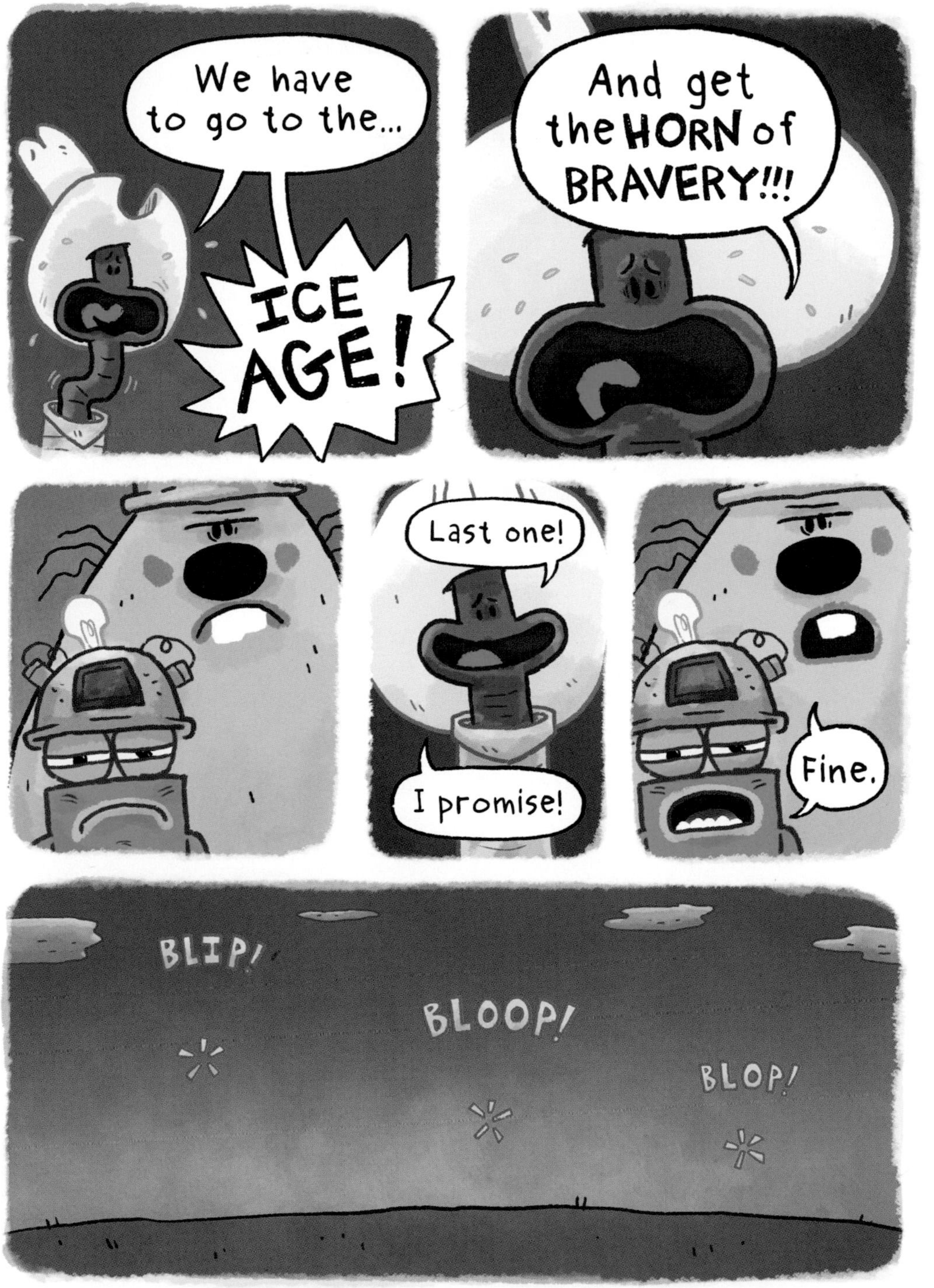

We have to go to the...
ICE AGE!
And get the HORN of BRAVERY!!!
Last one!
I promise!
Fine.
BLIP!
BLOOP!
BLOP!

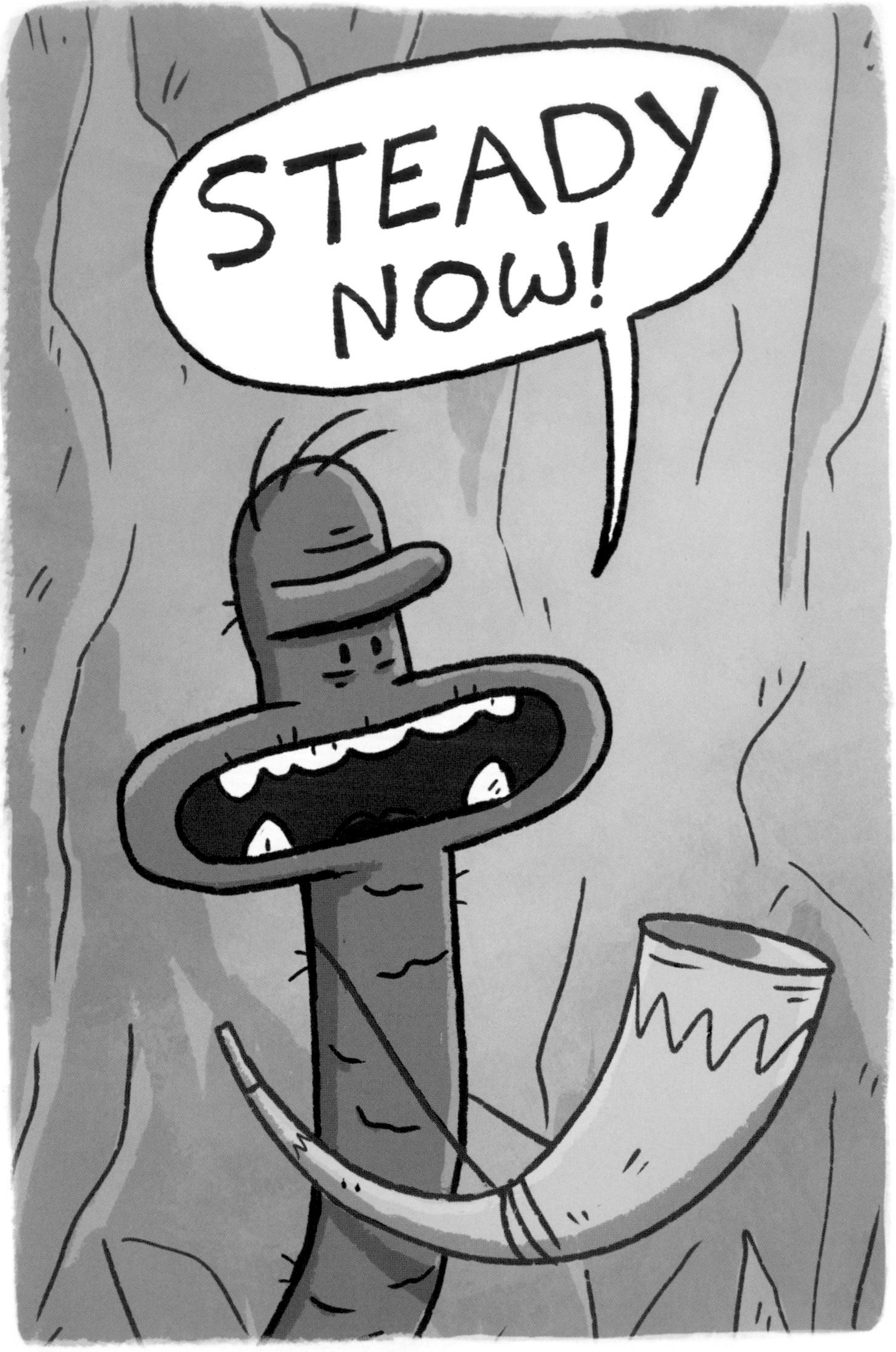
STEADY NOW!

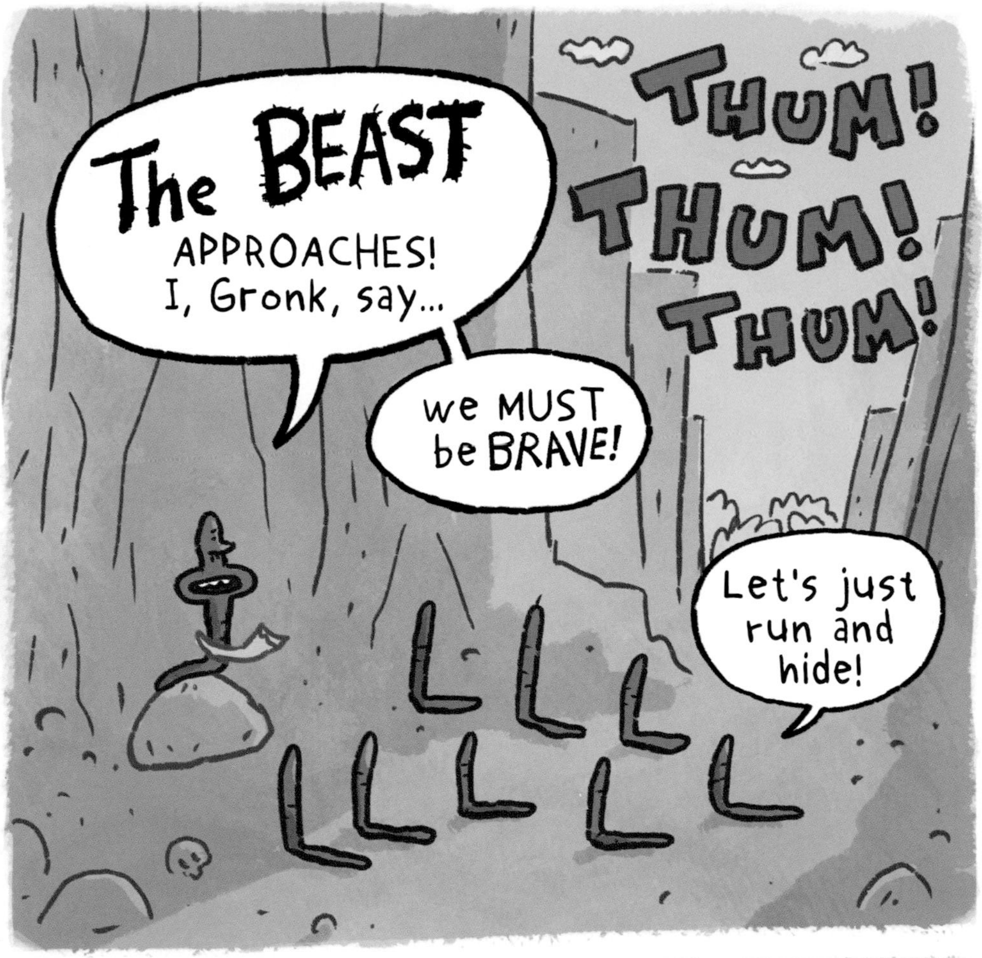
The BEAST APPROACHES! I, Gronk, say...
we MUST be BRAVE!
THUM! THUM! THUM!
Let's just run and hide!

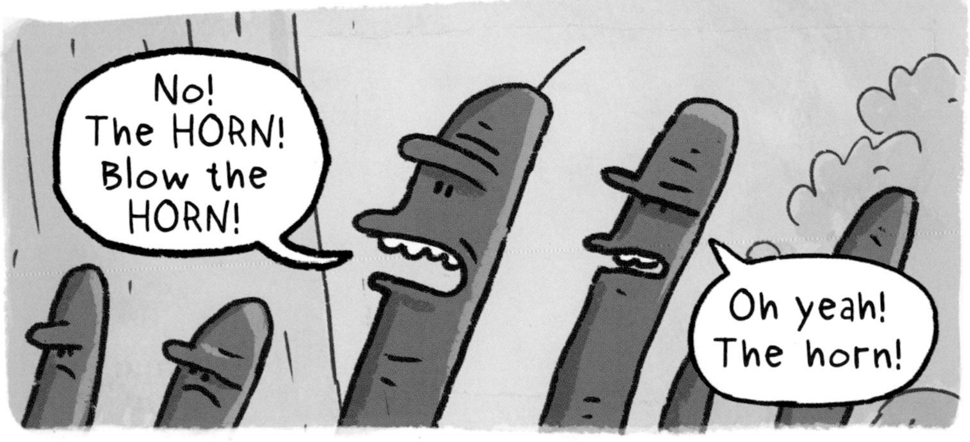
No! The HORN! Blow the HORN!
Oh yeah! The horn!

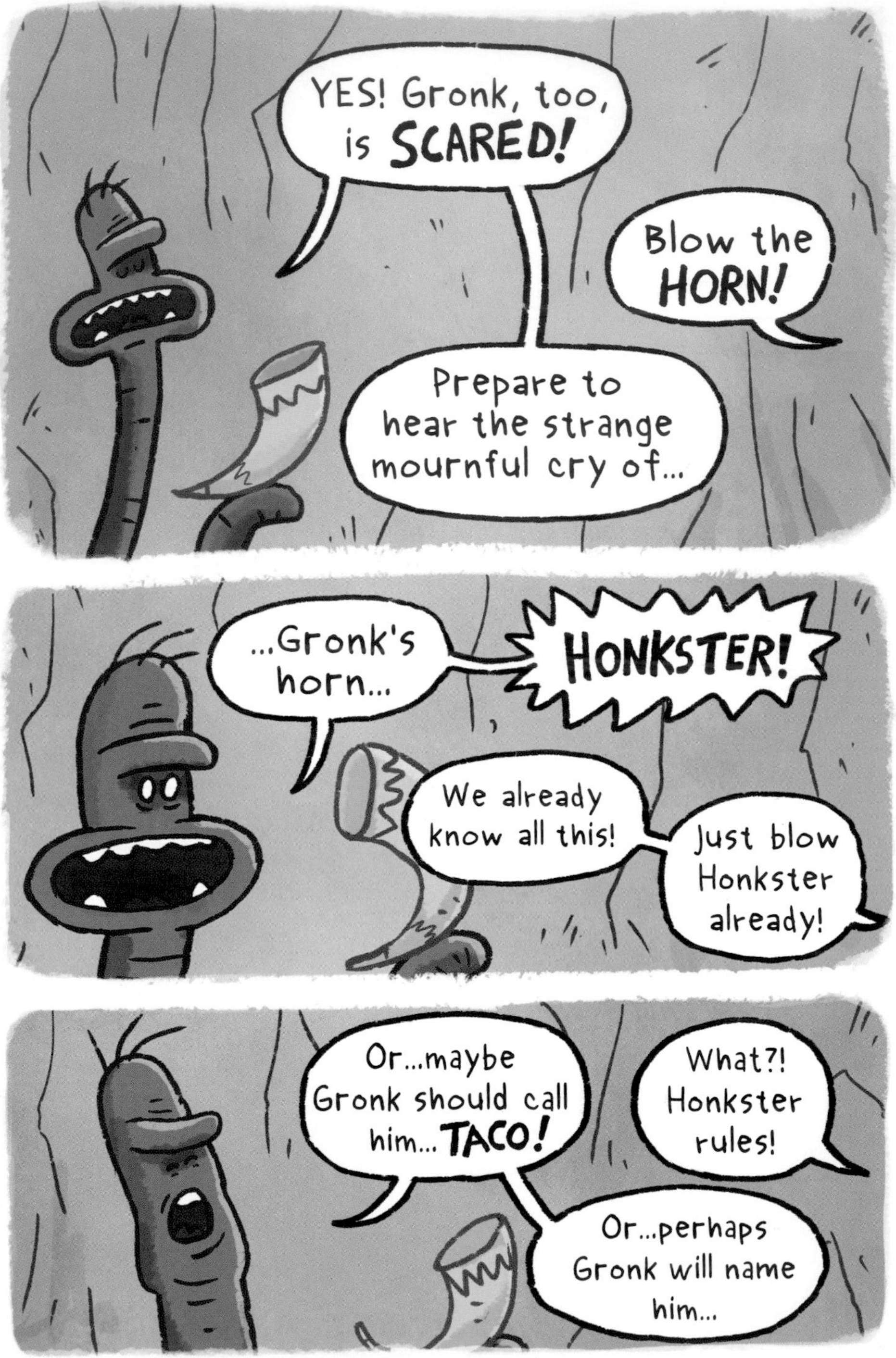
YES! Gronk, too, is SCARED!
Blow the HORN!
Prepare to hear the strange mournful cry of...
...Gronk's horn...
HONKSTER!
We already know all this!
Just blow Honkster already!
Or...maybe Gronk should call him...TACO!
What?! Honkster rules!
Or...perhaps Gronk will name him...

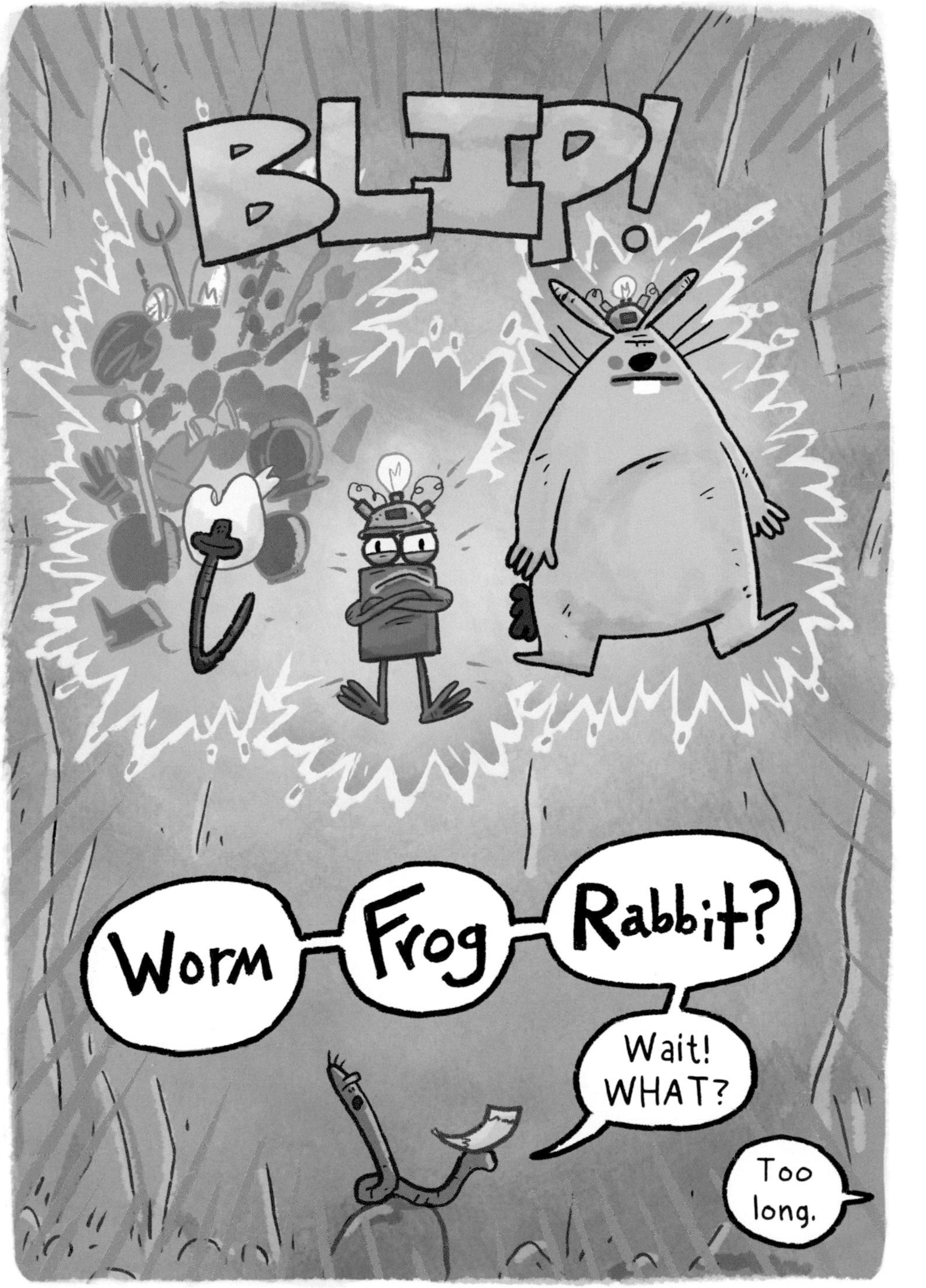
BLIP!
Worm
Frog
Rabbit?
Wait! WHAT?
Too long.

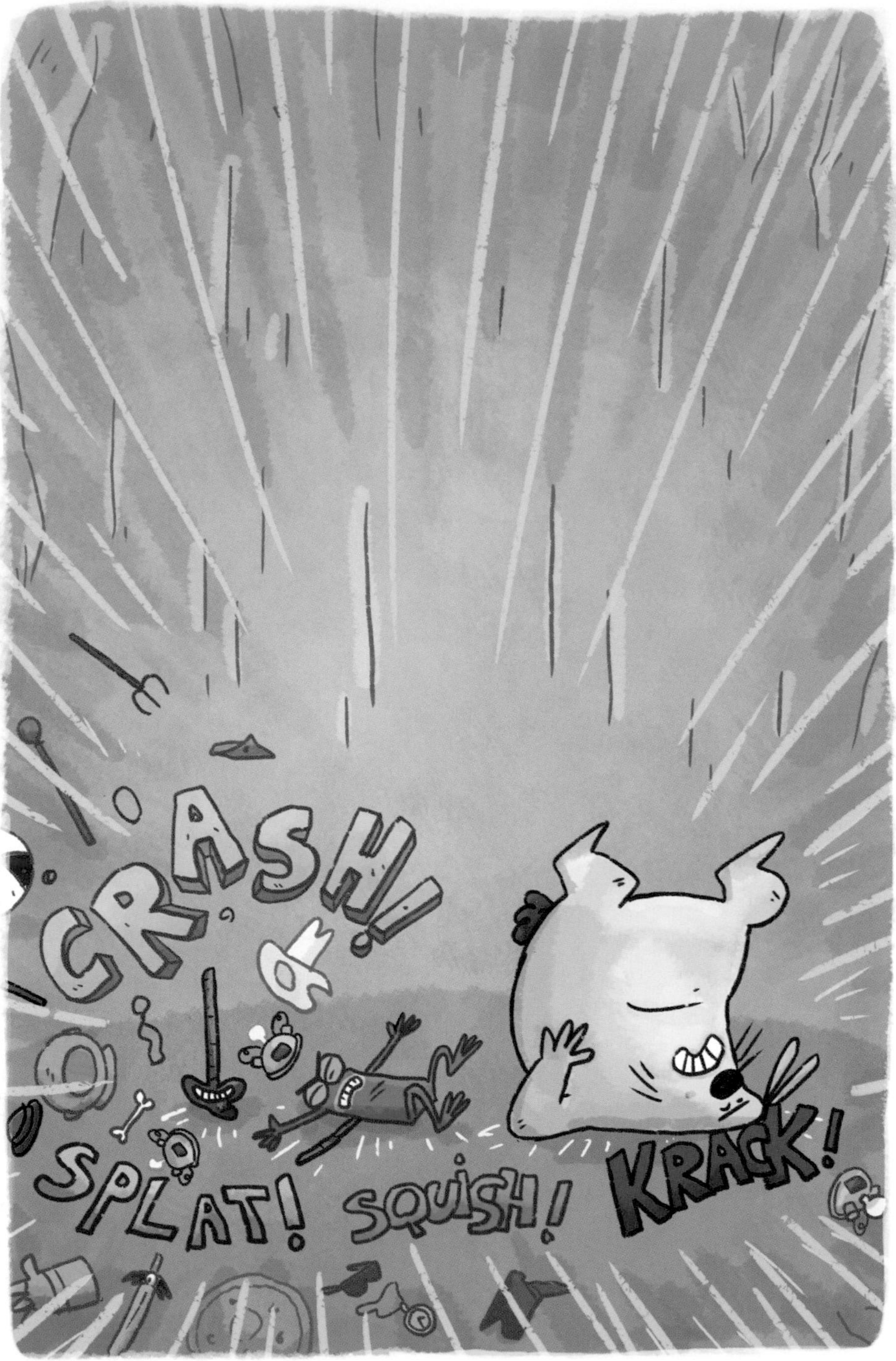
CRASH!
SPLAT!
SQUISH!
KRACK!

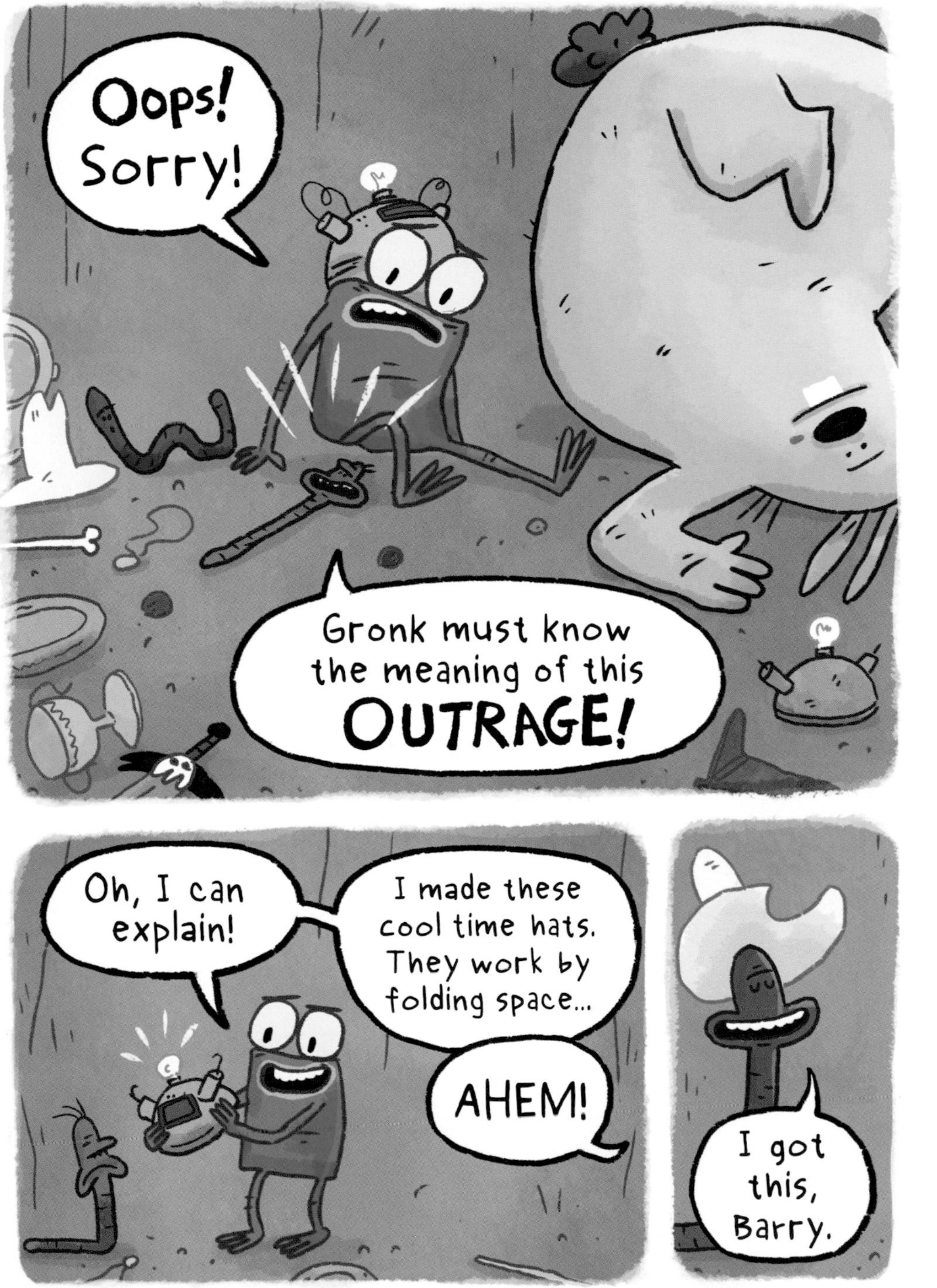
Oops! Sorry!
Gronk must know the meaning of this OUTRAGE!
Oh, I can explain!
I made these cool time hats. They work by folding space...
AHEM!
I got this, Barry.

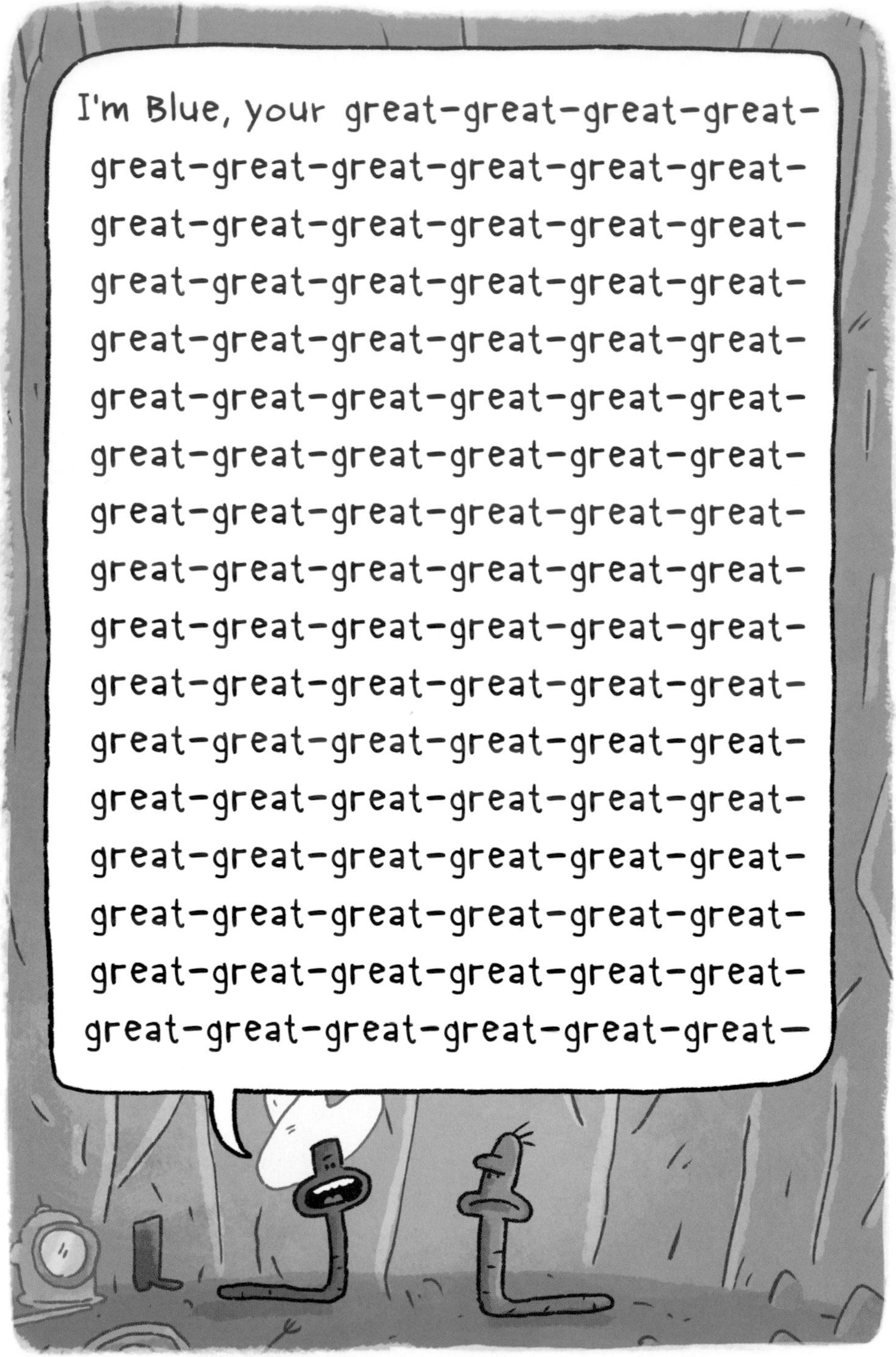
I'm Blue, your great-great-great-great-
great-great-great-great-great-great-
great-great-great-great-great-great-
great-great-great-great-great-great-
great-great-great-great-great-great-
great-great-great-great-great-great-
great-great-great-great-great-great-
great-great-great-great-great-great-
great-great-great-great-great-great-
great-great-great-great-great-great-
great-great-great-great-great-great-
great-great-great-great-great-great-
great-great-great-great-great-great-
great-great-great-great-great-great-
great-great-great-great-great-great-
great-great-great-great-great-great-
great-great-great-great-great-great—

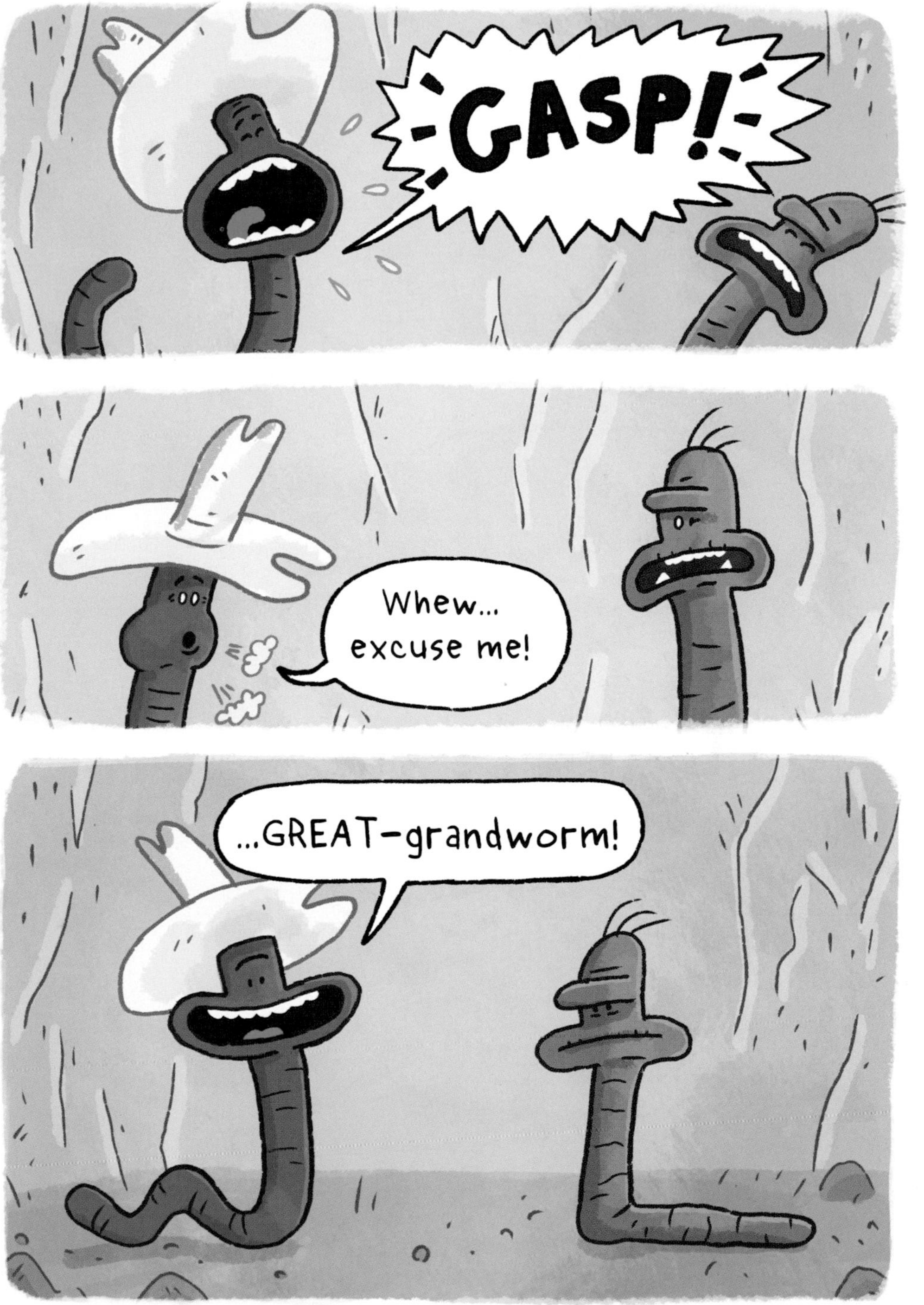
GASP!
Whew... excuse me!
...GREAT-grandworm!

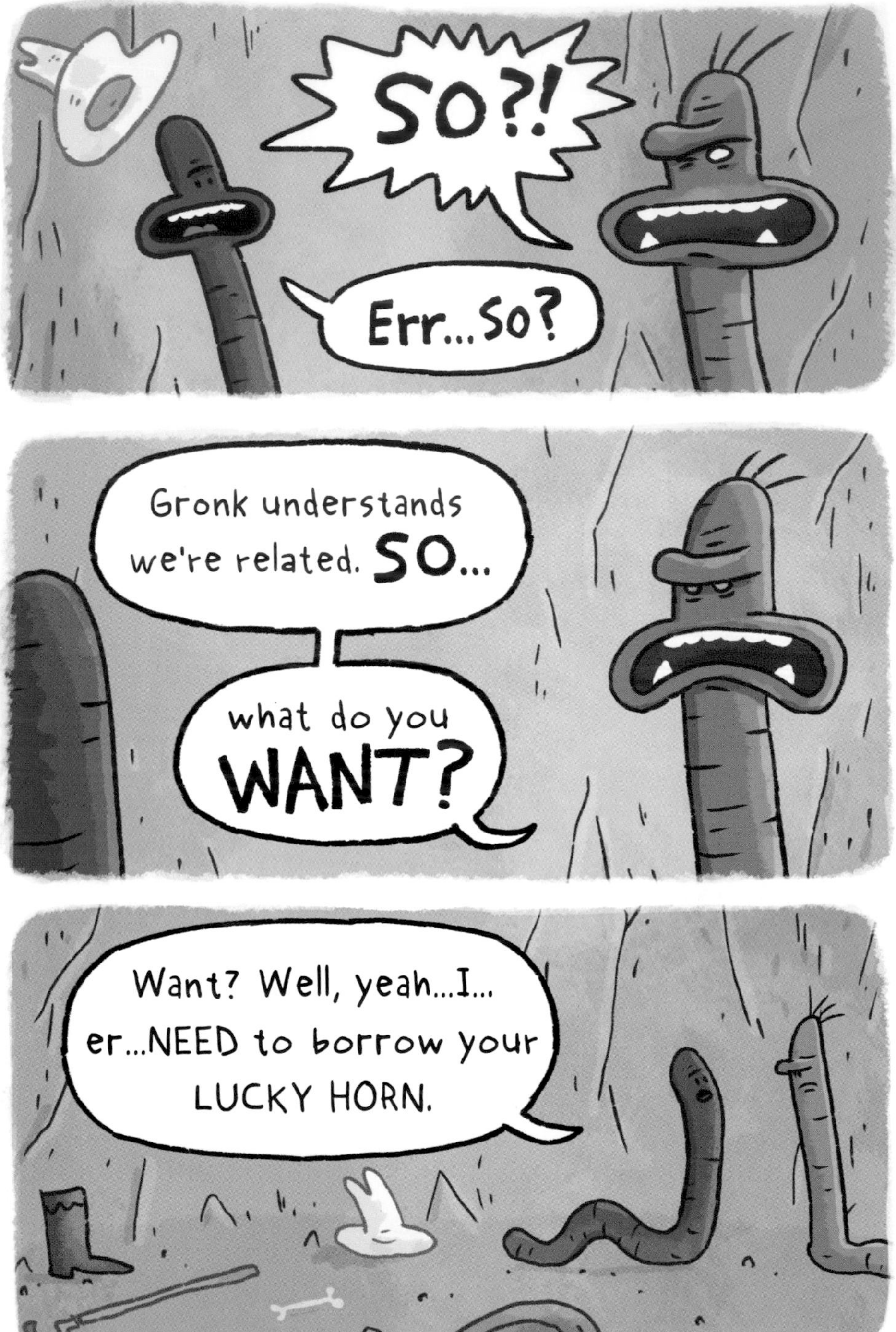
SO?!
Err...So?
Gronk understands we're related. SO...
what do you WANT?
Want? Well, yeah...I... er...NEED to borrow your LUCKY HORN.

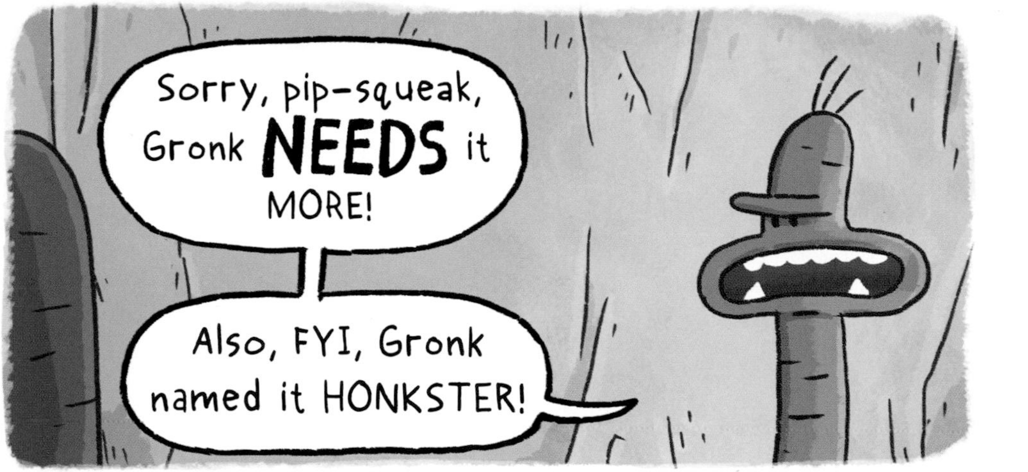
Sorry, pip-squeak, Gronk NEEDS it MORE!
Also, FYI, Gronk named it HONKSTER!

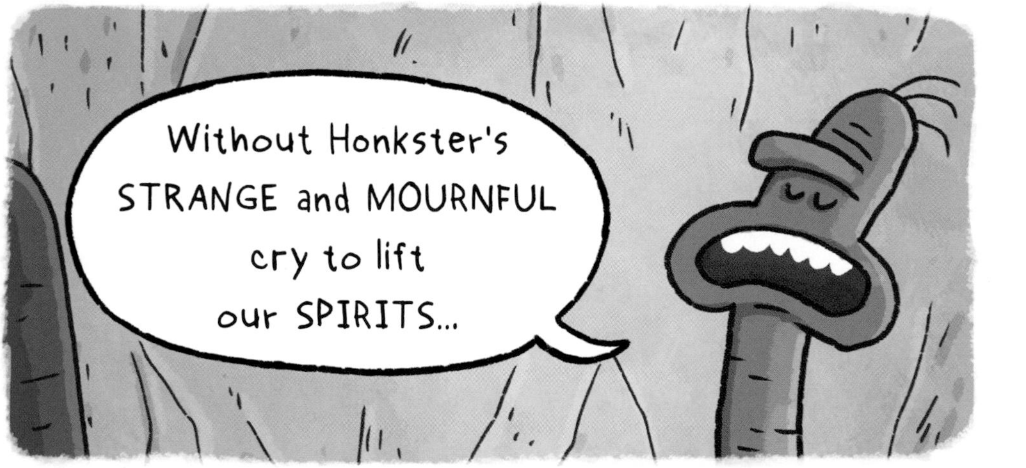
Without Honkster's STRANGE and MOURNFUL cry to lift our SPIRITS...

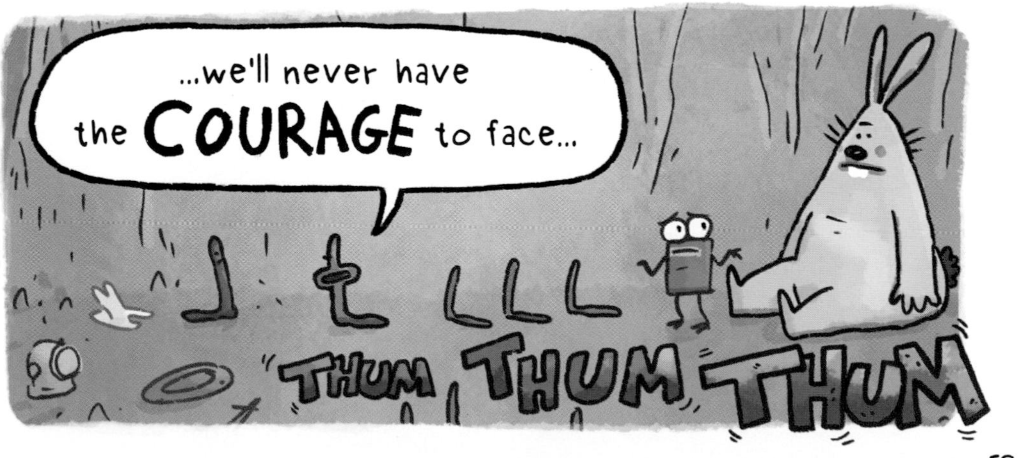
...we'll never have the COURAGE to face...
THUM THUM THUM

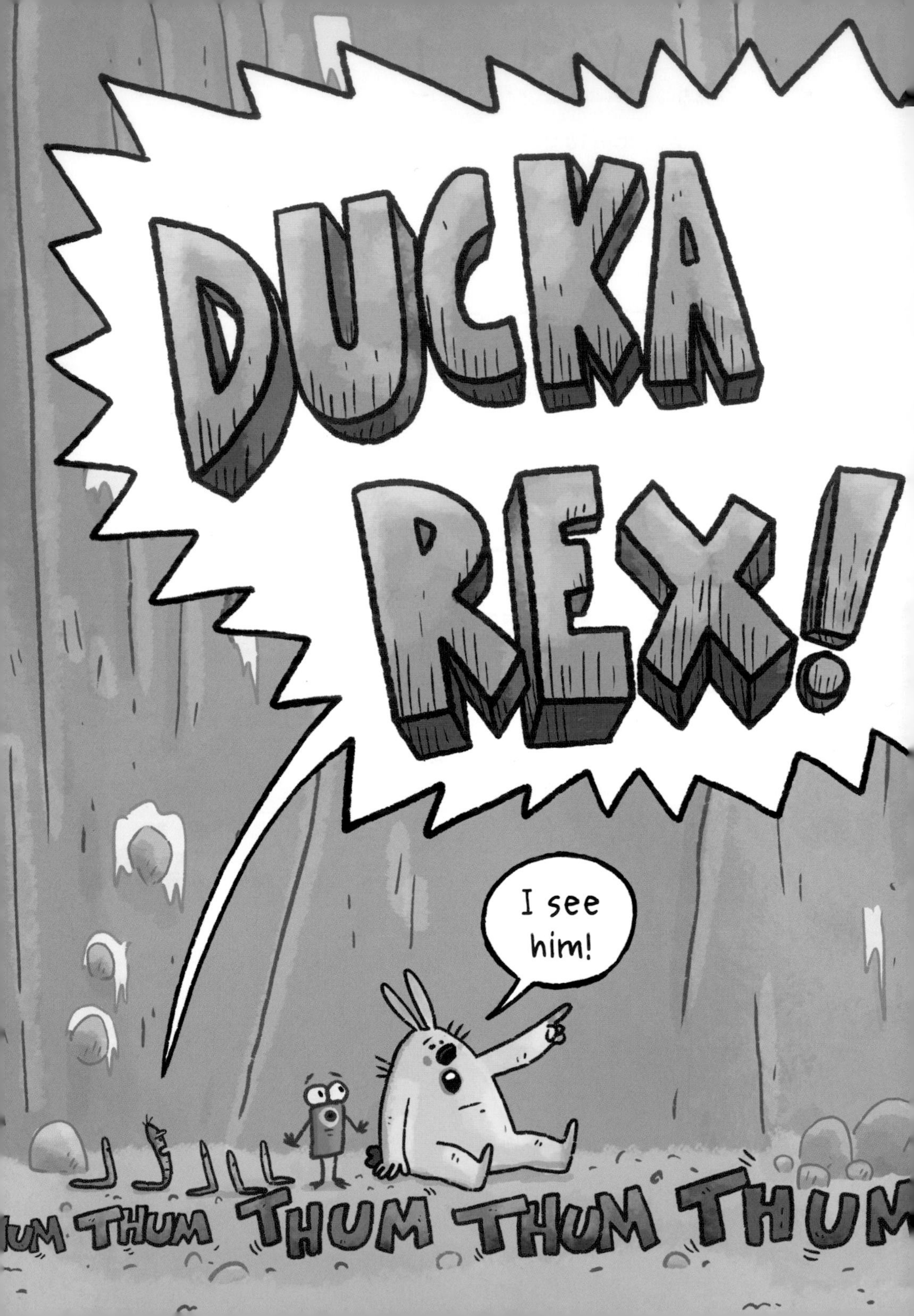
DUCKA REX!
I see him!
UM THUM THUM THUM THUM

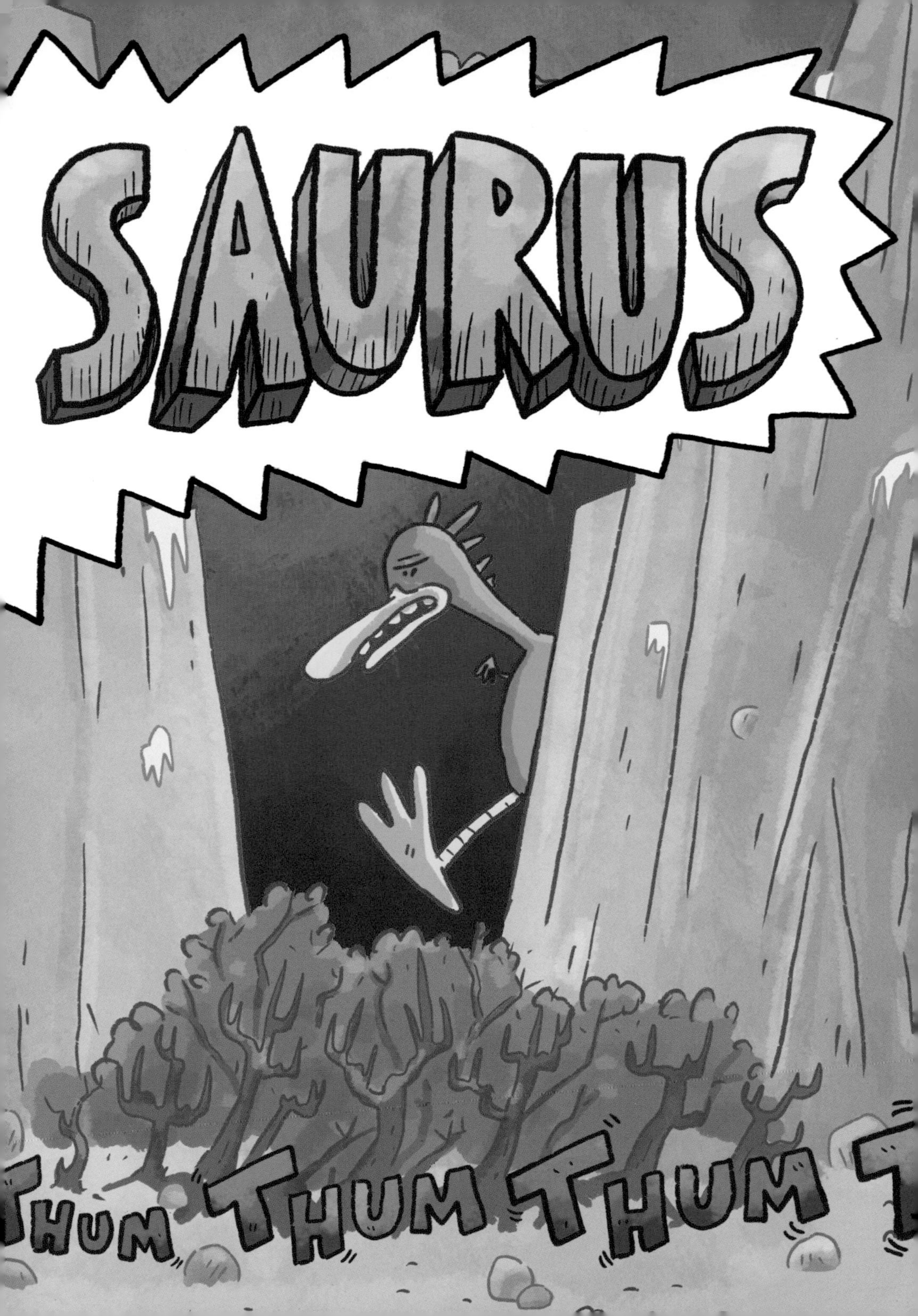
SAURUS
THUM THUM THUM

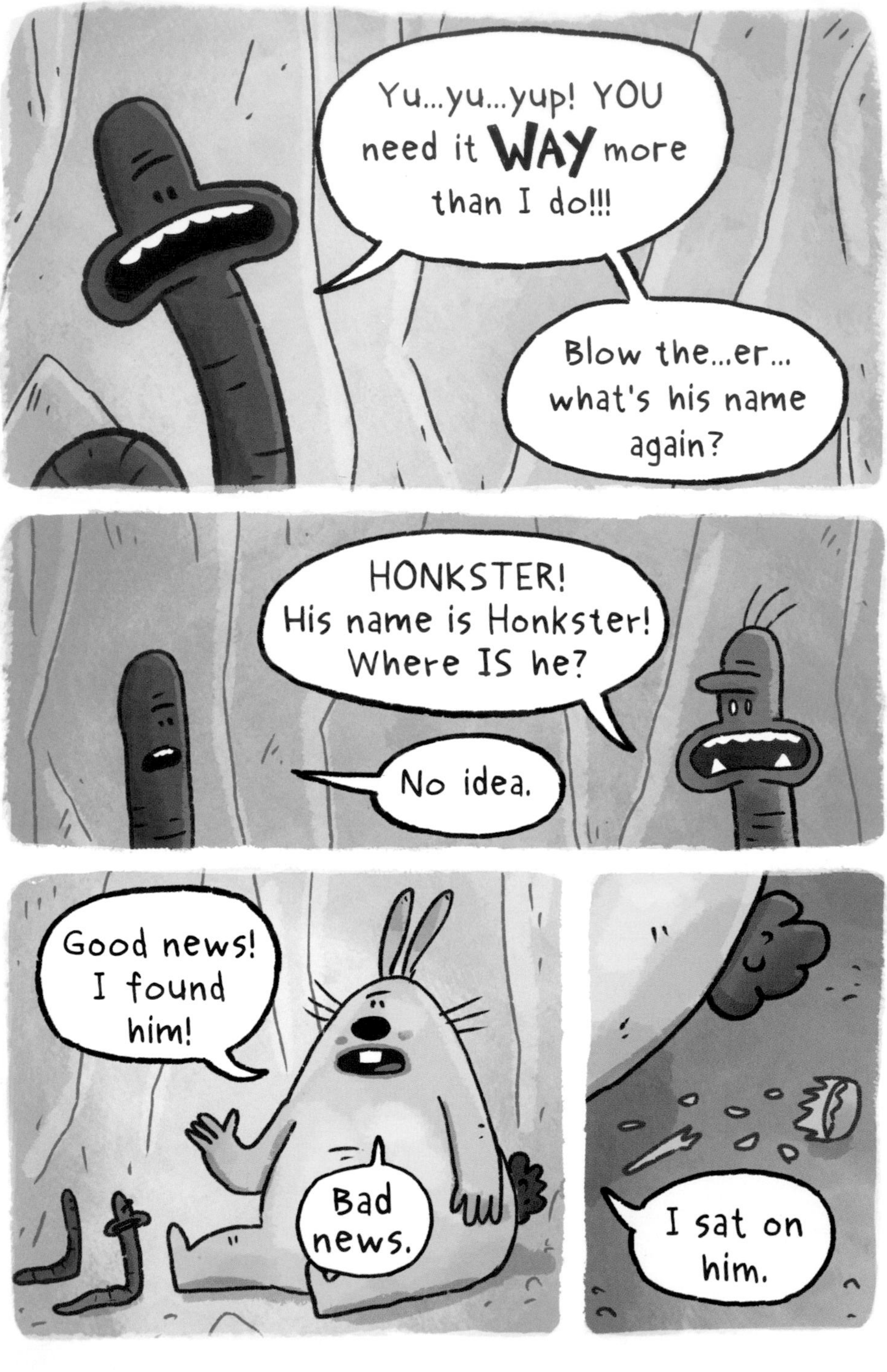
Yu...yu...yup! YOU need it WAY more than I do!!!
Blow the...er... what's his name again?
HONKSTER! His name is Honkster! Where IS he?
No idea.
Good news! I found him!
Bad news.
I sat on him.

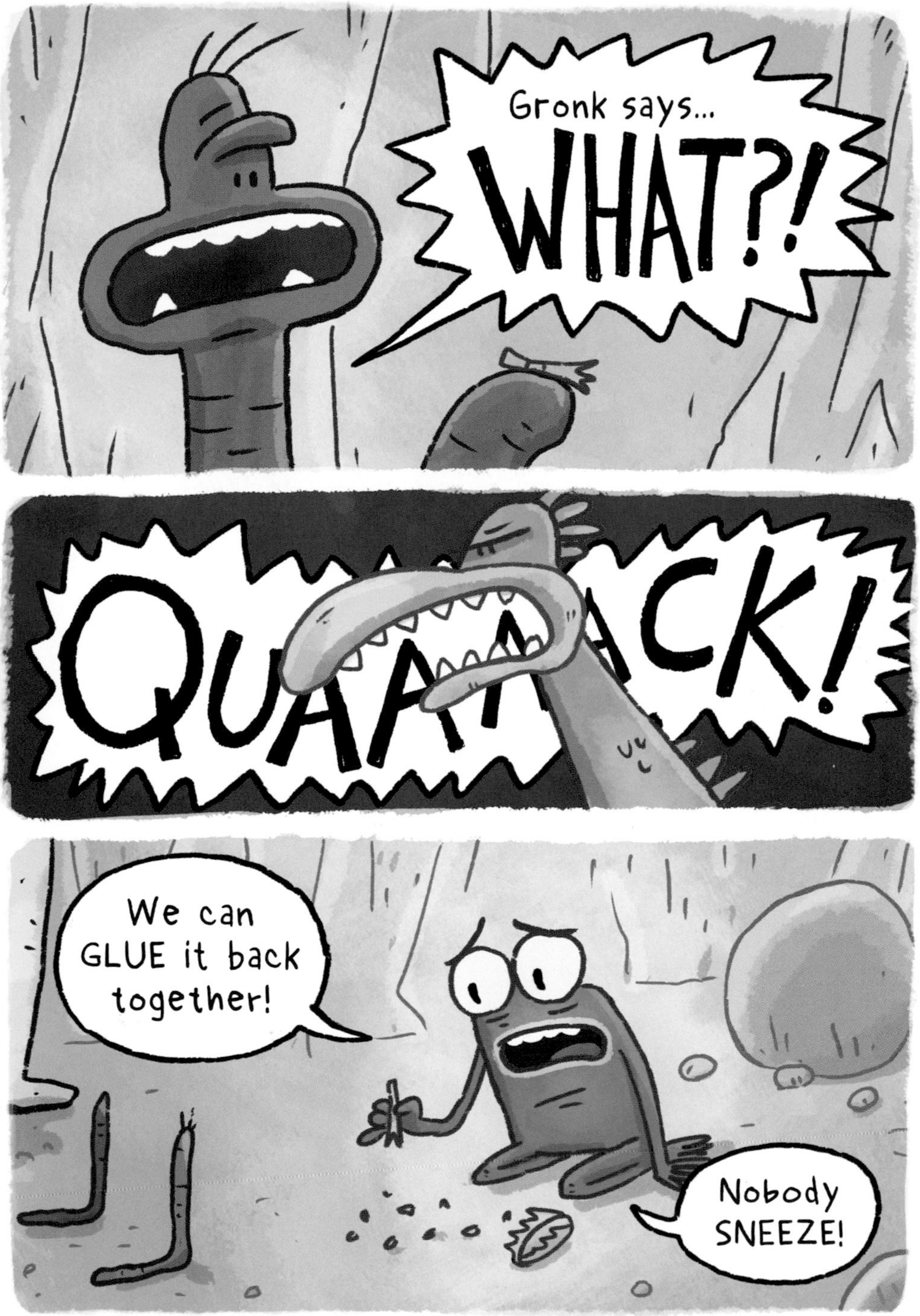
Gronk says...
WHAT?!
QUAAAACK!
We can GLUE it back together!
Nobody SNEEZE!

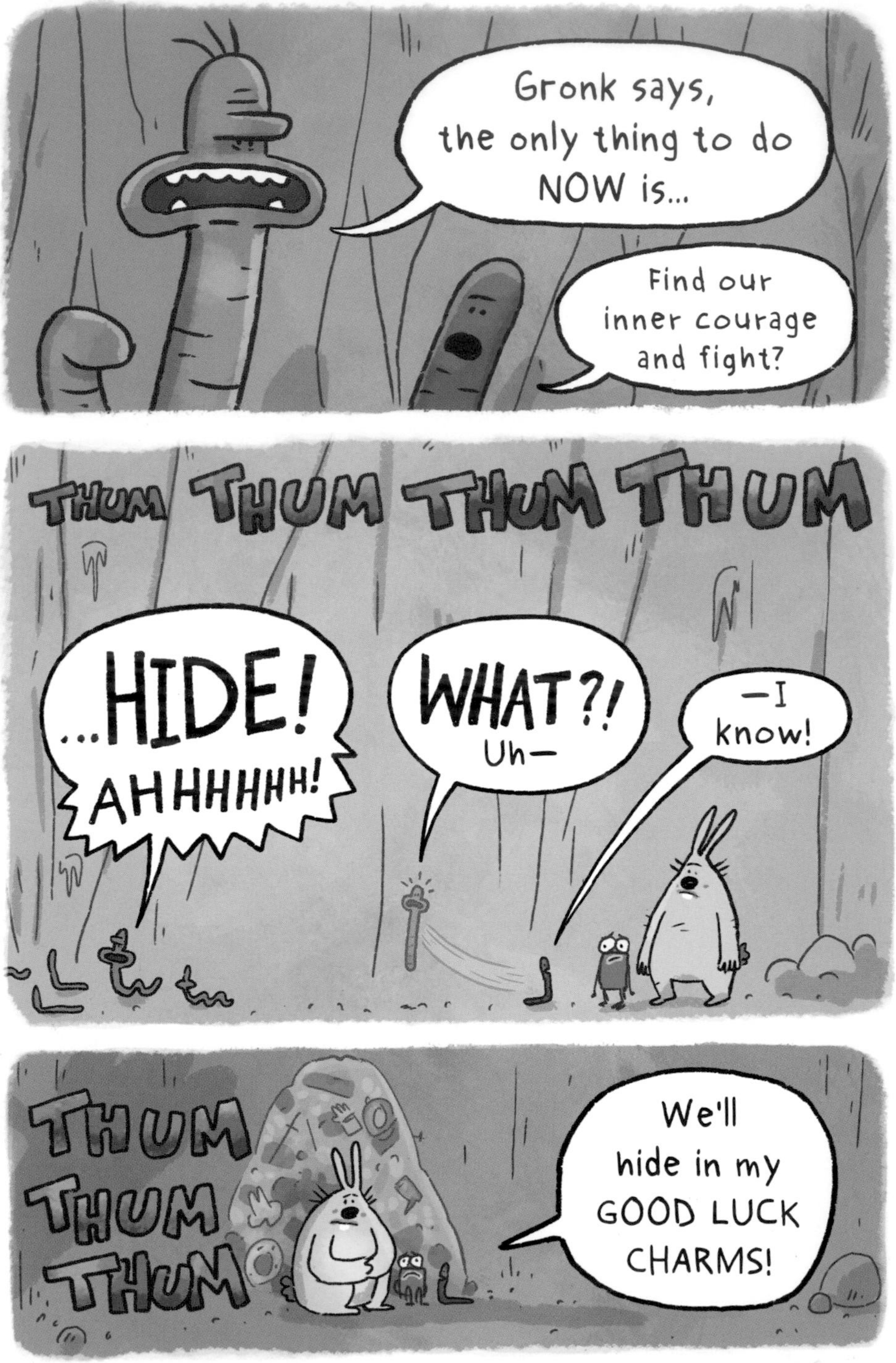

Gronk says, the only thing to do NOW is...
Find our inner courage and fight?
THUM THUM THUM THUM
...HIDE! AHHHHHH!
WHAT?! Uh—
—I know!
THUM THUM THUM
We'll hide in my GOOD LUCK CHARMS!

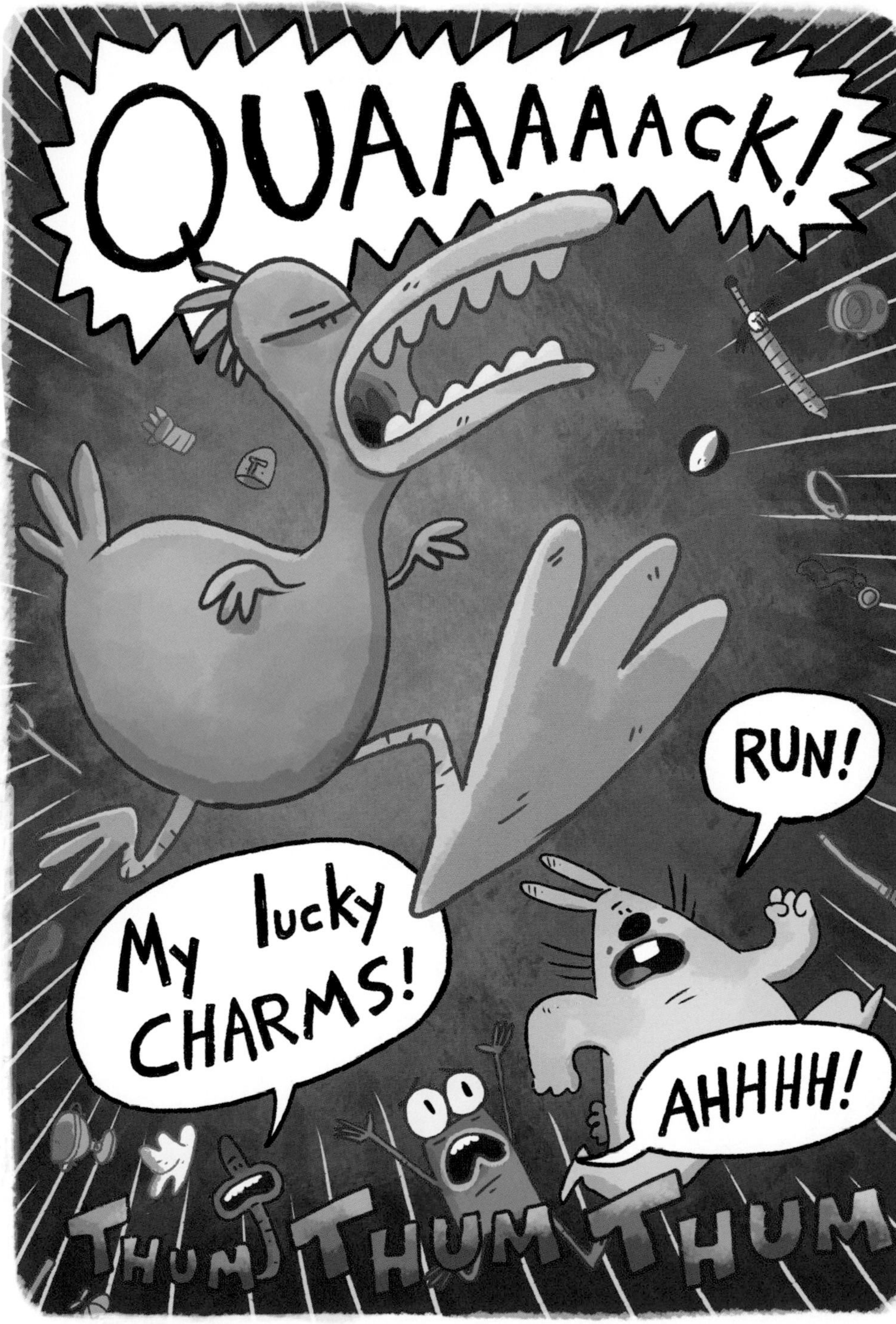
QUAAAAAACK!
My lucky CHARMS!
RUN!
AHHHH!
THUM THUM THUM

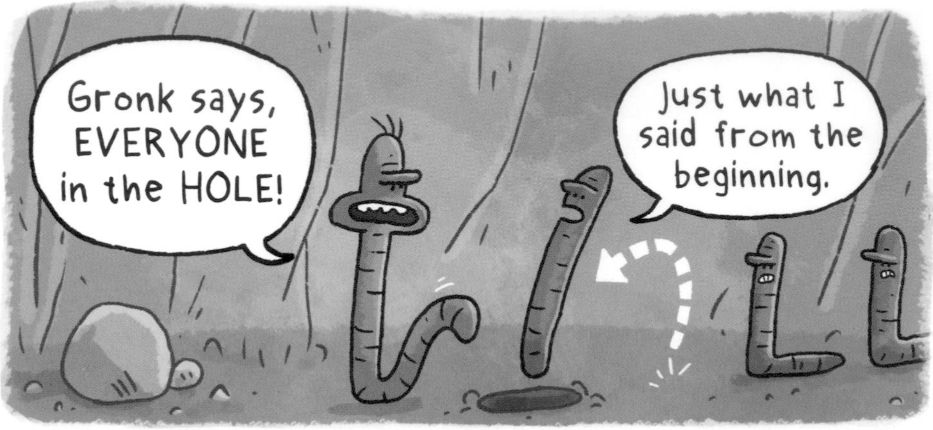
Gronk says, EVERYONE in the HOLE!
Just what I said from the beginning.

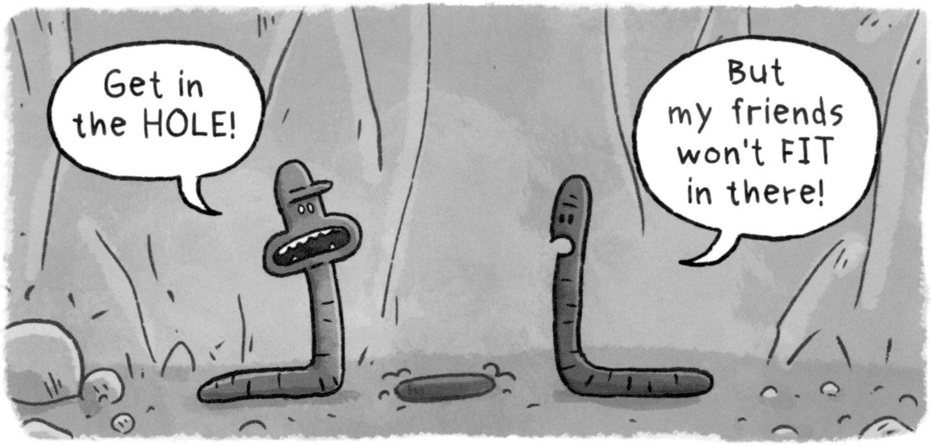
Get in the HOLE!
But my friends won't FIT in there!

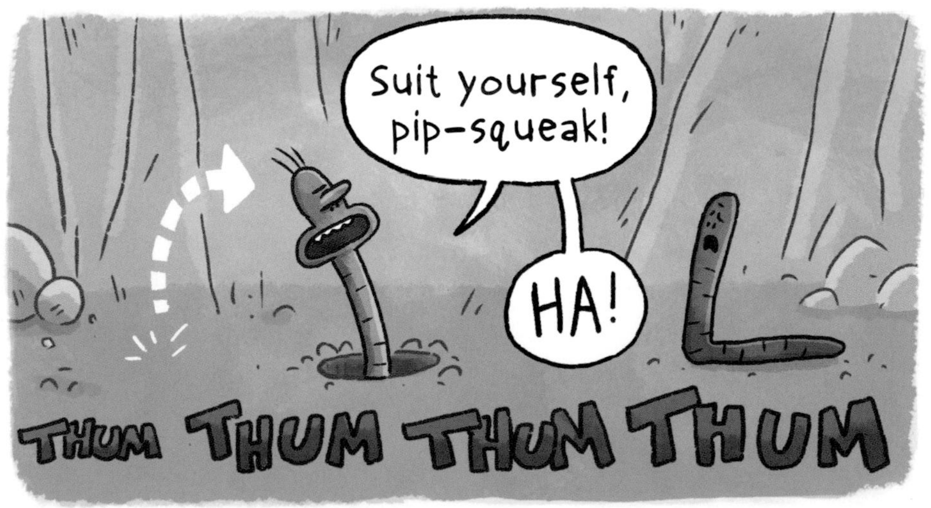
Suit yourself, pip-squeak!
HA!
THUM THUM THUM THUM

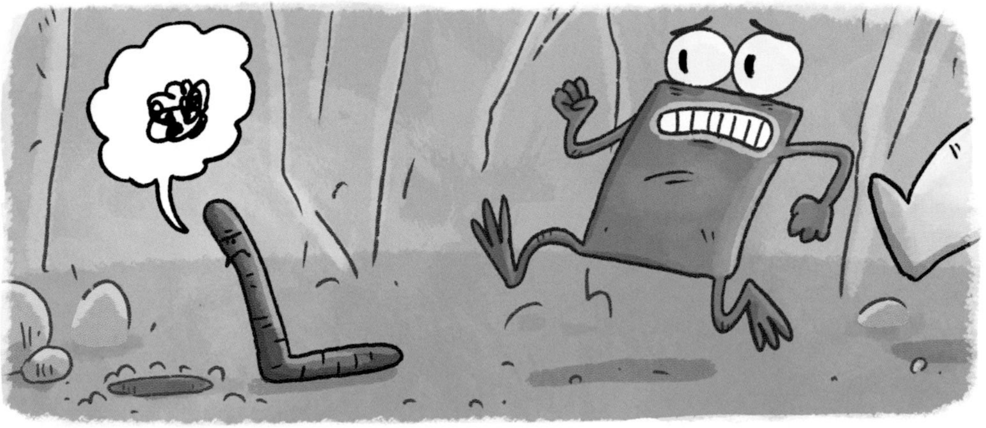

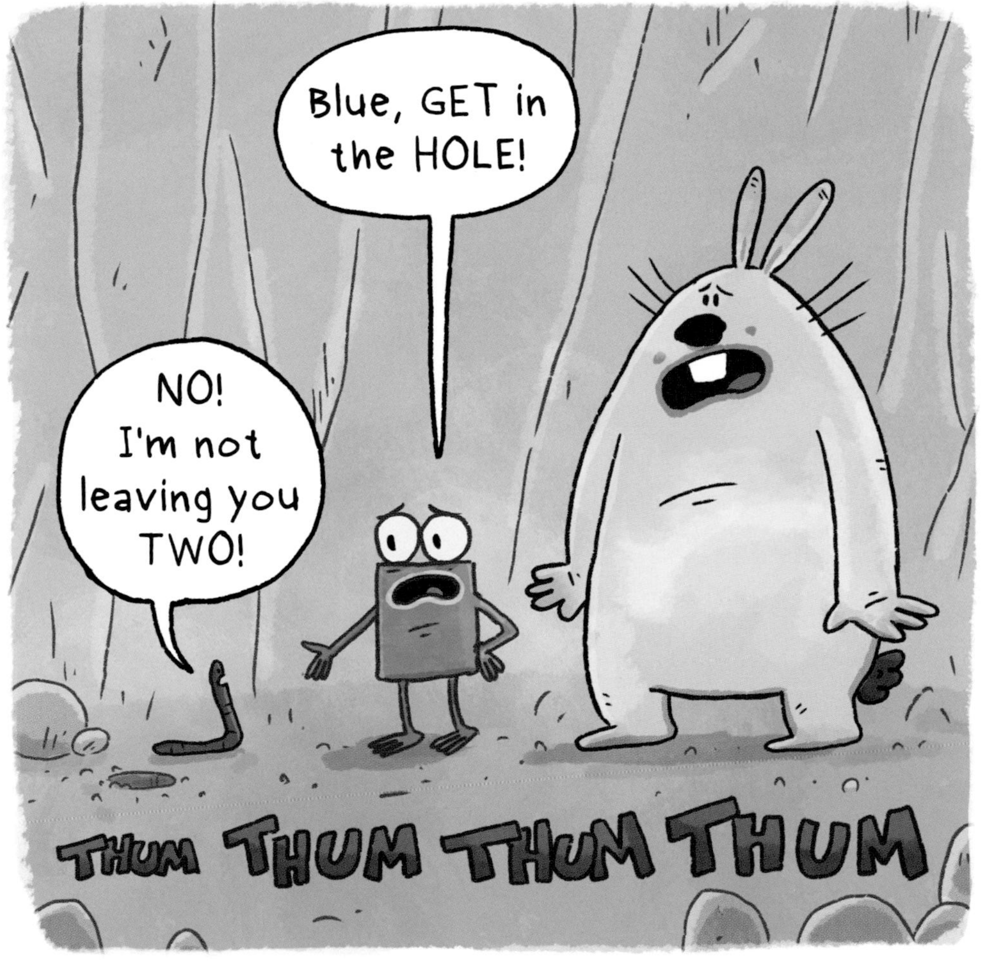
Blue, GET in the HOLE!
NO! I'm not leaving you TWO!
THUM THUM THUM THUM

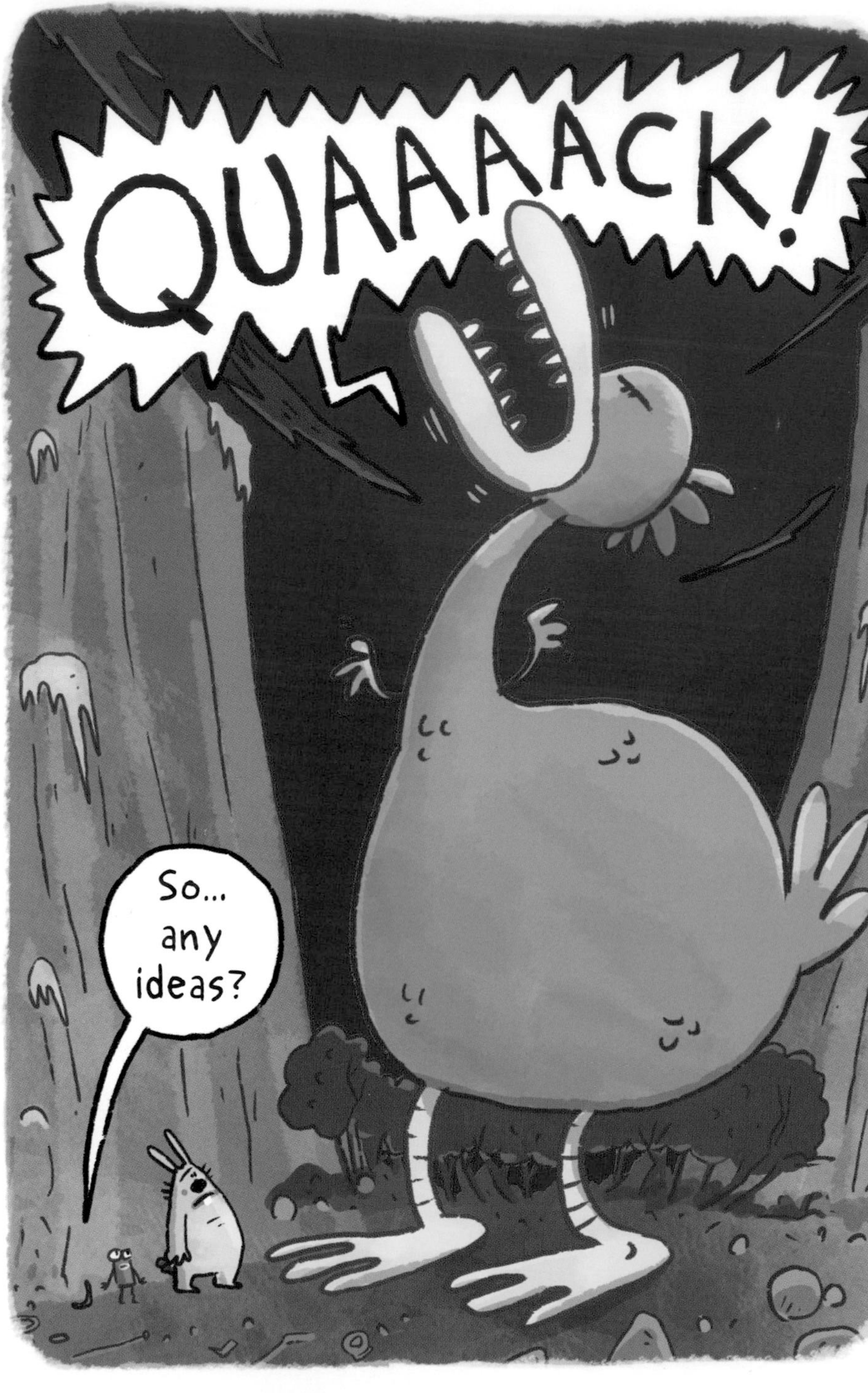
QUAAAACK!
So... any ideas?

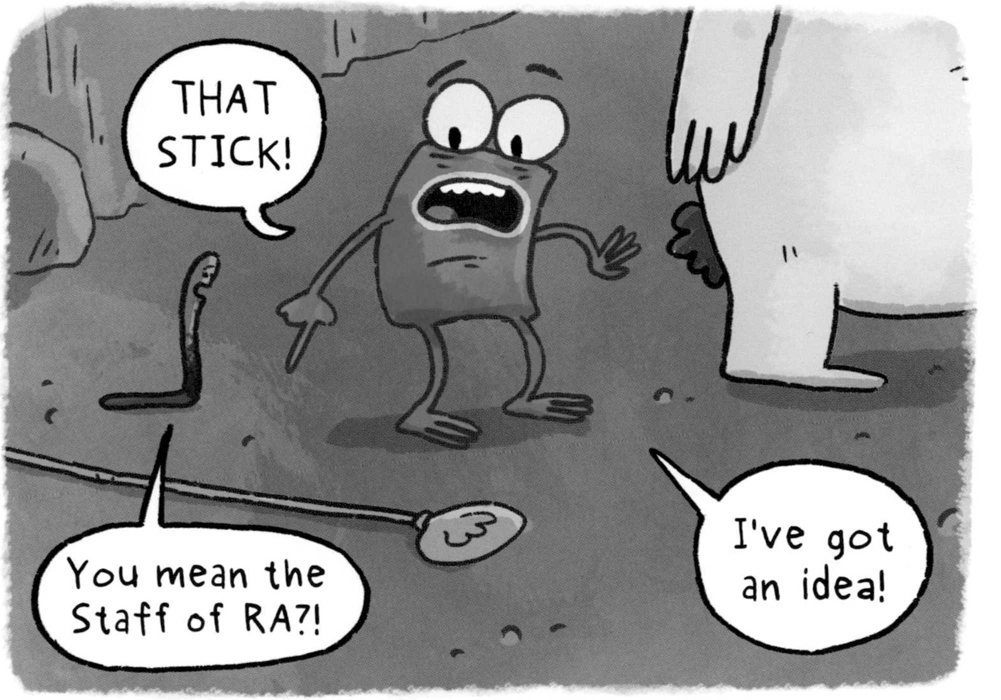
THAT STICK!
You mean the Staff of RA?!
I've got an idea!

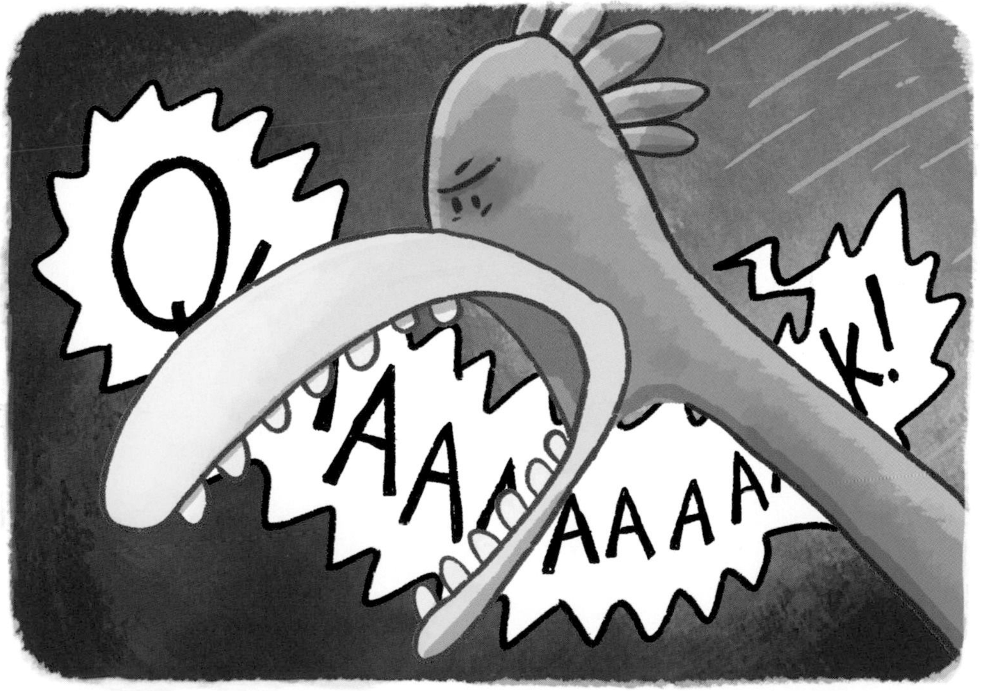

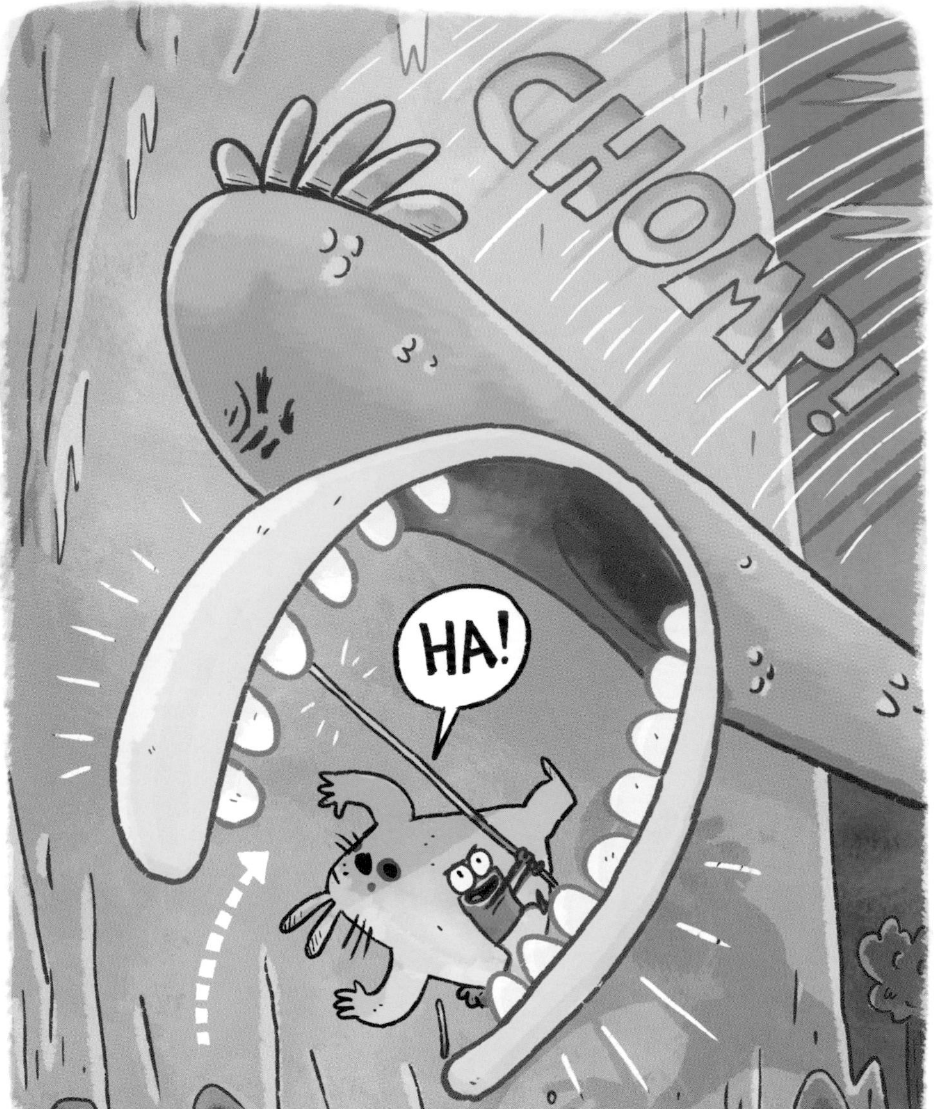
CHOMP!
HA!

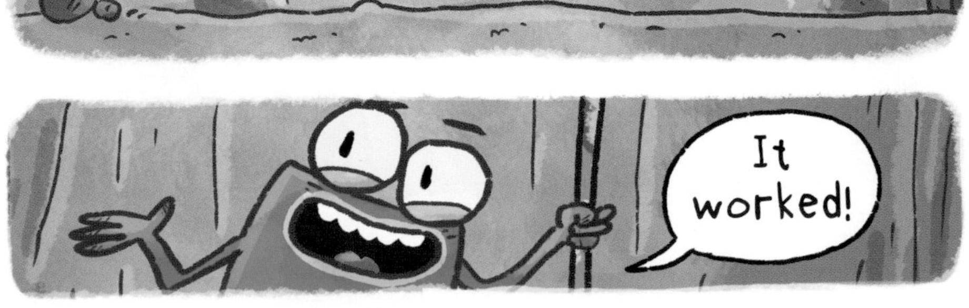
It worked!

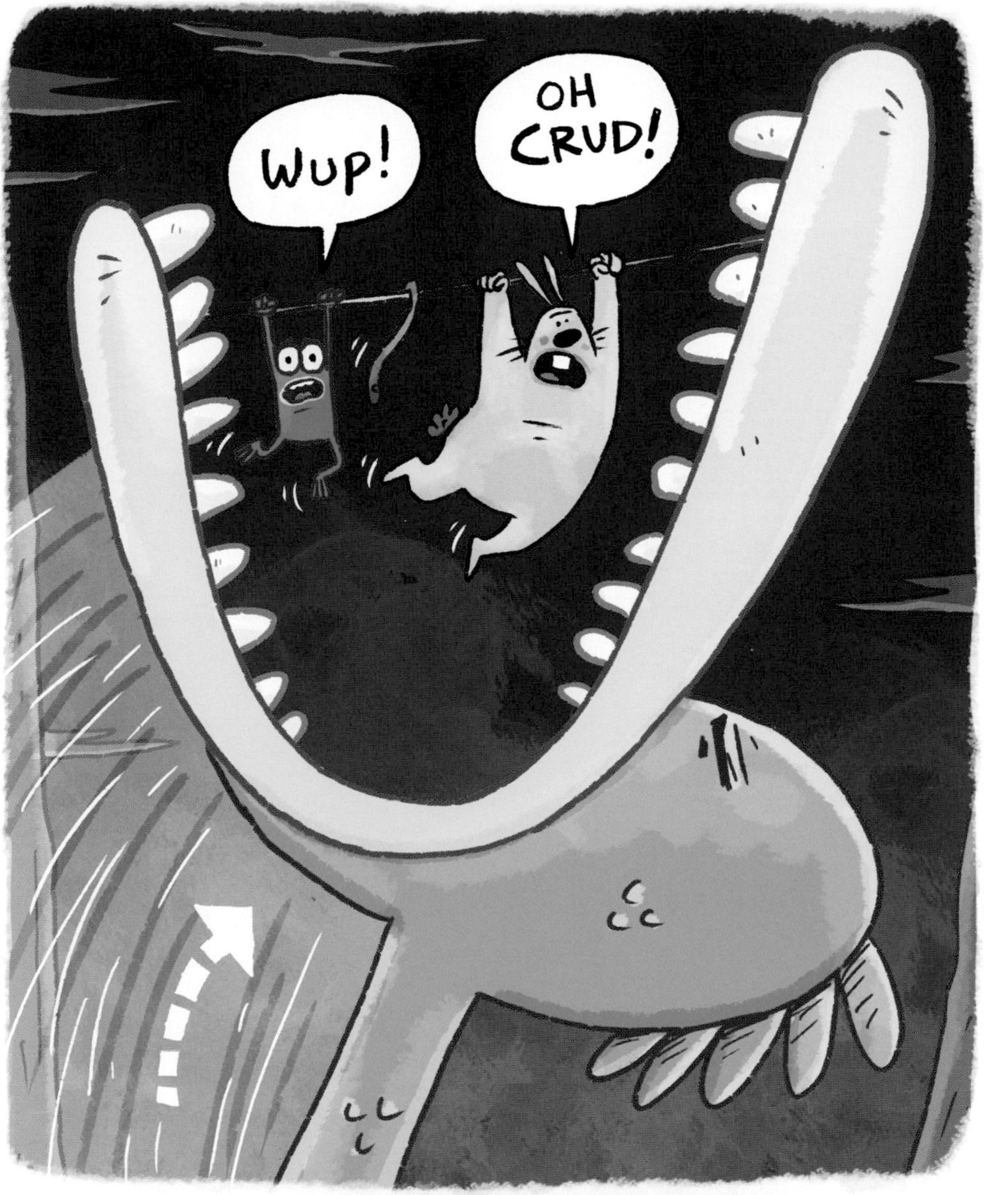

WUP!
OH CRUD!

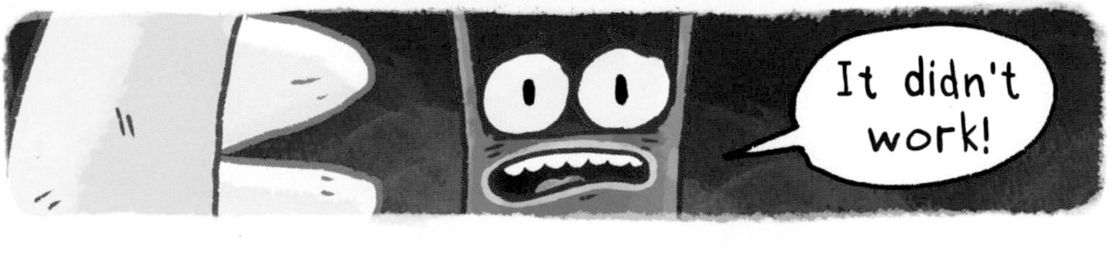

It didn't work!

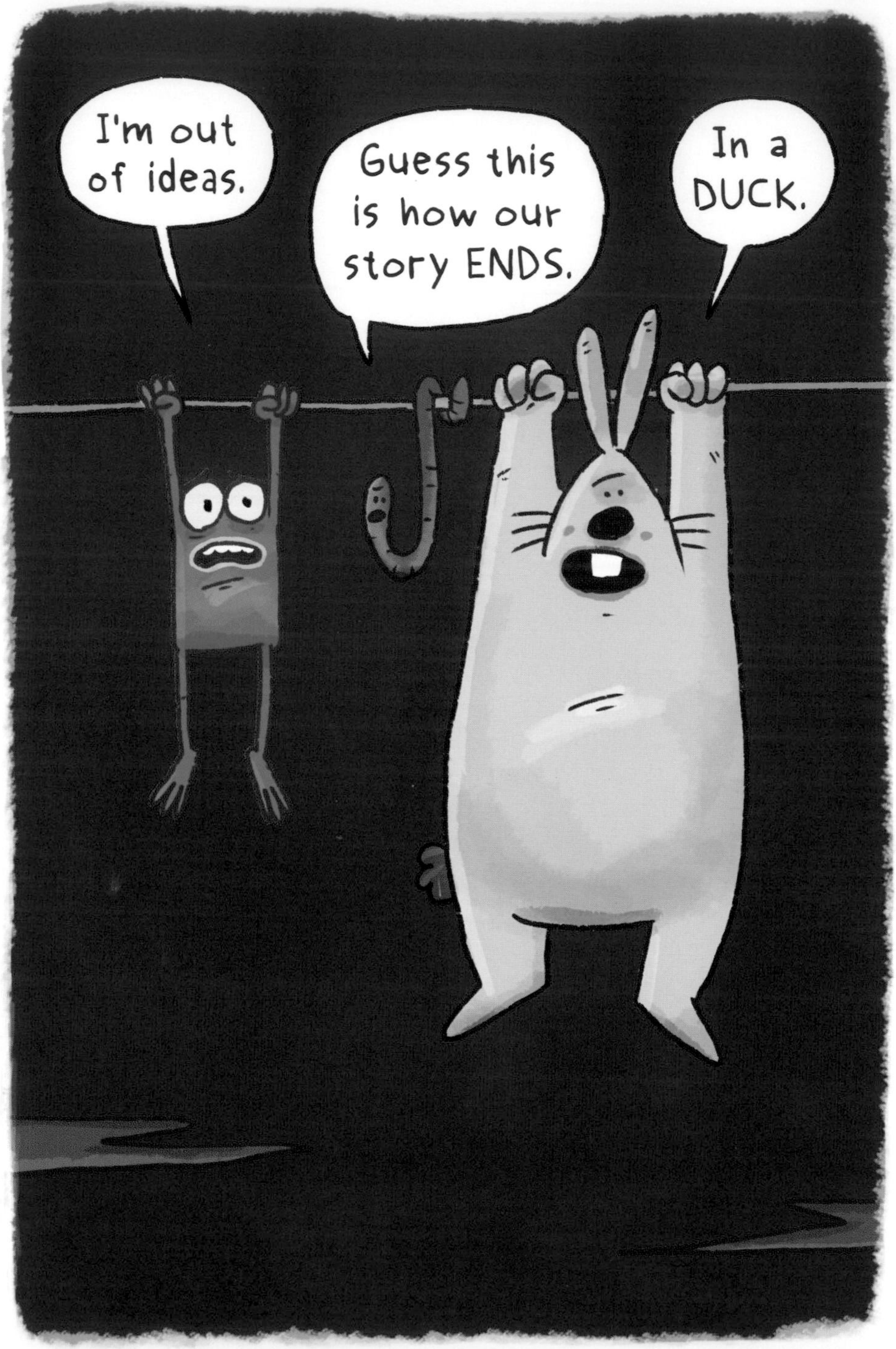
I'm out of ideas.
Guess this is how our story ENDS.
In a DUCK.

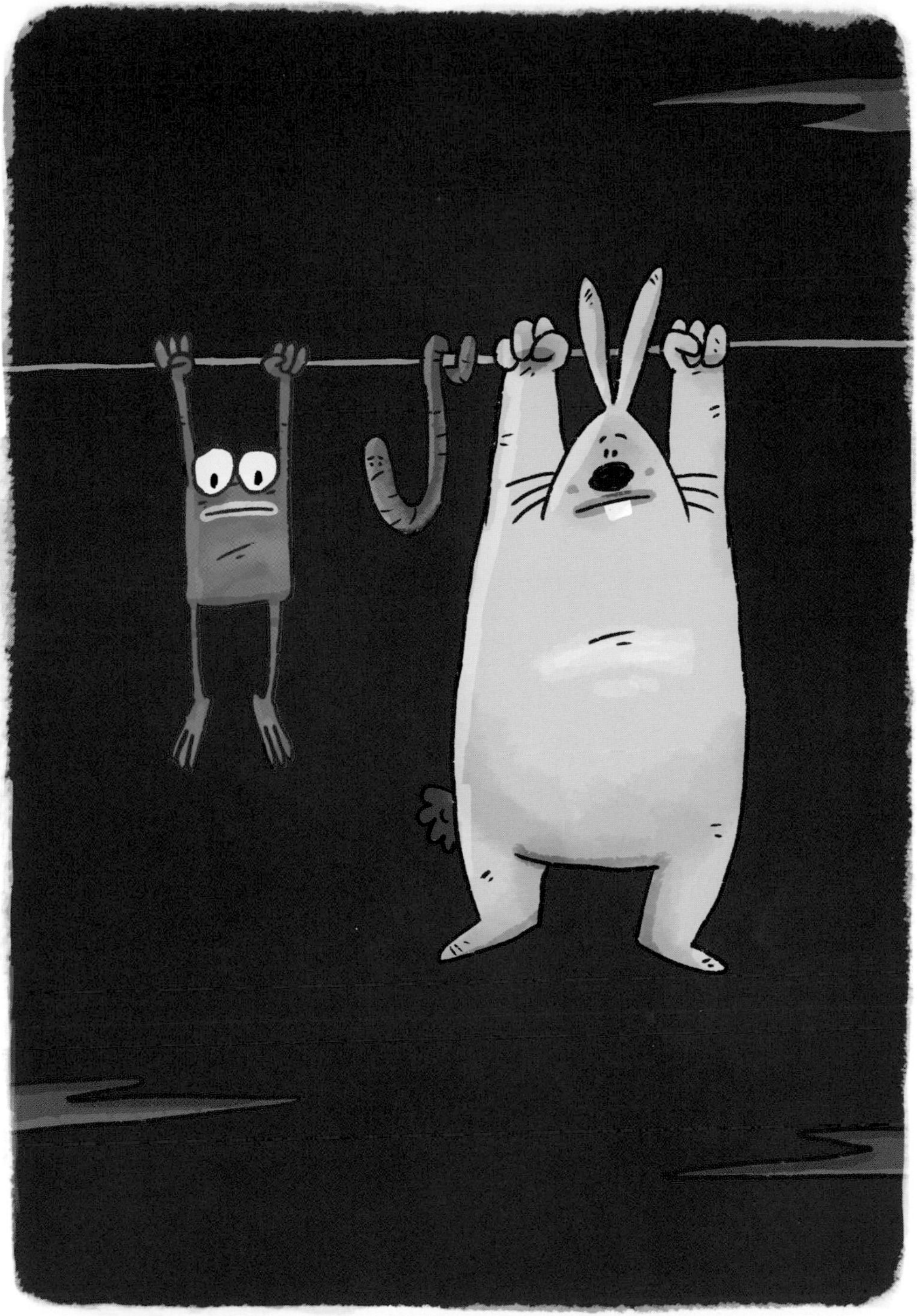

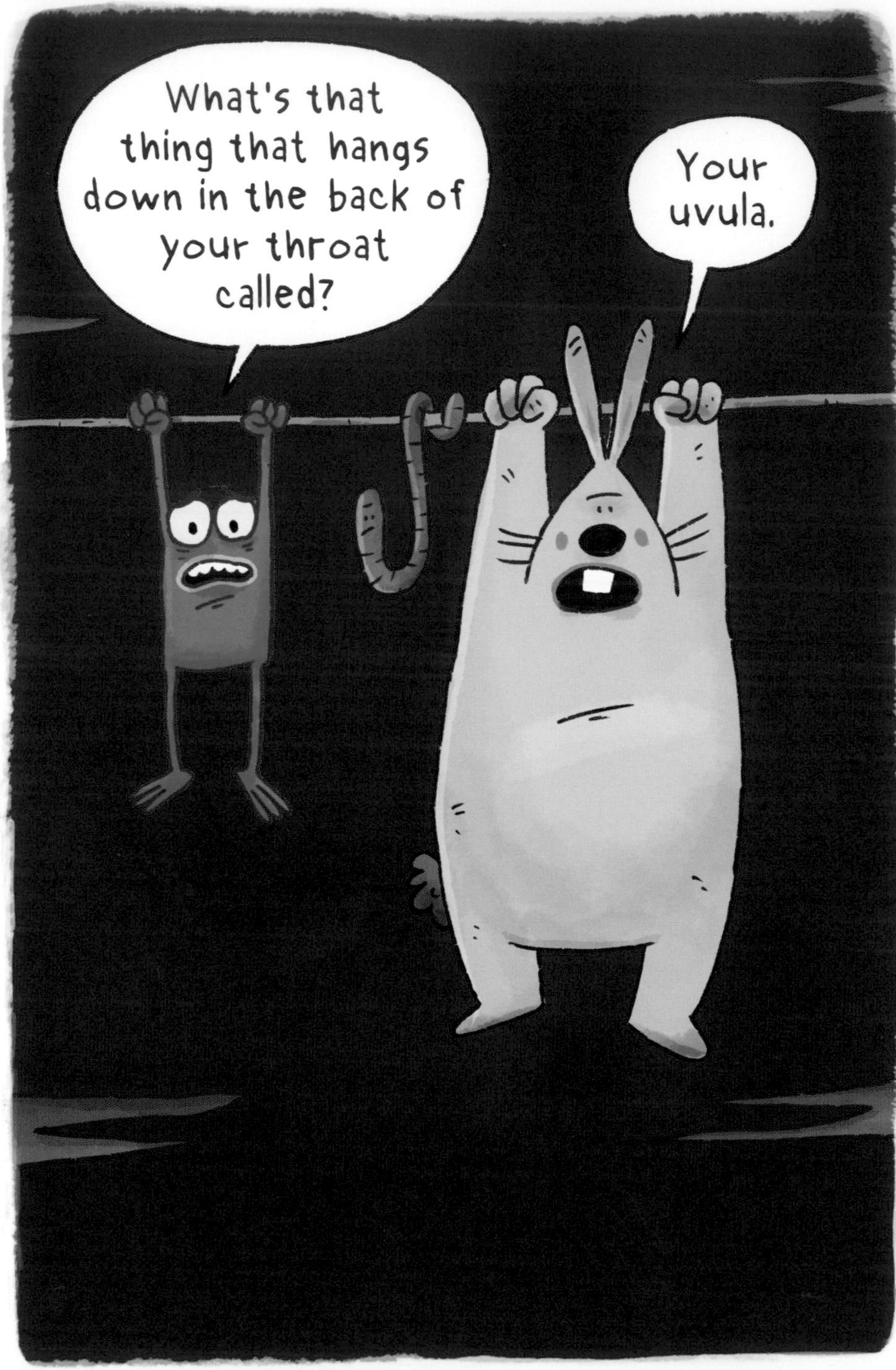
What's that thing that hangs down in the back of your throat called?
Your uvula.

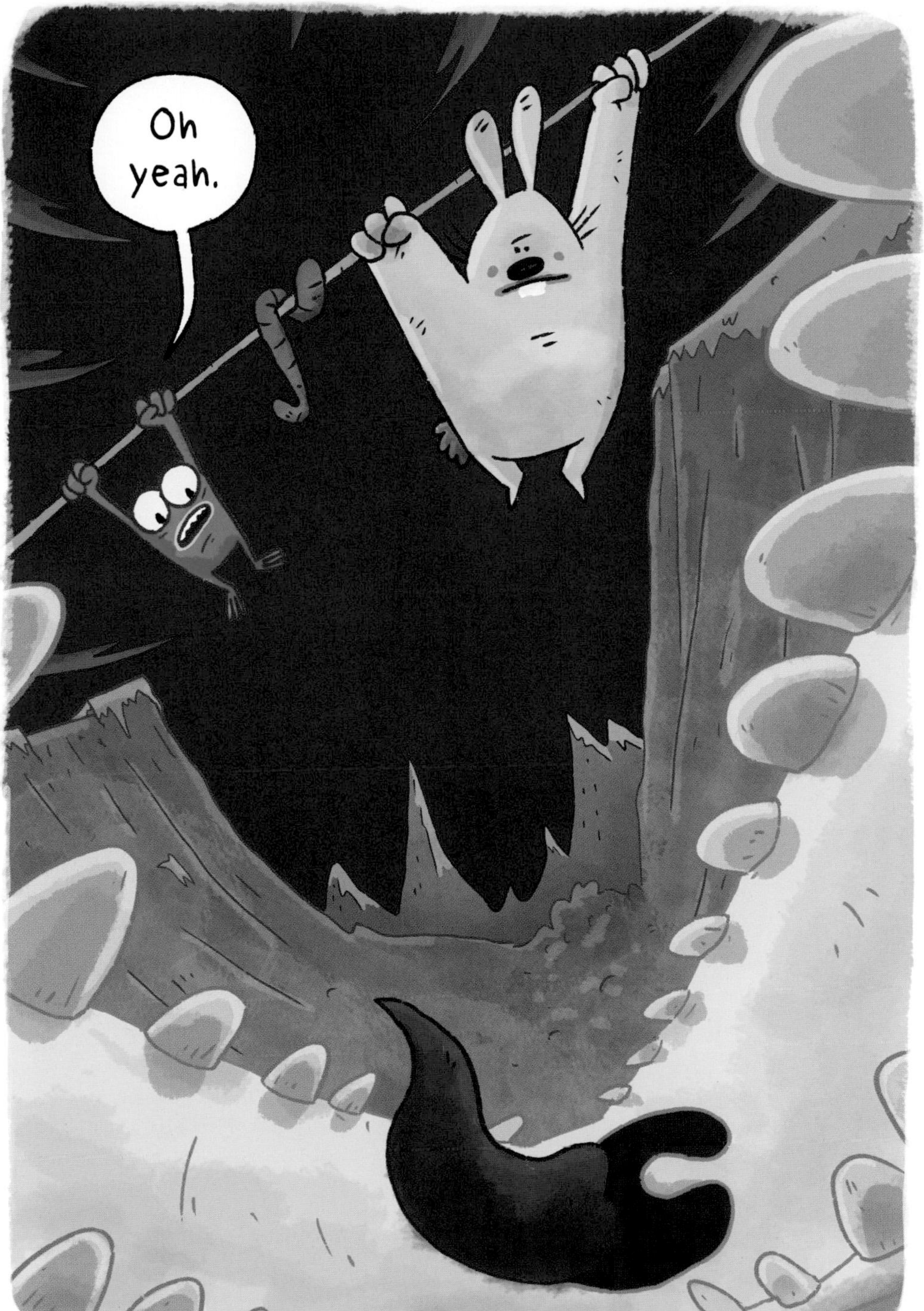
Oh yeah.

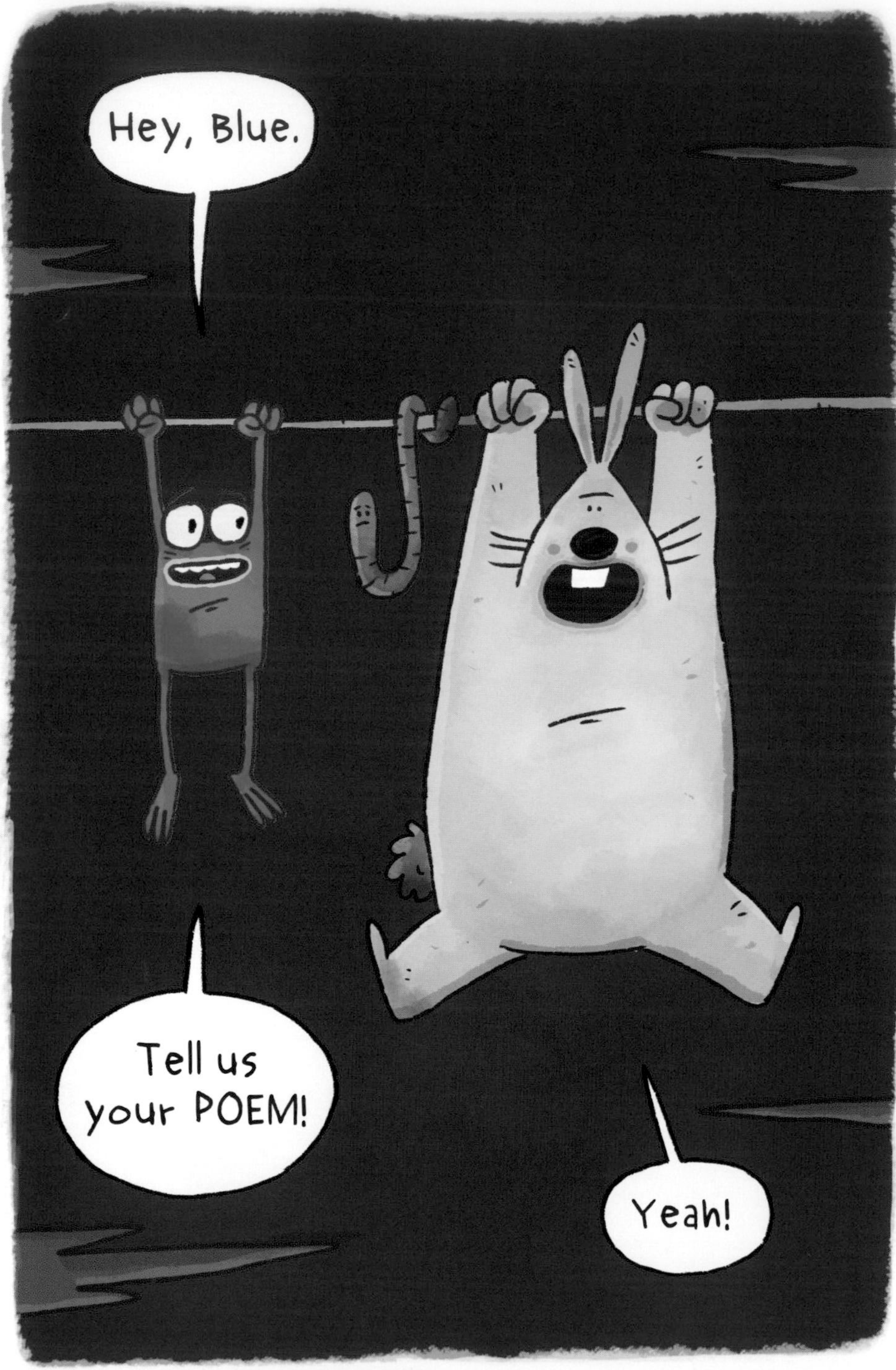
Hey, Blue.
Tell us your POEM!
Yeah!

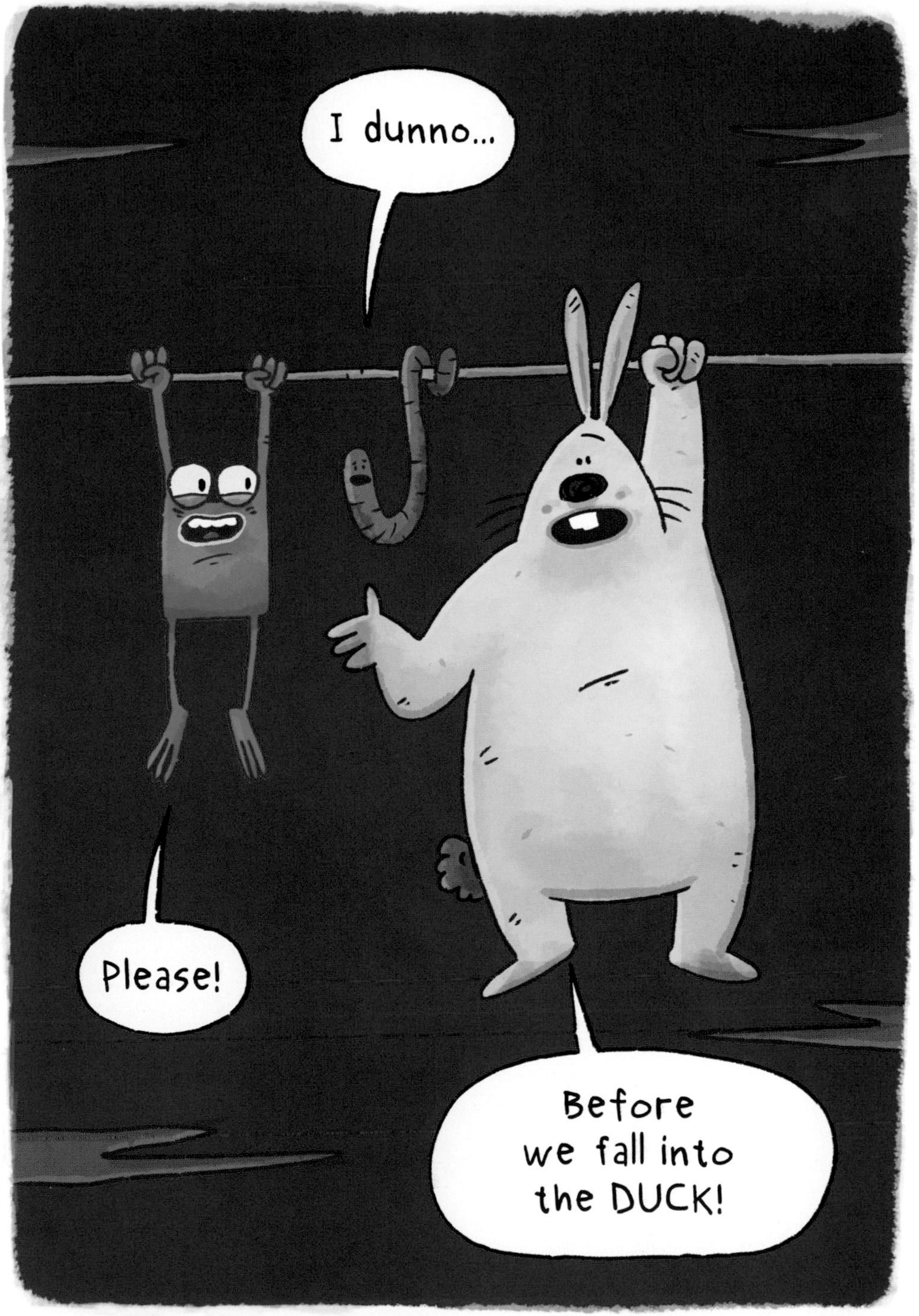
I dunno...
Please!
Before we fall into the DUCK!

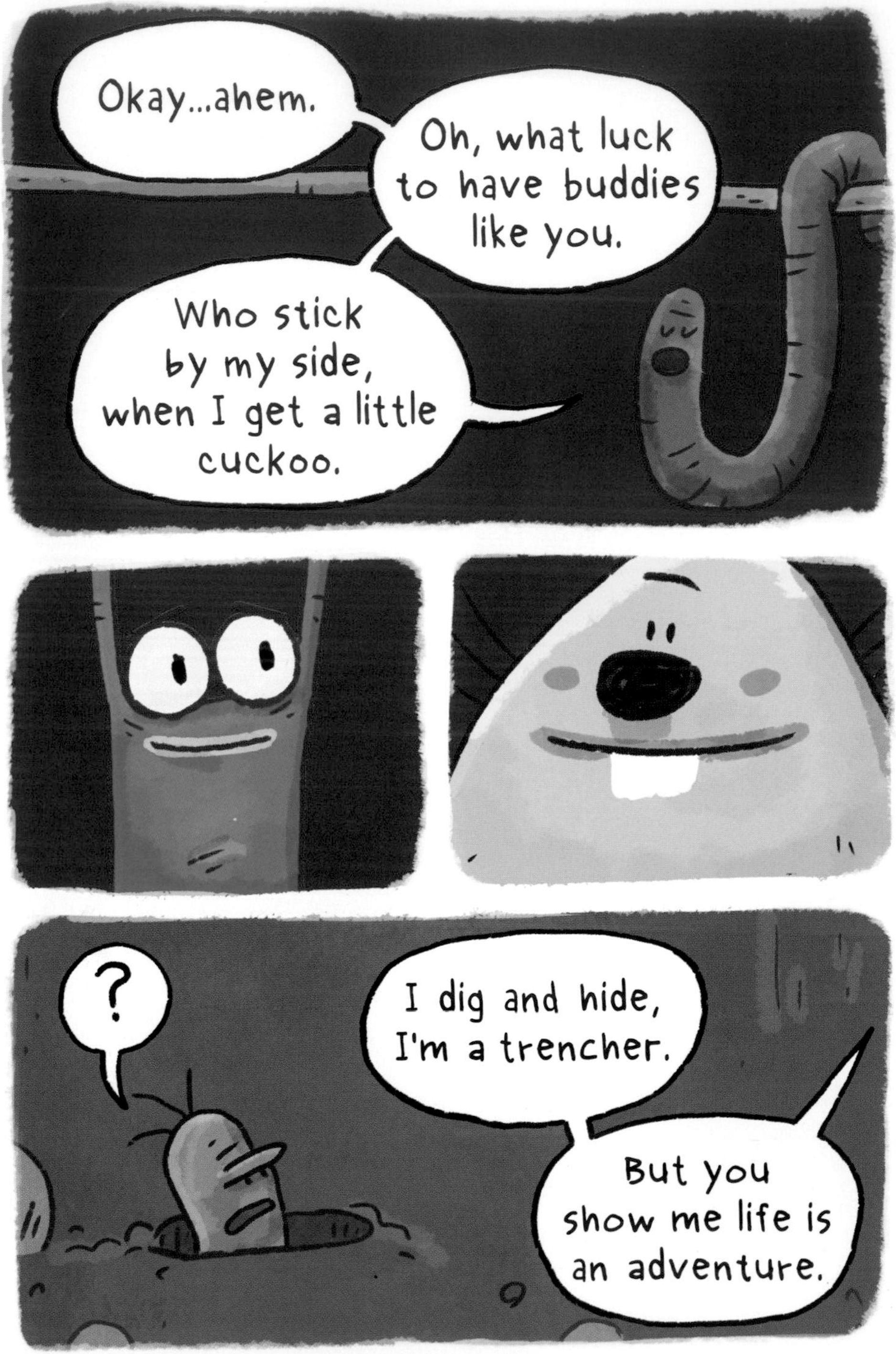
Okay...ahem.
Oh, what luck to have buddies like you.
Who stick by my side, when I get a little cuckoo.
?
I dig and hide, I'm a trencher.
But you show me life is an adventure.

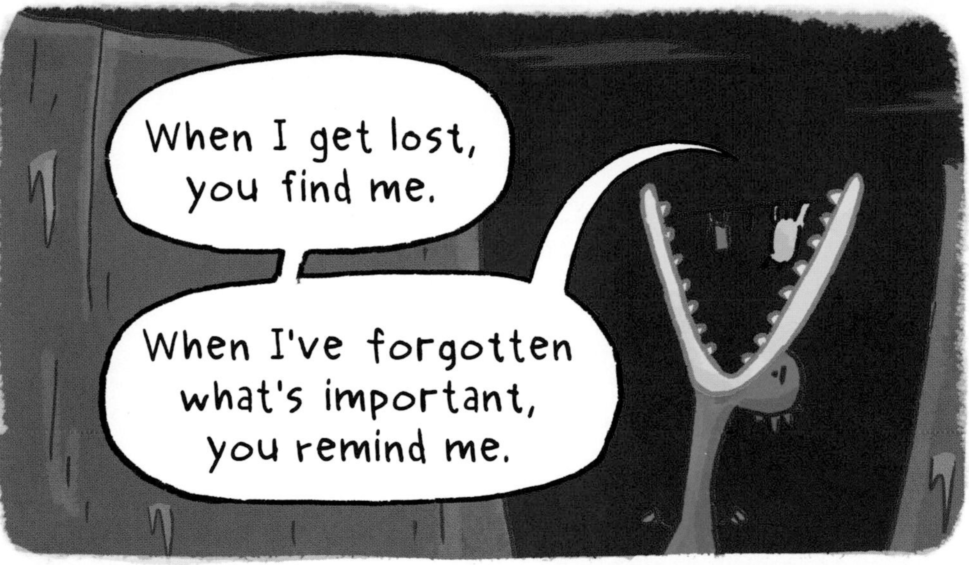
When I get lost, you find me.
When I've forgotten what's important, you remind me.

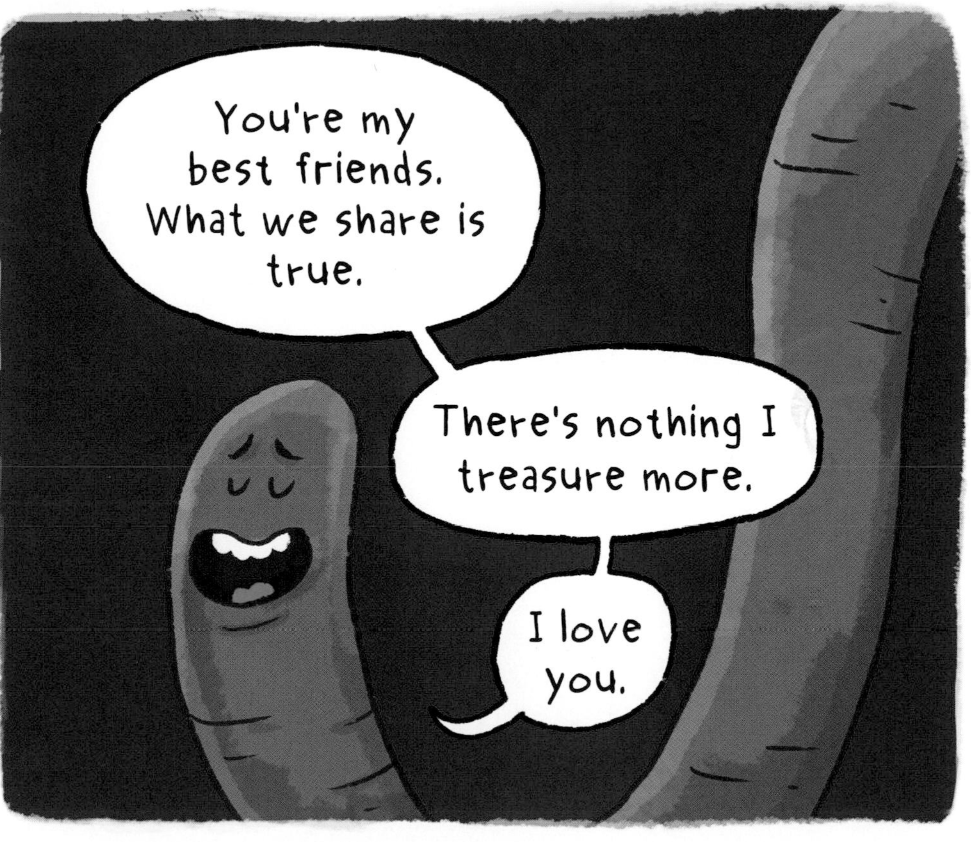
You're my best friends. What we share is true.
There's nothing I treasure more.
I love you.

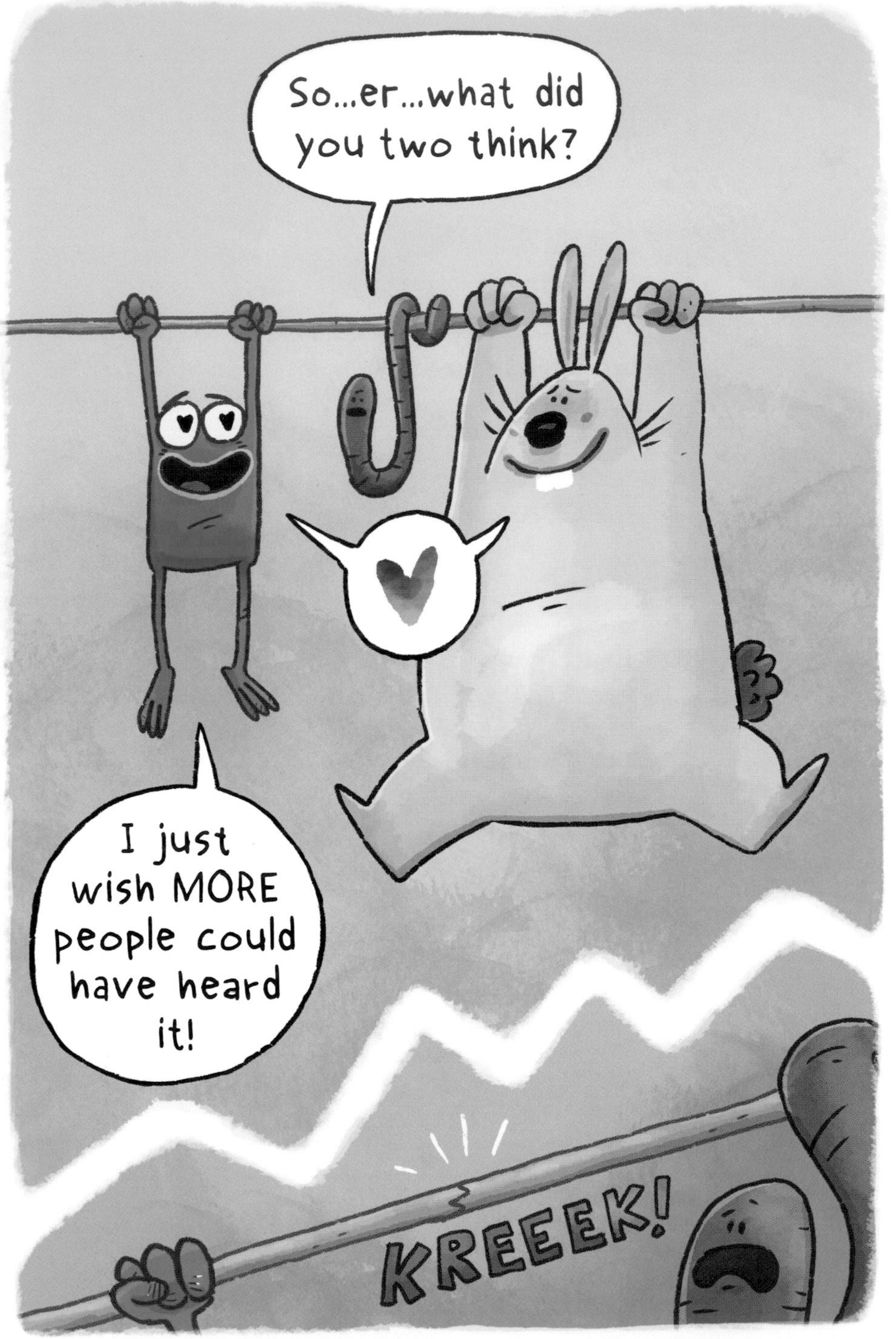
So...er...what did you two think?
I just wish MORE people could have heard it!
KREEEK!

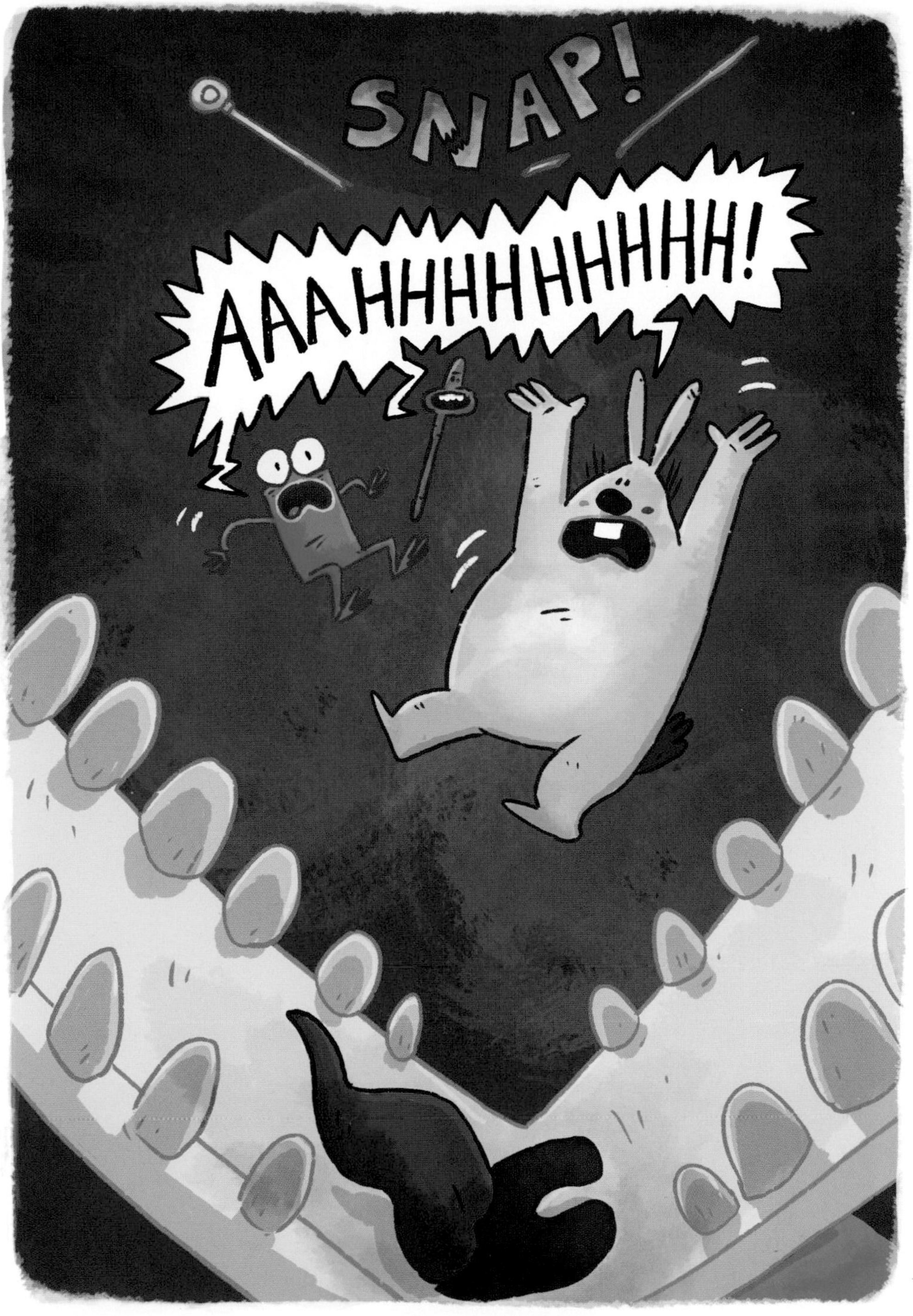
SNAP!
AAAHHHHHHHHHH!

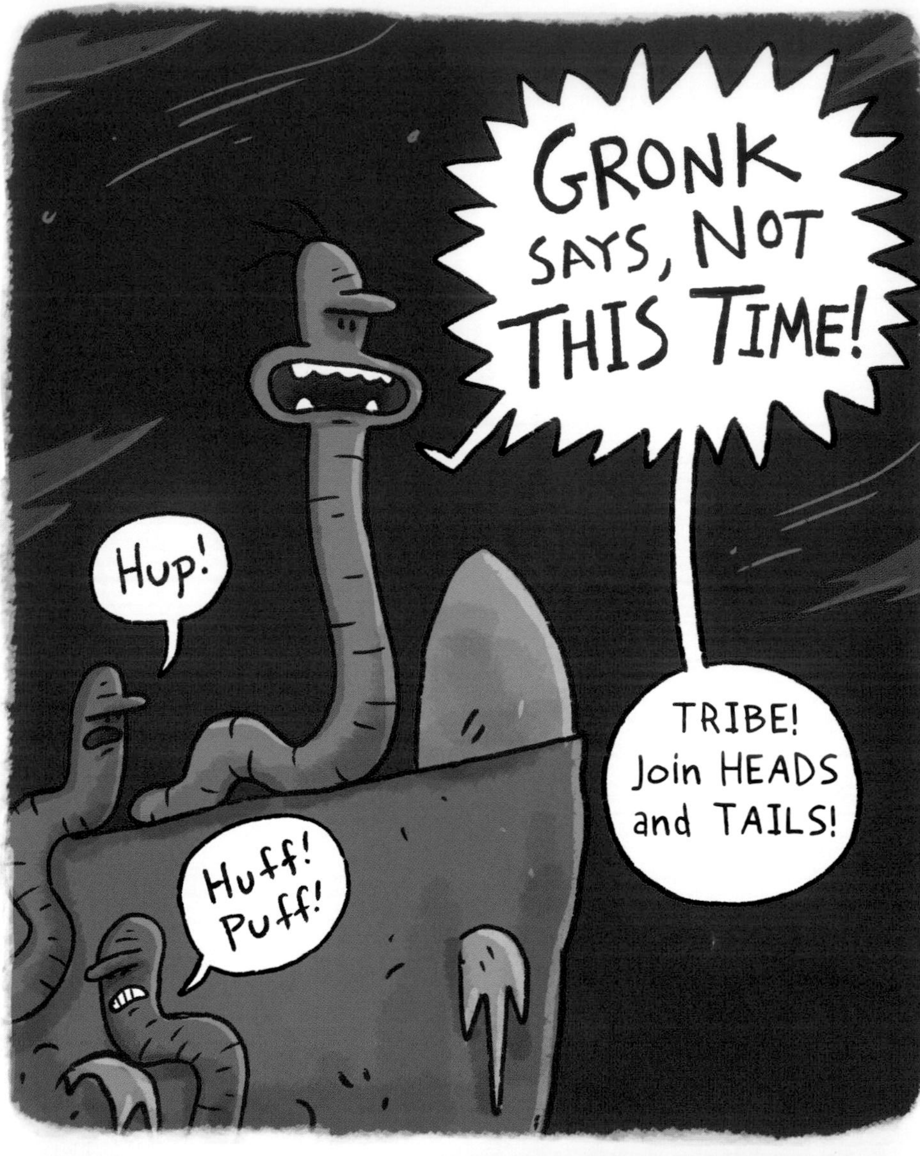
GRONK SAYS, NOT THIS TIME!
TRIBE! Join HEADS and TAILS!
Hup!
Huff! Puff!

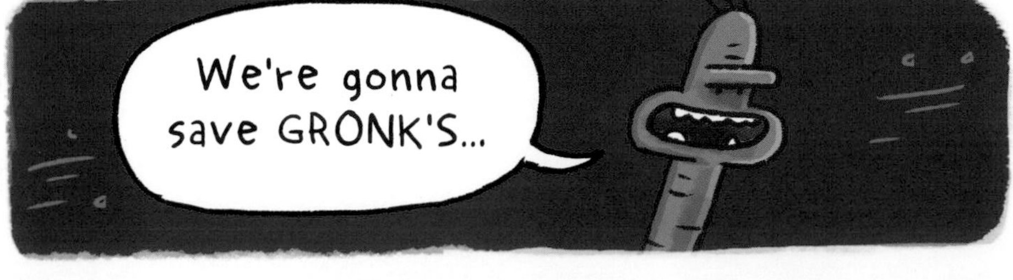
We're gonna save GRONK'S...

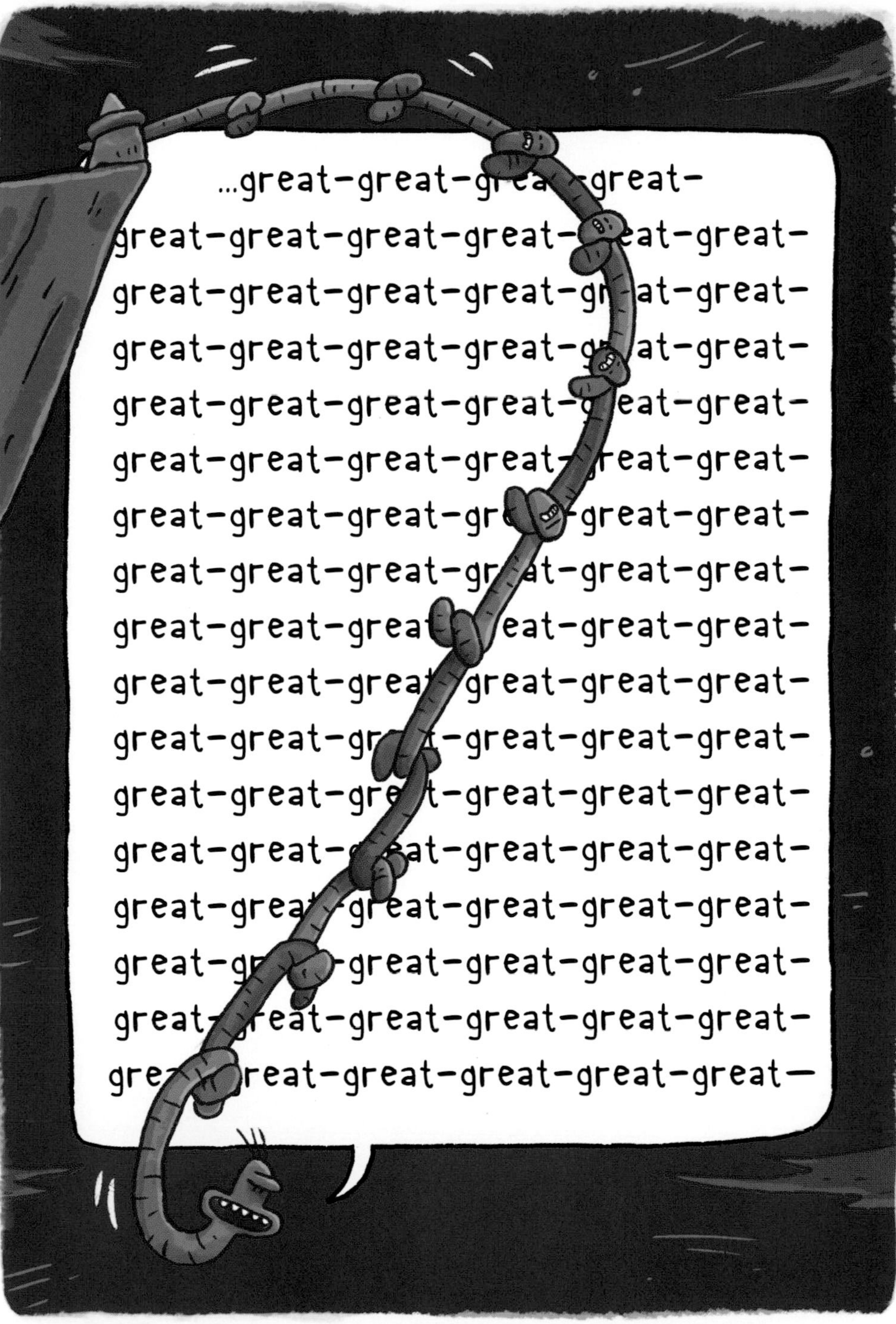
...great-great-great-great-
great-great-great-great-great-great-
great-great-great-great-great-great-
great-great-great-great-great-great-
great-great-great-great-great-great-
great-great-great-great-great-great-
great-great-great-great-great-great-
great-great-great-great-great-great-
great-great-great-great-great-great-
great-great-great-great-great-great-
great-great-great-great-great-great-
great-great-great-great-great-great-
great-great-great-great-great-great-
great-great-great-great-great-great-
great-great-great-great-great-great-
great-great-great-great-great-great-
great-great-great-great-great-great—

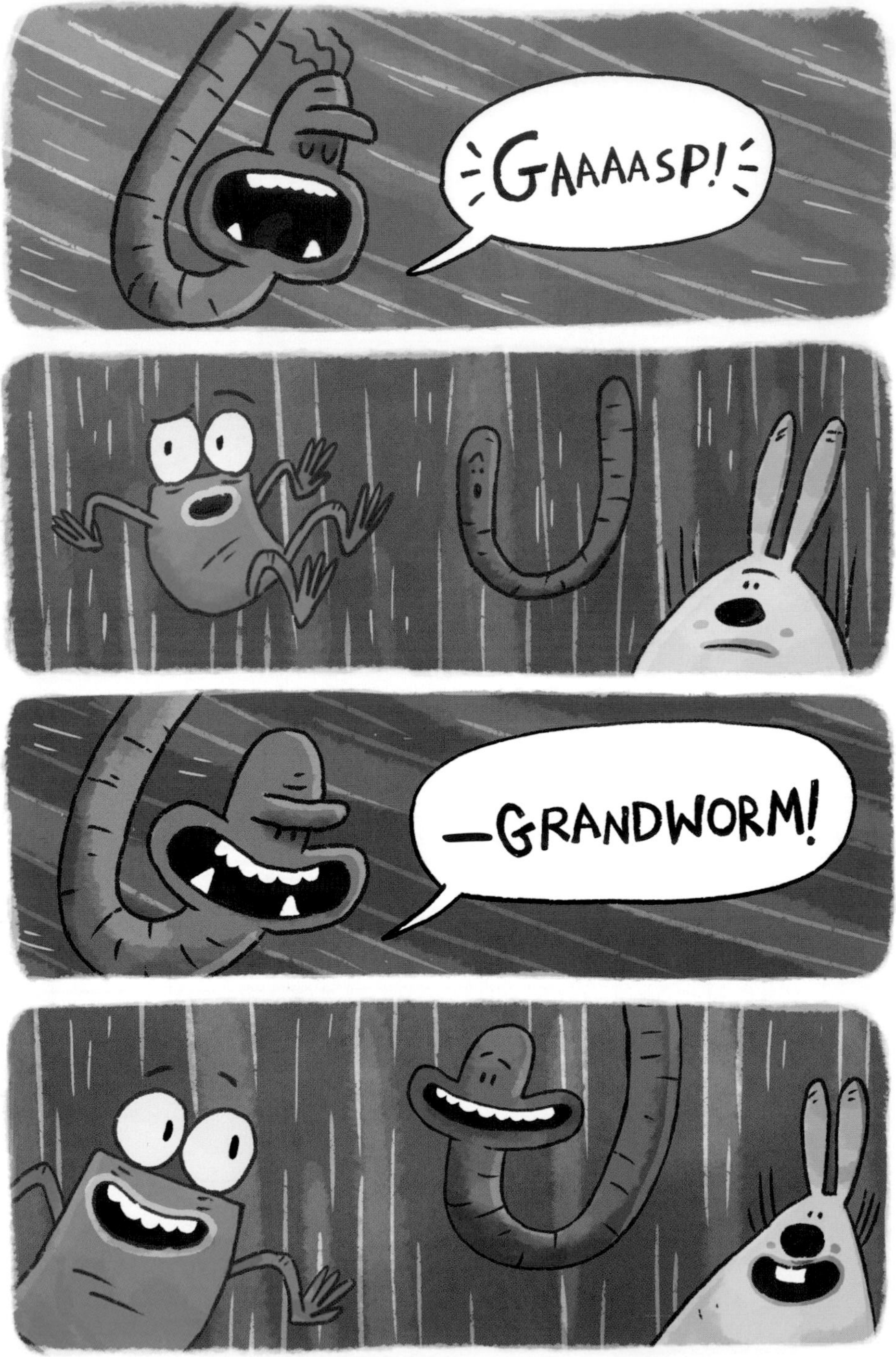
GAAAASP!
—GRANDWORM!

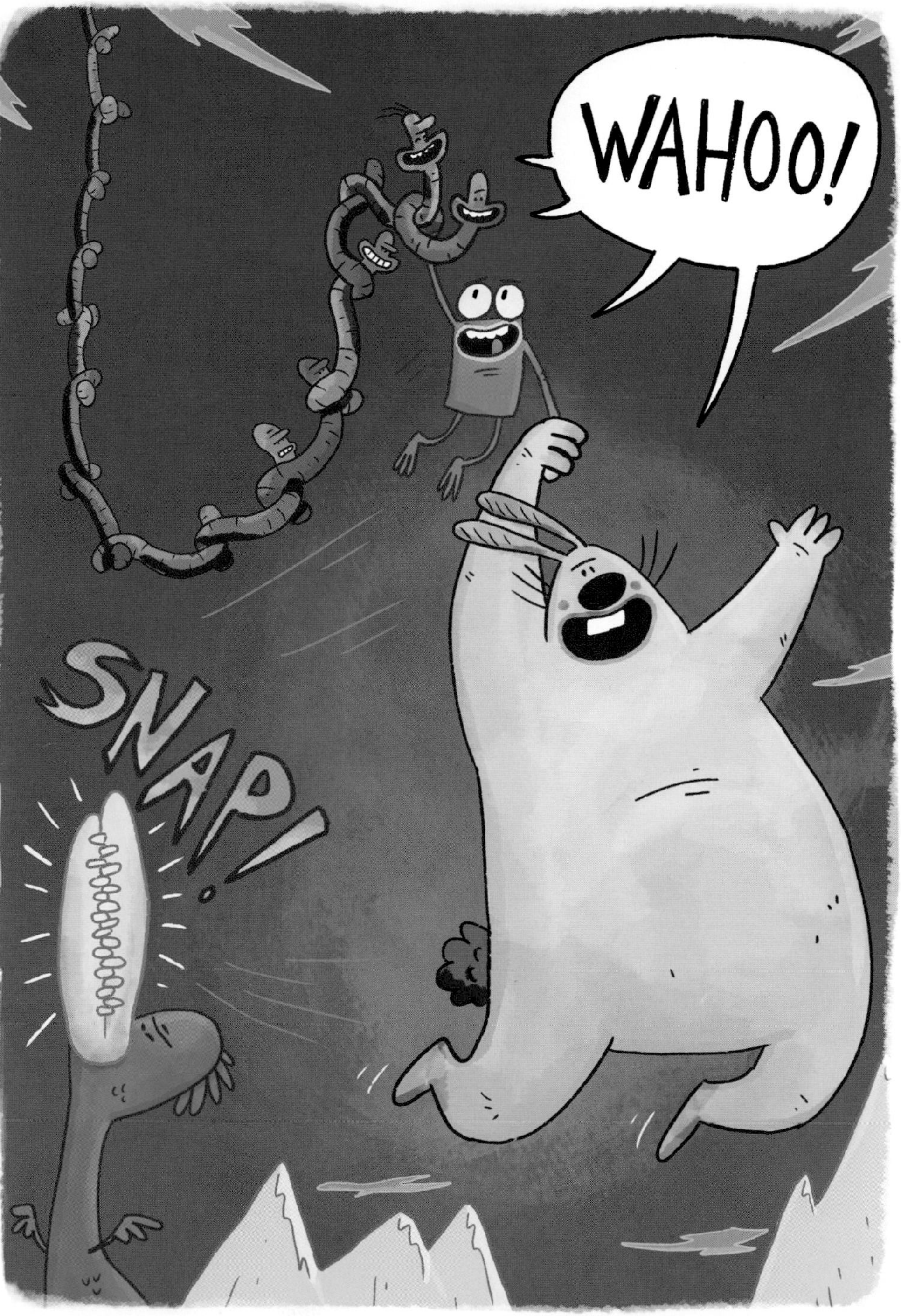
WAHOO!
SNAP!

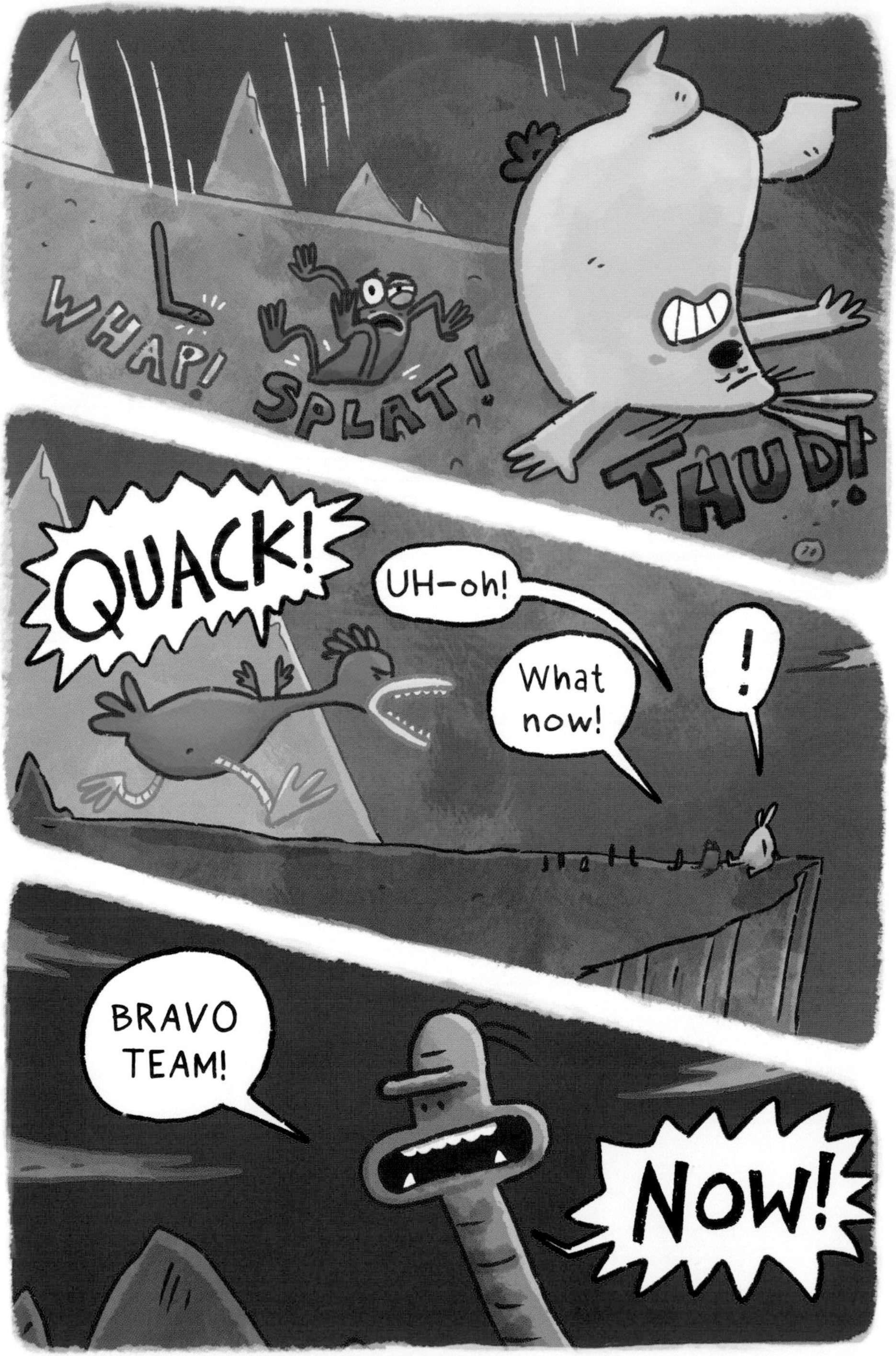
WHAP!
SPLAT!
THUD!
QUACK!
UH-oh!
What now!
!
BRAVO TEAM!
NOW!

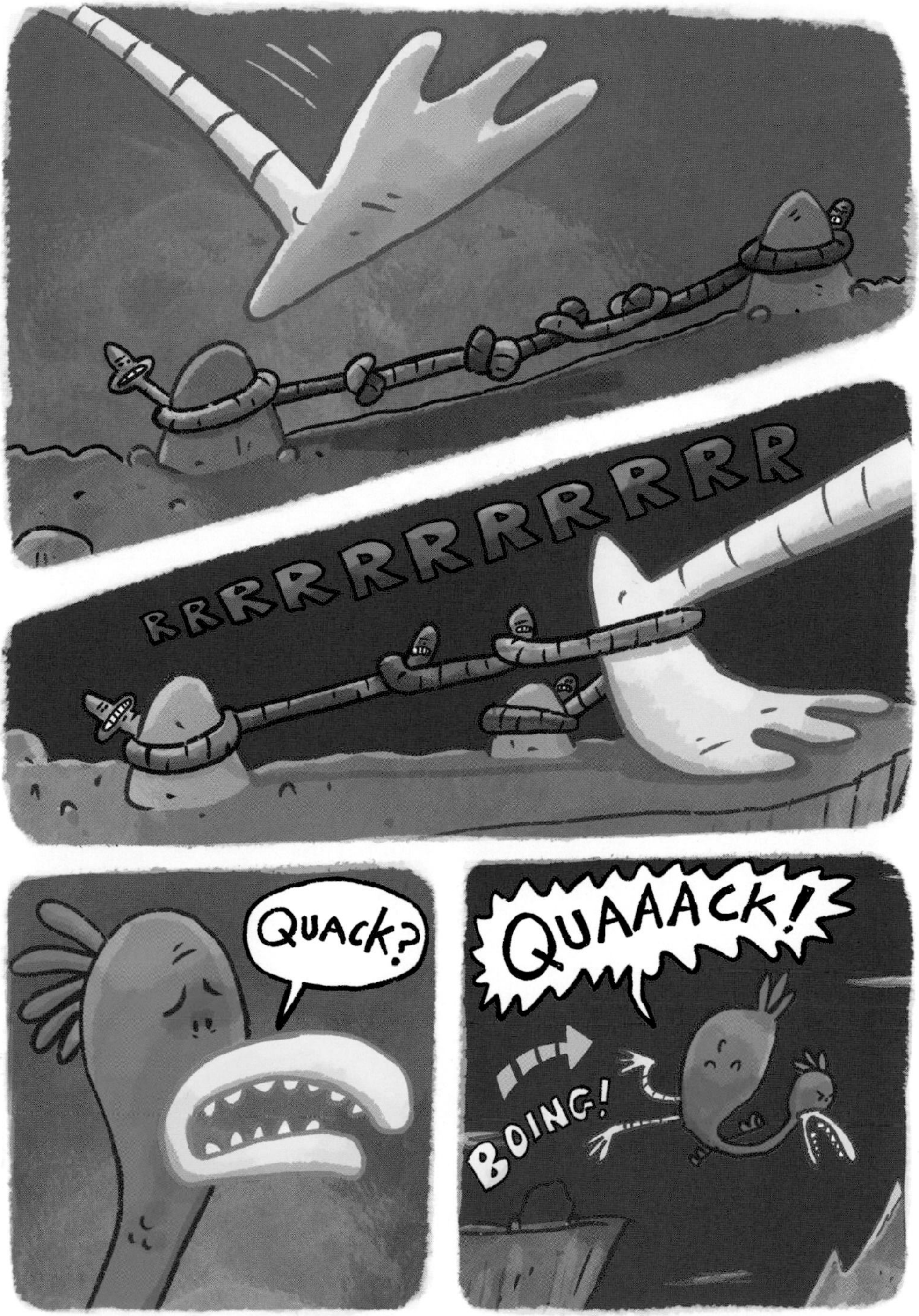
RRRRRRRRRRRRR
QUACK?
QUAAACK!
BOING!

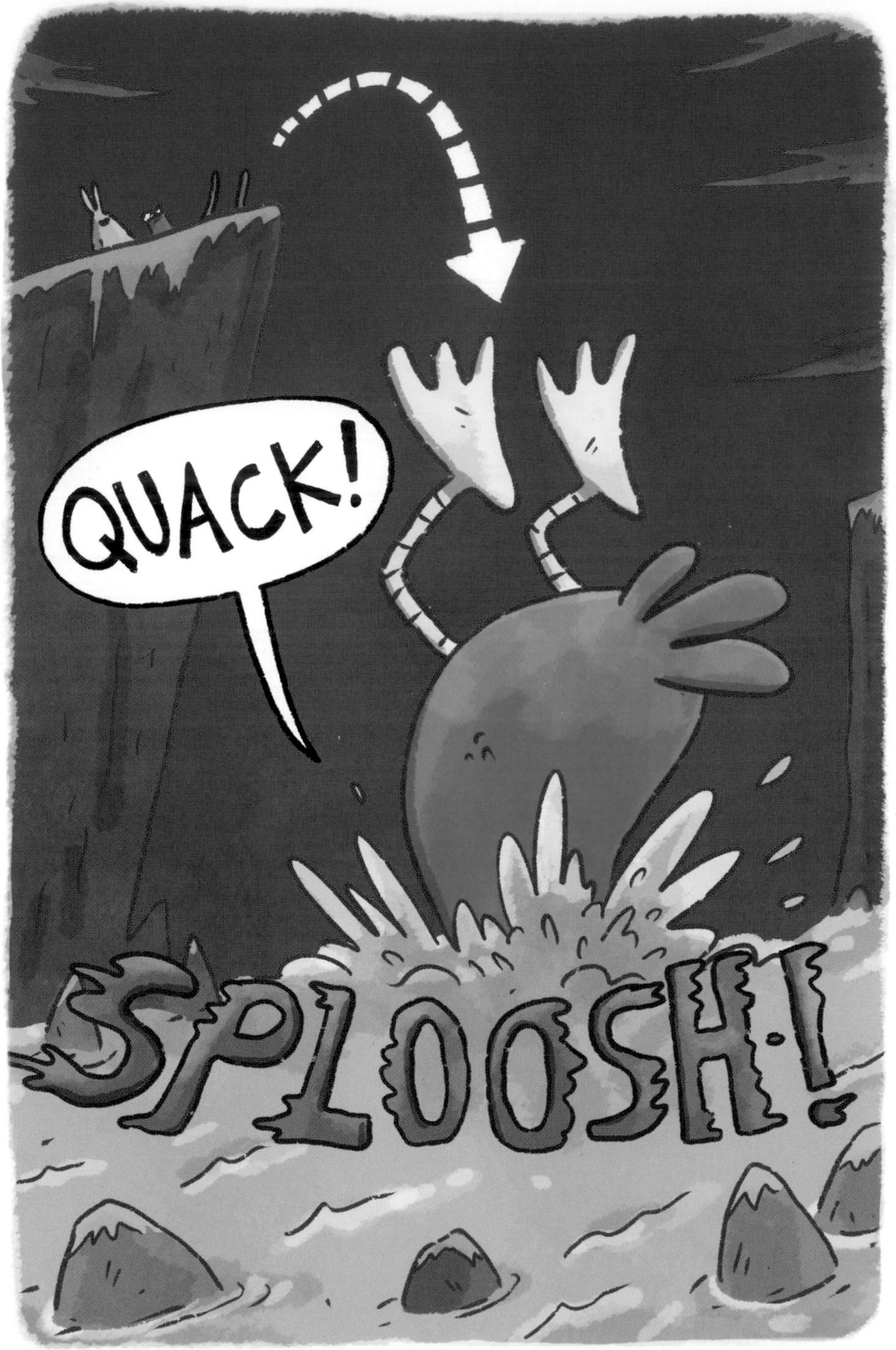
QUACK!
SPLOOSH!

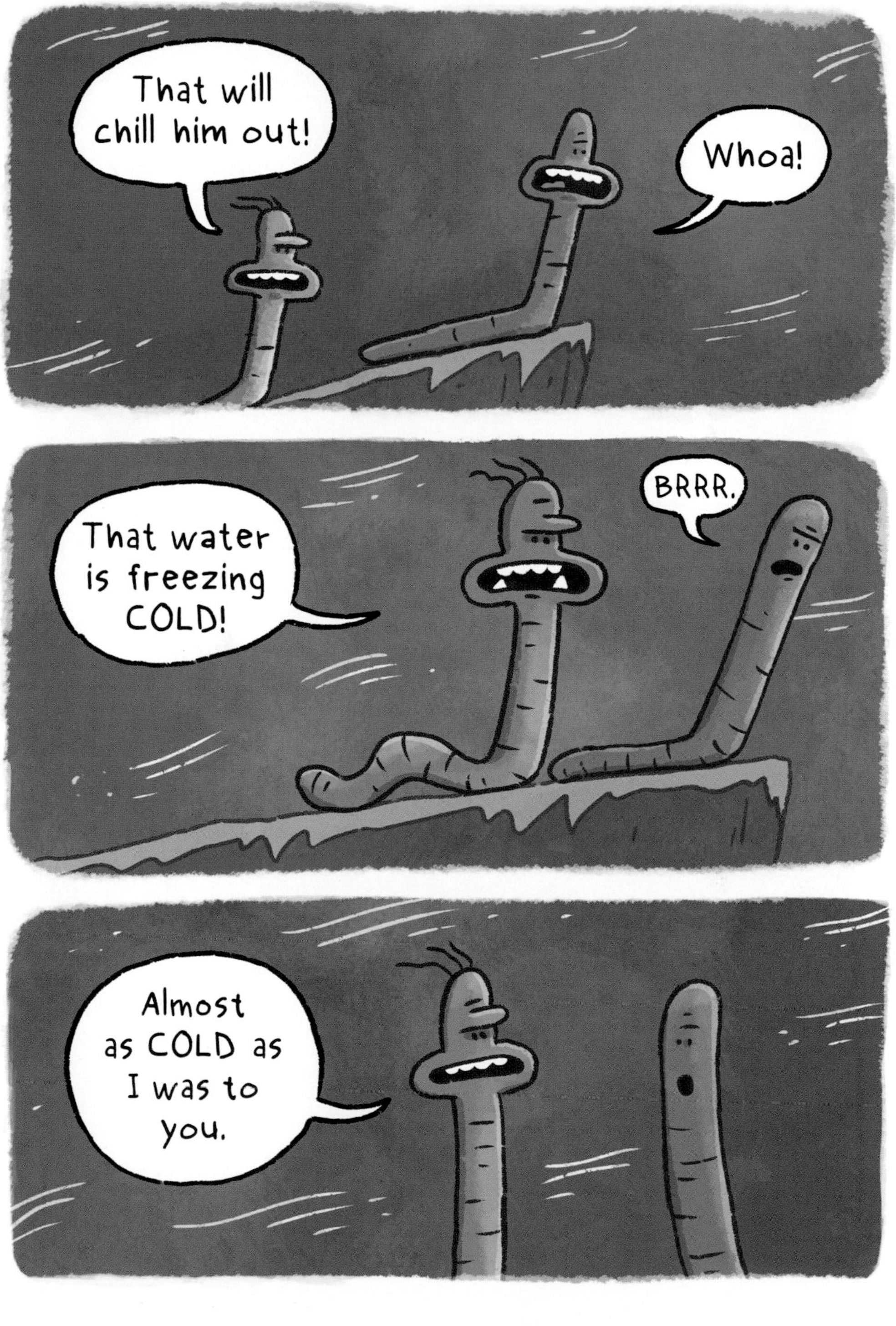
That will chill him out!
Whoa!
BRRR.
That water is freezing COLD!
Almost as COLD as I was to you.

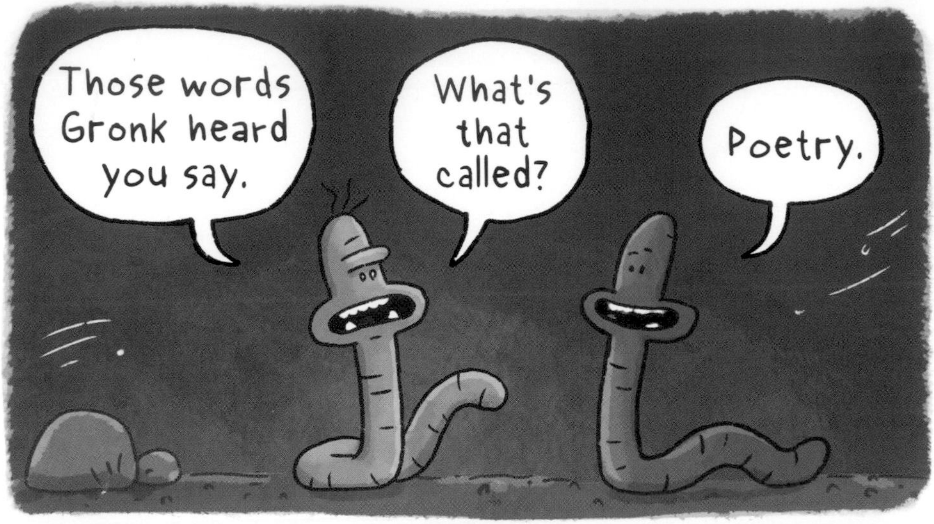
Those words Gronk heard you say.
What's that called?
Poetry.

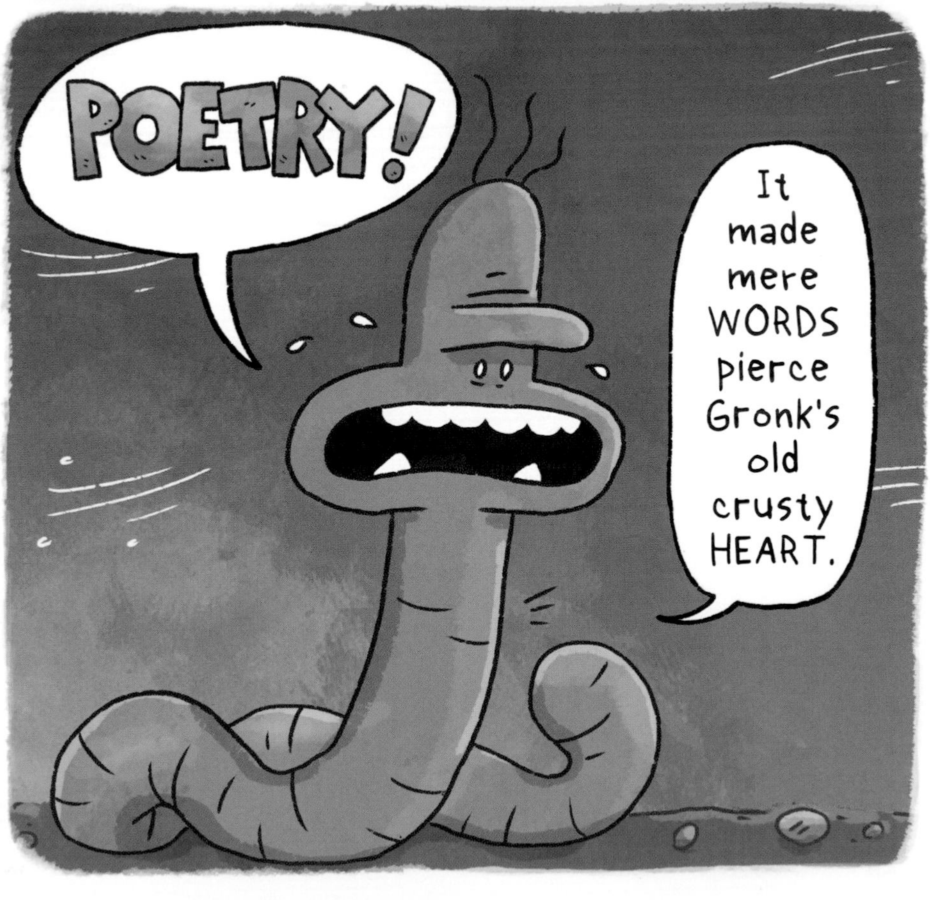
POETRY!
It made mere WORDS pierce Gronk's old crusty HEART.

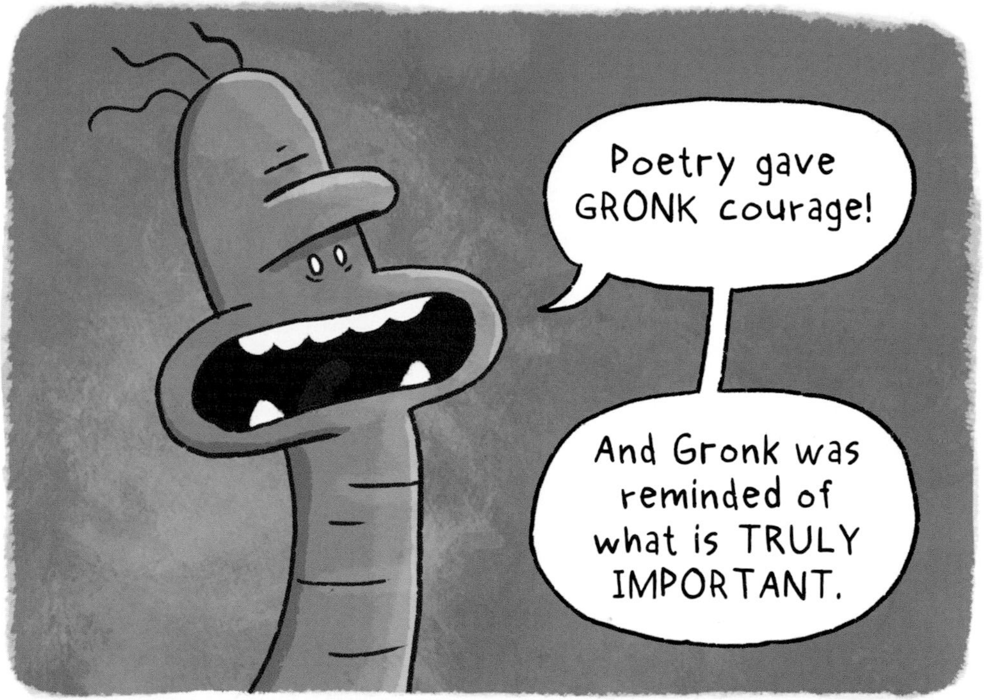
Poetry gave GRONK courage!
And Gronk was reminded of what is TRULY IMPORTANT.

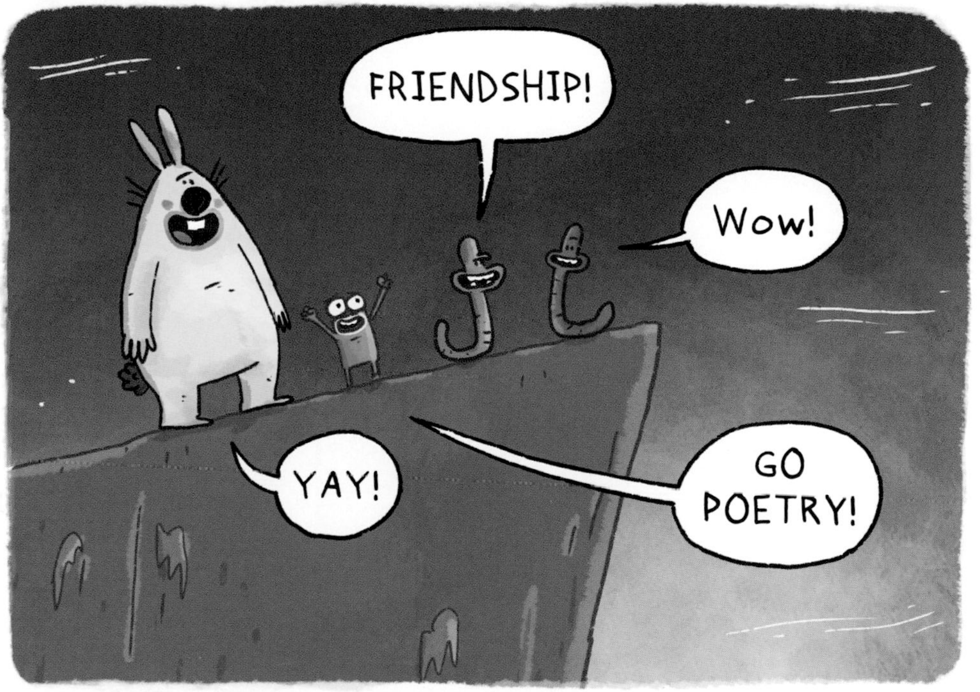
FRIENDSHIP!
Wow!
YAY!
GO POETRY!

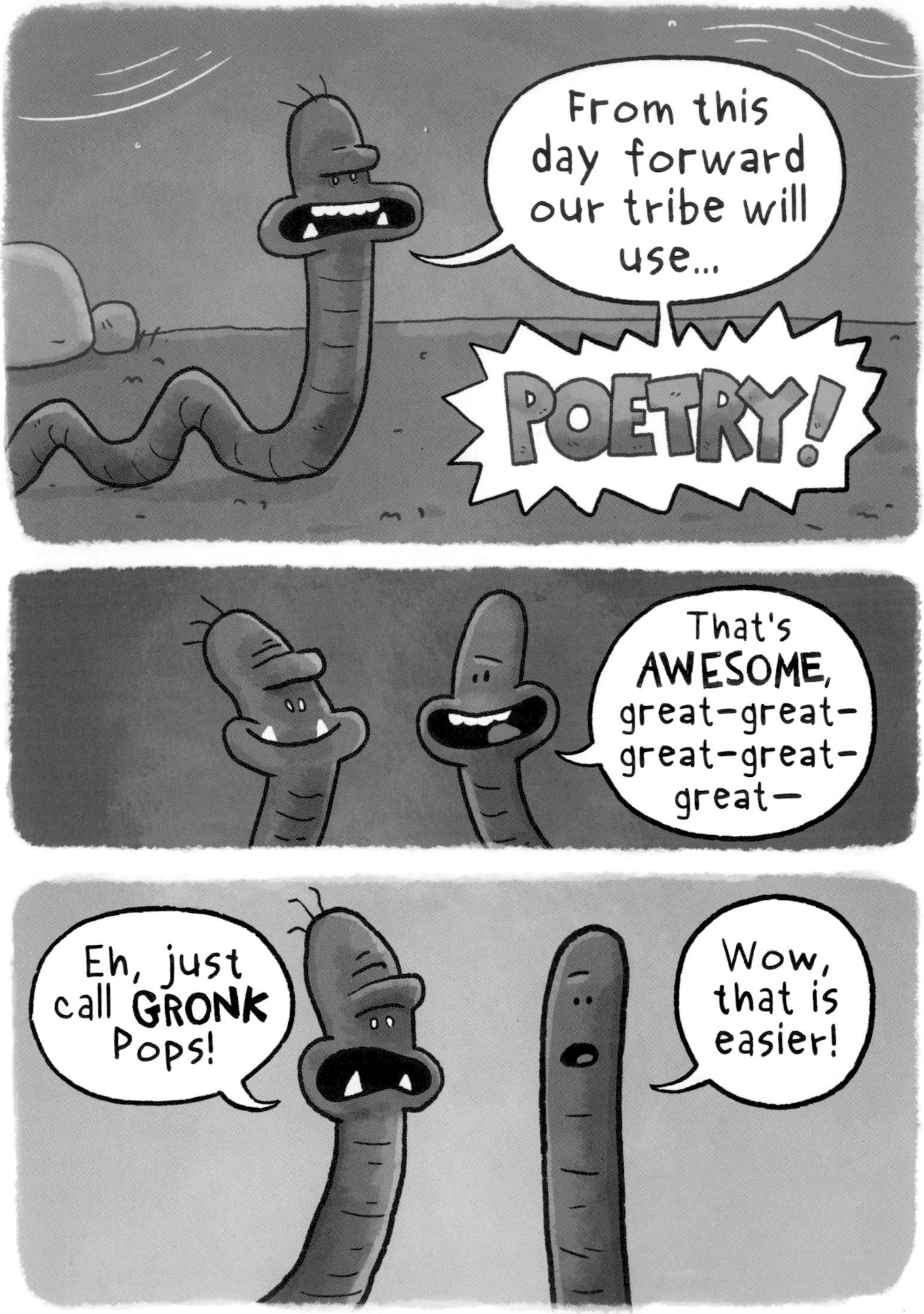
From this day forward our tribe will use...
POETRY!
That's AWESOME, great-great-great-great-great—
Eh, just call GRONK Pops!
Wow, that is easier!

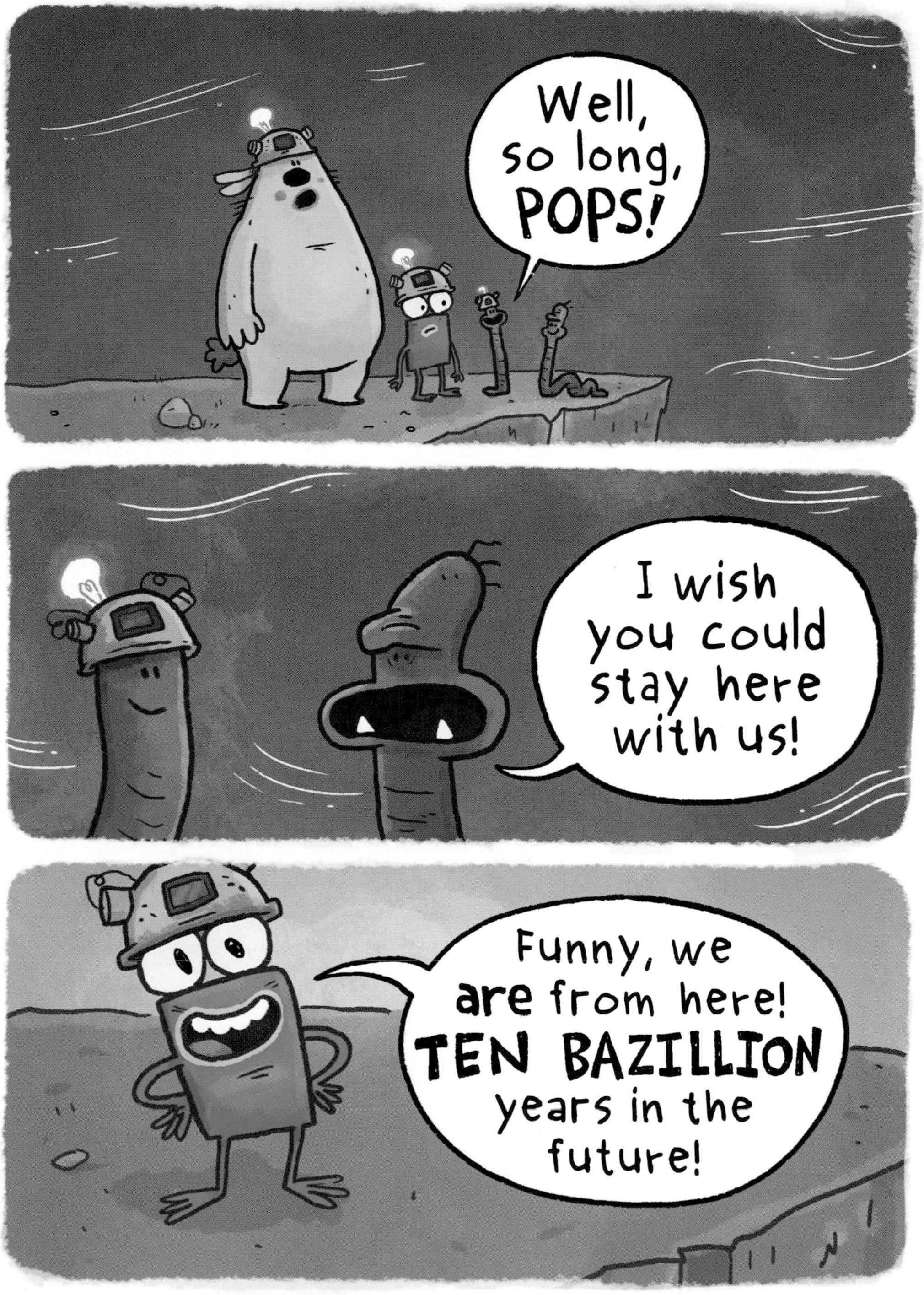
Well, so long, POPS!
I wish you could stay here with us!
Funny, we are from here! TEN BAZILLION years in the future!

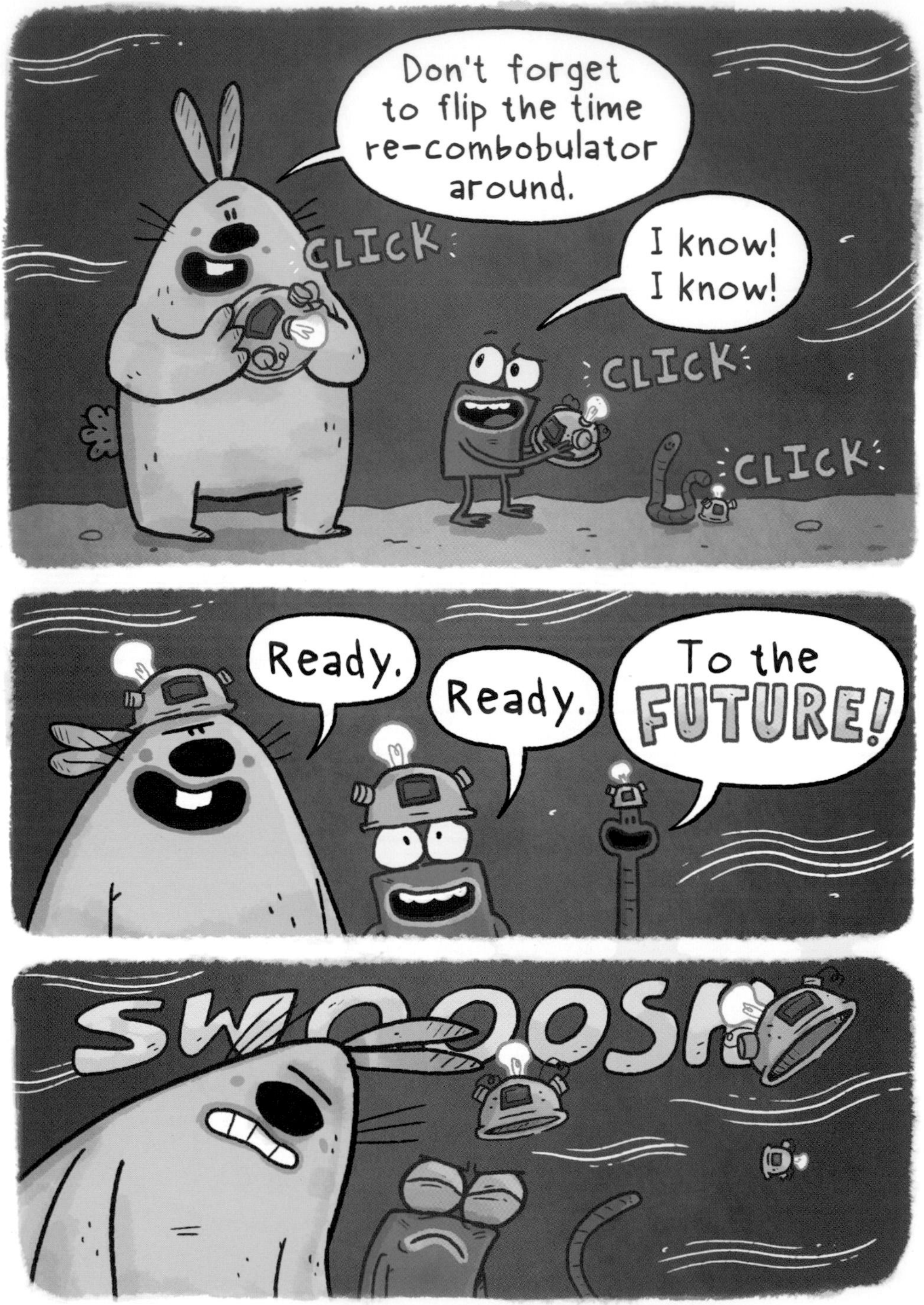
Don't forget to flip the time re-combobulator around.
CLICK
I know! I know!
CLICK
CLICK
Ready.
Ready.
To the FUTURE!
SWOOOSH

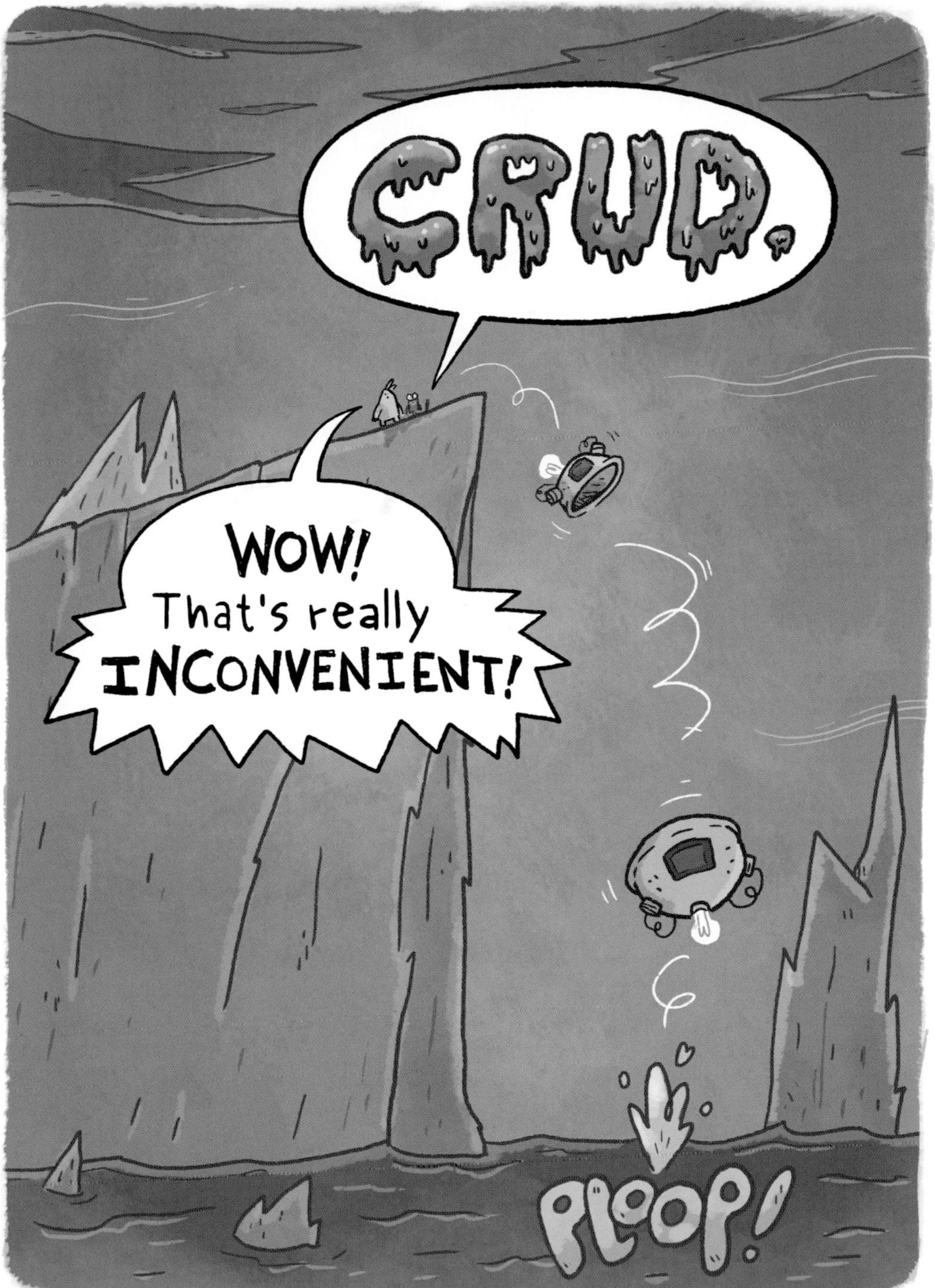
CRUD.
WOW! That's really INCONVENIENT!
PLOOP!

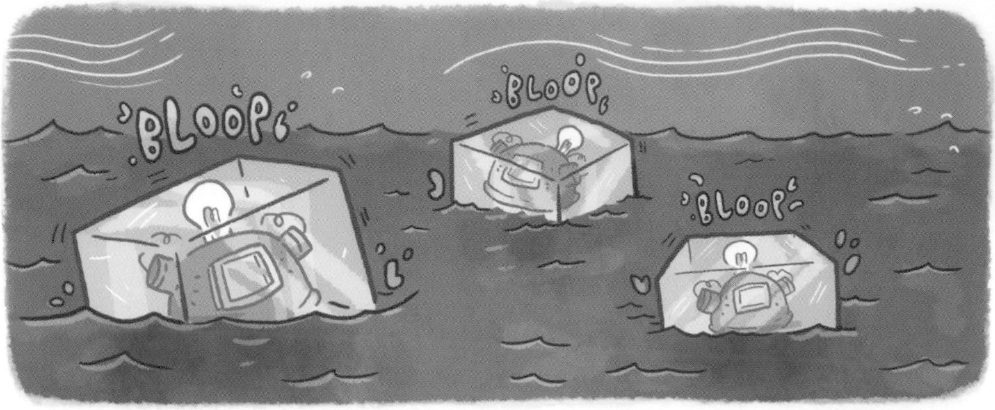
BLOOP
BLOOP
BLOOP

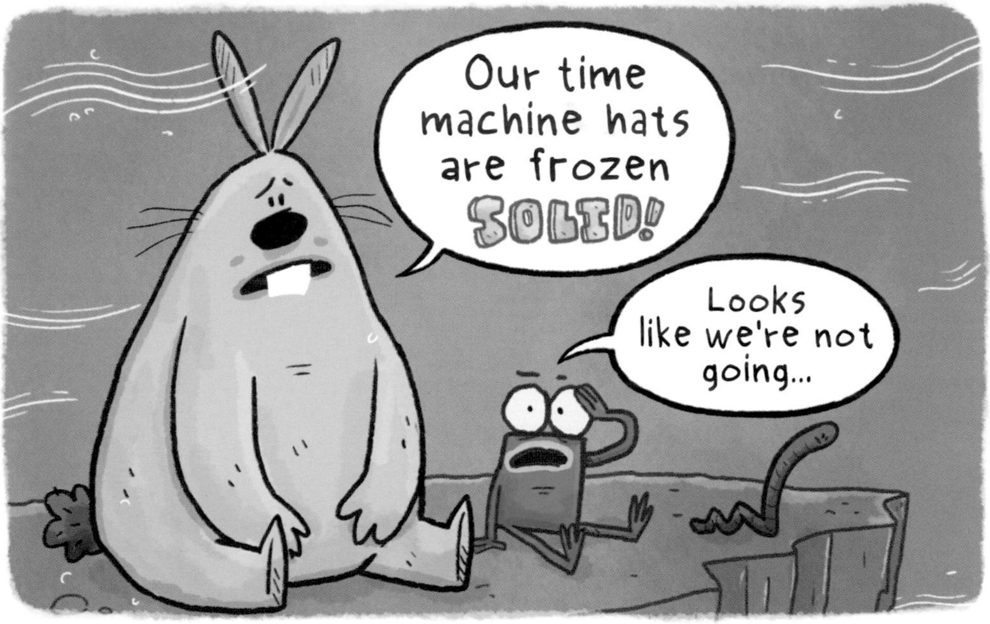
Our time machine hats are frozen SOLID!
Looks like we're not going...

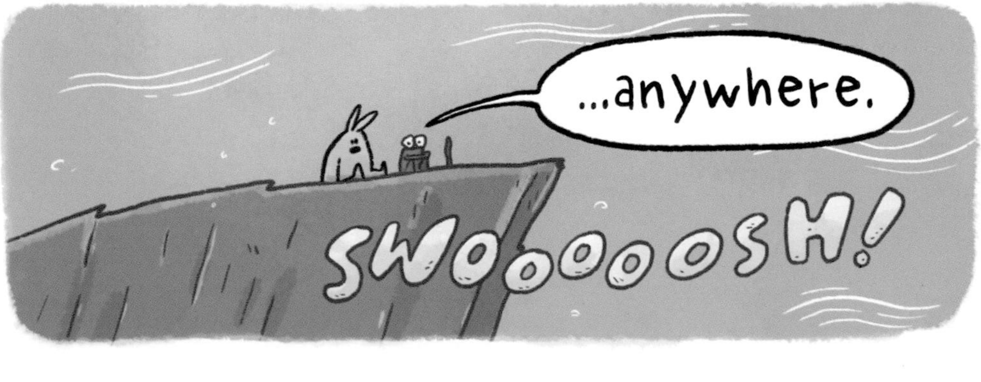
...anywhere.
SWOOOOOOSH!

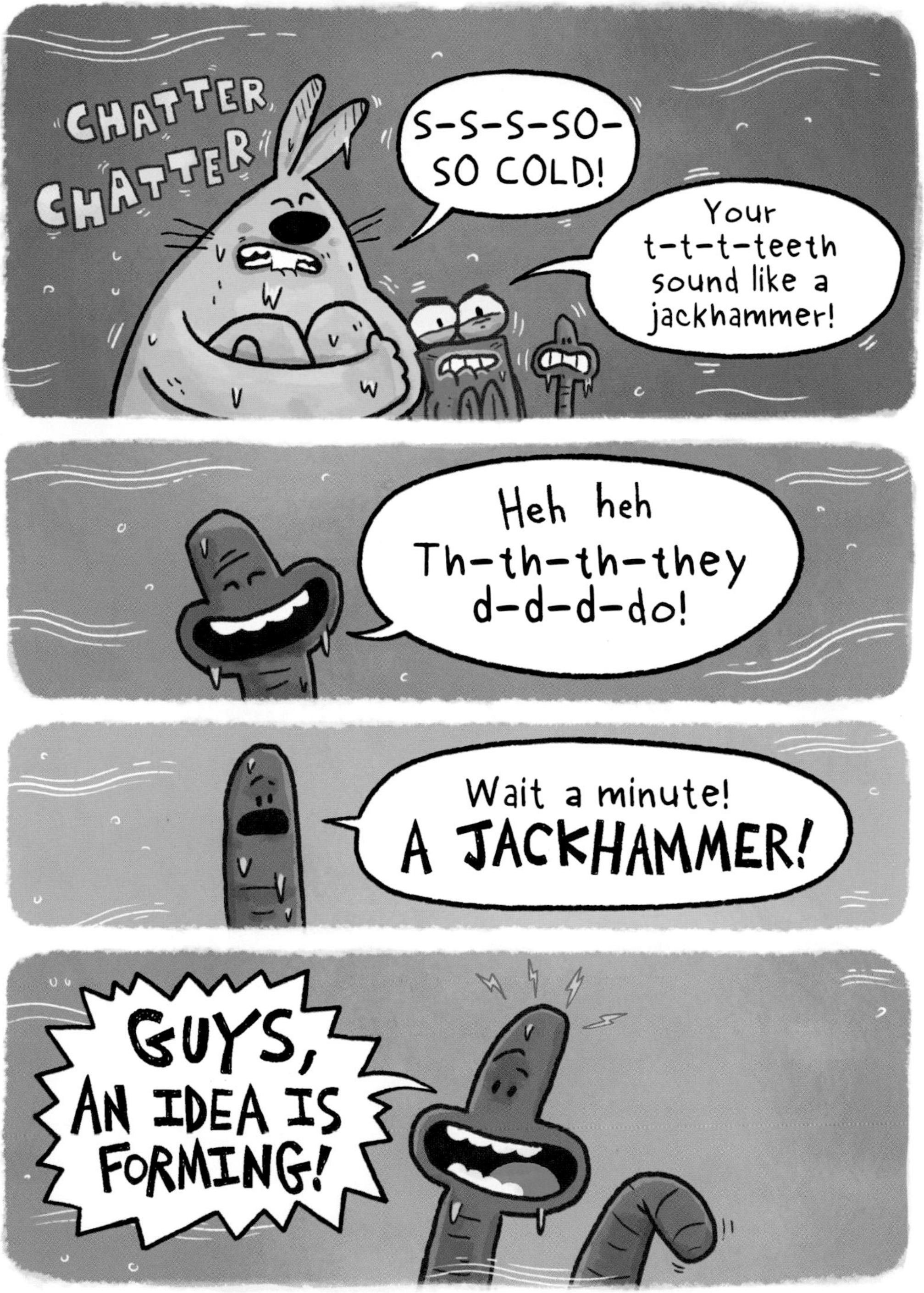
CHATTER CHATTER
S-S-S-SO-SO COLD!
Your t-t-t-teeth sound like a jackhammer!
Heh heh Th-th-th-they d-d-d-do!
Wait a minute! A JACKHAMMER!
GUYS, AN IDEA IS FORMING!

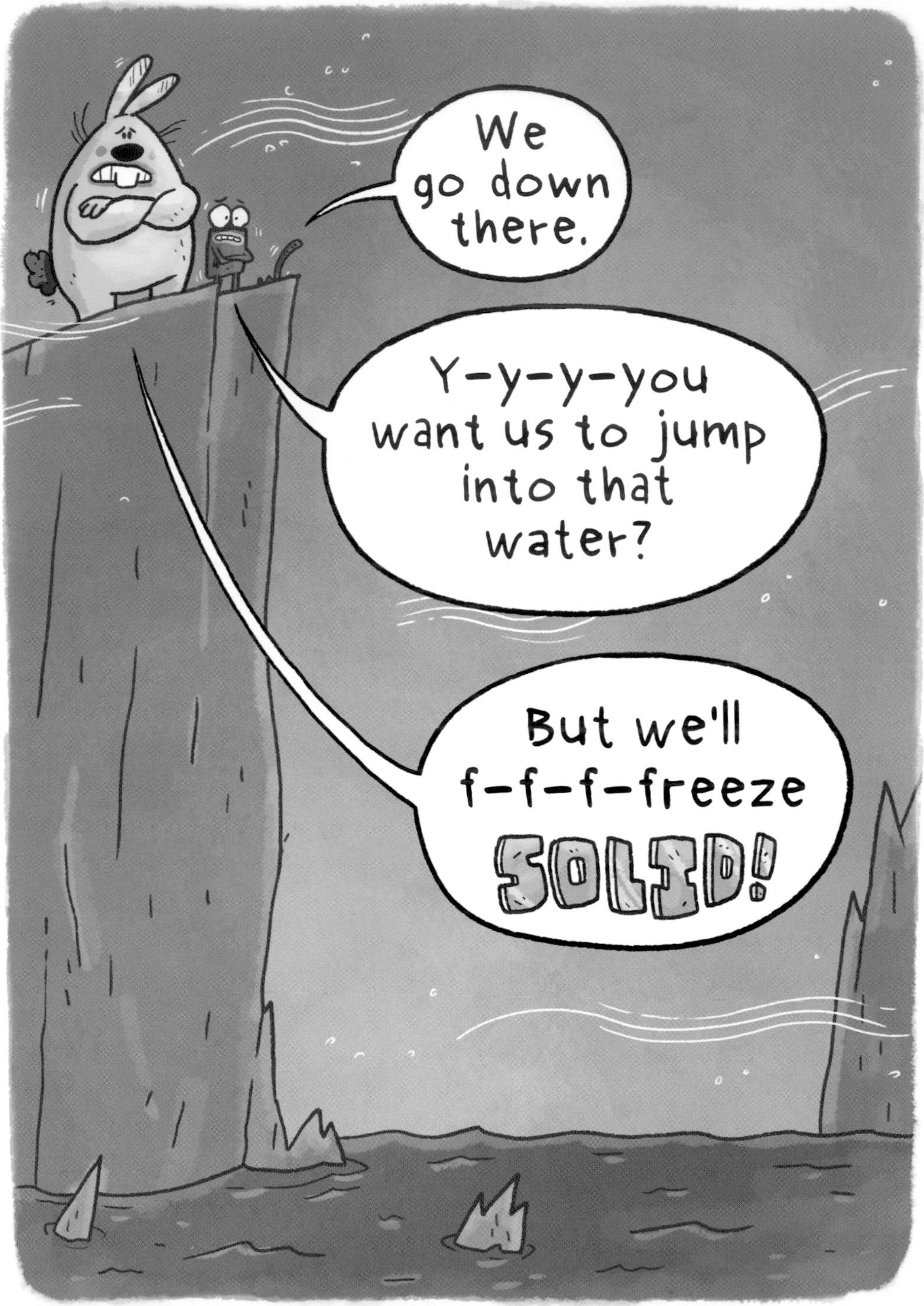
We go down there.
Y-y-y-you want us to jump into that water?
But we'll f-f-f-freeze SOLID!

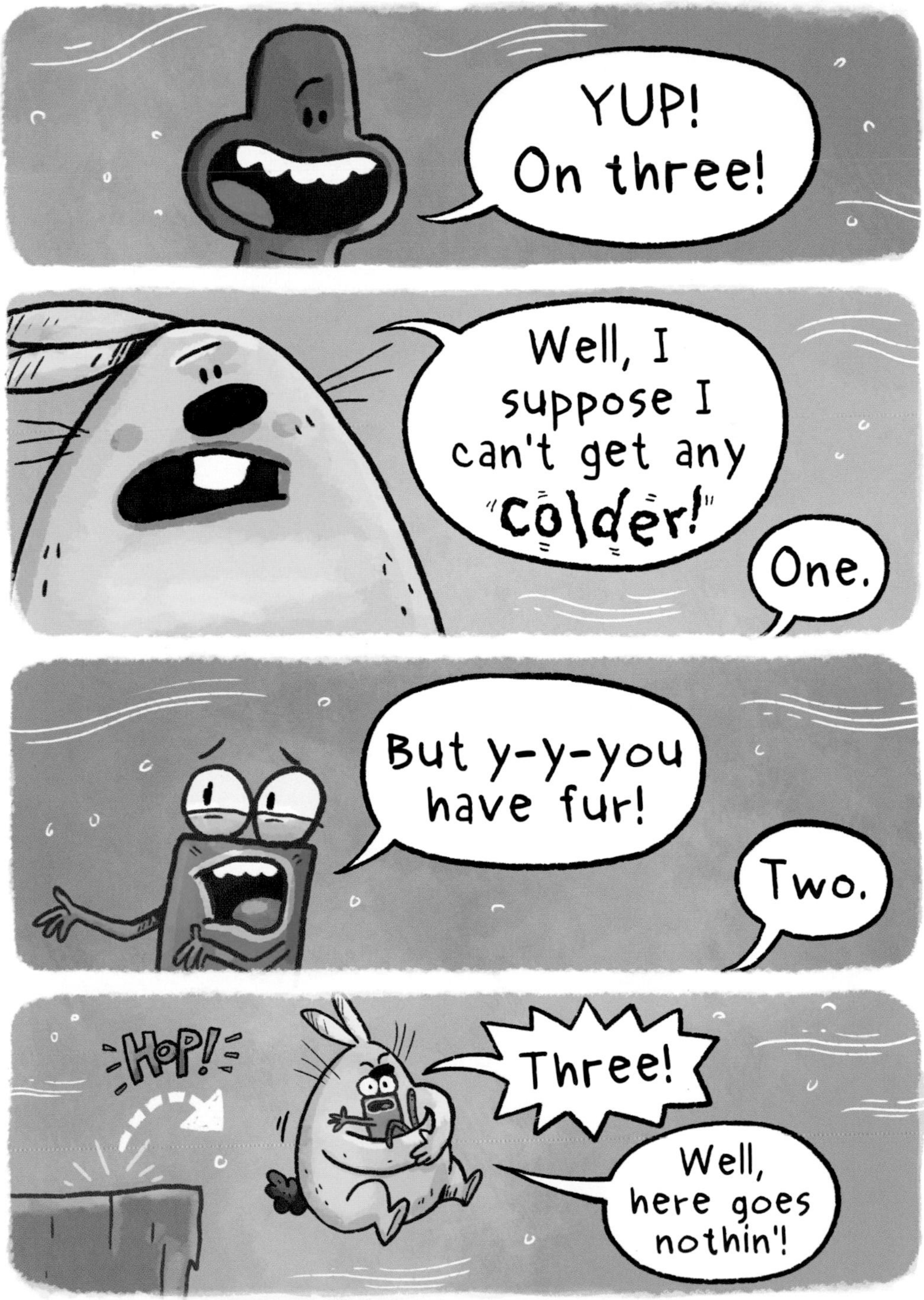
YUP! On three!
Well, I suppose I can't get any colder!
One.
But y-y-you have fur!
Two.
HOP!
Three!
Well, here goes nothin'!

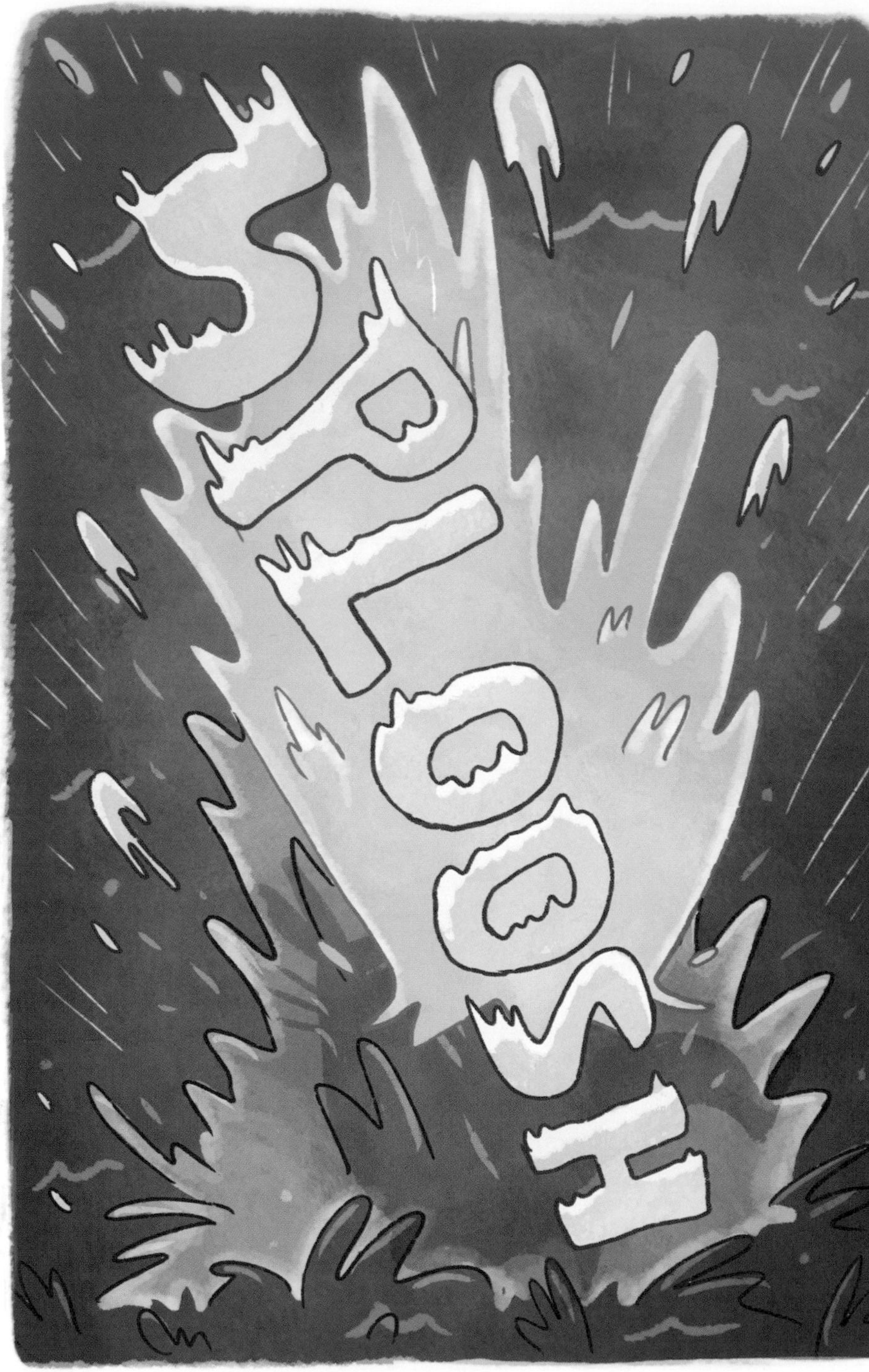
SPLOOSH

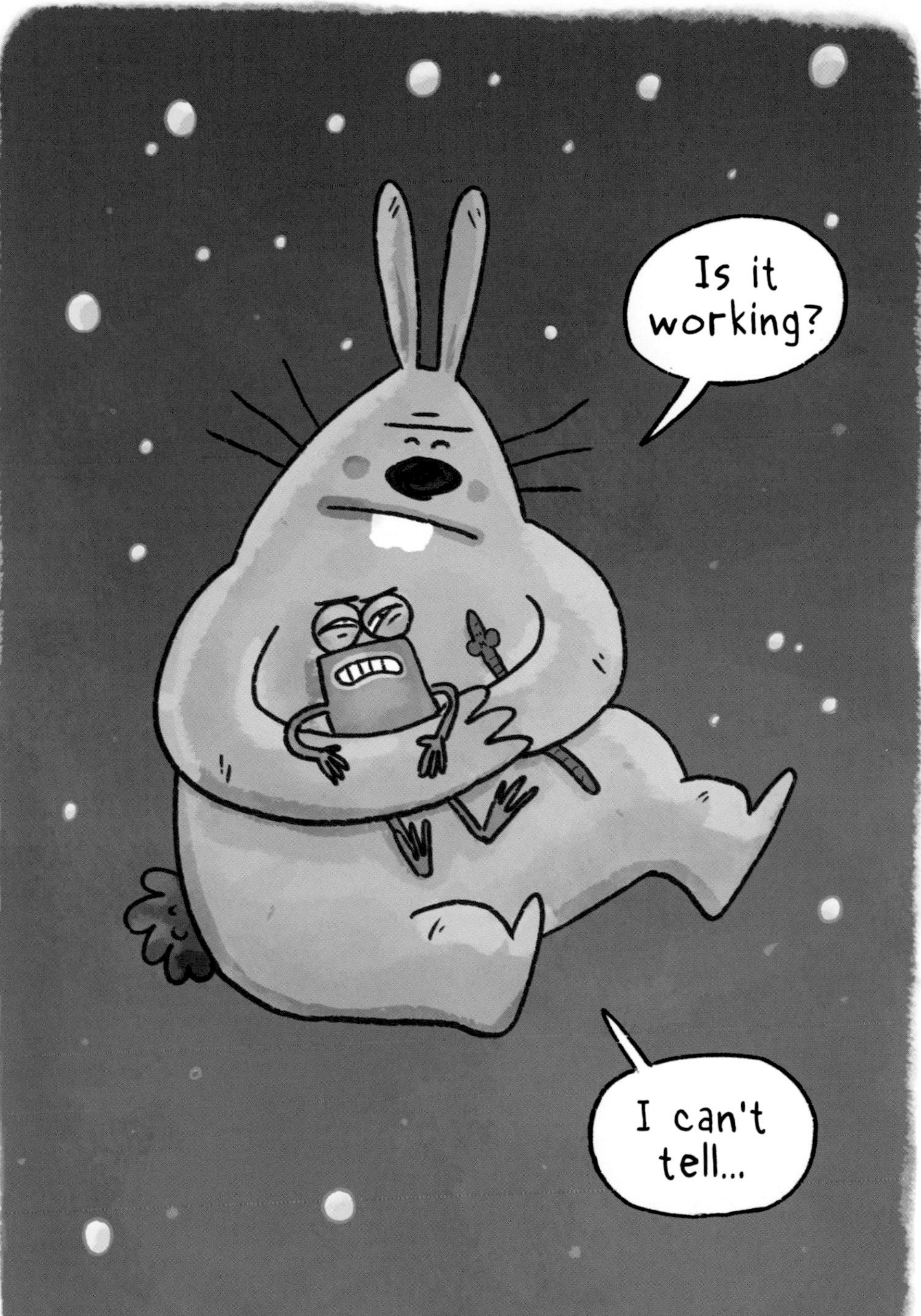
Is it working?
I can't tell...

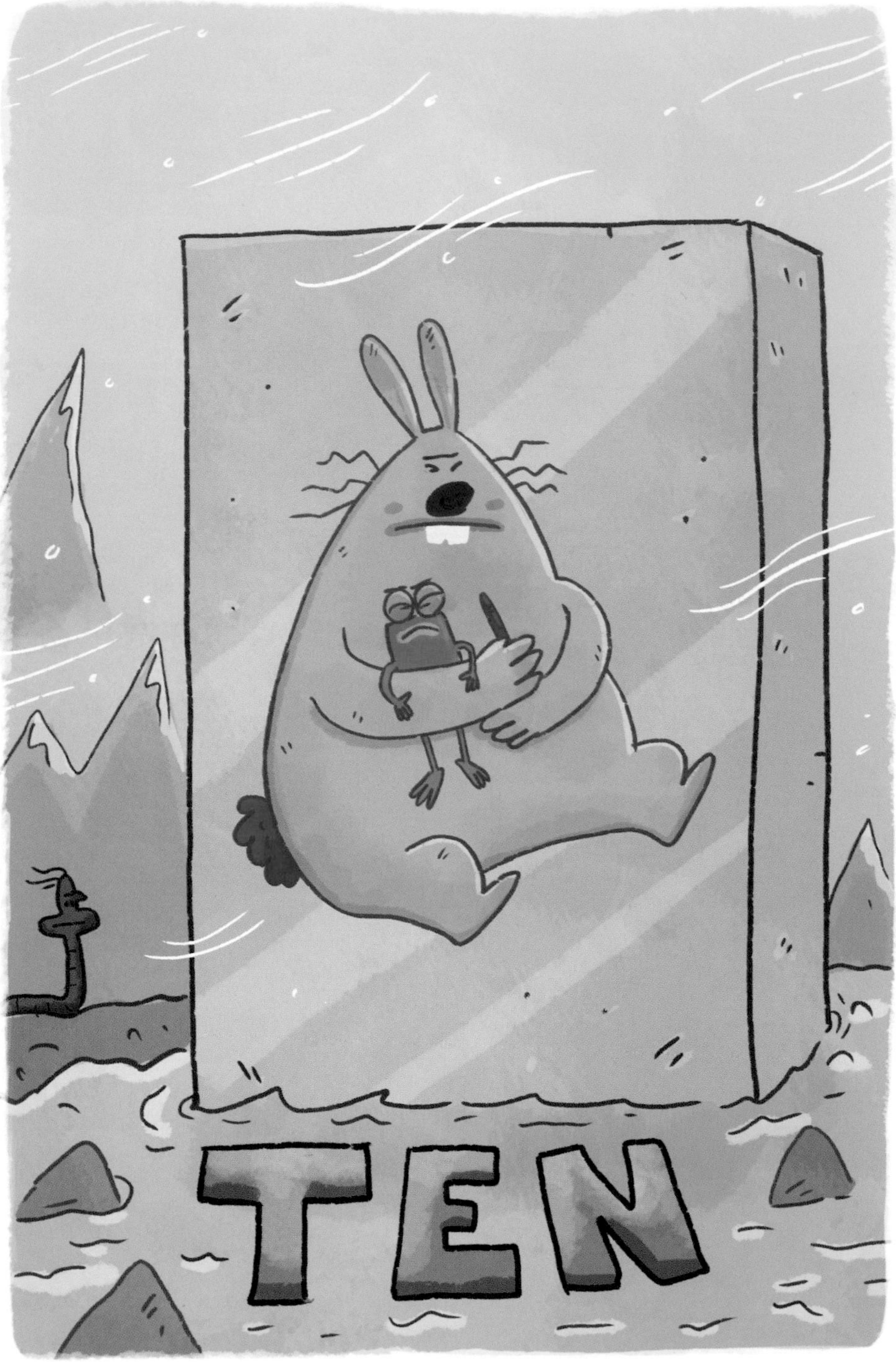
TEN

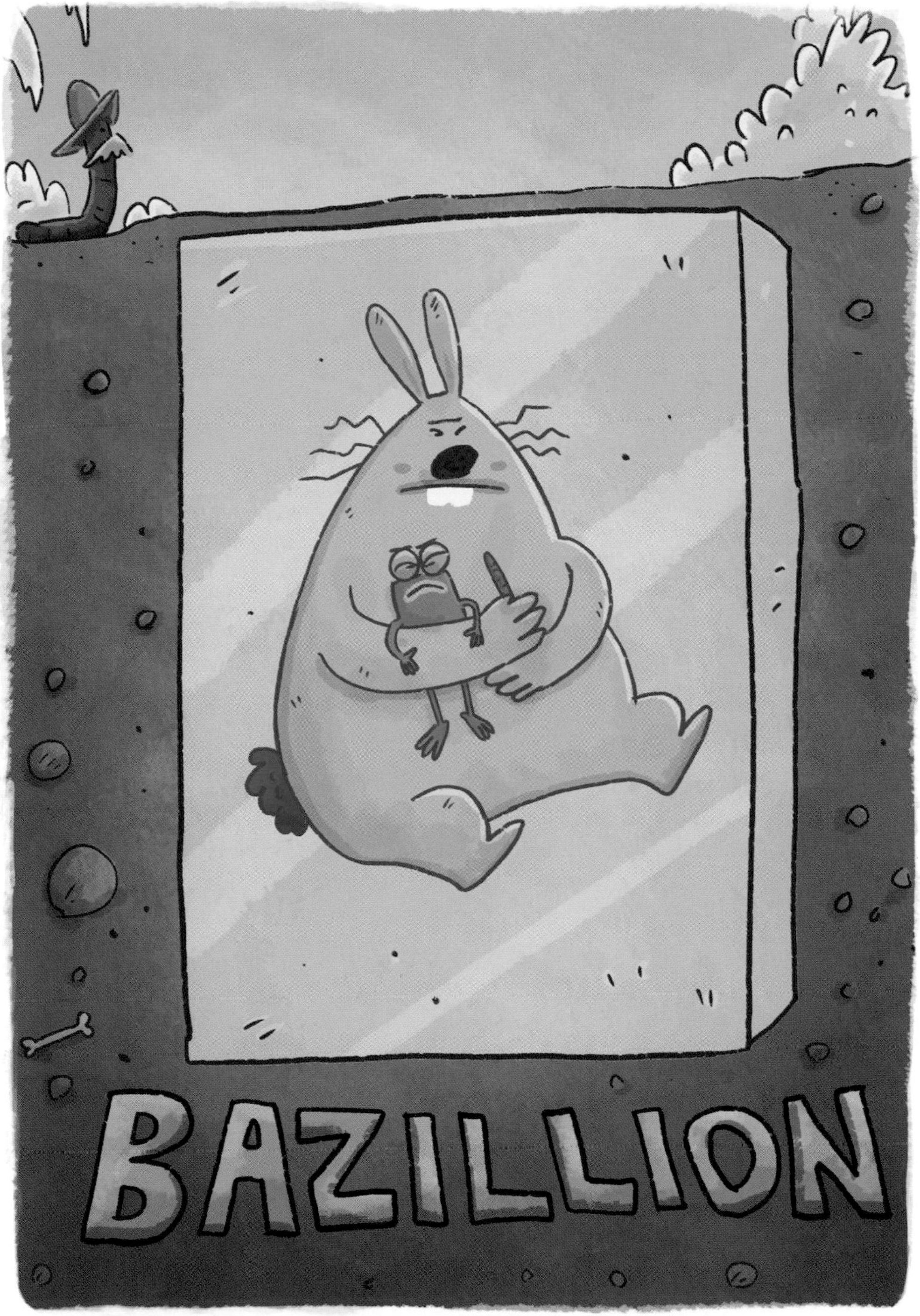
BAZILLION

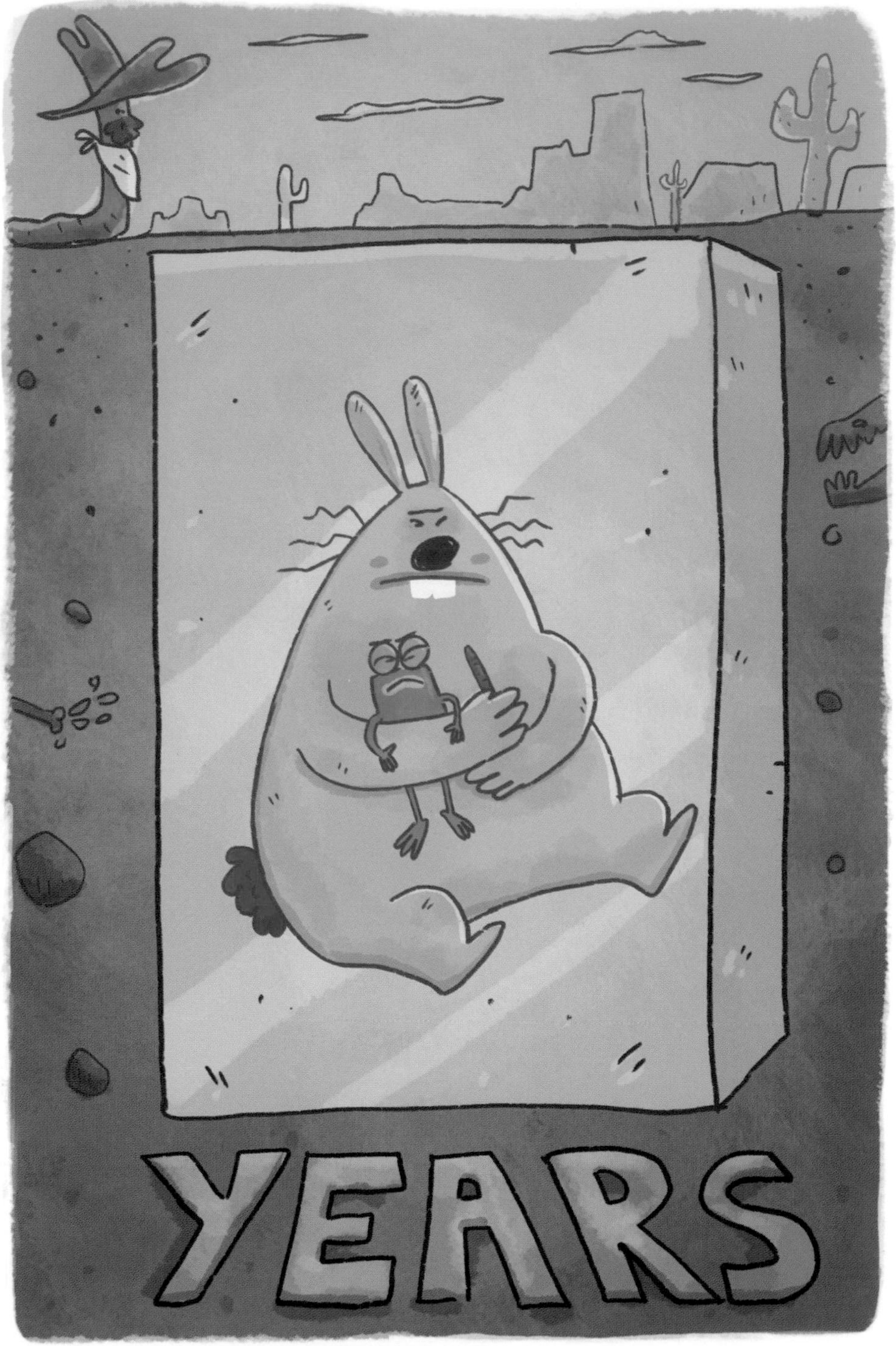
YEARS

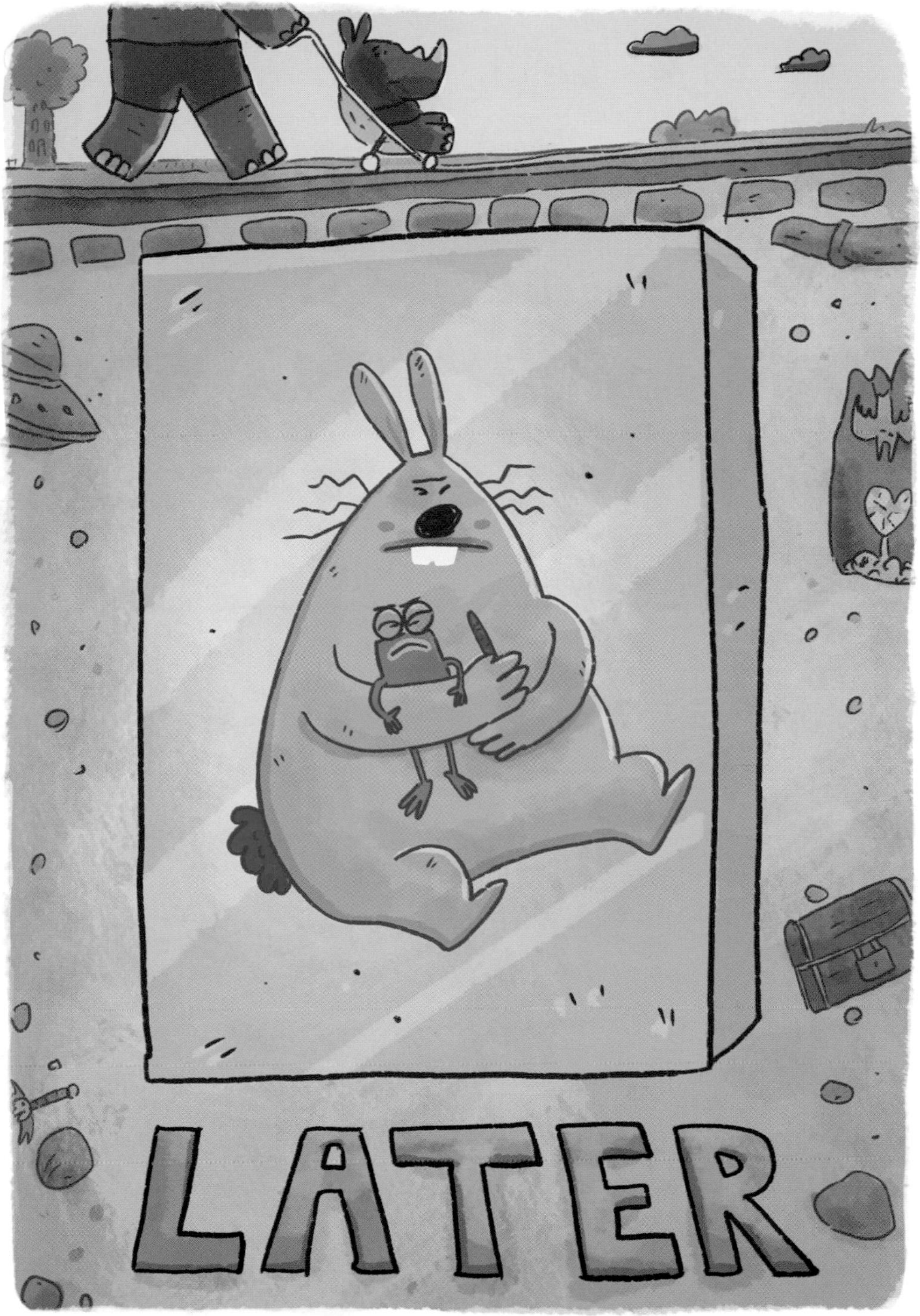
LATER

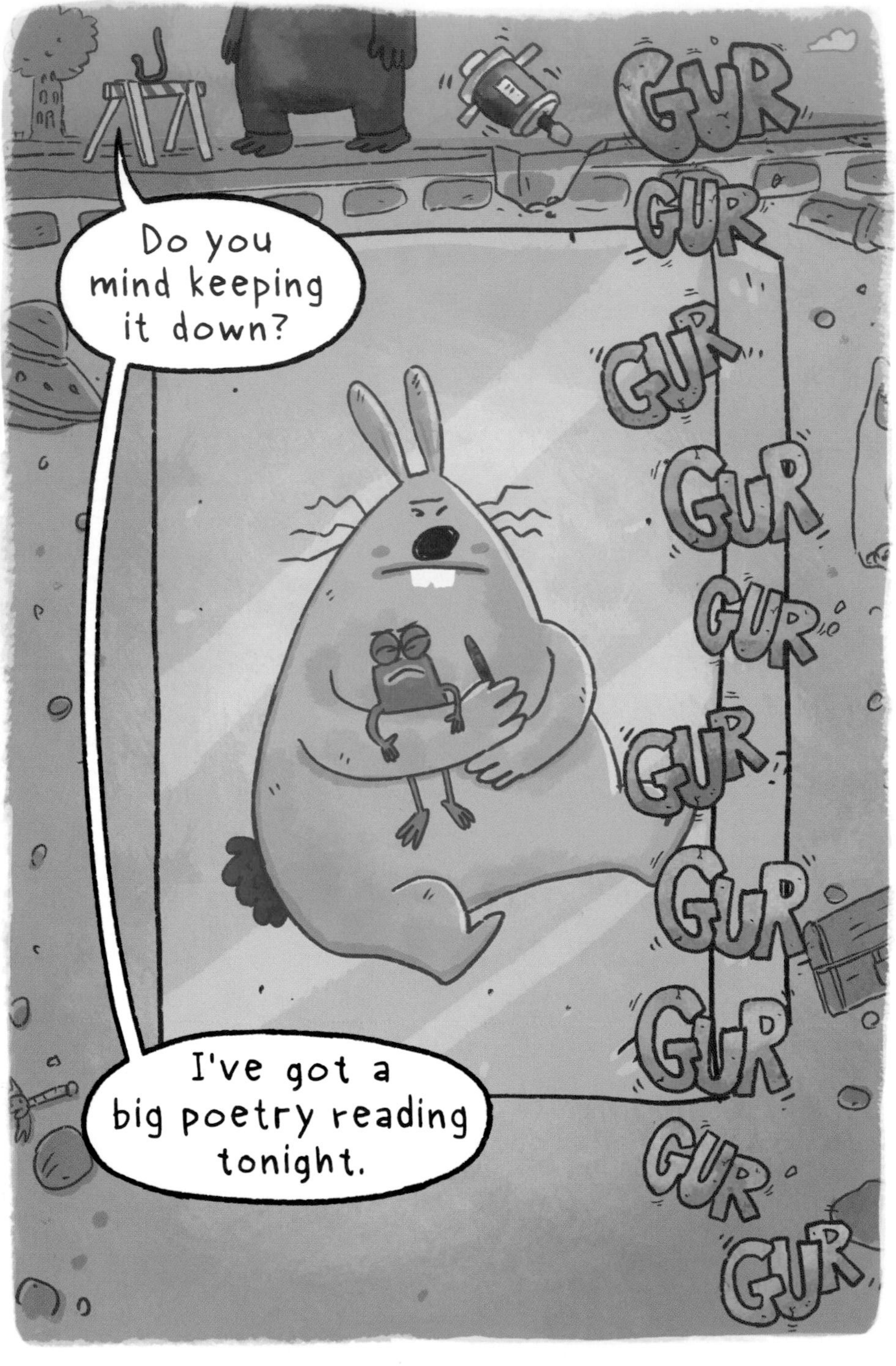
Do you mind keeping it down?
I've got a big poetry reading tonight.
GUR
GUR
GUR
GUR
GUR
GUR
GUR
GUR
GUR
GUR

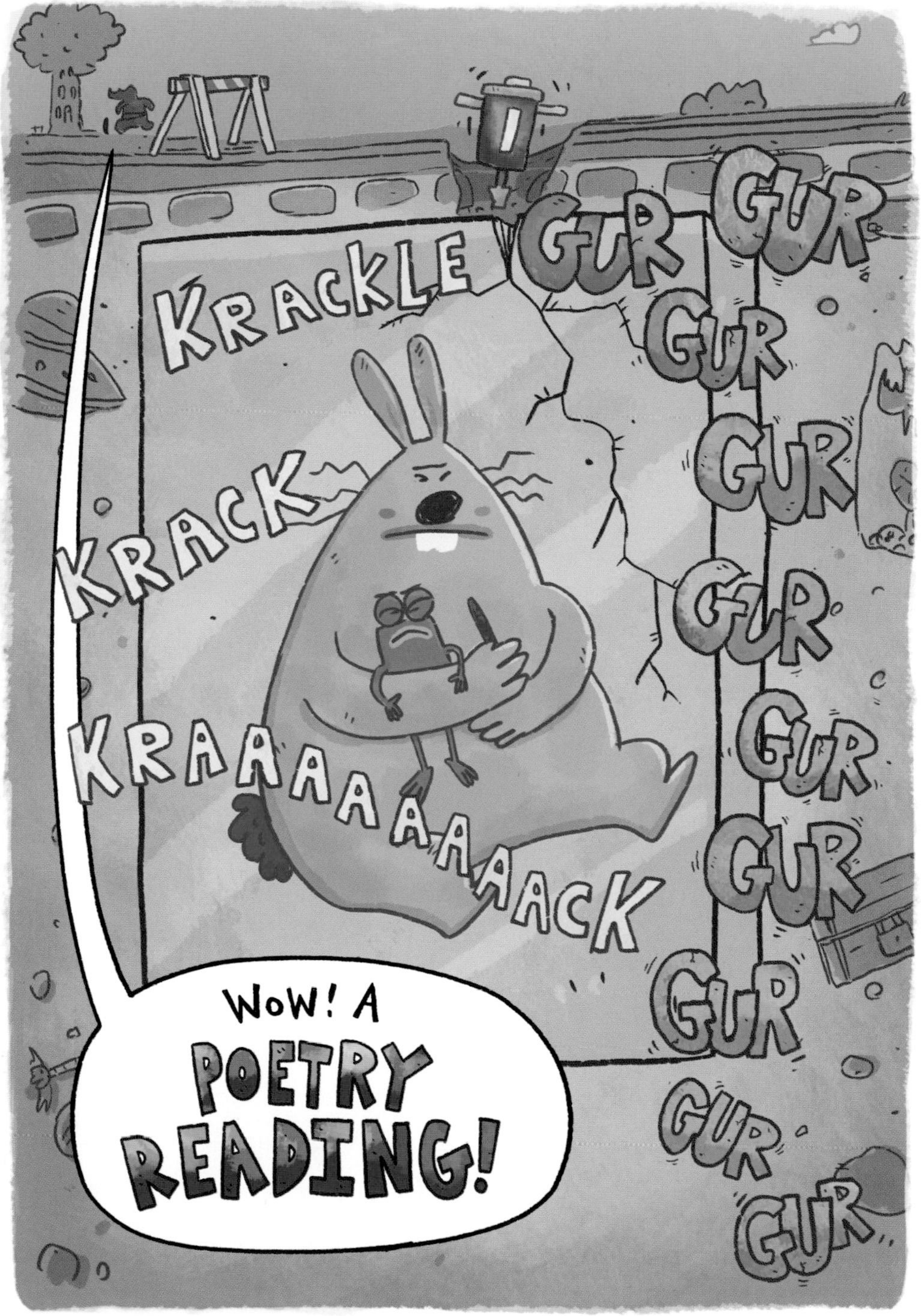

KRACKLE
GUR GUR
GUR
GUR
KRACK
KRACK
GUR
KRAAAAAAAAAAAACK
GUR
GUR
GUR
WoW! A POETRY READING!
GUR
GUR

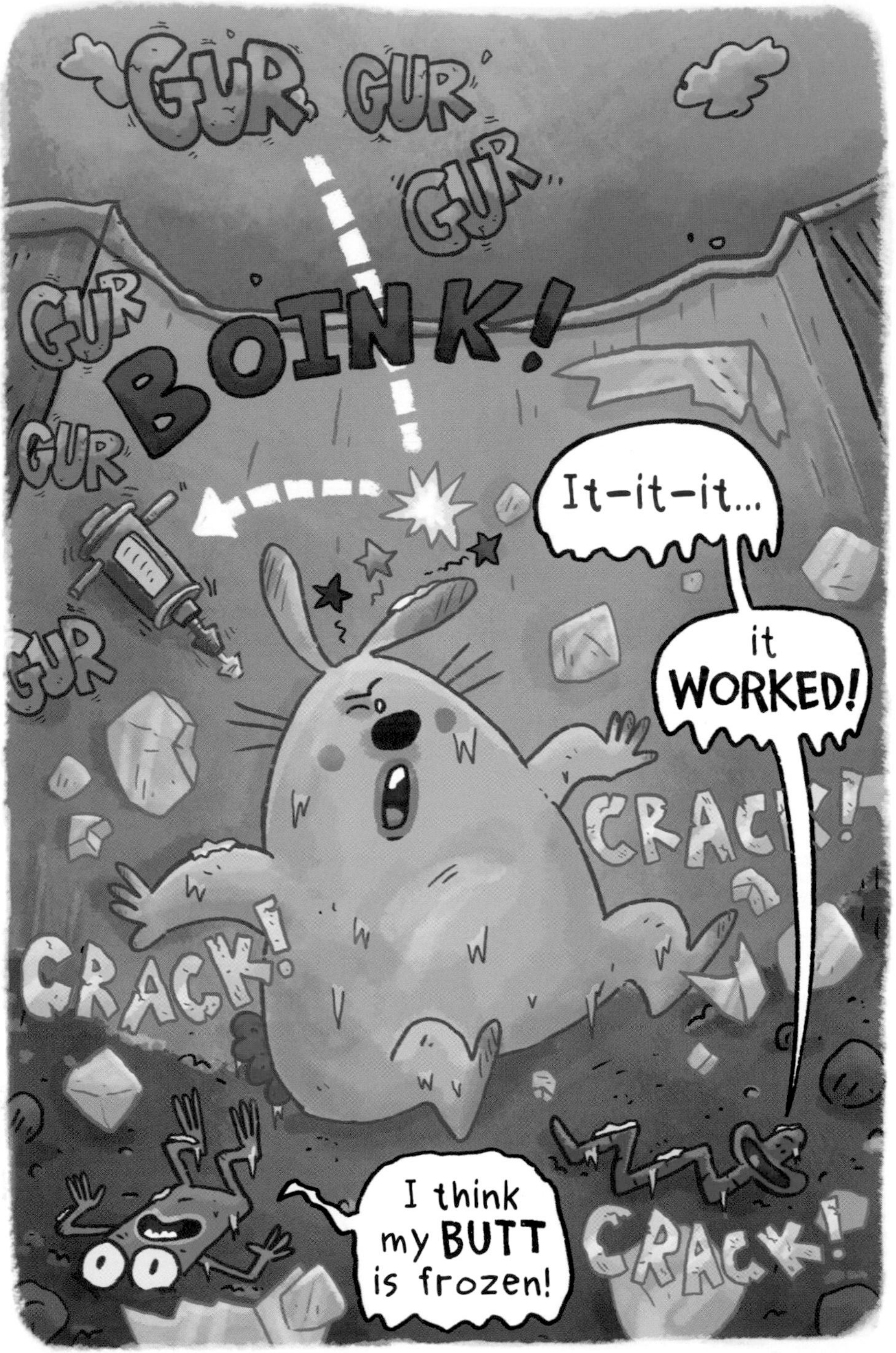
GUR GUR
GUR
GUR
BOINK!
GUR
GUR
It-it-it...
it WORKED!
CRACK!
CRACK!
I think my BUTT is frozen!
CRACK!

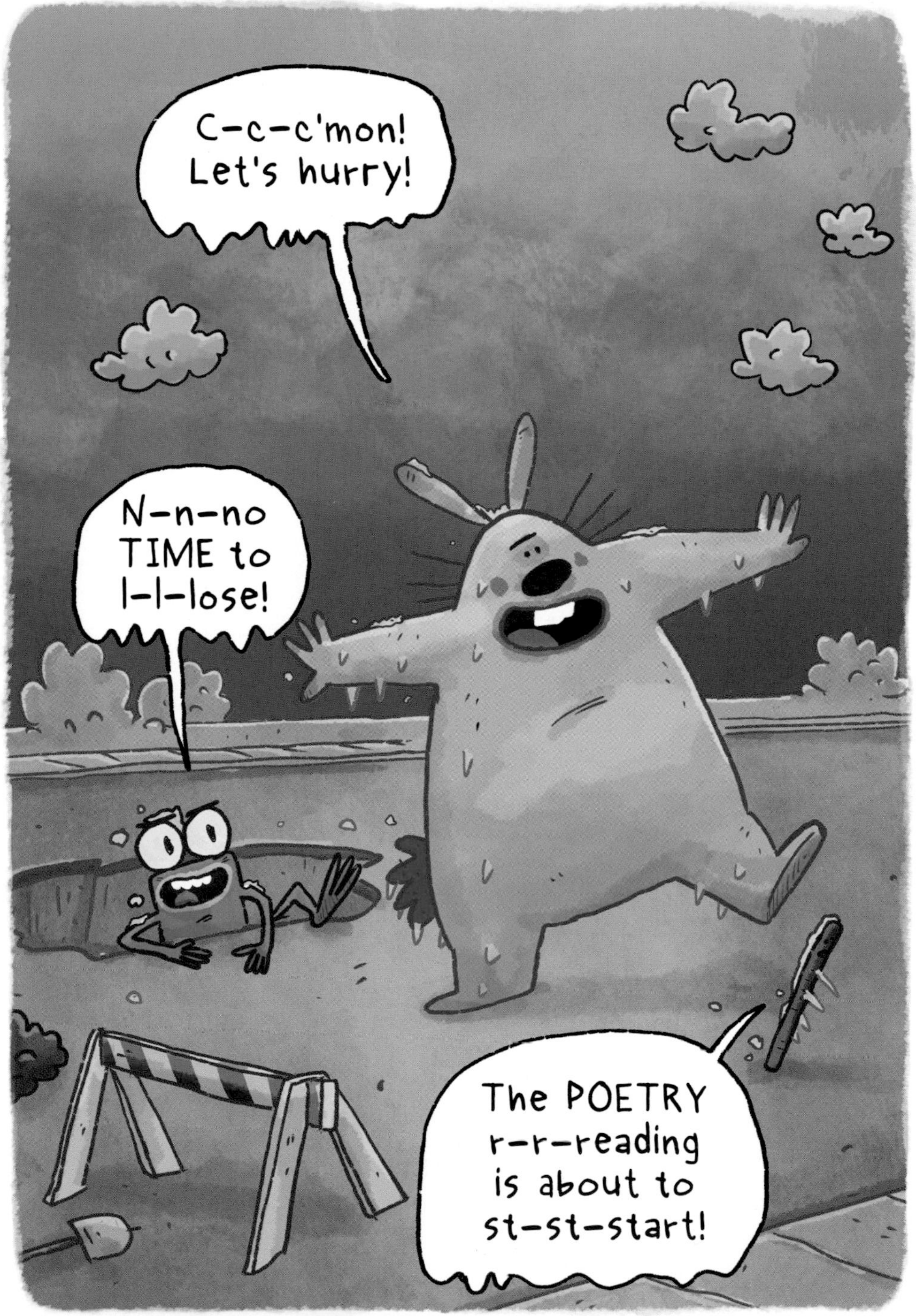
C-c-c'mon! Let's hurry!
N-n-no TIME to l-l-lose!
The POETRY r-r-reading is about to st-st-start!

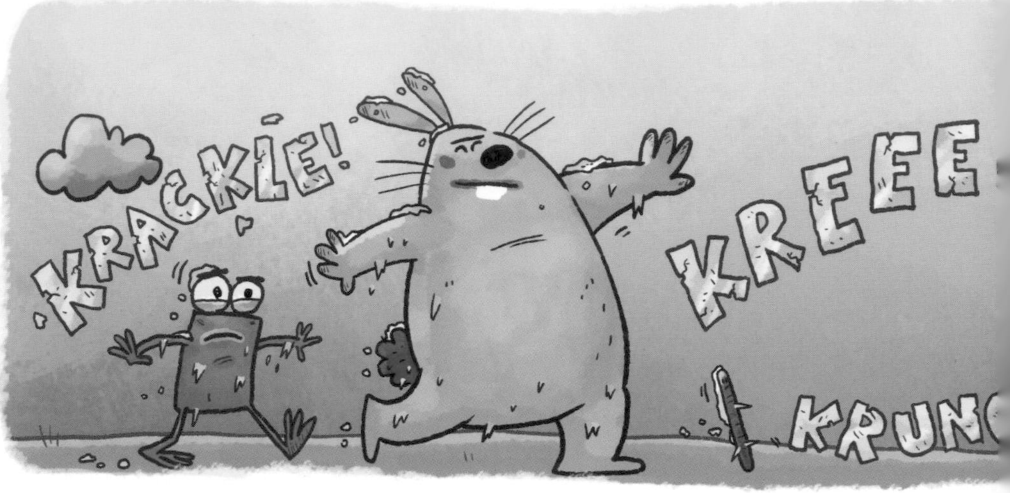
KRACKLE!
KREEE
KRUNC

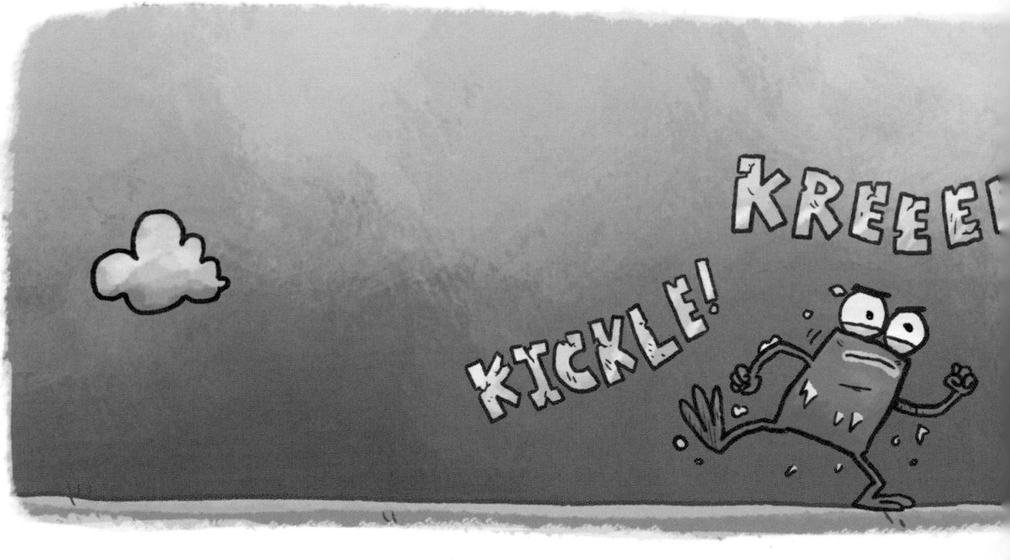
KREEE
KICKLE!

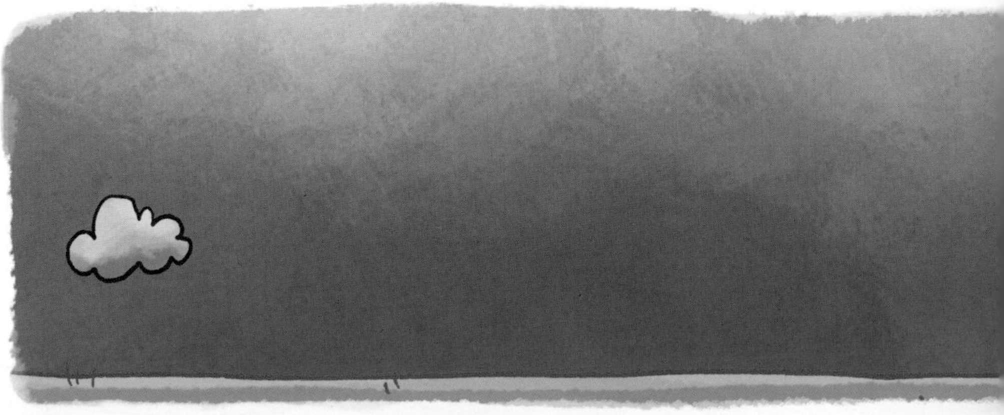

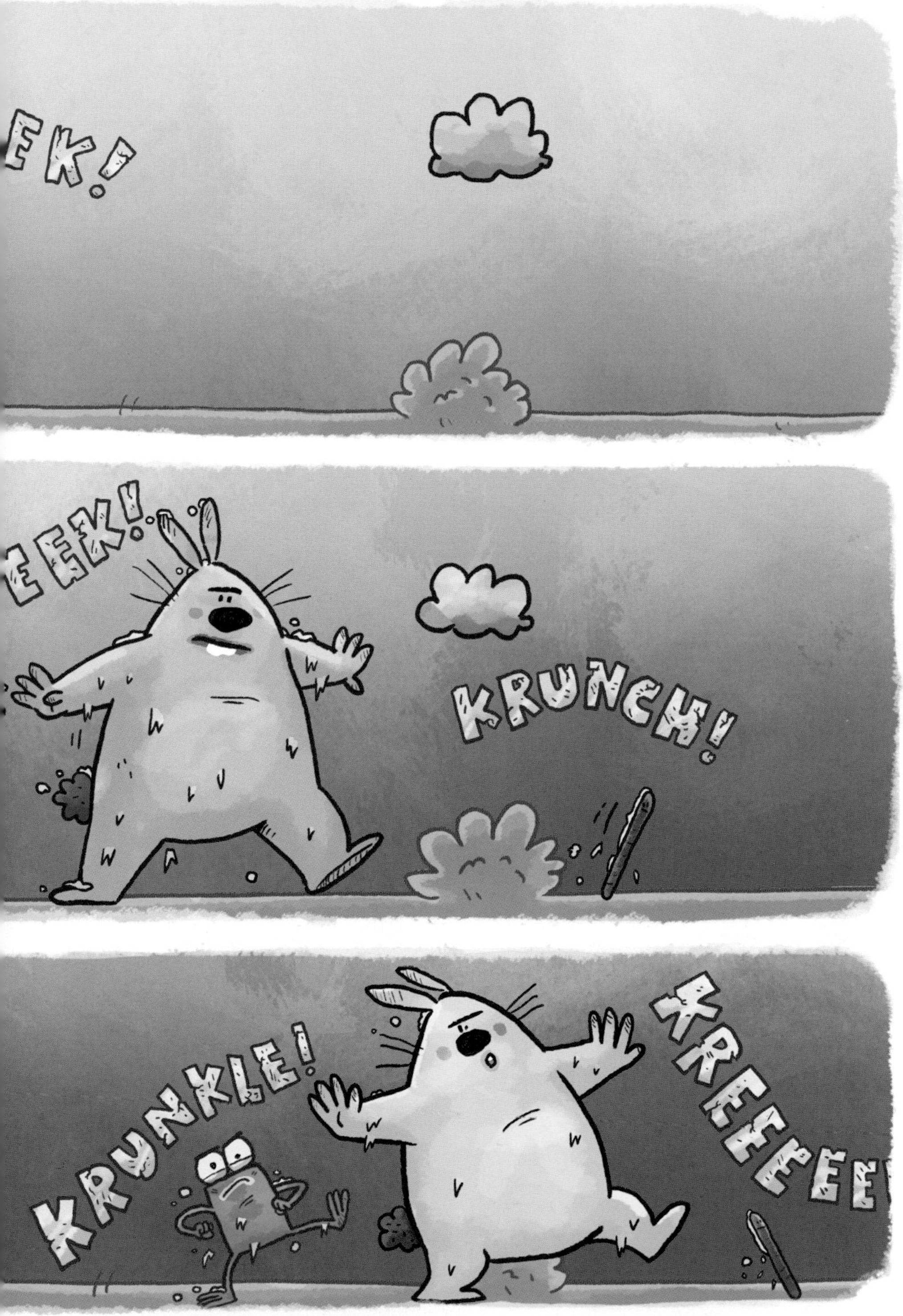
EK!
EEK!
KRUNCH!
KRUNKLE!
KREEEEE

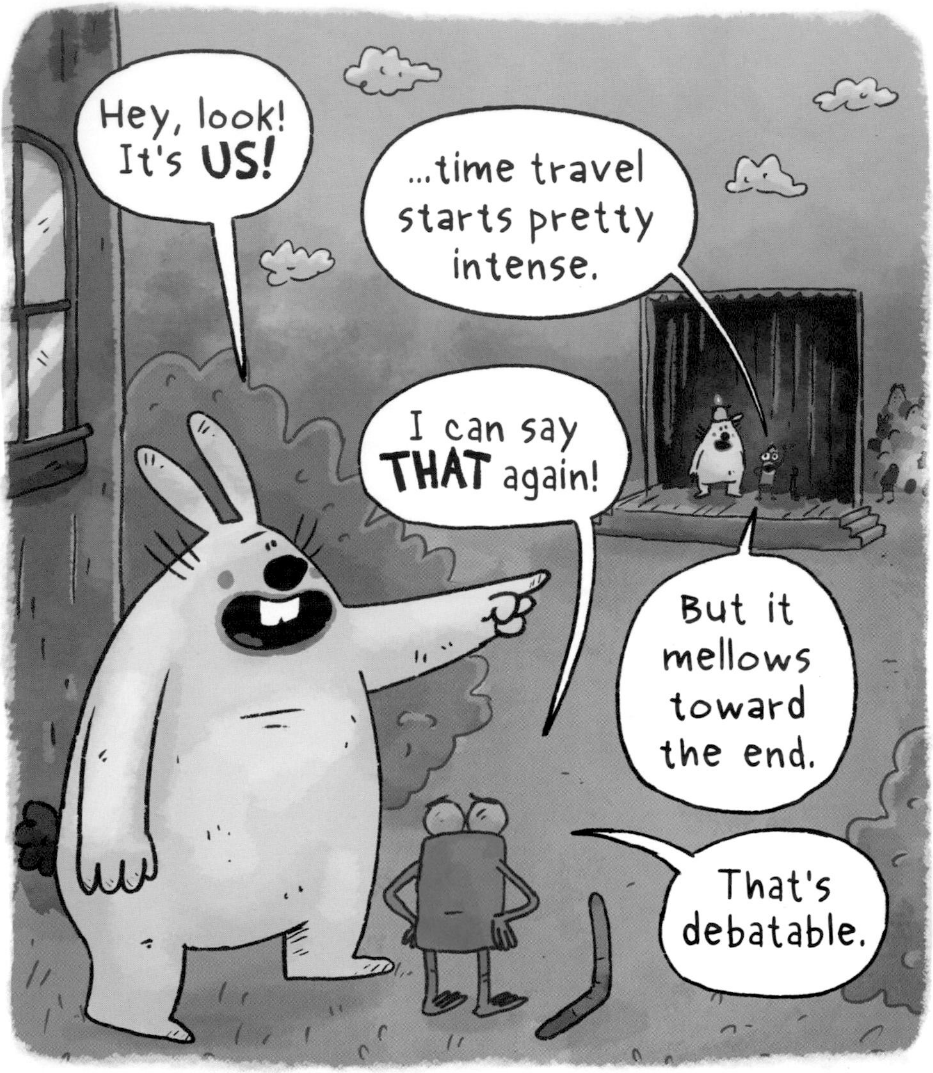
Hey, look! It's **US!**
...time travel starts pretty intense.
I can say **THAT** again!
But it mellows toward the end.
That's debatable.

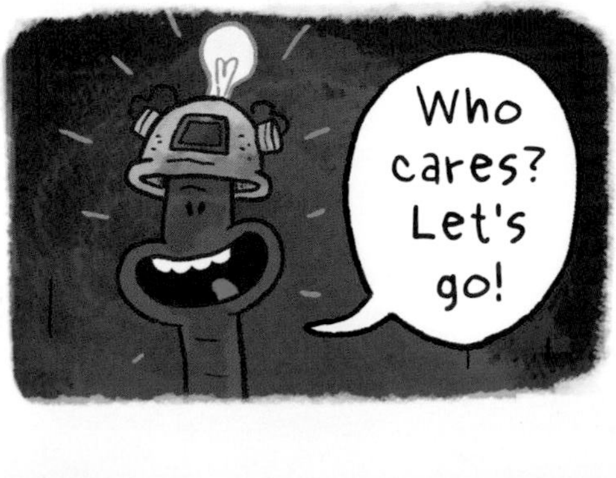
Who cares? Let's go!

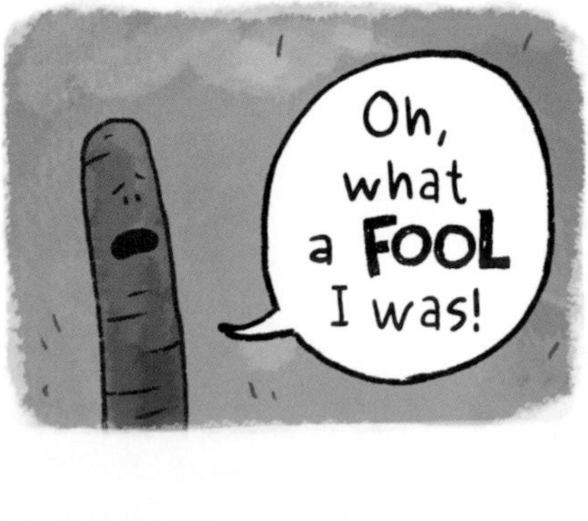
Oh, what a **FOOL** I was!

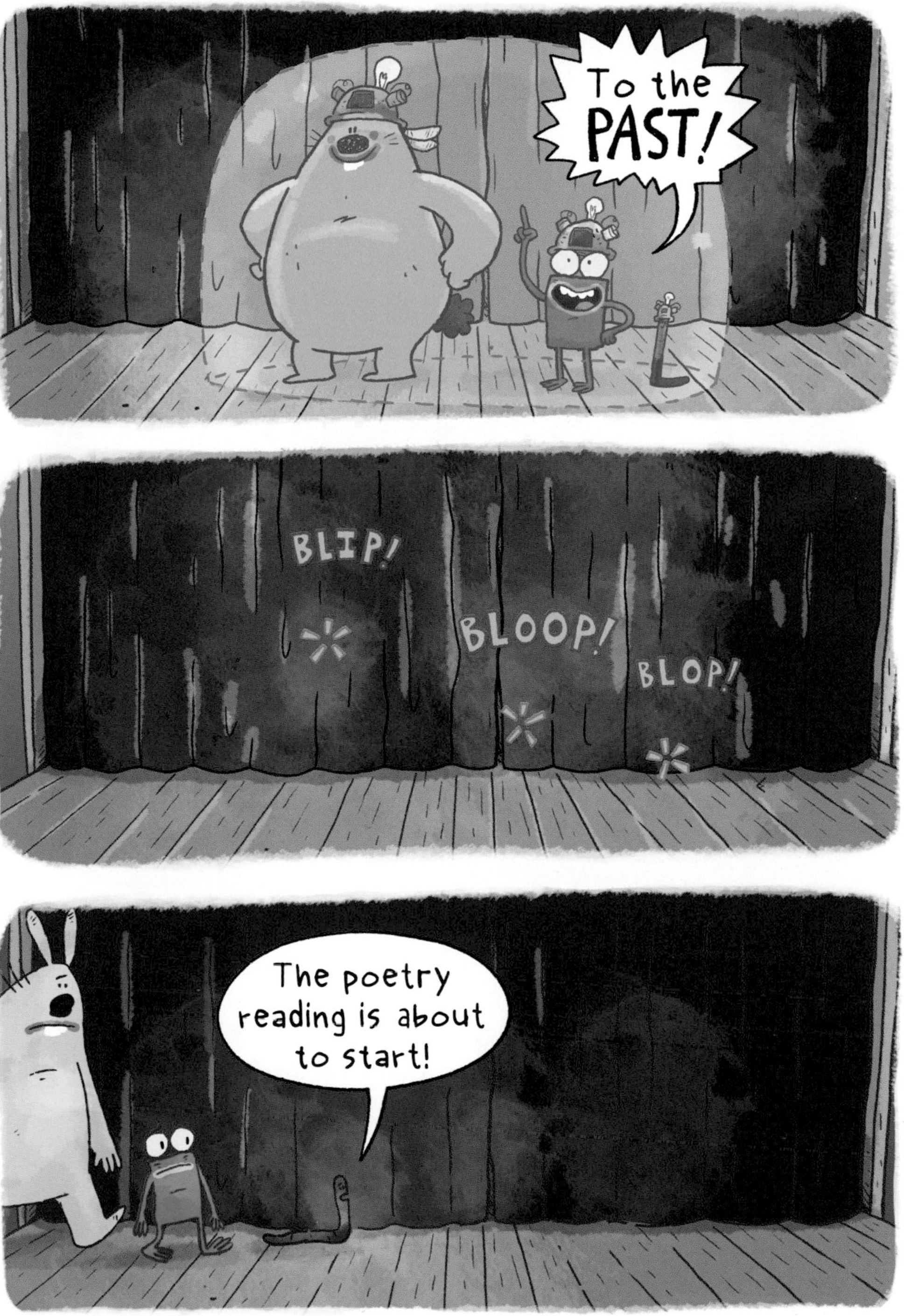
To the PAST!
BLIP!
BLOOP!
BLOP!
The poetry reading is about to start!

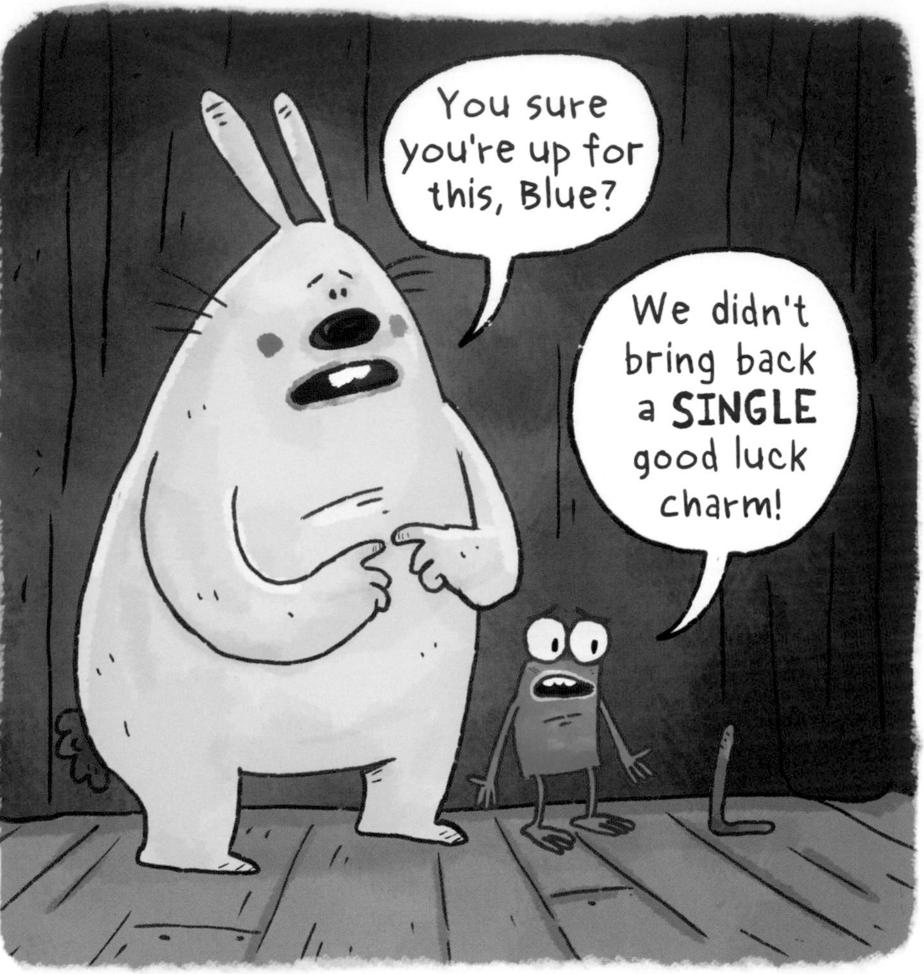
You sure you're up for this, Blue?
We didn't bring back a SINGLE good luck charm!
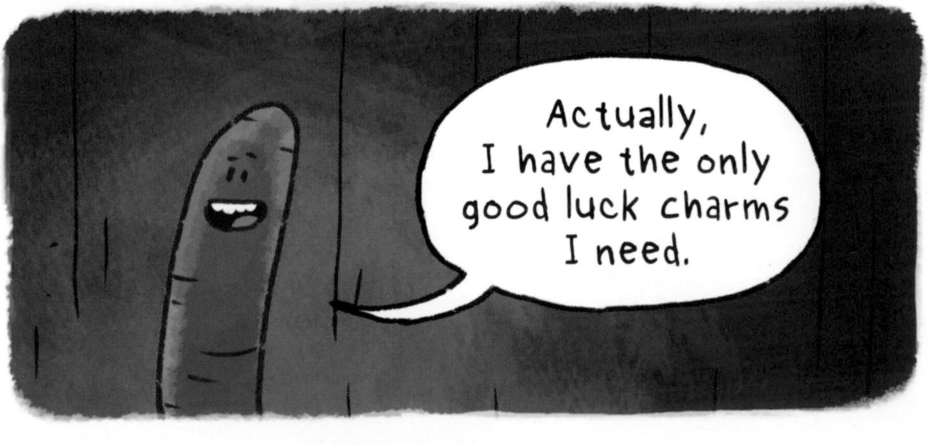
Actually, I have the only good luck charms I need.

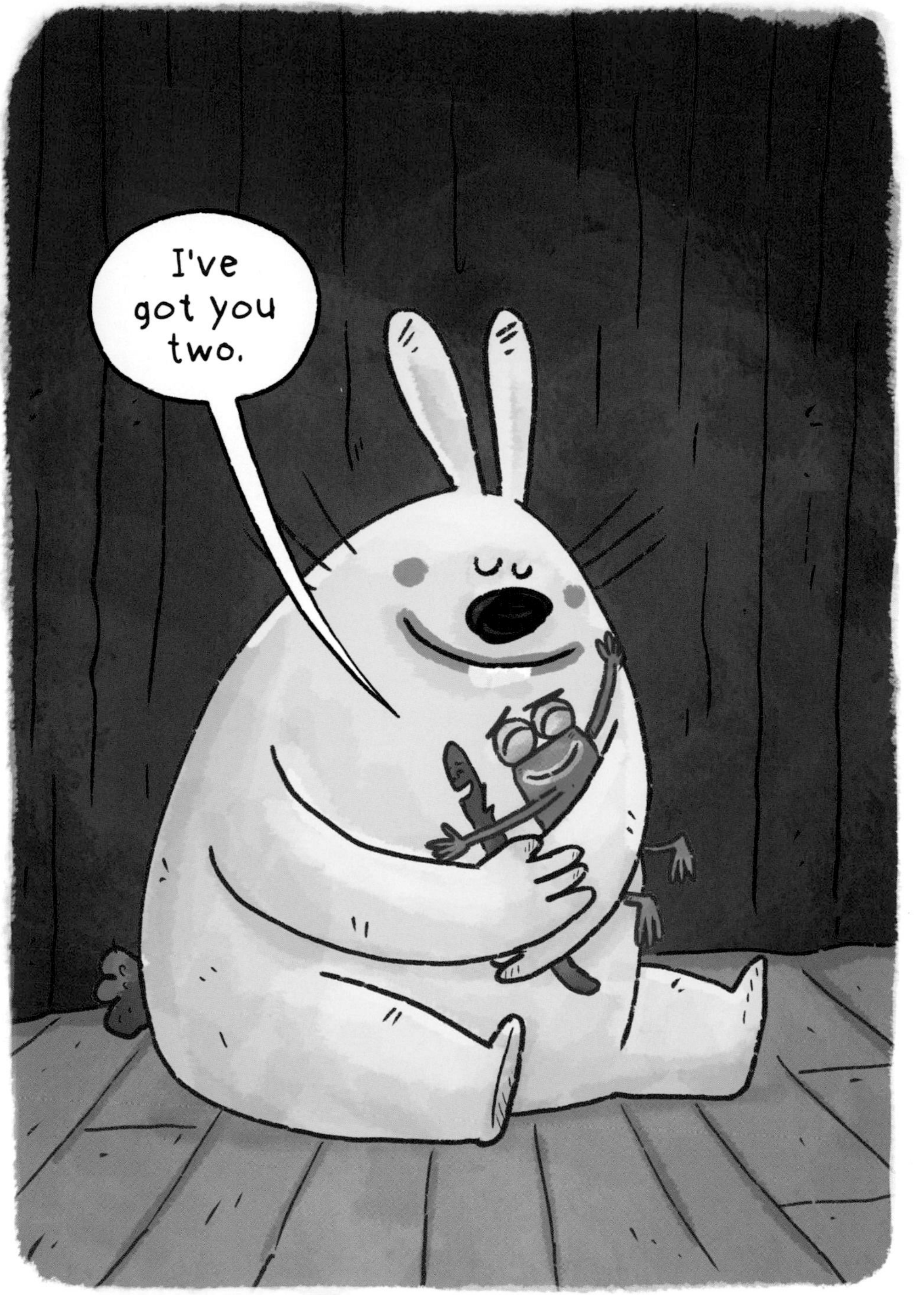
I've got you two.

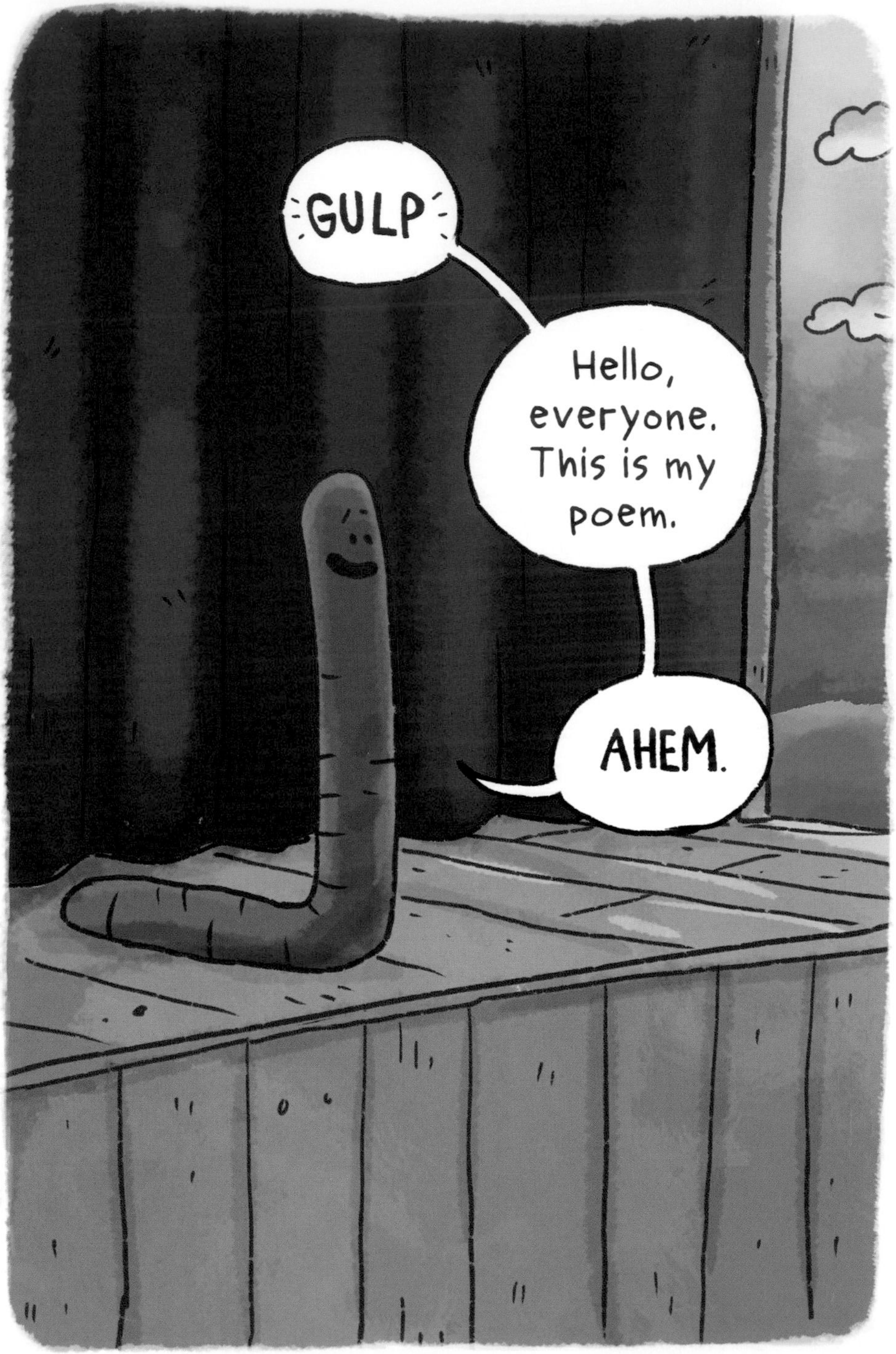
GULP
Hello, everyone. This is my poem.
AHEM.

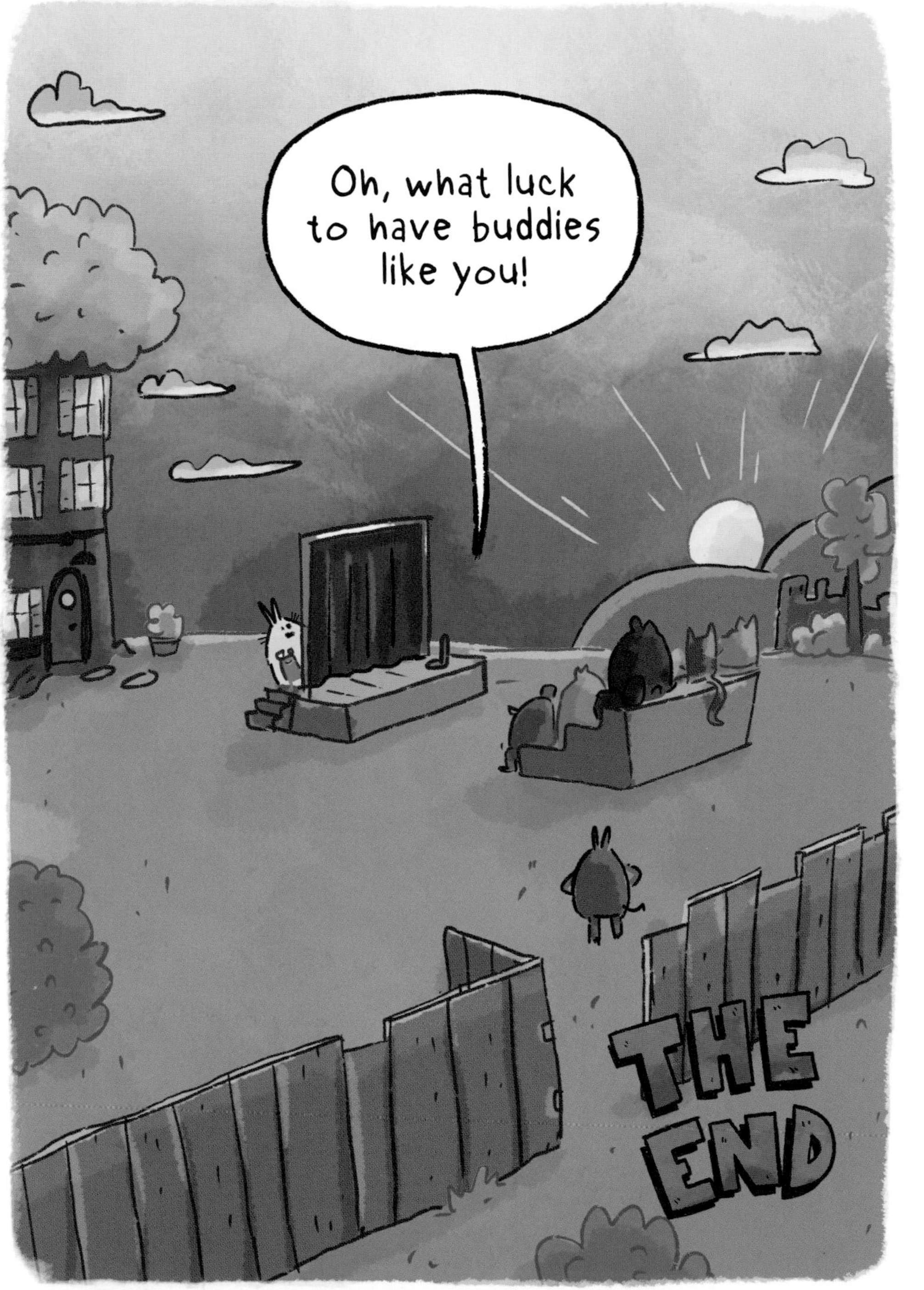
Oh, what luck to have buddies like you!
THE END

TRAVEL BACK IN TIME TO MOVE FORWARD TO THE BEGINNING!

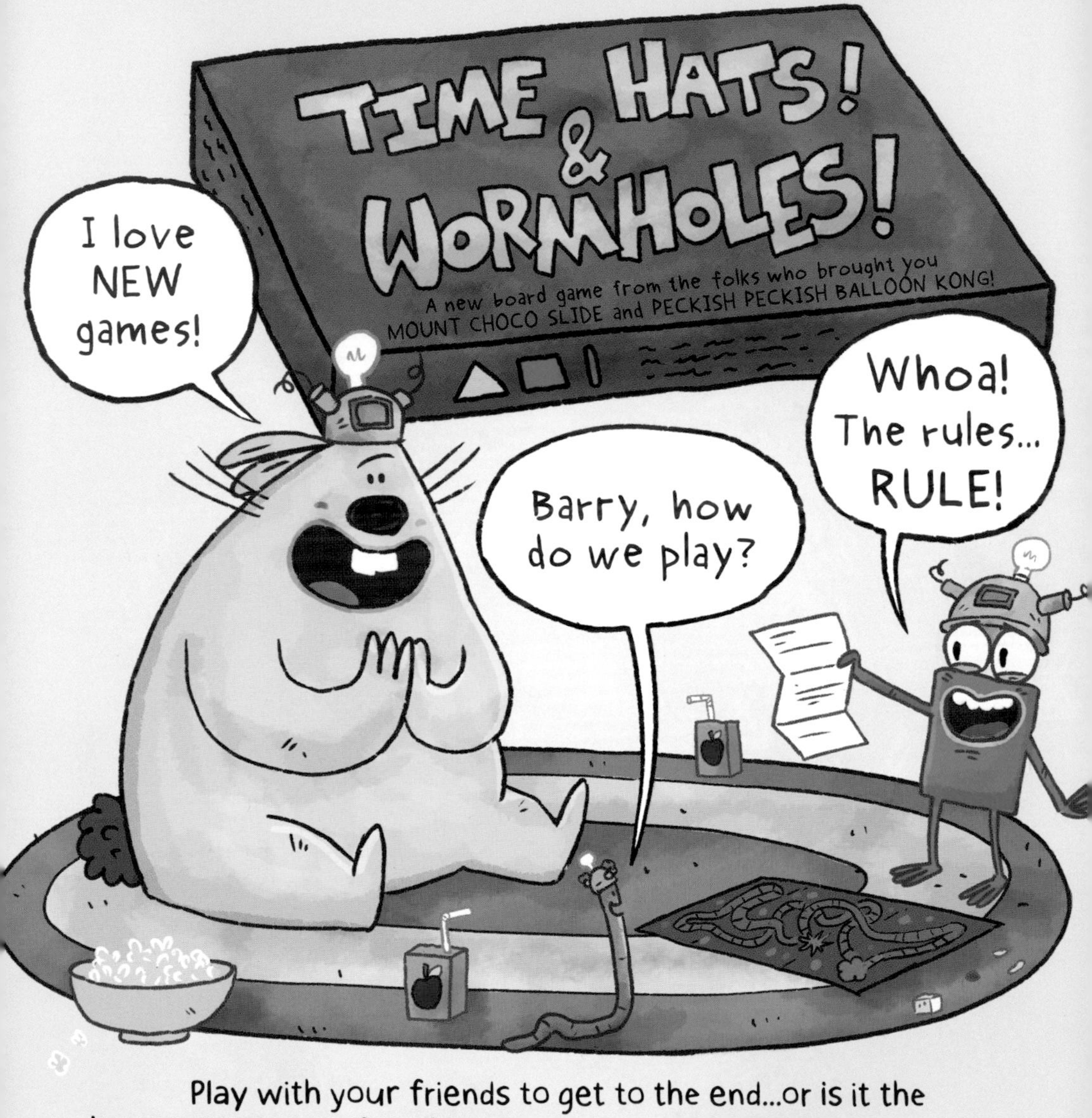
TIME, HATS! & WORMHOLES!
A new board game from the folks who brought you MOUNT CHOCO SLIDE and PECKISH PECKISH BALLOON KONG!
I love NEW games!
Barry, how do we play?
Whoa! The rules... RULE!

Play with your friends to get to the end...or is it the beginning? Be careful of time warps and wormholes as you jump along history's time line and encounter all sorts of wild critters and amazing places!

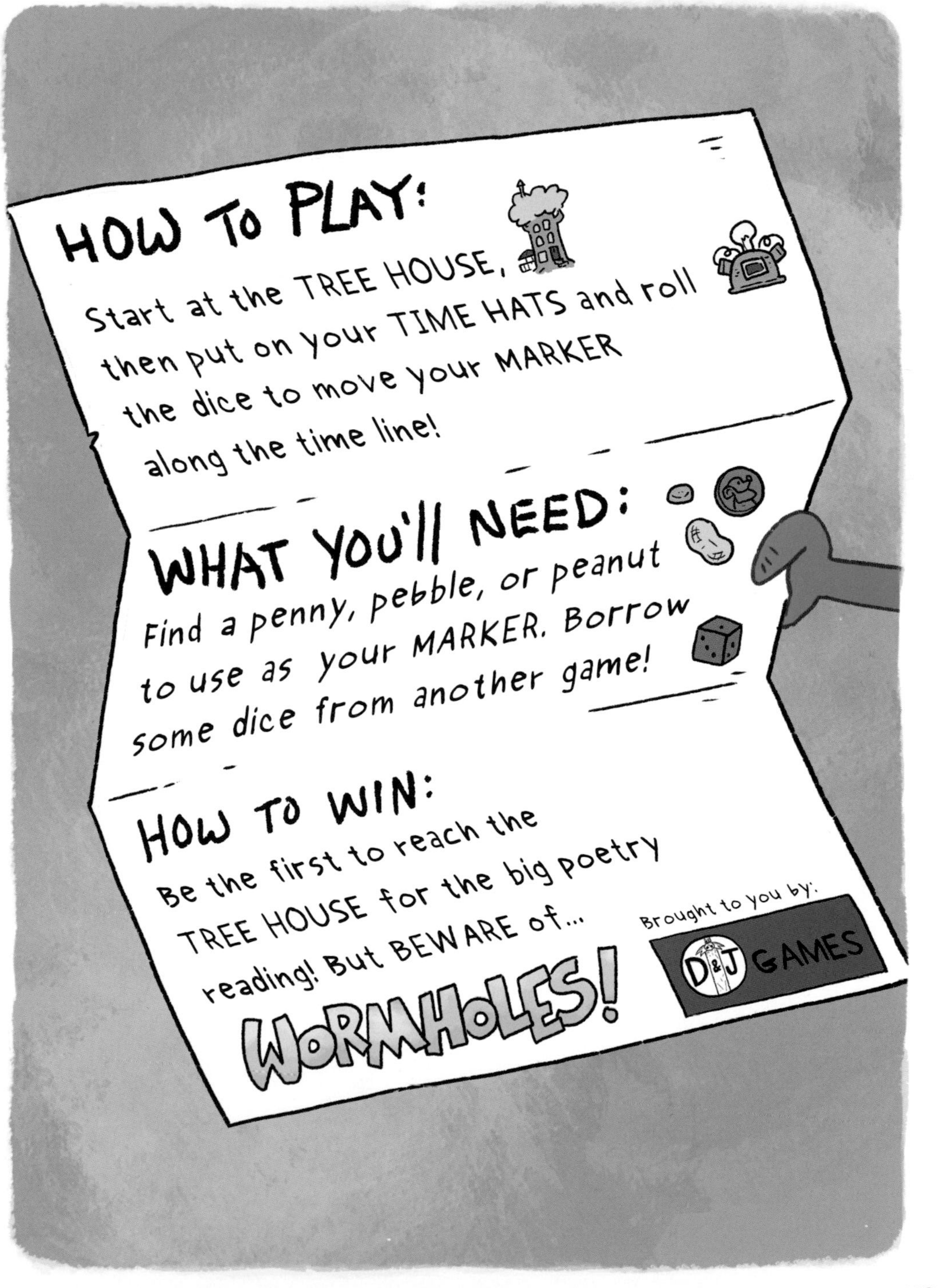
HOW TO PLAY:
Start at the TREE HOUSE,
then put on your TIME HATS and roll
the dice to move your MARKER
along the time line!
WHAT YOU'LL NEED:
Find a penny, pebble, or peanut
to use as your MARKER. Borrow
some dice from another game!
HOW TO WIN:
Be the first to reach the
TREE HOUSE for the big poetry
reading! But BEWARE of...
WORMHOLES!
Brought to you by:
D&J GAMES

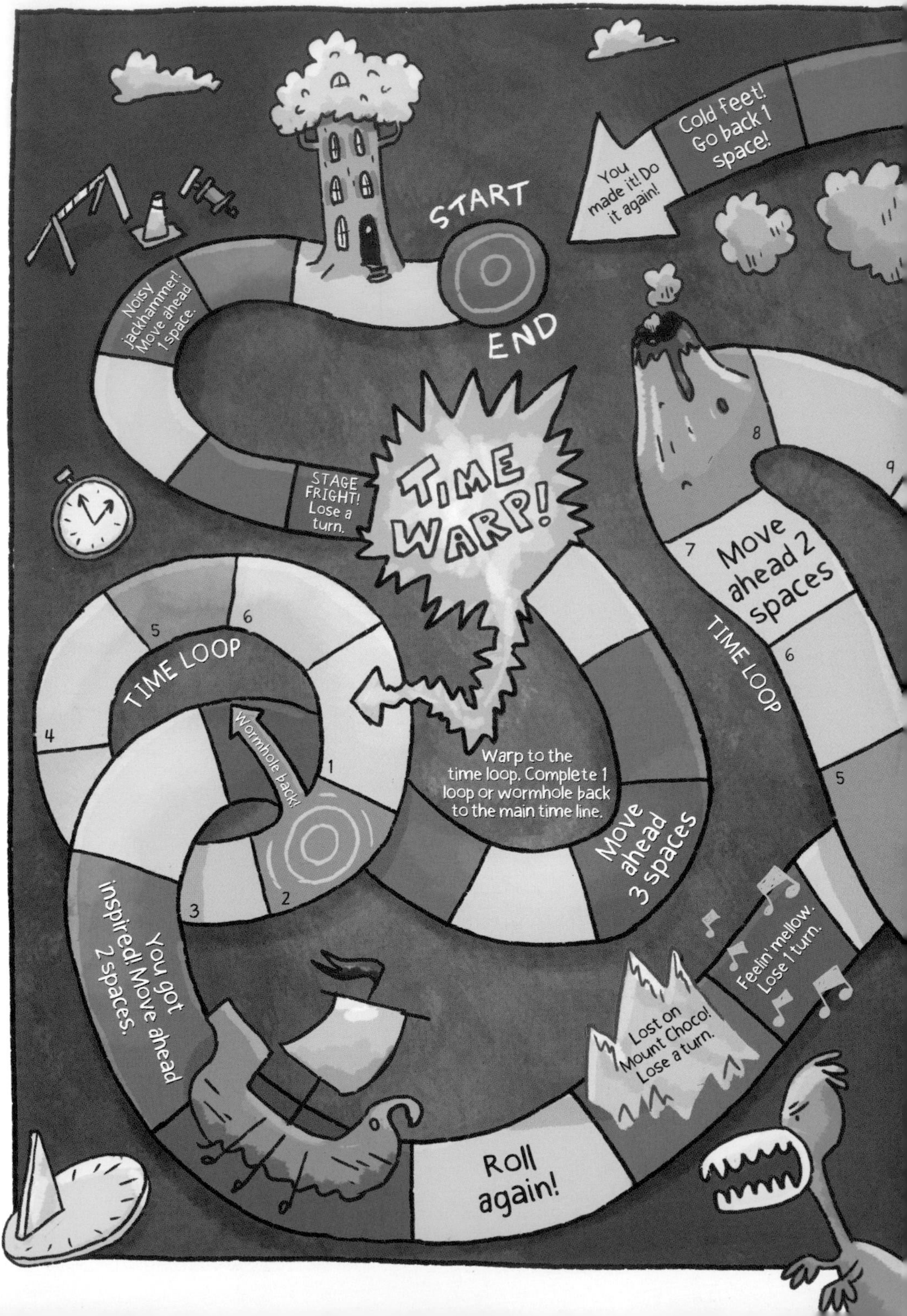
START
END
Cold feet! Go back 1 space!
You made it! Do it again!
Noisy jackhammer! Move ahead 1 space.
STAGE FRIGHT! Lose a turn.
TIME WARP!
Move ahead 2 spaces
TIME LOOP
TIME LOOP
Wormhole back!
Warp to the time loop. Complete 1 loop or wormhole back to the main time line.
Move ahead 3 spaces
You got inspired! Move ahead 2 spaces.
Feelin' mellow. Lose 1 turn.
Lost on Mount Choco! Lose a turn.
Roll again!
1
2
3
4
5
6
5
6
7
8
9

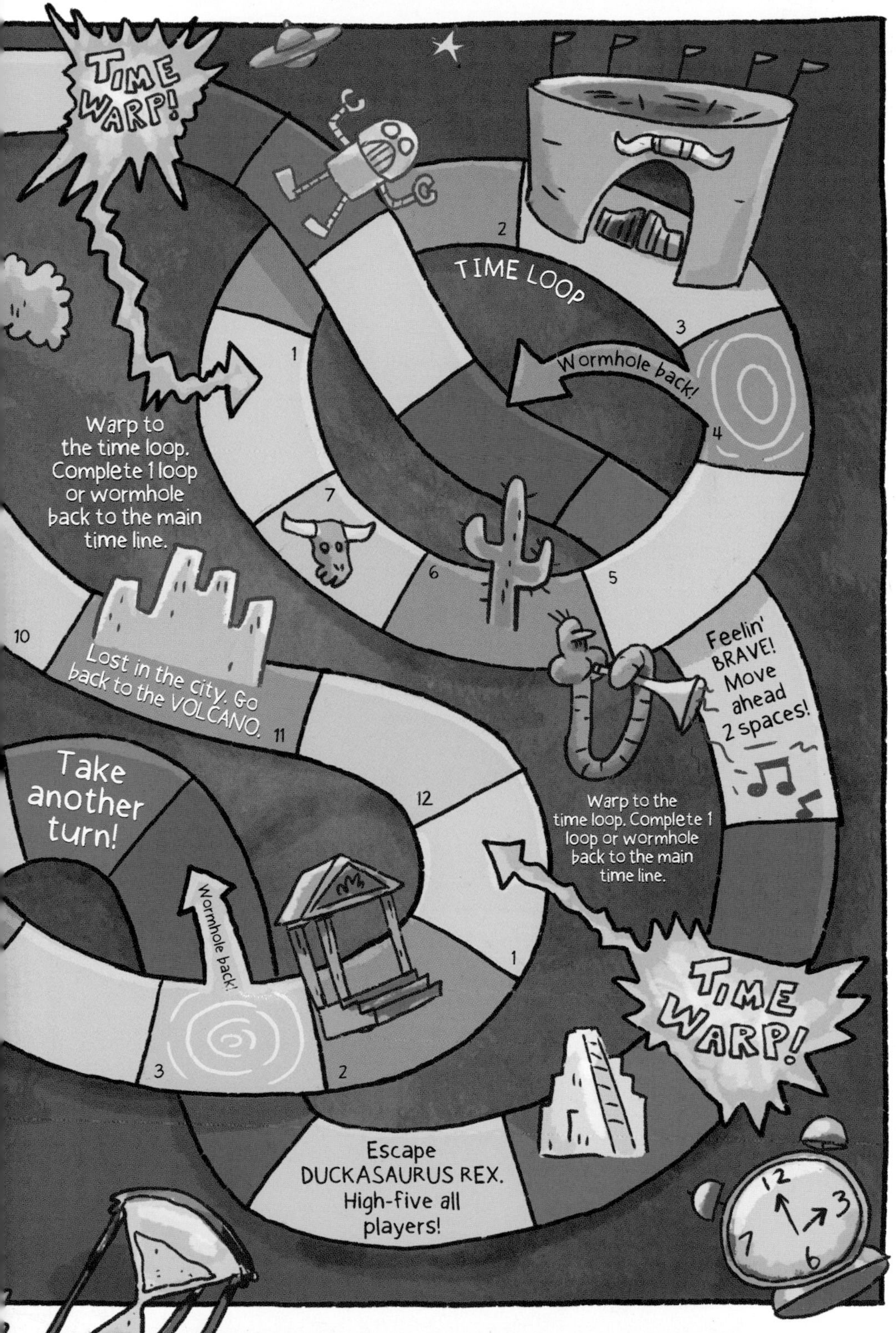

TIME WARP!
2
TIME LOOP
3
Wormhole back!
1
4
Warp to the time loop. Complete 1 loop or wormhole back to the main time line.
7
6
5
10
Lost in the city. Go back to the VOLCANO.
11
Feelin' BRAVE! Move ahead 2 spaces!
Take another turn!
12
Warp to the time loop. Complete 1 loop or wormhole back to the main time line.
Wormhole back!
1
TIME WARP!
3
2
Escape DUCKASAURUS REX. High-five all players!

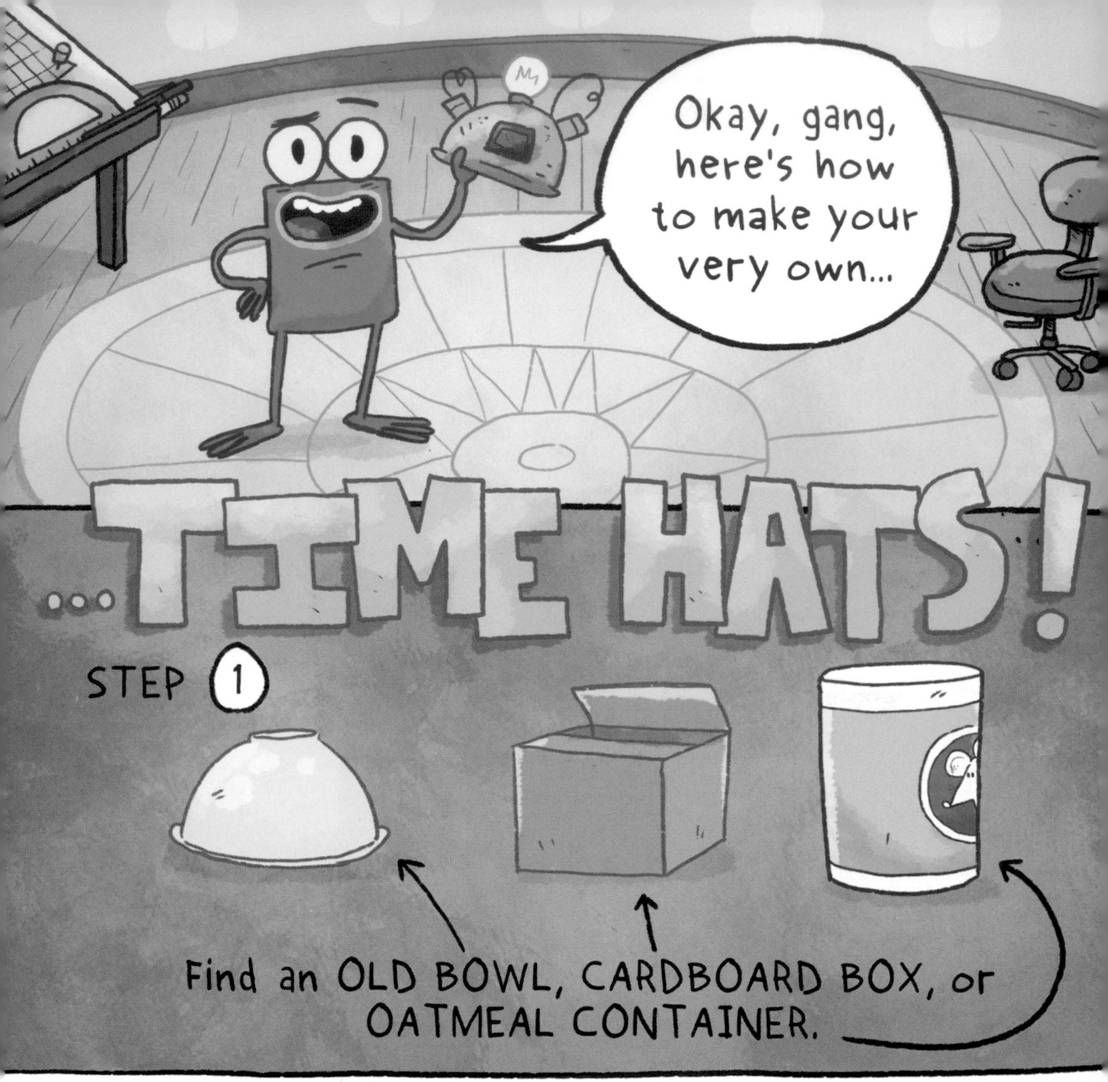
Okay, gang, here's how to make your very own...
...TIME HATS!
STEP 1
Find an OLD BOWL, CARDBOARD BOX, or OATMEAL CONTAINER.

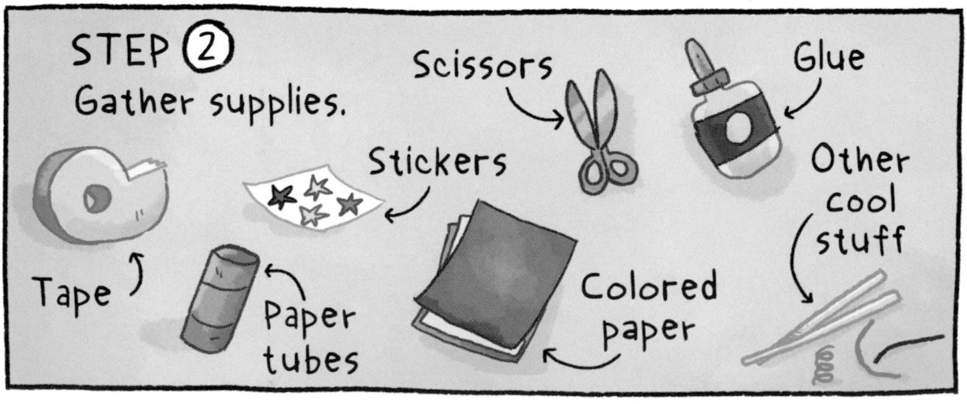
STEP 2
Gather supplies.
Scissors
Glue
Stickers
Other cool stuff
Tape
Paper tubes
Colored paper

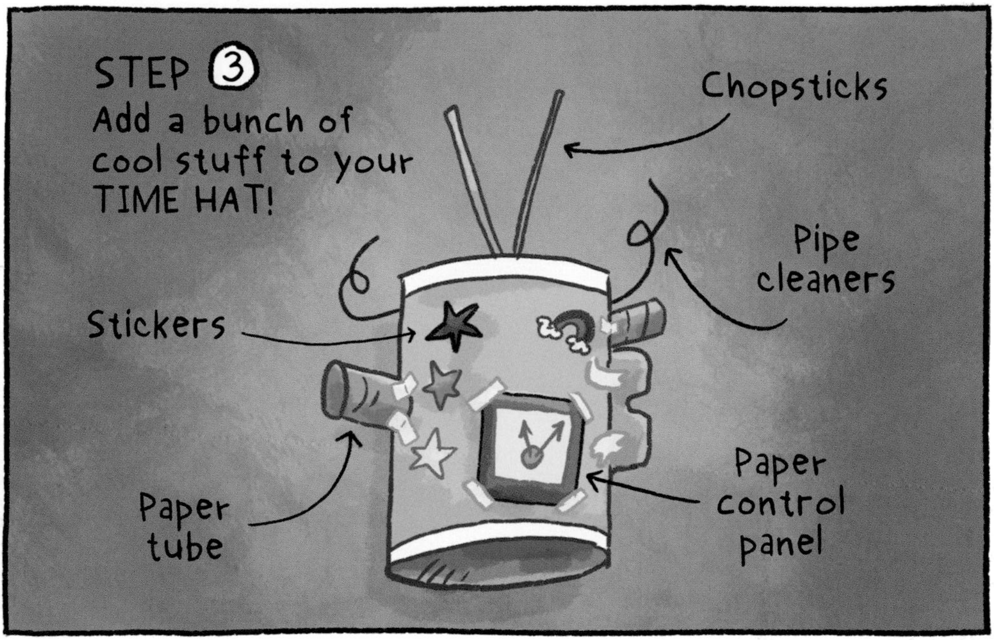
STEP 3
Add a bunch of cool stuff to your TIME HAT!
Chopsticks
Pipe cleaners
Stickers
Paper tube
Paper control panel

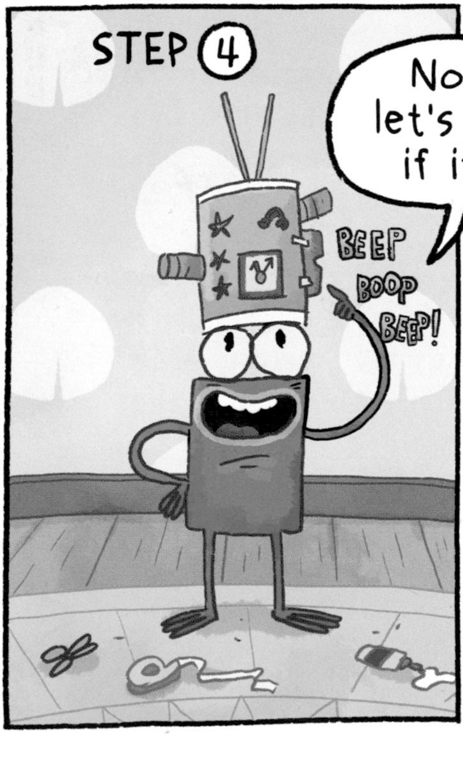
STEP 4
Now let's see if it...
BEEP
BOOP
BEEP!

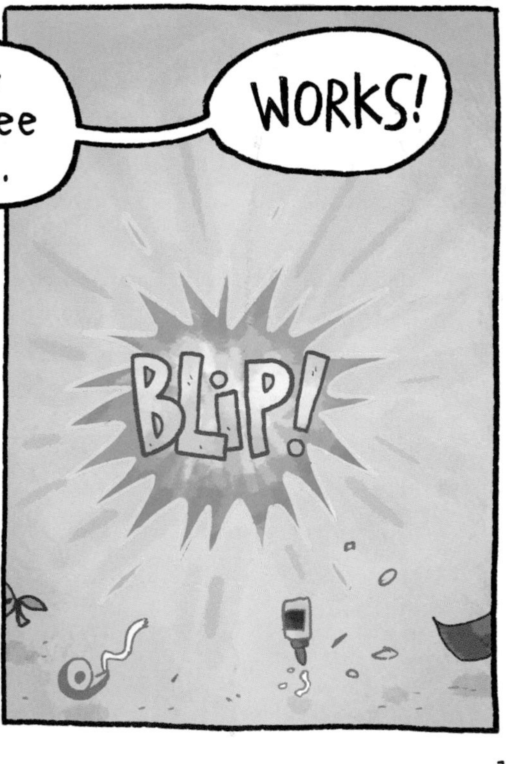
WORKS!
BLIP!

About the Authors

Jason

Dan

Dan & **Jason** go back. Waaaaay back. They got their start drawing and writing stories in what feels like the early Jurassic period, also known as the '90s, when they were making comics in the back of their high school art room. Annnnnd they never stopped!

The acclaimed cartooning duo live, breathe, and eat comics and animation. *Big Time Trouble* is their fifth Blue, Barry & Pancakes book. They love writing and drawing these stories more than anything else in the whole wide world, and they really hope you like reading them. Dan and Jason make everything together! They think it, write it, draw it, mix it, bake it, and serve it together. Just like Blue, Barry, and Pancakes, they're best friends!

JAN 2023

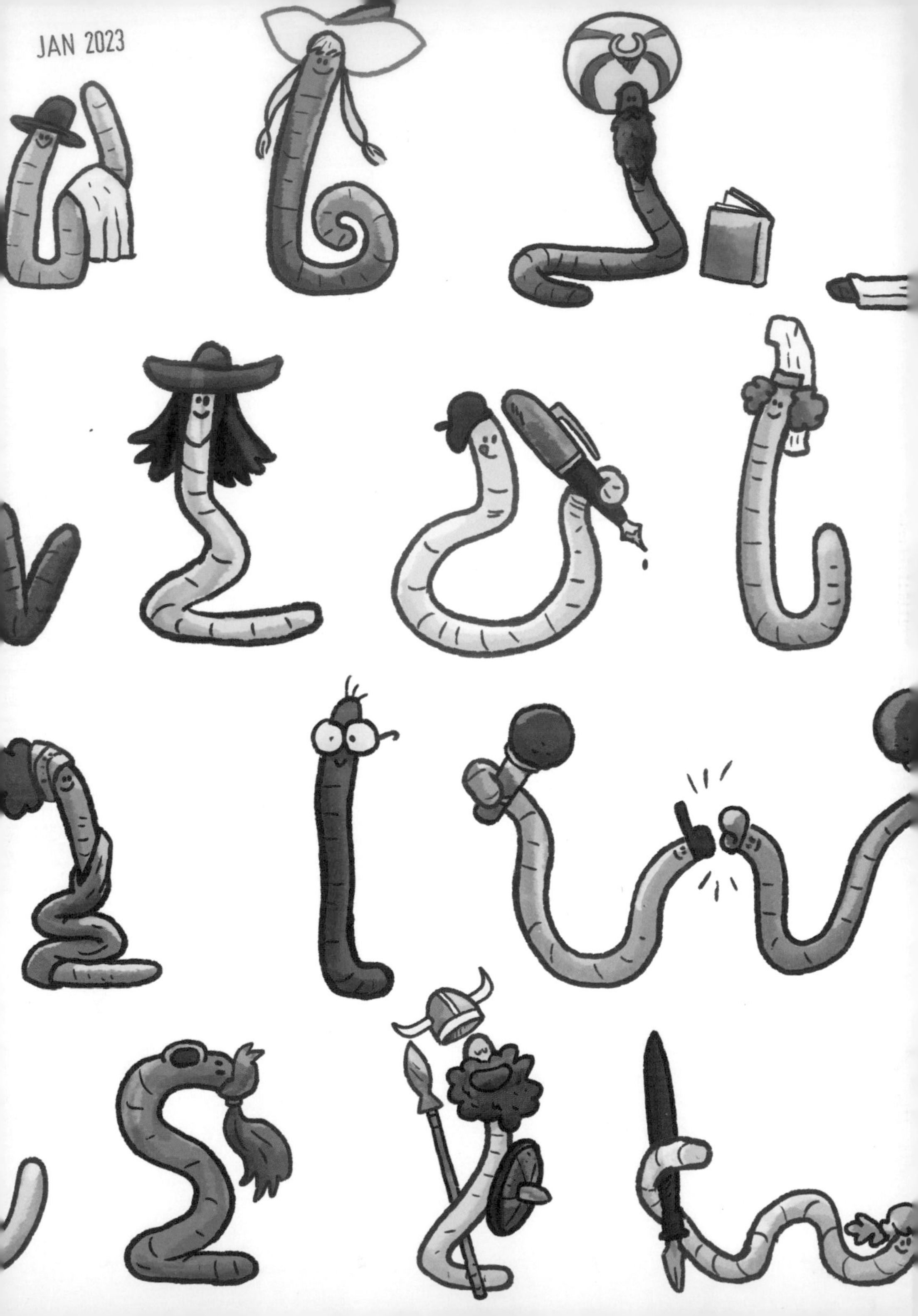